RAISED BY VENOM
ARGENTIUM VAMPIRE HUNTERS
BOOK ONE
P.S. NAIL

Written by P.S. Nail

Illustrations by P.S. Nail

Editing by Vanda O'Neill and Heather Shields.

ISBN: 979-8-218-09930-5

ASIN: B0B1Z6R5NZ (e-book)

First Edition: October 2022

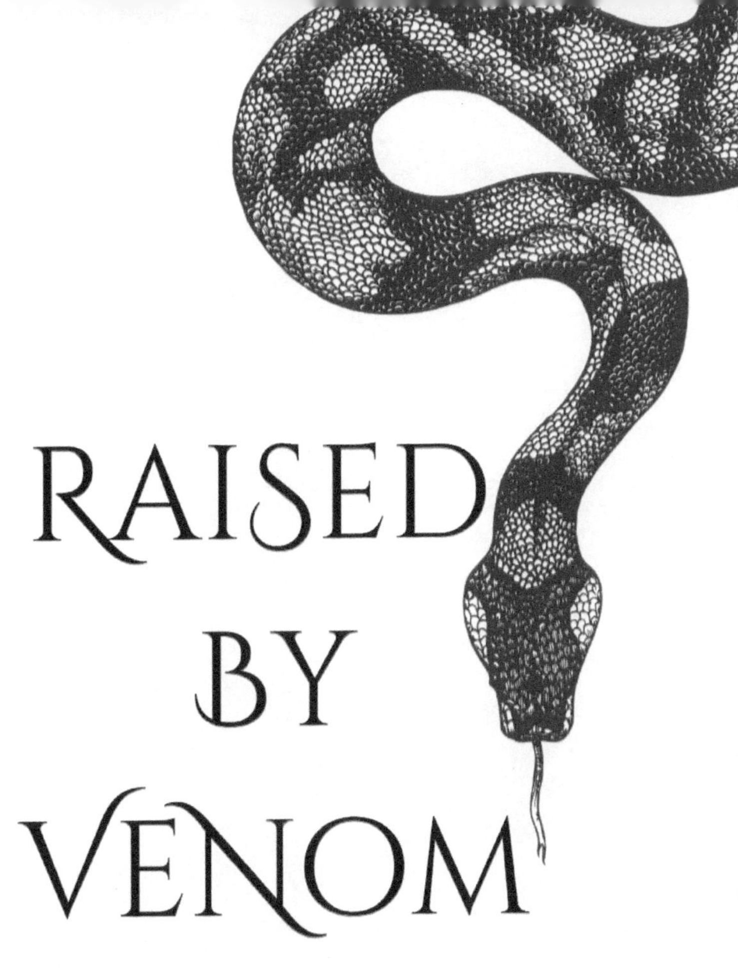

RAISED BY VENOM

ARGENTIUM VAMPIRE HUNTERS
BOOK 1

To my Uncle Paul Hogue
who I miss dearly.
I sing when I think of you.

"Oh, it won't rain all the time.
The sky won't fall forever.
And though the night seems long.
Your tears won't fall forever."
-Jane Siberry

CONTENTS

QUOTE

"If you would not be forgotten as soon as you are dead and rotten, either write things worth reading, or do things worth the writing."
- Benjamin Franklin

FOREWORD

If you're an asshole, my spell will cook.
Curse to all who steal this book.

Life will invert for the crook.
Curse to all who steal this book.

You have a pawn, I have a rook.
Curse to all who steal this book.

PLAYLIST

To help me get into the mood of each book, I make playlists to match the theme and feelings. Here is the one I listened to while writing Raised by Venom.

Listen on Spotify

Listen on iTunes

Paperback readers, visit psnail.org for playlists links.

INFORMATION

Warning: This book contains explicit language, alcohol consumption, fighting, choking, blood, gore, murder, graphic violence, attempted sexual assault, cult-like ceremonies, abduction, torture, and imprisonment.

It also contains explicit sexual content that includes unprotected sex, edging, bondage, spanking, and swapping of bodily fluids, e.g.semen and blood.

If you find a warning I missed, please email me at peggysue@primordialtree.com

For information on this book, please visit the author's website: psnail.org

To purchase officially licensed merchandise, please visit: primordialtree.com

A WAR HAS BEEN BREWING BETWEEN TWO OPPOSING GROUPS FOR OVER THREE HUNDRED YEARS.

V.E.N.O.M.

Vampire Eradicating National Organization of Malice

&

S.A.V.E.

Supernaturals Against Venom Elitists.

SAGE

I have wondered my whole life if those happily ever after stories actually exist. If they do, who are the lucky ones that get to experience it? Are we all just side characters in another person's story? Because that's what I have felt like, just a side character—not even a villain—a nobody, really. One whose death could be written off quickly with barely even a tear shed.

My life was boring, and I felt like it was going nowhere... until *he* came. He was the main character in his story—something I always wished to be. I loved to hate him, until I fell for him, taking sleeping with the enemy to a whole new level.

My name is Sagelynn Argent and the story I'm about to tell you is not one for the faint of heart. There is adventure, self-growth, denial lust, heartache, love, betrayal, and even death. Don't say I didn't warn you....

LUKA

Two hundred and fifty years ago, I was turned into a vampire. I was only twenty-six at the time and that's the age I will stay for eternity. My life wasn't perfect, but it was fun. It consisted mostly of drinking blood, fucking, and trying not to get killed... until *she* came.

I was ready to murder her after what she did—end her life in a slow, painful way. Then I couldn't bring myself to do it. She was the one thing I never wanted, but somehow, she was exactly what I needed.

My name is Lukas Draven and the story I'm about to tell you is a fucked up one. One of betrayal to my vampire family and to my own self-respect. Having enemies was easy, but trying not to fall in love with one was hard as shit. Grab a beer... you're going to need it.

CHAPTER I
SAGE

*I*t takes one incident, one moment, to change the outcome of history—the outcome of your life. You never know when it will happen, but when it does, you immediately wonder if you regret it, or if you would do it all over again.

Wandering down a dark alley alone at night was probably a bad idea, but it's what they instructed me to do. After ten years of extensive training, you'd think I would have been ready, but I felt no one could be prepared to kill their first vampire.

Part of my mission was spending the evening in a bar. Since I needed to be on my game for what I had to do, I ordered non-alcoholic drinks, so my head would stay clear. He had watched me at the bar—I didn't know his name. They trained us not to care about their names. Not to care about them at all.

They were evil creatures who needed to be eradicated, either by death or cure. The hierarchical organization I was born into taught me that.

The Vampire Eradicating National Organization of Malice. Commonly known as Venom.

As a teenager, I didn't get to hang out at the mall or go on random camping trips with friends from school. Instead, I was educated by the Venom society and spent most of my time training to be a vampire hunter. I was twenty-five and, up to this point, it was all my life had consisted of.

Doing the same mundane tasks over and over left me pretty jaded. Little did I know how much my life would change after this night.

The requirement to be "fully" inducted into Venom: kill my first vampire and survive. Since there was no leaving the organization, if I succeeded, I would be in it until death. If I failed? Well, if I failed, I would be dead, which was pretty much the same, only on a shorter timeline.

A small part of me almost wished I *would* fail. Spending my life hunting vampires wasn't what I wanted. If I had my way, I would tour the world visiting small villages, see all my favorite bands in concert, and possibly learn how to play the guitar.

Or maybe just be fucking normal.

My cell phone rang, and I quickly reached for it. The distraction call was supposed to make me look like a vulnerable girl alone.

"Hello?"

"Is he still following you?" It was another member of Venom.

"Yes, Mom, I'm okay."

"Are you prepared?" Marcus asked.

"Yeah, I ordered an Uber and I'm walking down to meet it now." I hoped I was good at playing the clueless victim.

"Call as soon as he's dead. Be careful, Sage."

"I will, Mom. Love you, too." The call ended.

A shadow in my peripheral caught my attention, so I dropped the phone to my side but kept it in my hand.

My high-heeled boots clicked on the concrete as I tried to steady my breathing. If my adrenaline kicked in, my heart would speed up and the vampire would hear it.

Halfway down the alley, he made his move and landed directly in front of me. I'm sure he had expected me to scream or run, but that wasn't me. I lifted my cell phone and clicked the button on the side of the case, turning on a bright UV light. He screamed and fell to his knees.

Taking advantage of his momentary weakness, I ran up and swung my leg toward his face. He caught my ankle mid swing, causing me to fall flat on my back knocking the wind out of me. And, unfortunately, the phone fell from my hand. He tried to crawl on top of me, so I kicked him in his chest and rolled away before quickly jumping to my feet. He did the same.

"This will be fun," the vampire said, as the skin on his face healed before my eyes.

"Yes, it will." Raising my fists, I went into a defensive stance. "Well, come on," I taunted with an arrogant grin.

Without hesitation, he lunged for me. Though I tried to dodge him, he plowed into my shoulder, knocking me down again. As quickly as I could, I scrambled away from him. If he got on top of me, he would have the upper hand and I would be dead.

A fist came at me as I sprung to my feet, but I dodged it, instead counterattacking with a roundhouse kick to his chest. He stumbled back, but came at me again. A blinding pain radiated through my face as his fist landed, making me fly back and hit the hard pavement. The impact had me gasping for air while he stood over me before I had a chance to even move.

As I lay on my back, I frantically tried to think of how to get out of this situation. He put one foot on each side of my body, blocking me in.

There were no magical breathing techniques to calm my adrenaline surge now. My heart threatened to beat out of my chest as the fear of death ran through me. Perhaps I didn't want to die after all.

"You're pathetic."

"Fuck you," I spat as blood dripped from my busted lip. The metallic taste filling my mouth.

"I probably would if you weren't a Venom member. You *are* rather pretty." He tilted his head with a smile, which dropped with quickness.

More pain radiated through me from a kick to my stomach, making me roll to my side. A second kick caused me to cough as it expelled the air from my lungs. Through squinted, watering eyes, I found my phone a foot out of reach, so I rolled over on my back to give myself time to devise a plan.

"Please don't kill me," I whimpered as tears streamed down my cheeks. They weren't fake—I was hurting.

He squatted over me, almost sitting on my stomach, and ran a finger across my bloody lip. "Oh, poor little Venom member." With his fangs half-extended, he slid his tongue across his finger, licking my blood. "You taste delicious."

Vampire or not, I knew a man's weakness. With a last-ditch effort to save my life, I punched him straight in the dick. He grabbed his crotch and yelled before falling to his knees, now completely straddling me. The weight of him sitting on my stomach made it impossible to move quickly. I squirmed out from under him enough to reach for my phone. I clicked on the light, aiming it at his face.

He used his hands in an attempt to shield himself. "You bitch."

Ignoring his remarks, I held the light only inches from him as I sat up. The stench of burning flesh filled the air along with the sound of his screams.

Even though it was hard with only one free arm, I managed to pull my legs out from underneath him. After hopping to my feet, I kicked him in the face and he fell to the ground. I dug my high heel into his chest while I held the light on him.

"Where is your den?" I asked. Getting no response, I clicked the UV light up to level two, and he screamed as I tried to steady my shaking hands. "I said, where is your den?"

"Like I would tell you!"

I clicked the UV light to level three. He screamed louder as I dug my heel in so far I felt the skin break. The feeling made me nauseous.

"This has five levels and each one gets worse, so I would start talking if I were you."

"Stop. Please," he begged. His voice cracked and a part of me felt bad, so I turned the light back to level one.

"Then tell me where it is!"

"Fuck off! I hope you all die!"

"Tell me where your den is or you will be the one dying!"

It honestly didn't matter whether he told me. My mission stated I had to kill him, otherwise I wouldn't be inducted in. But pumping him for more information could be helpful.

"I would rather die than tell you!"

"Your call."

His screams echoed through the alley as I returned the light to level three. After removing my heel from his chest, I pulled a silver stake from the waistband of my jeans. My bright light kept him still as I slammed it into his chest.

It was harder than I expected, puncturing through the layers of skin and muscle to get to the heart. The practice dummies I had worked on were hard, but this was worse. I was glad my aim had been perfect and I missed the bones. No matter how skilled you are, they're incredibly difficult to stake through.

He gasped as his mouth fell open in shock. My hands trembled as his skin turned gray, then his body slowly disintegrated to ash.

For a second, relief flooded me when I didn't die. Then I felt like a piece of shit. We were taught they were evil creatures we weren't supposed to feel sorry for, so why did I? My whole body shook as remorse filled me. I pushed my feelings aside, turned off the UV light, and clicked the button on my earpiece.

"Done," I said, trying to keep my voice calm.

"Copy," Marcus answered.

Thanks to the locator on my watch, the van would be here in less than two minutes to pick me up. With the tip of my boot, I spread the ash around a little, trying to make it look less noticeable. If somebody stumbled upon it, they would assume someone made a bonfire. Even though it was barely autumn in Saint Angelo, New Mexico.

Something on the rooftop caught my eye, and I looked up to ensure no one had been watching me. Waiting for more movement, I glared at the spot. My eyes stung as I tried not to blink, worrying I would miss it. Maybe I imagined the shadows dancing, but I had an overwhelming feeling I was being watched. My heart raced, so I took slow, deep breaths, willing myself to stay calm.

As a black van pulled up next to me, its door slid open, startling me. I quickly hopped inside before the vehicle sped off.

"Great job," Marcus said from the seat across from me. His mahogany cheeks glowing with pride.

"Thanks." My adrenaline was still running high. I took a deep breath, trying to relax myself.

"How did it feel to finally kill your first vamp?" Erik asked. He was our getaway driver.

"Okay, I guess." I swallowed hard. It wasn't okay, more like terrifying. I had never killed anything before in my life and it made my chest ache—even if it *was* a vampire.

Marcus furrowed his eyebrows. "What do you mean, 'okay?'"

I rolled my eyes. "Oh, excuse me, it was fan-fucking-tastic. Better?"

"Much better." Erik locked eyes with me in the rearview mirror as he laughed.

"Unfortunately, not everyone makes their first kill. Your dad will be proud, Sage."

"I know, Marcus."

"You're injured. Let me clean your wound." Marcus grabbed the first aid kit and dug through it.

"Are you okay?" Erik asked. I looked up into the mirror again.

"I'll be fine." I smiled, hoping he would relax. He nodded before turning his eyes back to the road.

Marcus moved over to my side of the van and I clenched my fist tight so he wouldn't notice me shaking.

"Look at me." Marcus's brown eyes were kind as he dabbed a cloth wetted with an antiseptic solution on my lip. "You will be sore tomorrow, but it doesn't look too bad."

"Thanks, Marcus."

"You're welcome." He smiled proudly before kissing the side of my head. "Welcome to Venom, sweetie."

Every mission we went on, we had to have a senior member with us to lead. I was grateful I had gotten Marcus as my commander on my first night out. I loved him with all my heart. He was second in command in our society and like a father to me. He was, in fact, also my godfather.

"I can't believe you are officially part of Venom," Erik gushed.

"Born with Venom, dies with Venom!" Marcus said.

"Until death!" Erik added.

"That's what *dies with Venom* means, dummy," I retorted, and Marcus and I both laughed.

Marcus took a deep breath and stilled his face. "Anyone following us, Erik?"

"No, Marcus. I've been watching."

"Good. Let's get back to the base."

Marcus returned to the side of the van he was previously on and began typing on his tablet. I knew he would be busy recording the notes from tonight's events, so I crawled into the front seat. After a ten-minute drive on the highway and another twenty on back roads, we finally made it to base camp.

The Venom compound was an extremely secure piece of land in the middle of nowhere, surrounded by an electrified fence topped with barbed wire. It housed multiple buildings, each with their own use. We always had a full staff of security guarding the campus even though we had never been attacked. As far as I knew, the vampires didn't even know where we were located.

Everyone in Venom had a job. Other than security, we had secretaries, bookkeepers, IT, nurses, trainers, and multiple other positions. Then there were hunters, like me and Erik. We would hunt vampires so they could be sent off to the research lab in the hopes of one day finding a cure for vampirism. Unfortunately, sometimes we would come across some uncooperative ones we would have to kill.

We pulled up to the barbed wire-topped gates. Erik rolled his window down and placed an index finger on the security scanner to make them open. I glanced up at the guard tower and saw a woman dressed in full black holding a rifle. I couldn't tell who they were in the dark, but I had a sneaking suspicion, based on her silhouette, it was my friend Lyric.

Erik pulled the van in and the gates shut behind us. Another armed guard gave us a nod as we drove by. We headed toward the main building where we held ceremonies, meetings, and where all the clerical offices were located.

He turned down a small alley, which took us to an oversized garage. As soon as Erik parked, we hopped out and headed toward the elevator. The smell of the garage calmed me. It reminded me of my childhood since I was raised in this compound.

Pushing the button on the wall, the elevator doors opened and we stepped inside. Marcus put his finger on the scanner and the red light turned green. After tonight, I would be fingerprinted and have limited access to certain areas, as well. My security clearance would only be a level two, but someday, I would run Venom and be a level six. Even if it wasn't what I wanted.

We stayed silent as we rode the elevator down to the basement. As soon as the doors opened, my mother was waiting with an anxious look on her face, which faded to relief when she saw me.

"Sagelynn." She pulled me into a hug as soon as I stepped off the elevator. "I knew you would be fine. I'm so proud of you." She looked over my face and gasped.

"I'm fine, Mom," I whispered, and she gave me an empathetic smile.

"Sagelynn, darling, welcome to the society," my father said as he walked up. "I knew you could do it, however, it took longer than I expected from you. You will learn someday that you can't leave people waiting, but we can talk about that later. Let's get the induction started." My father slid his mask over his face and turned away. As the respected president of our society, as soon as he did anything, people followed. Including me.

I sighed as quietly as I could, hoping he wouldn't hear me. Erik gave me a sad smile.

It took longer than I expected from you. His words repeated over and over in my head. It was common for my father to compliment me and put me down all in the same minute. Sadly, I was used to it.

We entered the ceremonial room packed with people. Every single person was wearing a mask and a dark green cloak with the hood up. Each mask was hand-carved into a face, which I found to be rather creepy.

Two society members were at the door and laid the same type of heavy cloak on me. As my dad took the stage, I glanced up at our banner hanging behind him. It was the same deep green as our cloaks, and it had our logo on it in white. The symbol was a viper with the words Venom on it—not very original, to be honest.

"Welcome, members of the Vampire Eradicating National Organization of Malice," my dad announced. "It's time for the induction of our newest member. Please welcome my daughter, Sagelynn Argent."

The crowd clapped as I ascended the small set of stairs and made my way up to him.

"My distant grandparents founded our society over three hundred years ago. Control of it has been passed down each generation to the eldest child. As you all know, my only child is Sage, so she will one day lead you. This makes tonight extra special because she will also be the first female president." The crowd roared as my father turned toward me. "Kneel."

I kneeled before him as two cloaked members walked up, both had masks on, but I could tell by the design of them who they were. Marcus handed my dad a wooden mask as Deren set a large golden urn in front of me.

"This mask was carved with the strengths of the wearer in mind. You must stay masked and cloaked at every ceremony. Do you understand being a Venom member is an honor and a job you will do until death?"

"I do." My dad placed the mask on my face and then pulled my hood up. He then put a silver necklace with our symbol engraved on it around my neck.

"The ceremonial dagger, please." My father held out his hand as a knife with a handle made from the bone of a vampire was given to him. "Your hand."

Nervousness filled me as I placed my hand in my father's. He ran the blade across my palm and sliced it open. Thankful for the cover of the mask, I winced at the stinging sensation. He turned my hand over and held it above the urn. I watched every drop of blood as it fell, making a slight thud sound in the room's quietness. After giving enough blood for the ritual, my father let go of my hand.

"Rise." I did as he bade and rose from the ground, turning toward the crowd. Everyone silently stared at me through their creepy masks.

"Born from the blood of Venom!" my father shouted, and the group repeated. "Now, let's celebrate in the dining hall."

Most of the crowd had dispersed as my father left the stage. A hand reached out and grabbed my wrist making my gaze wander upward. Erik had his mask on top of his head and a scowl on his face as his gorgeous brown eyes inspected my bloody hand.

"Let's clean this," he said kindly as he pressed a cloth into my hand.

We strolled to the bathroom and he held the door open for me before we headed toward the sink.

"Did he have to go so damn deep?" He grabbed my hand and stuck it under the warm water and I hissed. "Sorry."

"I'm okay. It's not bad."

"Lies. Mine hurt like a son of a bitch and he went much deeper on you."

I was sure he did it on purpose. My father wanted to ensure I was stronger and better than anyone else. In his eyes, I should be impervious to everything.

I rolled my eyes and sighed. "It won't kill me, unfortunately."

"No negative talk, Sage."

"Sorry. I hate my life."

He smirked. "I know you do."

"I don't want to be the leader of this society!"

"I know you don't." A small laugh left him because this was the same conversation we had at least once a week.

He grabbed a clean washcloth from the closet and pressed into my hand before his eyes met mine. "I can't take you seriously with your mask on." He lowered my hood and lifted my mask onto the top of my head before he pushed my short black hair behind my ears and smiled. "That's better."

"Thanks." I let out a deep breath, the sound echoing in the bathroom.

"You have a long time before worrying about taking over," Erik reminded me as he headed to the first aid cabinet. He grabbed some supplies to bandage my hand and returned.

"I know."

He gently took my hand and removed the cloth. "This definitely needs to be bonded."

"I'll be fine."

"Sage."

"Okay, but can we do it after the feast? You know my dad will be pissed if I go now."

"Fine, but immediately after."

"Yes, sir, drill sergeant, sir!" I saluted him with my good hand.

He wrapped the gauze around my wound, then smirked. "You're a brat."

"You love me." I stared up into his eyes and smiled mischievously.

"Of course, I do. You're my best friend."

Erik and I were only two years apart and had been raised in the society together. He was a good-looking man—clean-shaven, and stylish. His hair was brown, his skin was golden, and he was muscular. Of course, I loved him too, but my feelings were like ones you would have for a brother. He felt the same way about me. Erik's sister,

Lyric, was my other best friend. She was like a sister to me as well, since I had no siblings of my own.

He taped my gauze down. "All done. Let me see your face." He lifted my chin and ran his thumb lightly across the cut on my lip. "It's noticeable, but it's not bad. It could have been worse."

"I know."

He dropped his hand and sighed. "We better get back before—"

"Before my dad gets mad. I know." He laughed and held the bathroom door open for me as we exited.

CHAPTER 2

LUKA

Screams were echoing through the night air as I hurtled myself from one rooftop to the other. A light flashed in the night sky seconds before I heard another scream. Jumping onto the last rooftop by the alley where the screams were originating, I ran to the edge in time to watch a woman slam a stake into my brother's chest. Not wanting to watch him die at the hands of a Venom member, I immediately glanced away,

My heart sped up in grief and disbelief—then anger.

"Done," I heard her say, so I looked back down.

Since she was alone, this must be her induction night. I should do her a favor and kill her now before she knows what kind of organization—or should I say *cult*—she's in.

The other members will be here any minute and I won't risk my life over vengeance. Avenging our other brother is what got Andrei killed. I needed to engrave her face in my memory so I could kill her when the time was right. I took in every single detail about her I could, as I patiently waited to get my revenge.

The woman looked young, maybe mid-twenties. Around five and a half feet tall without her boots. Her hair was black and shoulder length.

She spread the ash around with the tip of her shoe—the ash which was once Andrei.

She must have seen some movement since she glanced up at the rooftop. Even though I knew she couldn't see me—not with human vision—I stepped back into the darkness. She glared right at me like she knew I was there.

In the quietness of the night, I could hear her heart racing. She was nervous and she should be. I was going to rip her heart out and eat it after I slowly drained her dry.

A black van pulled up and slid its door open. She jumped inside and they sped off.

Footsteps fell against the rooftop as the scent of another vampire filled my lungs. "Luka."

I turned around and met his eyes. "Yeah, Finneas."

He was a short man, with brown hair and a face which screamed asshole.

"Did you find Andrei?"

I nodded my head and swallowed hard. "Yep."

"Where is he, then? Did Venom take him?"

"It was an inductee."

"Shit! I kept telling the fool to stop hunting them down or he would get sent to that treacherous research lab or end up staked. He didn't listen!"

"Well, you won't have to tell him anymore, since he's fucking dead!" With a clenched jaw and tightened fists, I walked away.

"I'm sorry, Luka, but you know he was—"

I whipped around and pointed a finger in his face. "I don't give a shit about what you have to say right now, Finneas!"

If I didn't get away, I was going to kill him. Before I did something stupid that would get me killed, I turned and took off running.

"Luka, wait!"

With a long jump, I landed on the rooftop of the next building over as anger rushed through me. Running and jumping again, I landed onto the next roof, then again, and again. Needing to put distance between us, I continued to do it until I was sweating my ass off, tired, and at least a few blocks away from the inconsiderate asshole.

Finally, in my favorite spot with the city's best view, I took a seat on the roof's edge and looked up at the moon. My brain failed to believe Andrei was dead. As I sat with my thoughts, I realized I had lost all my family.

One brother was captured, the other now dead, leaving me alone. If it wasn't for my friends, Winnie and Drag, I wouldn't even stay in this town.

After a while, my cell phone rang, bringing me back to reality. Winnie's name was displayed across the screen.

"What's up, Winnie?"

"Dude, you know I hate that nickname."

"That's why I use it."

He let out a long sigh. "Did you find Andrei?"

"Yeah. An inductee got him."

The phone went silent for a few seconds. "Shit, man. I'm sorry."

"We will avenge his death, don't worry."

"Hold on, Finneas just got here." There were muffled sounds of Winnie talking to Fin in the background.

"Finneas said there's an emergency Save meeting."

"Be there in ten minutes."

I ended the call with a sigh and made my way down to the council meeting. Ironically, we held our gatherings in an abandoned church. Finneas was already talking when I entered the hall. I wondered where Viktor was, since Fin was second in command.

"As some of you already know, Andrei was staked tonight." The room was mostly quiet as he spoke except for sobs coming from Laren, Andrei's wife.

"We have rules around here for a reason. We all know Venom is always out to imprison us in that awful research lab, and believe me, as a survivor who escaped, you *do not* want to be a lab rat."

As I listened to the bullshit, I leaned against the back wall and crossed my arms.

"If you are going to be a part of Save, you need to follow our rules. We *will not* retaliate."

"That's bullshit!" Winnie protested.

"There are rules we need to follow, Winston. We only engage if they engage or to save another."

My anger was getting the best of me and I spoke up. "So, we should just sit back and let them kill us, one by one?" Everyone looked over their shoulder when they heard my voice.

"We don't engage first, Lukas."

"They engaged first when they staked Andrei," Laren choked out before sniffing back tears.

"We aren't savages. We are a group that helps bring awareness to—"

"So, our name means nothing?" I asked, as I stepped farther into the room.

"Our name means—"

"Aren't we the Supernaturals Against Venom Elitists?" Since everyone was expecting a show anytime I was at a meeting, I threw my hands out for dramatics.

"Well, yes, but—"

"So, we *aren't* against them. We just let them do what they want."

I didn't give a shit about our rules. Even if it meant going against my own moral code and killing out of anger instead of defense, I wouldn't let them get away with kidnapping and murdering my family.

"Lukas, we can't go killing them each time—"

"So, why are we here if we aren't going to fucking do anything?"

"Every meeting, you have something to say. You need to watch your tone!"

"My tone?" My body stiffened and my jaw clenched. The air was thick as I stared at Finneas, waiting for him to say something even more foolish.

"Luka is right," Drag interrupted. "We can't keep letting them kill our people or take them for lab rats."

Mumbles of agreement and disagreement filled the room, as each person tried to express their feelings on the situation at the same time.

"Enough!" The room was silenced as Viktor's word rang through the basement. He was the oldest and most respected vampire I knew. Everyone sat up straighter as he made his way to the front and took the stage.

"I have it from here, brother." He nodded to Finneas, who quickly moved aside.

Stepping to the front of the stage, he looked over the crowd.

"What happened tonight was a tragedy, but Andrei knew better than to hunt down a Venom member. He couldn't let go of the fact they took one of his brothers and look where it got him." More anger filled me, and I shook my head before he continued.

"We must protect our members. Vampires and wolven alike. We can't have everyone going rogue. Our numbers are dwindling because of Venom. Please don't give them another reason to come after us." He let out a sigh as his eyes scanned the room. "Make sure you are mindful of your surroundings, especially this week. They will have the new inductee in the field to show them the ranks. They will be dying to capture us, so be careful. We will discuss this later when everyone's emotions aren't as high. You're all dismissed." Viktor left the stage and Finneas followed behind him.

Most of the crowd started conversing about their opinions on what we should do as Laren made her way toward me.

"Luka." She squeezed her bright blue eyes shut and tears rolled down her pink cheeks. I immediately pulled her in for a hug.

"I'm sorry, Laren. I tried to save him as soon as I was told what he was doing . . ." I got quiet, unable to finish my sentence.

"I know you did. Don't be sorry." She let go of the hug and looked at me with pleading eyes.

"I will avenge him, no matter what they say," I whispered.

She nodded and gave me a sad smile. Her thick, curly, auburn hair swayed slightly as she walked away.

"I'm sorry, friend," Drag said as he put a hand on my shoulder. "But don't do anything stupid."

I turned toward him. "You know me. Every move I make is extremely calculated."

"I know you, and I know exactly what you're thinking, Luka." He ran his hand through his thick beard.

"That I'm going to kill them all?"

He glanced nervously around the room. "Yep. But you can't go against Viktor."

"I know. That's why I will make sure they engage first." Murder wasn't normally on my agenda, but when your heart had just been broken, your moral compass didn't always point in the right direction. They would be slaughtered.

"The pack has your back. All you have to do is let us know when and where."

The best thing about having a shifter as a best friend is wolves run in packs and kill together. They are also extremely loyal.

"I know." I gave him a fanged smile.

"Want to get a drink in honor of your brother?" he asked.

"Have I ever said no to alcohol?"

"Winnie, it's beer time," Drag said over his shoulder.

"Sweet. I'm coming!" Winnie made his way over to us. "Who's driving?"

"I am," Drag said.

We all made our way outside, got in Drag's truck, and headed downtown to Drifter's bar.

CHAPTER 3
SAGE

We strolled down to the dining hall and joined the party. We didn't have to have our masks on outside the ceremony room so they were still on top of our heads. Wanting to avoid everyone, I immediately hit the food table.

"Yes! There's chicken," Erik said as he grabbed a plate.

"Leave some for me."

"If you're lucky."

"I was born into Venom, so not likely."

"Stop being a negative Nancy," he said, as he put some chicken on his plate.

"Don't you dare call me that again, or the next time I practice staking vampires, you will be the practice dummy!"

"You kill one vampire, and suddenly you're a badass." He held out the tongs, clicking them in my face.

"Pretty much." I smiled teasingly as I took the tongs from him and got chicken for myself. "Where are we sitting?"

"Sage, you know you have to sit at the head table tonight."

"No one will notice if we hurry past. There is a place in the back, right there." I headed toward the empty two-seater and Erik followed.

I took a seat as he gave me a disapproving look.

"Sit down and block people from seeing me."

"You're so demanding," he said as he took a seat across from me.

"Where is Lyric?" I asked.

"She's on tower duty tonight."

"I figured that's who I saw on the way in." I took a bite of my chicken as I scanned the room and saw Deren approaching us.

He was a good guy, with darker hair and eyes, who had been my friend since birth. He looked like your basic computer gaming nerd.

"Marcus told me you would be hiding," Deren said to me as he strolled up.

"Did you expect anything less?"

"Not from you, Sage."

I smirked as I looked up at him. "Am I that notorious?"

"Yes," both men announced in unison.

Ignoring them, I took another bite.

"Are you ready for tomorrow?" Deren asked.

"What do you mean?" I mumbled with a full mouth.

"You're on the roster."

Dropping my food, I met his eyes in shock. "What? Already?"

"Sage, your dad." I glanced in the direction Erik was nodding his head.

"Shit, shit." My dad was making his way over to us, and I shifted uncomfortably as I wiped chicken grease off my fingers.

My father's face was filled with disapproval as he glared at me. "Sagelynn, what do you think you are doing?"

"Eating chicken." I shrugged and gave him an adorable smile.

"You aren't funny. You *will not* embarrass me tonight. Grab your food and go sit at the head table."

With a sigh, I stood and picked up my plate. Looking over my father's shoulder, I caught Deren sneaking off. *Pussy.*

"Erik, I expected more from you since you are older than her," my father scolded.

"My apologies, sir." Erik glanced up at me. I gave him an empathetic face and mouthed 'sorry' before turning away.

My dad led me to the head table and took a seat. I sat next to him. I picked up my chicken, and someone came up to congratulate me, so I set it back down. After they left, I tried again to eat, and someone else came up. I eventually gave up and sat there talking to random people with a plate of cold food.

After an hour of extreme boredom and small talk, I got up to find my mother. She was mingling with the other women who were married into the society when I caught up to her.

"Mom, can I go home?"

"You know you can't leave, Sage. It's your induction ceremony."

"I have a nasty headache," I whispered as I rubbed my forehead. It was a blatant lie, but I wanted to get the hell out of there.

"Oh. I will let your father know and I'll take you home."

"It's okay. Erik can take me. He's going to bond my cut first, anyway."

Her face filled with shock as she grabbed my bandaged hand.

"Is it bad?"

"Erik said it is."

She sighed and dropped my hand. "Very well. Be safe." She kissed my cheek and sauntered off.

Looking around for Erik, I spotted him by the bar, so I pushed my way through the crowd and over to him.

"I'm sorry," I said the instant I approached.

His smile told me he wasn't mad. "It's fine, Sage."

"Can you take me home?" I asked. "I need to get the hell out of here."

"I can, but where's your car?"

"At my apartment. My mom insisted I ride with them so we could chat before the mission. Probably in case I died." I sighed.

"Okay, but we need to bond your hand first."

"I figured."

"Come on." He led the way to the infirmary, and I followed close behind, ensuring I didn't make eye contact with anyone. I was tired of conversing. I had hit my limit of small talk.

As we walked, I couldn't stop thinking about what I had done. Killing a vampire was what I was trained to do—born to do—but I had an uneasy feeling about it. I was glad I would be capturing them from here out unless I had no other choice but to kill them.

"Why do we have to kill a vampire to get inducted in?"

"Sage, you already know why. It's so they can see our skills are good enough, but also, so they know you will *actually* do it. If you hesitate, you could get yourself or someone else killed."

"I understand, but why don't we just capture them like we do the others?"

"Capturing them is a lot harder. If you can't kill one, you won't be able to capture one."

"I get it, I guess." I sighed because I didn't get it. "I hope I'm good enough to capture one. I would rather them go to the Vampire Research Center than to stake them."

Erik pushed the button on the elevator and the doors popped open. We stepped on and he hit the floor for the infirmary.

"Maybe you will get to take your first vamp to VRC tomorrow."

"Possibly. I'm super nervous."

"You will be with Deren and me, so you'll be good."

The elevator doors opened and we stepped off.

"I wasn't expecting to be thrown in the field so quickly, other than to shadow."

"You know how your dad is," Erik reminded me as he opened the door to the infirmary. "He wants you out there as soon as possible."

"Yeah, I know." After taking my cloak and mask off, I threw them on a chair.

Caught up in my thoughts of anger, I wandered over to the examination table and stood next to it. I couldn't believe my dad would throw me on the roster my first week. New inductees usually shadowed trained members for a while. They observe the squad to see how missions are done before getting put on the roster.

Not me, though. Not the future president of Venom. He held me to higher standards than everyone else, so of course, I would be thrown to the wolves. More like thrown to the vampires. We had a truce with the wolven. They were shapeshifters who could turn into wolves on command. I had never met one, but I wasn't scared of them since most honored the pact we had made.

"Sit up here." Erik grabbed my waist and set me on top of the table.

"Thanks for doing this," I said as he walked away.

"Not a problem." He retrieved some items from the medical supply fridge.

After setting the supplies down next to me, he headed to the sink and washed his hands. He dried them off, then snapped on some gloves.

"Oh, kinky," I said sarcastically.

Erik laughed and shook his head. He picked up my hand, unwrapped the bandages he had put on, and disposed of them. After grabbing the antiseptic spray, he squirted it on me. It burned for a second, but the coolness from it being refrigerated felt soothing on my wound.

Using some gauze, he wiped the cut dry. Then he picked up the can of skin bonding spray called bondcoat—a medically engineered wound bonding solution. Venom worked closely with the government, which gave us access to many medically enhanced products. And also military-engineered devices and weapons.

Erik sprayed the bondcoat on my hand, and I watched closely as the cut sealed itself, leaving behind a pink mark.

Erik ran his thumb along the scar. "It looks good. The scar will fade in a few weeks." He let go of my hand and removed his gloves.

"I hate that stuff. It creeps me out."

"You should be grateful. It's an amazing medical innovation only a select few have access to." He cleaned up the mess he made and disposed of all the waste.

"Which makes it worse. Hospitals everywhere should have—"

"Are we going to have this conversation again, Sage?"

"No, I guess not," I huffed as I jumped off the table.

"Let's get you home so you can rest for tomorrow."

With a sigh, I grabbed my cloak and mask, and we left the infirmary. We stopped at the lockers down the hall to store our items until the next meeting before we made our way out to the garage.

I was grateful we didn't see anyone on the way out except for a few guards who congratulated me. After getting into Erik's Mustang, he drove me back to my apartment in the city. We pulled up to the curb around four a.m.—early for a Venom member.

"Thanks for the ride," I said as I opened the car door.

"Do you want me to come up?" Erik's kind eyes told me he actually didn't want to come up and hang out with me while I binge-watched TV.

"No, I'm going to feed Chewy and go to bed."

"Alright. I'll see you tomorrow, then. Love you."

"Love you. Bye." I shut the car door.

The sound of a motorcycle purring got my attention. The rider's head was turned toward me, so I smiled at him. I couldn't tell if he smiled back or not because he was wearing a helmet. Turning away, I headed toward my apartment building. The doorman held the door for me and I thanked him.

Living in a luxury apartment in the middle of downtown was terrific, but my father hated it. Somehow, I had convinced him this one had good security and, since no one knew who I was, I would be safe.

Exhaustion filled me as I hopped on the elevator, took it to the top floor, and made my way to my apartment. After opening the door, I flipped the lights on. Upon entering the room, I made one quick sweep with my eyes. Everything looked normal, so I shut the door and locked the three locks my dad had installed.

"Chewy. Here kitty, kitty." My cat, Chewbacca, came strolling out of the bedroom. "Are you hungry?"

He weaved between my legs and purred as I grabbed his bowl and filled it with dry food. I opened a can of wet cat food and scooped half of it on top. Chewy started meowing as I set it on the ground.

As I stored the leftover food in the fridge, I realized I was hungry because I never got to eat. I peeped around the bare shelves as I held the door open.

"Shit." I grabbed a piece of cheese and shut the fridge. I shoved it in my mouth as I headed down the hall to my room.

Dying to get out of these jeans, I got undressed and threw on a long, comfy sleep shirt. I crawled into bed, grabbed the remote, and turned on the TV. Chewy eventually came to cuddle with me. While I was petting him, my eyes got heavy.

CHAPTER 4

LUKA

Drowning my feelings about my brother's death seemed like a good idea a few hours ago. Now, as I sat at Drifter's Bar, not so much. My brother may not have made the best decisions, but he was my blood and I would do anything for him—even kill for him. My emotions were getting to me, and I was ready to go. I could still get drunk as a vampire, but it took a lot more alcohol to affect me, so I was safe to drive.

"Another round?" Winnie asked.

"Not for me," Drag responded.

After digging in my wallet, I threw some cash on the bar. "Me neither. I'm taking off."

"Do you need a ride?" Drag asked me.

"No, I'm going to rooftop it for a bit. I left my Harley on the other side of town, so I'm going to grab it and head home."

"We are going to my apartment to play video games. Do you want to come?"

I got up from the barstool I was sitting on. "Not tonight, Winnie. Thanks, though."

"See you tomorrow," Drag said. His face was still empathetic.

Winnie held out his tan fist and I bumped mine against it.

"See ya, Ollie," I said. He was the owner of Drifter's bar and the wolven father of Drag.

"Bye, Luka," he called out from behind the bar.

As soon as I was outside, I found a way to get up to the roof. We used rooftops a lot. Humans couldn't jump from roof to roof, so it was a great way to escape if Venom tried to capture us. I used them mainly because I hated people.

Twenty minutes later, I was across town and back to my motorcycle. After throwing on my helmet—to hide my identity, not to keep me safe—I mounted my bike, started it up, and hit the main street which ran through the city.

A few blocks away, I was a couple vehicles back awaiting a red light when a blue Mustang pulled up on the curb to the right of me. The shapely figure of the woman who got out grabbed my attention, but when she turned around, my mouth dropped open.

"No fucking way," I mumbled to myself.

Disbelief hit me when she glanced in my direction and smiled, making ice shoot through my veins. She was the Venom member who killed my brother. Not having any clue who I was, she turned and entered the building.

The car behind me honked his horn, bringing me out of my shocked state. Glancing up, the light had turned green. The Mustang pulled out behind me as I went through the intersection. I pulled over to the curb, waiting for it to pass. As it did, I noticed there was only one person in it. Not sure if he was a Venom member or not, but I knew she was. I quickly pulled out my cell phone and made a call.

"Hello."

I killed the engine on my bike. "Drag, take down this number."

"For what?"

"Hurry!"

Shuffling of paper came through the phone. "Okay, okay. Go."

"AWJ55F."

"License plate?"

"Yes, a Hispanic male in a blue Mustang. Possible Venom member. Give the info to Winnie and let him work his magic." Already deciding what I was going to do, I took my helmet off and tucked it under my arm.

"Damn. We haven't had a lead on a member in a long time."

"I got even better information, and it's kind of shocking."

"Like what?" he asked.

"I just watched the Mustang guy drop off a girl in front of the Silver Pines apartment building."

Hopping off my bike, I set the helmet on it.

"And that's shocking because?"

"Because it was the same girl who staked Andrei."

He sucked in a large breath. "Holy fucking shit!"

"Yeah. Holy fucking shit."

"Don't do anything foolish, Luka," Drag warned.

"I won't. I just want to say hi." I grinned mischievously to myself as I threw the keys in my jeans pocket and headed toward the alley behind the apartment building.

"Luka, you know—" I hung up my cell and pocketed it.

Drag was my best friend and someone I looked to for advice, but when I was hellbent on doing something, no one was going to stop me . . . not even him.

My cell rang, so I pulled it out. It was Drag calling, so I silenced my ringer and shoved it back in my pocket. He wouldn't talk me out of this. It wasn't like I was going to kill her—not yet.

Making it to the back of the building, I tried to find a way up. It seemed like a secure place, with no fire escapes or ladders hanging down. So, I went down a few buildings, made my way up to the rooftops, and jumped across them until I got to hers.

After I was up here, I realized I didn't know which apartment she was in, and there were eleven floors.

"Shit." I took a seat on the ledge.

If I couldn't find a way to her, I would fail him. My brother wouldn't want me to fail. Trying to develop different strategies to find out her apartment number, my phone vibrated in my pocket again. This was the fourth time. I pulled it out and answered it.

"I'm fine, Drag."

He let out a huge sigh of relief. "Just checking. You know I worry about you."

"I'm going to head home. I promise."

"Okay, I'm at Winnie's apartment, looking into your lead."

"It's Winston," Winnie protested in the background.

"Let me know if he gets a hit. Later." I clicked the phone off.

Tonight wouldn't involve me getting my revenge on the woman who killed my brother. I wasn't ready to kill her right now, anyway. The need to meet her, scare her, and let her know she was being stalked by a vampire was stronger. The *fear* of death is worse than death itself, I always said.

Getting up from the ledge, I made my way across the rooftops and back to the ground. I had almost made it to my bike when my phone buzzed in my pocket again. Pulling it out, I answered it.

"Seriously, Drag. I'm headed home now."

"Winnie got some info on your license plate."

"On my way." I hung up the phone, mounted my bike, and headed toward Winnie's.

Ten minutes later, I pulled up to his apartment. Both of my friends were sitting on the outside steps, waiting for me.

"What did you find?" I asked.

"Not a huge amount of info, but it's the reason I'm a hundred percent sure he's a Venom member. Let's head up and I'll show you."

Winnie stood up and went into the apartment building, Drag and I followed. We climbed two flights of stairs and entered his unit.

Winnie was a hacker, but you wouldn't know it unless you knew how to get into the secret room.

"Cave, avow," Winnie said, and then there was a clicking sound.

He walked over to the picture on the wall, swung it open, and typed in a code. Hearing more clicking sounds, the bookcase which appeared to be built into the wall, slid out and then opened. We entered the space.

His hidden office, which he called the cave, was filled with high-tech equipment. He had multiple computer monitors, keyboards, and other things with a purpose beyond me. I had no clue what he did when he was hacking, but I knew he was good at it.

Winnie took a seat at his computer and started pulling up information.

"Okay, so I ran the license plate and came up with the name Jim White." He pointed at the screen.

"That's a super common name," I said.

"Almost *too* common," Drag added. "They might as well have called him John Doe."

"I assumed it wasn't his real name, so I dug some more. I found the address where the car was registered and did a property check. Turns out it's an abandoned warehouse in the meatpacking district." Winnie pointed to the screen.

"Interesting. Do you think it's the Venom headquarters?" I asked.

"Not at all. They aren't *that* stupid, bro. So, I did some Google image searches, hacked into some cameras in the area, and watched some footage. No one has been in that building in the last month."

I crossed my arms. "So, what does it mean?"

"It means they more than likely own the property and registered the vehicle under the address, but no one actually lives there."

"So, it's a dead-end?"

"Not yet. I'm doing record searches right now for the property owner. I should have a name soon."

He pointed to another monitor with a bunch of things scrolling across it. I didn't know what any of it meant.

"Thanks, Winnie. You're a beast." I patted his back.

"It's Winston."

Ignoring his protest, I turned toward Drag. "Can we get someone on lookout at the Silver Pines apartment building?"

"I can. Suspect?"

"Female, Caucasian, 5'5, shoulder-length black hair. I'm assuming she is at least twenty-five, since it's how old they have to be before they let them hunt."

"Is she hot?"

My head whipped toward Winnie. "What the hell kind of question is that, man?"

"There could be multiple twenty-five-year-old women with black hair living in the apartment building. It helps me narrow it down."

I shook my head with a disgusted look on my face. "I don't know. I guess. She stabbed my brother, so I refrained from looking at her with anything other than hatred."

"What time did you see her?"

"Around four a.m."

Winnie started typing and pulled up some street video surveillance. And then she popped up on the video.

I pointed at the screen. "That's her."

"She's totally hot. Too bad you have to kill her," Winnie blurted.

"Winnie," Drag warned.

"I took some screenshots of her for reference," Winnie said, ignoring Drag.

"I'm going to head home before sunrise. Let me know if you find anything else." I left the office and headed back down to where I parked.

Mounting my bike, I had a thousand thoughts going through my mind. I pulled into traffic and headed home. After taking the long dirt road to my house, I pulled into my garage and went inside.

"Annie," I called out. My dog came running out and greeted me, happily wagging his cute little tail. I opened the back door and let the tiny beast out.

Today was a messed-up with too many events happening. It's never boring in the supernatural world, I guess. Grabbing a beer out of the fridge, I popped the top off the bottle. Annie scratched at the back door, so I let him in.

"Alexa, shut it down." The metal shutters which kept the sunlight out of my house during the day closed, all the doors locked, and the alarm set while I grabbed another beer.

Downing it quickly, I threw it in the trash before heading to my bedroom and flopping down onto my bed. Annie followed behind me.

Laying with my hands behind my head, I couldn't stop thinking about Andrei or the girl who killed him. My dog whined, so I reached down and picked the spoiled chihuahua up, who immediately burrowed under the covers.

"Alexa, sleep." The house went pitch black. I rolled over and continued to think about the day's events.

CHAPTER 5

SAGE

My alarm went off and my cat was purring in my face. I hit snooze and covered my head with my blanket.

A few minutes later, there was a knock. With a sigh, I crawled out of bed and headed to see who it was. When I opened the door, Erik and Lyric were smiling at me.

"Why are you here?"

"Nice to see you too, Sage," Erik said as he entered my apartment.

"I didn't mean it like that."

He held up a bag. "I brought you breakfast."

"And I brought coffee," Lyric said.

I reached out and grabbed a cup. "Thank you."

"There are bagels and cream cheese in here," Erik said as he set the bag on the counter.

"Yum." I dug into the bag, grabbed one, and popped it into the toaster. "So, what's up?"

"We were in the area and Lyric wanted to bring you breakfast."

"Because I haven't seen you in three days," she said as she took a stool at the counter.

"I know. I missed you," I confessed, and she winked at me.

"Are you excited about tonight?" Erik asked.

"Should I be?"

"Sage, this is our life. You will—"

"Do *not* tell me I will get used to it, Erik. I will never get used to having to do something I didn't have a choice in doing."

"I agree with Sage," Lyric said before taking a sip of her coffee.

Erik shook his head, a disapproving look on his face. "I don't know why you both hate this job. We get paid over six figures a year, and you will get even more when you take over."

"And what good does money do for me when I have no free time or social life?"

"Hear, hear!" Lyric held up her coffee cup in agreement with my statement.

Erik ignored her as he continued. "You have a social life. What happened to the one guy you were talking to? What was his name? Umm . . . Alberto?"

"Roberto, and he dumped me." My bagel popped out of the toaster and I spread cream cheese on it.

"Why?" he asked.

"She didn't have enough free time to give him what he needed," Lyric said. She knew more about my relationships than Erik did.

Erik furrowed his eyebrows, a smidgen of brotherly anger showing on his face. "And what was that?"

"He wanted me to hang out with him all day and night. Wake up next to him, cuddle, and—"

"That's information I don't want to hear."

"You asked." I shrugged and took a bite as Lyric laughed.

"What about Tara?"

"She went back to her ex-girlfriend," I said with a full mouth.

"Unfortunate. She was sexy," Erik said.

I smiled at my memories of her. "Yes. Yes, she was."

"And what about the guy who was always calling? What was his name?"

"Kevin," Lyric answered.

I cringed at hearing his name. "He was too suspicious. Always wanting to know where I was going and what I was doing, so I broke up with him."

"He would have put a tracker on her if she would have let him," Lyric added.

"Disgusting," Erik said before popping a bagel in the toaster. "That probably wasn't fun for you."

"He was fun, though. Most psychos are," I said with a wink. Lyric giggled, and Erik gave me an appalled look.

"By the way, I saw your name on the booster sheet. You're due for your weekly shot today," Lyric informed.

"Shit, I forgot I would have to get them weekly now."

"Yeah, we should leave early so you can receive it before we head out," Erik said. "Mine's today, as well."

"I have to shower and get dressed first."

"I'll wait for you."

That was one thing about Erik that made him a fantastic guy. He cared enough to patiently take care of me, making me wish sometimes he wasn't practically family. It would make it easier to love and marry your best friend.

"I'll be gone before you get out. I have to pick up my dry cleaning before guard duty tonight," Lyric said.

"Aww, okay. I'll see you later. I love you."

"Love you, too!"

Shoving the last piece of bagel in my mouth, I headed down the hall into my bedroom. After showering, I wrapped a towel around myself while picking out clothes.

"Erik, what should I wear?"

"Are you covered?"

"Yeah. Come in."

Erik opened the door and stepped in. He glanced at my towel-wrapped body and quickly averted his eyes. "Most of us wear jeans. Some girls wear leather pants. Just make sure whatever you wear, you have a full range of motion so you can kick and punch."

"Jeans and a t-shirt for the win."

He smiled. "Wear the light leather jacket . . . the black one. It looks good on you."

"I'm not trying to look good, Erik."

"I know, but leather helps keep you from getting scraped up. Plus, this time of year it can get chilly at night."

I nodded, and Erik left the room, shutting the door behind him.

After getting dressed, I threw on my lace-up black combat boots—the ones *without* the heels. I also threw on a little black eyeliner and mascara before I emerged from my bedroom.

"I'm ready."

"You look too pretty to be hunting vampires."

I laughed and shook my head. "Thanks."

It was still daylight when we left my apartment building. We got into Erik's Mustang and headed for the facility.

We arrived right before dusk. Erik parked his car into the garage. We stepped inside the elevator and went up before making our way down the hall. We mainly stayed quiet during the walk.

"After you," Erik said as he opened the door to the infirmary.

As we entered the room, Doctor Jayne was preparing our immune boosters. As hunters, we are required to receive these shots weekly. They give us more strength, agility, and prowess. Without it, we wouldn't stand a fighting chance against the vampires.

"Hello, Sagelynn." She smiled at me. She was tall, fair skinned, and blonde. She was pretty and probably could have been a model if it wasn't for the long bird nose she had.

"Hi, Dr. Jayne."

"Take a seat," she said while she snapped on some gloves.

I took my jacket off, rolled up my sleeve, and took a seat in her chair. I watched as Erik rolled up his sleeve, too.

Dr. Jayne grabbed an alcohol wipe and prepped my skin. She stuck me quickly and injected me with what I like to call the "super potion."

A warm, blissful feeling washed over me, and my heart sped up a little.

"All done."

I hopped up and Erik took a seat. She injected him as well. By the time he was done, my blissful feeling had slowed down, but it left me with super energy.

"What's all in the shot?"

"It's a bunch of vitamins, minerals, and other immune boosters. Nothing for you to worry about, Sage."

Erik furrowed his eyebrows at me, silently telling me to stop being nosey. I rolled my eyes at him and put my jacket back on.

"Alright, I will see you both next week."

"Thanks, Doc," I said before we left the infirmary. As soon as we were in the hallway, we ran into Deren.

"What's up, guys?"

"We just got our shots," Erik said.

"I have to get mine. I'll meet you down in the van."

We continued our journey through the halls until we came upon the armory where we each grabbed some weapons. I picked up a full-size crossbow.

"You don't want that," Erik said.

"Why not?"

"It's slow to load, and it's heavy. Try the mini one."

Taking his advice, I turned around and grabbed a mini crossbow off the table. It held three small silver stakes, and you could shoot them consecutively without reloading.

Grabbing a satchel, I threw a full-size silver stake and the mini crossbow into it. I also strapped a silver dagger onto my hip. Silver would kill not only vampires but wolven, too. Even though we had a treaty with them, there were a few rogue wolves who were vampire sympathizers and would sometimes engage with us in battle.

"You ready, Sage?"

I nodded. Physically, I was ready—meaning I was trained and packing weapons—mentally, I wasn't.

Erik left the armory, and I took a deep breath as I followed him. We went back to the garage, got in a black van, and waited.

"Are you losers ready?" Deren asked as he slid the van door open.

"Just get in, asshole," Erik said and I laughed.

Erik was driving and I was in the passenger seat when we left the parking garage. The guards let us through the gates and we headed for the highway.

Deren's tablet beeped. "I just got a lead," he informed us.

"Where?" Erik asked.

"Southside. Drifter's bar."

"What was the lead?" I asked.

Glancing back, he was typing on a tablet. "Wolven sighting, so there might be vamps around."

"Alright, Drifter's it is." Erik pulled onto the highway and we headed downtown.

Once we parked, we made sure to hide our weapons before heading into the bar. Since I was a girl, it was normal for me to carry a satchel. People would just assume it was a purse. I left my dagger and crossbow in the van, taking only the stake with me.

Unfortunately, we didn't have any unique way to tell if a person was a vampire, other than some of them will make themselves known when we meet them by trying to kill us. The only other failsafe way was to stab them with silver. Even touching their skin wouldn't work. It had to be inserted into them and I had no idea why.

"IDs," the bouncer at the door commanded.

We all pulled out our IDs. They were fake to keep our names and addresses secret, but we were of age. I handed him mine, and he took a flashlight to it. He gave it back, then gestured for me to go.

I started through the door when the bouncer said, "We are at full capacity. You two will have to wait."

Stopping, I made eye contact with Erik. He shook his head no.

"In or out?" the bouncer said. I quickly decided and continued into the bar without my team.

Within seconds, my phone rang, and I answered it.

"Sage, are you crazy?"

"I can't hear you, Erik. The music is loud."

"Come back outside."

Deciding I would be fine in a bar packed with people, I hung up the phone. I figured they would eventually have to let them in.

There was a long bar on the left side, a few tables on the right, and pool tables further back. The jukebox was going, and the place was packed, so I made my way to the bar and took a seat.

"What can I get ya?"

I looked up into a gray-haired man's eyes. "I will take, umm, a beer." I rarely drank beer, but this place didn't look like it would serve anything other than that and hard liquor.

"What kind, doll?"

"Whatever's good." I smiled at the bartender, trying to seem relaxed.

"Coming right up." He slid open a cooler, grabbed a beer out of the ice, popped the top, and set it in front of me.

"Thanks."

"Do you want me to start a tab?"

"Sure." I took a swig of my beer and it tasted like shit.

"I need a card to put on file."

Reaching into my bag, I pulled out my wallet and gave him my debit card. Like my ID, it had the name Marie Adams on it.

"What brings you to this neck of the woods?" a male voice asked. Turning to look at the man, he was middle-aged with scruffy blond hair.

"How do you know I'm not from this neck of the woods?"

"Because I've never seen you here before and I would remember a pretty face like yours." His arrogant grin repulsed me. It seemed mischievous in a gross way, making me feel uneasy.

"That's because this is my first time visiting this fine establishment." I took a swig of my beer to keep from rolling my eyes.

"Fair enough. I'm Jack." The man extended his hand to me.

I extended my hand back. "Sage."

Shit, I was supposed to say Marie, and I accidentally told him my real name. It's my second night out and I'm already failing.

"Nice to meet you, Sage. Let me buy you a beer."

I held up the bottle I knew he had seen. "I already have one. Thanks."

Pulling my phone from my pocket, I started a game on it, hoping he would get the hint and leave. He stayed quiet as he ordered himself a beer before heading back to his table. I was grateful.

My eyes did a sweep of the room and I spotted some slot machines, so I made my way over to one and sat down. It took less than ten minutes for me to lose twenty bucks and get bored. Wondering if my friends were ever going to get let in, I checked my phone and saw multiple texts from Erik on the screen.

Erik: *They won't let us in.*

Erik: *Sage, leave.*

Erik: *Come on.*

Erik: *Please.*

Erik: *Damn it, Sage.*

Erik: *Come outside!*

Erik: *LEAVE NOW!*

Erik: *If you aren't outside in five minutes, I'm calling your dad.*

"Shit," I exclaimed as I got up from the slot machine. Erik was furious at me and I needed to get out of here now.

After pocketing my phone, I looked around. The guy who was trying to buy me a beer, Beer Jack, I was now calling him, was watching me. He gave me a wink. An uneasy feeling washed over me since I couldn't tell if he was a vampire or not. Plus, he was creepy. I tried to stay calm, so I gave him a kind smile before turning away and heading toward the bartender.

"Another beer?"

"Not yet. Where's the bathroom?"

"In the back, to the left."

"Thanks." I headed back, scoping out the place as I wandered there.

Beer Jack stood up and smiled at me while I passed him. More gross feelings filled me. I was almost to the back door when a hot guy entered through it, so I couldn't escape just yet. He was lightly tanned with dark hair. His fully tattooed arms stood out to me, and I immediately wondered where else he was tatted. He was sexy as hell and I would have told him so if I wasn't trying to get the fuck out of there. I smiled at him before heading into the bathroom. After I shut the door and locked it, I sighed.

What kind of shit did I get myself into?

CHAPTER 6

LUKA

The sun had set, so I headed out the door. Wanting to see if Winnie got any more leads, I planned on heading to his apartment. After opening the garage and hopping on my bike, my cell rang.

"What's up, Ollie?"

"Hey, Luka, there are some out-of-place people here."

"How out of place?"

"They smell of cult."

"How many?" I asked as I latched my helmet.

"Three. One woman is at the bar, and two men are at the door."

"What does the woman look like?"

"Young, short black hair, pretty. Her debit card says Marie Adams, but she told Mannie her name was Sage."

"Shit! Don't let her leave. I'm on my way." I hung up the phone and called Drag.

"Hello?"

"Venom is at Drifter's."

"On my way!"

"Bring Winnie." I pocketed my phone and started my Harley.

Once I was at Drifter's, I decided to go into the back entrance. I pulled my bike into the alley and parked. I took off my helmet and threw my keys in my pocket before entering the back, right by the bathroom.

As I was closing the door, I looked up and there she was. Locking eyes with the woman who killed my brother made me go rigid. She smiled and the sweet scent of her flowed into my nostrils. I froze in shock as she entered the women's restroom. As the door closed, I wondered if I should go after her.

Taking a deep breath and calming myself, I moved into the supply room across the hall from the bathrooms. After shutting the door all but a crack, I flipped off the light. My hands balled into fists and my jaw clenched as I patiently waited for her to come out.

After a few minutes, she emerged from the bathroom and went toward the exit. She glanced over her shoulder to make sure no one noticed before she snuck out the back door. I waited thirty seconds and then went after her.

When I stepped into the alley's darkness, I didn't see her anywhere. There was no way she took off running and made it to the end of the alley that quickly. She had to be hiding. The sweet sound of her heartbeat filled my ears—she was nearby.

Being as casual as possible, I strolled to my bike like I wasn't looking for anyone. I leaned against it and pulled out my phone, texting Drag that I was in the alley while I waited for her to make a move or a noise, whichever came first.

The light scuff of a shoe on the pavement came seconds before I saw her shadow. I jumped out of the way, and she tumbled to the ground.

She recovered quickly, hopping to her feet like a pro with a stake in her hand.

"What the fuck are you doing?" I asked with an annoyed voice.

Her face looked dumbfounded as she halted herself. "What?"

"Why are you out here? And why are you holding an ice pick?"

"What?" she repeated as she eased her body, dropping the stake to her side.

Perfect. She was easy to manipulate and trusting.

This will be fun.

"I said why are—"

"I know what you said, fucker."

Man, she was snarky. It made me smirk. "Then why did you say *what*?"

"I thought you were someone else. Sorry."

She turned to leave and I needed to keep her from finding her friends.

"Were you trying to steal my bike?"

"No, I wouldn't know how to ride that death trap if I wanted to," she mumbled as she kept walking.

She wasn't taking my bait, so I needed to piss her off.

"Oh, you're a hooker." That got her attention.

She whipped back around toward me. "First thing, it's escort or sex worker and no. I'm *not* one!"

"Then why are you in a dark alley by yourself?"

"It's really none of your business, but I was looking for my friends."

"Are they hookers, too?"

Her face was angry as she strolled toward me. "I said I'm not a fucking hooker!" She pointed her finger like she was scolding a child. I smiled, finding it rather amusing.

"It's escort or sex worker," I reminded her with an arrogant grin.

Her face reddened as more anger took over. "What's your deal, man?"

"What's yours? I was just chilling next to my bike, and you sprang out of the darkness with an ice pick in your hand."

"It's not an ice pick, it's a stake!"

I smirked. "Oh, are you a vampire hunter?"

"Sorry I scared you. Have a good night," she called over her shoulder as she strolled away.

"Don't go through the field. There are snakes at night."

"I'll be fine," she said with a wave of her hand.

"I have some antivenom if you need it."

Her body tensed as she stopped dead in her tracks.

She whipped around toward me, but I was already close behind her—I was fast. Grabbing her arm, I halted it as she tried to plunge the stake into me. Twisting her wrist, she cried out in pain as she dropped the weapon.

She brought her knee up and shoved it into my groin. I let go of her for a split second when I felt the pain radiate through my balls and toward my lower abdomen. I may be a vampire, but that shit still hurts.

She yanked her phone out of her pocket and I smacked it out of her hand. "No, no. I've seen what that light can do."

She lunged for the stake on the ground as I lunged, shoving her. She fell onto her back, and I laid on top of her, pinning her wrists above her head. She twisted and turned, trying to get away from me. She may be strong, but I was stronger.

"Get off me!" she screamed.

"Quiet down, and I might think about it."

Figuring I won, I grinned at her mere seconds before she slung her head forward and head-butted me in the face. I won't lie, it also hurt.

"Shit!"

"Get off me!"

"You are a part of Venom, so tell me why I would do that?"

Her response was to lean forward and bite my shoulder. This girl was feisty and it thrilled me. She was a fighter, that was for sure. It almost felt like a waste to murder someone with such spunk.

"Stop before I hurt you!"

Unrelenting, she continued to struggle free. "You're trying to kill me, why are you worried about hurting me?"

"Why would you think I'm trying to kill you?"

"Because you're a killer!"

"*I'm* the killer? You're the fucking killer! You killed my brother!"

She finally stopped fighting, her eyebrows furrowed in confusion before a look of realization came across her face.

Her chest rose and fell below me as she tried hard to catch her breath. "Then kill me," she said through gritted teeth.

"Oh, I'm not going to kill you. Not yet, anyway."

"Then why are you laying on top of me, fucker?"

"Because I want you to know you should watch your back. I know who you are now and everywhere you go, I'll be there."

"Death by fear, huh? That might work if I was actually scared of you, but I'm not." She smiled like she didn't give a fuck about anything.

"You should be." I opened my mouth, showing her my fangs as they elongated.

"Fuck you!" She struggled again to get free.

A slight clicking sound came from behind me, I rolled to the side, taking the girl with me as a stake flew past us. Yanking her off the ground, I carried her as I ran down the alley. Once we were a few blocks away—which was roughly thirty seconds because vampires are super-fast—I slowed down.

"Let me the fuck go!"

I stopped running and dropped her to the ground. She scrambled to her feet and immediately took a defensive stance.

I nodded my head in the direction we came from. "Get the fuck out of here."

"What kind of game are you playing?"

"I'm not playing a game."

Her brows furrowed as she struggled to catch her breath. "Why aren't you killing me, then?"

"I already told you that—"

"I know what you said, fucker. You're going to stalk me, blah, blah, blah." She rolled her eyes.

"Yeah, pretty much."

"Why?"

Closing the distance between us, I looked down into her eyes. "Because you killed my fucking brother!"

She threw her hands out to the side. "Then why not just save yourself some time and kill me now?"

"Because it would be too quick and less fun for me," I whispered in her face.

Her eyes searched mine, looking for a shred of humanity. Currently, I had none. I could see the fear in her eyes, but she kept it contained, instead swallowing hard before running her mouth again.

"Like I give a rat's ass about your fun!"

"I said you can go, I'm not killing you. Not tonight." I took a step back, giving her room to flee.

"But you will eventually?" she asked, tilting her head.

I smirked. "That's kind of how revenge works."

"Good. See ya." She leisurely strolled down the alley.

Confused by her, I needed to know more, so I sprinted up to her.

"Fuck. What now?" she asked with a frustrated face.

How the hell is she not running from a vampire? I wondered. "Are you not afraid of death?"

"Not really."

"Do you want to die?"

She stopped, crossed her arms, and glared at me. "Not particularly, but I would rather you get it over with if you're going to do it."

"You're weird as shit, you know that?"

She shrugged. "Yeah, I've been called an anomaly before."

At the sound of footsteps, I glanced down the alley. Her teammates were almost here.

While standing there for a few seconds, deciding whether I should kill them, I caught her shift out of the corner of my eye.

"Don't," I said as I made eye contact with her. Her hand was in her bag. "I'll see you around." I gave her a wink.

After I made my way down the alley, I headed to the rooftops. As soon as I was up on one, I pulled out my phone and called Drag.

"Yeah?"

"Hey, there are three in the alley. I'm on the roof three buildings down."

He sighed. "Winnie and I are in the bar."

"Okay, stay inside. I'll head down as soon as they're gone."

After ending the call, I took a seat on the roof's edge and watched the city below me.

CHAPTER 7
SAGE

The soulless creature looked down the alley, so I glanced in that direction. With only human vision, I could barely make out two figures, and I hoped they were Erik and Deren. If they weren't, I needed to get out of here fast. I guided my hand into my bag to grab my stake, but remembered I dropped it.

"Don't," he said, and I froze as his blue eyes burned into my soul, making my breath catch.

It was like they were trying to steal secrets I didn't want to reveal. Secrets I didn't even know I had. He was standing too close for me to move—to breathe.

"I'll see you around," he said with a wink.

In a flash, he was gone, leaving me breathless with a racing heart. Of course, I was scared of him and had completely lied. I was also fearful of being stalked and not knowing when he would murder me. But I wasn't lying when I said I would rather die now than wait out the death coming to me.

Footsteps slamming against pavement brought me back from staring at the space where he once stood. I turned around and waited as my team got closer.

"Sage, are you okay?" Deren asked as he ran up to me.

Erik's reaction was less nonchalant—he plowed into me with a hug.

"Did he bite you?" he asked frantically.

"No, I'm fine," I said. He pulled away and grabbed my arms while looking me over. "Erik, I'm fine, I swear."

"I was worried to death, Sage!"

"Why didn't he kill her?" Deren asked as he handed me my stake and phone.

Erik shook his head. "I don't know." A look of confusion and relief played upon his face.

"I know why," I whispered, and both of their heads whipped towards me.

"Why?" Erik asked.

I stuck my phone in my pocket but kept the stake ready. "He told me I should watch my back."

"What?" Erik's face scrunched up as anger took over.

"He also said he knows who I am and he will be everywhere I go."

"Because you're a Venom member?" Deren asked.

"No, because the vampire I staked last night was his brother."

"Oh shit, let's get you out of here." Erik grabbed my arm and tried to escort me to the van.

I didn't like being treated like I was weak, so I yanked my arm away from him. "I can defend myself, Erik. I don't need you to do it!"

"Really, Sage? Because it didn't look like it when we found you on the ground with a vampire on top of you!"

His words not only hurt, but pissed me off. "You're an ass!" I shook my head and turned away.

"Sage, stop! I didn't mean it like that."

"Shut up, Erik! We aren't talking right now."

"I'm going to go get the van," Deren said uncomfortably and took off jogging.

"Sage, stop walking!" Erik grabbed my arm halting me from my furious stomping and I immediately yanked it out of his grasp.

"What, Erik? What else do you want to say?" I crossed my arms, waiting for his response.

"I was scared, and I didn't mean to hurt your feelings. I know you can protect yourself."

"Whatever." I started walking again, and he followed close behind me.

"Please don't be mad at me, Sage. You're my best friend. I'm sorry."

I stopped and met his eyes as I pointed the stake at him. "Don't say shit like that to me again! It's my first night in the field and I already have enough pressure trying to please my dad. I don't want to worry about pleasing you, too!"

"I won't. I promise." He grabbed my free hand and placed it over his heart. "Blood of the coven."

Looking into his eyes, I knew he was sorry, and I knew he didn't mean it. Fear makes people say the wrong words sometimes.

"Okay." I took slow breaths as I tried to calm my racing heart.

"I love you, Sage."

"I know. I love you, too."

Deren pulled up in the van. Erik opened the sliding door and we got in.

"Where to next?" Deren asked.

"Find an empty parking lot. We will regroup and figure out where to go," Erik said.

"No. Take me home, please."

"Sage, you're on shift until dawn. Your father will—"

"I don't give a shit what my father says! Take me home, Deren!"

"You got it."

I looked at Erik, daring him to say something. He pressed his lips into a tight line and stayed quiet.

Twenty minutes later, we pulled up to my apartment and I got out of the van.

"Sage," Erik called. I said nothing as I shut the door and went into the building.

Tears filled my eyes as I headed to my apartment. I almost died, and that reality hit me hard. Erik was right. I couldn't protect myself, which disappointed me.

Unlocking my door, I entered my home. Everything looked fine, so I shut the door and locked all the locks. After flipping on the light, I plopped down on the couch. Sitting there for a mere thirty seconds, my cell vibrated. It was my father.

"Hello?"

"Sagelynn, why are you at your apartment?"

I was surprised that he knew where I was. "How did you know?"

"You know we track everyone's heart rate and location when they're in the field. So, why did you go home?"

I hated the fact the *health monitors* kept track of us.

"I almost died, Dad," I whispered. He was quiet for a few seconds like he was trying to decide what to say.

"Since you disregarded your shift, you will make it up by taking a shift tomorrow."

Anger filled me since that was my normal day off. "What? You can't be serious!"

A long breath of exasperation left him before he spoke. "Sorry, but you know that's how it works."

"You don't care I almost died?"

"Of course, I do. Unfortunately, that's part of the job, Sagelynn. We *almost* die *every* night."

I wanted to say there is *no we* because he doesn't go in the field, but I kept my mouth shut. "Whatever," I mumbled instead.

"Your actions have also caused there to be an infraction mark on your records and, as punishment, you will come in early the rest of the week for extra training."

"Seriously?!"

"Don't take that tone with me, Sagelynn. Just because you're the president's daughter doesn't make you impervious to the rules. You will be marked!"

Deciding I was too mentally exhausted to fight with him, I ceased. "I'm sorry, dad."

"Take the rest of the night off and rest. I'll see you tomorrow."

The phone went silent, so I threw it on the couch next to me and put my face in my hands. I wasn't mad I got an infraction, I cared little about that, but I didn't want to go in early for extra training.

Disappointment in myself filled me as I headed into the kitchen and made a sandwich. Chewy purred at my feet, so I fed him and then ate while standing there, staring into space. Frustrated with the night's events, I took two shots of tequila before I made my way back to the couch. I turned the TV on and flipped through the channels until

I found a murder mystery marathon. Chewy crawled up on me and purred while I vegged out and pretended this wasn't my life.

CHAPTER 8

LUKA

After a while of chilling on the rooftop, I had a text from Drag saying it was clear to come down. I entered the back door of the bar and my friends were sitting at a table with three women and a man. Humans.

The lustful smell radiating off them, let me know they were fangasizers or fangsters—people who fantasized about being bitten. Winnie called this group of men and women the fangdom. Kind of like a fandom for vamps. Some believed the want or need to be bitten stemmed from the whole therapeutic phlebotomy thing, like bloodletting. I, on the other hand, assumed it was because the venom in our bite causes the bitee to have an instant orgasm. Not just any regular orgasm—a euphoric, long-lasting one that's sought after like a rare diamond. A powerful drug, really. They say our venom existed so we could seduce our victims and kill them before we were caught. As humans evolved and decided they liked it, it became easier for us to feed, and that's how the fangdom was born.

Luckily for us, the fangsters loved to be fed on during sex. So, I would give them what they wanted in return for feeding me. I always wondered if it made me a slut . . . or perhaps more like a sex worker, since I'm getting paid in blood. My eyes darted across each of them as I decided what meal I was eating tonight.

"What's up, losers?" I asked as I approached.

"What the fuck happened, Luka?" Drag asked. The look on his face told me he was not only pissed, but worried.

"I was just having fun, man." I grinned, showing him my fangs. Well, it was more for the fangdom.

One of the girls shifted and rubbed her thighs together—dinner.

"You're not a sadistic bastard. I know this because I have been your friend for ten years, so stop fucking around. Either kill the girl or let her be. I'm not going to sit around and worry about my best friend getting staked!"

"Okay, Drag. Fuck. Chill out, man."

"Sorry. It's just frustrating enough having to always watch everyone's back, but I never have to worry about you. I know you can handle yourself, but I was worried about you tonight, and it scared the shit out of me, Luka."

Drag was an open and honest man. He wore his heart on his sleeve and he didn't care who knew—unlike me. I wasn't a man to talk much about his feelings, so I nodded to acknowledge his concern, hoping he would drop it.

"Do you want a beer?" Winnie asked, breaking the tension.

"What kind of question is that?" I took a seat next to Thigh Rubber. She smiled at me, and I gave her a wink.

"Libby," Winnie called to the server walking past our table, "can you get us another round, please? Bring an extra one for the bloodsucker."

"Dude, you're a bloodsucker, too!"

"Yeah, but I'm just a hacker, I don't stalk people for fun. I don't play with my food. Right?" Winnie looked over at his date who blushed.

A hand slid onto my leg—the thigh rubber wasn't wasting time. Reaching my hand down, I guided hers to my now hardened cock. A small gasp came from her and I couldn't help but smirk.

"Here you go, Luka," Libby said as she set my drink down. "I'll go grab the rest."

"Thanks, Libby." The blonde-haired wolven smiled before sliding back behind the bar.

Thigh Rubber leaned in close to me and blew in my ear before whispering, "Do you want to feed?"

It only took me a few seconds to decide whether a beer or blood sounded better. Warm blood washed down by a cold beer sounded great, so I took her hand and stood up.

"Abso-fucking-lutely."

Ollie respected our alliance and was even nice enough to have a feed room set up for us, which made me grateful for the old bastard. I headed toward the back of the bar, pulling my date—dinner, whatever—behind me.

"Hey, Luka," Ollie hollered as he came from behind the bar. "I got something you may want." He handed me a debit card.

"Marie Adams? Who's that?"

"That girl left it behind."

"What did she tell Mannie her name was again?" I asked. The woman hanging on my arm was getting antsy.

"Sage. She didn't give a last name."

"Thanks, Ollie." I pocketed the card as I continued walking.

After opening the door to the supply closet, I pulled Thigh Rubber inside. Running my hand down the seam on the back wall, I pushed and the secret door to the feed room popped open. Before we even made it in, she was already letting out light moans of excitement.

Shutting the door to the small six-by-six room, it got dark. She couldn't see anything, but I could, and I watched as she bit her lip in anticipation.

My throat was dry from hunger, so I wasn't going to waste time. My hands were instantly on her, pulling her toward me, and she gasped as her body pressed against mine. Her hands slithered up the back of my shirt as I slammed a kiss on her. More moans of excitement left her mouth, ringing loudly through the tiny room. I was never more grateful for it being soundproof.

I grabbed her hands, threw them off me, and spun her around, pressing her face up against the wall. She immediately stuck her ass out, trying to grind on me. Another loud moan left her lips as I pressed my hard cock against her.

Leaning down, I sniffed her. The lustful scent humans radiated when they wanted to be fucked or bitten was extremely intoxicating to vampires. We called it their *lure*. This woman's lure smelled like musk and berries, not my favorite, but all lures smelled delicious.

Yanking up her skirt, she shifted as she lowered her panties as fast as she could. I immediately unzipped my jeans and pulled my cock out. My balls were tight and ready.

I ran my nose across her ear and whispered, "Spread your legs."

She did, so I slid my hands between her thighs and up to her core. The anticipation of my bite already had her soaking wet. Good. Less work for me to do.

Lifting her leg, I slammed my cock into her, and she moaned loudly. One of my hands snaked around, grabbing her tit and squeezed as I pounded into her.

I could last hours in bed, but when it's just for a feed, I tried to give the fangsters what they were anticipating. Moving her hair to the side, I ran my free hand down her neck.

"Yes, bite me, please!" she cried out.

My hand moved to her hair, and I tightened my fist into it, using it to tilt her head. Opening my mouth, my fangs elongated, ready to strike. The flesh was soft as my fangs pierced her skin. The warmth of her blood filled my mouth, and I swallowed rapidly.

Her pussy clenched around my cock, and she moaned again as she started coming from my venom. Her warm blood snaked down my throat, making my balls tighten even more. Once I felt her heartbeat slow, I knew it was time to stop. I broke free of the bite before I killed her.

As I continued to slam my cock into her, pictures of the Venom member filled my head. I envisioned being inside of her and her warm blood in my throat. The blonde was still orgasming hysterically when I came.

Laying my forehead against the wall as I caught my breath, she slunk out from between me and the wall. After she pulled her panties up, she opened the door.

"Thank you," she said before shutting it.

"What the fuck is wrong with me?" I asked myself. I put my cock away and tried to pretend like I *didn't* have the fucked-up thoughts about the Venom girl.

Blood-filled and satisfied, I went back to the table for a few more rounds of drinks.

Not long before the sun came up, Drag took off alone. Winnie went somewhere with one girl and the guy, so I made my way home. After sleeping away the daylight, I was awoken by my cell ringing. It was Finneas.

"What the fuck does he want," I mumbled to myself before hitting the accept button. "Yeah?"

"Lukas, I have a lead on some Venom members in the old meat-packing district. It seems like they're possibly setting up shop there. I was hoping you could check it out for me tonight."

I immediately sat up. "Of course. Address?"

Finneas gave me the full details about the lead, which I wrote down before I took a quick shower and got dressed.

As I sat at my kitchen table and waited until it was time to head out, I wondered why Fin gave me the lead. It had been the first one he offered to send me on. My suspicions rose higher the longer I sat there, and I wondered if I should call for backup. Not wanting to get any of my friends killed, I decided to go alone, but I made sure to take my gun in case I needed it.

Once it was time to go, I told Annie bye, and jumped on my bike. The whole drive there, I reminded myself to be on high alert tonight since I didn't trust Finneas.

CHAPTER 9

SAGE

Waking up early, I had already cleaned my apartment, done laundry, and read a few chapters of a book. I had three missed calls from Erik.

I had just gotten dressed and was ready to head in early for my mandatory practice when my phone rang again.

"Hey, Erik."

"Sage, I have been calling you all day." His voice sounded frustrated.

"I was busy."

"You're still mad at me, aren't you?"

"No, it's fine," I mumbled. Actually, I *was* still mad at him, even though I had already told him I forgave him.

"I know you better than you know yourself, Sage."

"Yeah, I'm still mad, but I will get over it. Just change the subject or something." Grabbing my socks, I slid them on as he spoke.

"Okay, here's a new one for you. Your father called me after he called you. I got an infraction for letting Deren take you home, since I was the lead on duty with you."

"What? You've got to be fucking kidding me."

"Yeah, no. It's okay, though. It's my first one."

"It's not okay, Erik. He shouldn't have done that!" Grabbing my boots, I took a seat on the bed. "I'm sorry."

"I forgive you. Now, will you forgive me for real this time?"

"Yes, I promise."

"Do you want me to pick you up? Or are you driving yourself?"

I tied my boots before standing up. "I'm going to drive in since I have to come in early for extra training as punishment."

"Yeah, umm . . . me too."

"Geez. My dad is completely ridiculous."

"Yeah, Deren was mad." A small laugh left him.

"He got punished too?"

"He just got training."

"I'm glad he didn't get an infraction. I will talk to my dad and try to get yours removed."

With a pat on Chewy's head, I left the bedroom.

"No, don't. I kind of feel like a badass now, going against the rules and all." He laughed, and it made me smile.

"I'll see you soon, Erik."

"Okay. Love you."

"Love you. Bye."

After gathering my things, I headed down to my car. I got off the elevator, made my way through the private parking garage, and entered my Jeep. Security knew me, so they raised the door, and I waved as I pulled out onto the main street.

It was a beautiful, sunny day. I didn't get to see the sun often, so it was nice to feel the warmth on my skin. Rolling my window down, I let the wind blow my hair back as I dreamed of another life—one where I could call off work and go to the beach. A life where slaying vampires wasn't a requirement, and I didn't almost get killed. Turning up the radio, I enjoyed my life with no worries in the world—just for a bit.

"You're in a great mood," a guard said to me as I pulled up to the compound's gates.

"It's a beautiful day," I said with a smile. I placed my finger on the pad and the gates opened.

"Stay safe," he called out as I drove in.

Since I had training today, I wasn't going into the main building. I was going to the trainer's arena, so I turned left and parked outside the building.

"Are you ready to get your ass kicked?" Deren asked as I walked up.

I laughed. "By you?"

"You got me in trouble, so it's only fair."

"I'm sorry. I didn't know my dad was going to punish everyone."

"It's okay, Sage. It gave me some badassery."

I stopped at the door and stared at him. "That's not a word, Deren."

"Yes, it is! Look it up."

With a shake of my head, I opened the door and Deren followed behind. I would look it up later when he wasn't around—in case I was wrong.

"Well, well. The delinquents have finally shown up," Marcus said as we entered the gym. Erik was standing with him.

"Oh, shit," Deren whispered. "We're about to get our asses kicked."

"So much for your badassery," I teased.

Marcus was a huge man—over six feet tall and two hundred and fifty pounds. He was extremely fit, fast, and trained a lot. We were both going to be murdered.

"Hey, Marcus." I gave him an uneasy smile.

"Hi, love." He kissed the side of my head. "Don't worry. I won't go too hard on you. This fool, maybe." He glanced at Deren, and I laughed as he seemed to shrink in fear. "You three change your clothes and get on the floor."

We headed to the locker room, Erik falling into step with me.

"So, we are getting slaughtered today. That'll be fun." He gave me a sympathetic smile.

"Thanks, Sage," Deren said with a sigh.

"I'm sorry, guys. I didn't know we were going to have Marcus training us."

"I barely made it through his class when I was a novice," Deren admitted.

"You're *still* a novice," I said jokingly. Erik laughed before turning serious.

"The more we train, the better we are. We all need a little refresher sometimes." Erik always had a way of seeing the silver lining—something I struggled with.

"I don't need a refresher. I just came off daily training," I reminded him.

"Me too," Deren added. "I have only been in the field for a few months."

Erik gave us a teasing smile. "Then you both should be able to handle it."

We parted ways as I entered the women's locker room where I changed into some athletic shorts and a tank top.

"We are training, not clubbing," Deren said as I walked out.

My shorts were short, but it gets hot while sparring and, honestly, I didn't care, so I shrugged.

"Are you staring at my goddaughter?" Marcus asked.

Deren's body stiffened, and I couldn't help but laugh. "No, sir."

"Good. You're up first."

"Shit," Deren mumbled. He knew he was about to take a beating. No matter how good any of us were, I didn't think we could ever take Marcus in a real fight.

Erik and I both stood on the sidelines as Deren took his stance. I did a little stretching as I watched, and Erik kept track of points. Marcus didn't hold back. He was the offense the whole time and, as I figured, Deren got his ass handed to him. Marcus got three points and Deren got one.

"Sage, you're next," Marcus said.

Walking onto the mat, I cracked my neck and shook my arms. It wouldn't help, but it made me feel better. Since I needed to get to three points before he did—and not wanting to follow Deren's mistake and be on the defense the whole time—I decided I wasn't going to hold back.

As soon as the match started, I darted out toward him and threw a kick, and he immediately blocked it. Spinning around, I swung my fist, and he caught my arm in mid-swing and twisted it, so I grabbed his arm with my other hand and pulled on it. While I used his body weight against him, I kicked the side of his leg. He went down, and I quickly tapped my fist to his chest like I was staking him.

"One point for Sage," Erik said.

Marcus got up off the floor and smiled before we went again. He lunged for me, and I dodged it. He swung a knife hand out and got me in the throat, making me fall to the ground where he instantly staked me.

"One point for Marcus."

Marcus smiled arrogantly as I tried to catch my breath. We started again, and this time I watched for his notorious preemptive strike. I knew he always threw a left punch before he kicked. When his left fist shot out, I dropped to my hands and knees. As he kicked out, I did the same and swept his other foot out from under him. As fast as I could, I staked him.

"Two points for Sage," Erik said with excitement.

Sparring with Marcus was fun because he was a phenomenal fighter. It kept me on my toes and made me think, which I loved. We have fought thirty or more times, but since I have only won twice, I was eager to take the win today. He might have said he would hold back, but he didn't mean it. He always told us how important it was to fight like your true self during sparring, and that's exactly what I did.

Both of us threw kicks and punches, the other side-stepping them flawlessly. Dodging one of his moves, I countered with a punch to his face, and he stumbled back, so I jumped up and spun a roundhouse kick into his chest. He caught my foot and yanked me to the left, making me fly a few feet away. Landing on my stomach, I immediately rolled onto my back, then his fist landed on my chest.

"Two points each. Final round."

Anxiousness filled me as I hopped to my feet, which was a big mistake and could cost me my life in a real battle. When I lunged for him, he grabbed me and twisted my back toward him before putting me in a chokehold. If he had been a vampire, I would have bitten his arm, but I didn't bite during sparring. Instead, I tried to punch him in the face as he choked me. He was much taller than me, so I only landed some weak blows to his neck and shoulder.

"Come on, Sage. You got this!" Erik cheered from the sidelines.

If I didn't get out of his chokehold, I was going to lose. Deciding to use his body weight against him, I grabbed onto his arm tight, brought one foot up, and kicked him in his knee. Once he felt the pain and eased forward, I pulled my knees up as far as I could and yanked down. I curled into a ball, making him lose his balance and tumble to the ground—along with me. As I was scrambling away, he grabbed my leg. Kicking my other foot out, I got him in the face. I felt terrible, but it wasn't enough to stop me. When he rolled onto his back, I flung myself on him and staked him.

"Three points. The winner is Sage!" Erik announced proudly.

"Yes!" Deren yelled as he clapped.

Exhausted, I laid my head on Marcus's chest while I slowed my breathing.

He patted my head. "Good job, honey."

"Thanks," I said breathlessly.

"Need a hand?" Erik asked as he reached one out to me. I took it and he helped me up. "You were wonderful."

"Thanks."

My heart was racing, and I was dying to wash the sweat off me.

"Erik, you're next," Marcus said. Deren and I took a seat on the sidelines.

"Need this?" Deren held out a bottle of water and a towel. I took it.

"Thanks."

"Come on, Erik," Deren encouraged as they started sparring.

We watched as the two went round and round. They ended up tied at two points each before Marcus prevailed in the last round.

"Good job today, everyone. Especially you, Sage. Being shorter has its advantages sometimes. You're quicker than most men. Make sure you always use it efficiently."

"Noted."

"You're all dismissed."

"Who is on the roster with me tonight?" I asked as we headed towards the locker rooms.

"I know it's me and you, but I don't know who the lead is," Deren said.

Looking at Erik, I wondered if he was on shift.

He shook his head. "I'm off. Sorin is leading tonight."

"Shit," I mumbled as I entered the locker room.

Sorin and I didn't quite see eye to eye—he was a little too aggressive for me. I also didn't like the fact he thought we should respect him, even if he didn't respect us. He was a bit pretentious and it always rubbed me wrong. Mostly, he acted like we were in the military, holding rank to high standards. We were paid by the government, but we weren't a military branch, except in Sorin's eyes. He was third in command behind my dad and Marcus, and he made sure everyone knew it by handing out infractions like they were parade candy.

Trying to get out of my overthinking head, I quickly changed and drove over to the main building, Deren riding shotgun. We went to the armory and grabbed our weapons before heading to the van.

Sorin was in the driver's seat when we walked up. Deren quickly got in the back, which forced me to get in the front.

"Hey," I said as I slinked into the seat and shut the door. Sorin was a man of few words. He gave me a nod before pulling out of the parking garage.

Sorin spoke once the whole ride. He told us we had a lead on a vampire nest in an industrial area, so we headed to the south side of the city.

"Is this the place?" I asked as we pulled up to a dark, abandoned building.

Sorin nodded.

"There's no electricity," Deren muttered.

Sorin didn't respond, silently hopping out of the van. Deren and I followed. He opened the back doors of the vehicle and dug in a bag before handing us each a UV flashlight.

"Don't use these unless you have to," Sorin said, his Russian accent was thick tonight. "Come on."

We followed him into the abandoned building. Once inside, it was mostly dark. We entered the massive main area that looked like it used to be an old factory of some sort.

"These, you can use." Sorin took out three tiny pen-style flashlights and handed us one, before he looked around.

"What are we looking for?" Deren asked.

Sorin held up his hand with a stop signal and then made a fist alerting us that we were switching to tactical hand signals.

We followed him through the warehouse where we stumbled upon a small room which looked like an abandoned office.

The half-empty file cabinets and papers strewn about made it look like someone had left in a hurry. I peeked through a few of the papers on the desk. There were invoices and other crap. Nothing useful.

We left the office and continued our search, checking a few more rooms. We found nothing—the entire place vacant. Heading toward the exit, we took the back door into the alley.

"That was a bust," Deren said as we emerged.

Sorin furrowed his eyebrows. "Did I tell you to talk?"

Deren's eyes met mine and I gave him a sympathetic smile.

Since Sorin was a *dick*, we both stood there quietly as he pulled out a small tablet. His eyes wandered around the screen for a few minutes before he finally spoke.

"Okay, there are two other buildings here we need to check." He turned the tablet toward us and pointed at it. I saw a detailed map of the block we were on and three flickering dots marking our location. "I'm going to go investigate this building. I want you two to check the other."

I glanced up at Sorin's face in disbelief. He could *not* be serious. He was first in command and shouldn't be sending two low-ranking members alone into a building. Even as a rookie, I knew that.

"Is that safe?" I asked. I didn't give a shit if he told me to be quiet, because that wasn't going to happen if I thought something was stupid or dangerous.

"Why wouldn't it be, Sage?" I thought he was joking for a second, but as my eyes searched his face, there was no sign of humor.

"I don't know, maybe because we are hunting vampires! We are both rookies and you're supposed to lead this team."

He pointed his finger at me. "First off, lower your voice and drop the tone. I don't give a shit who your father is. When I am in command, you treat me with respect. Understood?"

"Understood," I answered flatly, not wanting another infraction.

"Second, we rarely find a vampire so you two will be fine. Meet back here in twenty minutes." After a few seconds of intense eye contact, Sorin strolled away.

"Now what?" Deren asked.

"Don't ask me. This is literally my second day in the field, and I almost died last night, so hell if I know." I sighed as I watched the back of the idiot in charge round the corner of the building.

"I guess we should go in there." Deren pointed toward the building across the street. I knew the place because it used to be my gym.

"I guess fucking so, since his ass just left us!"

"Lead the way."

"Why do I have to? You have been in the field for months, Deren."

He shrugged his shoulders. "I have never led a team."

"I'm one person, not really a team. You walk and I follow."

"Yeah, I'm not about that life," he said as he crossed his arms.

"Shit." I shook my head. "Come on." I walked toward the building with him trailing behind.

We turned into a narrow alley, both of us taking slow, quiet steps until we got to the back door. There was a window next to it and I peeked inside. The glass was covered in years of dirt, so I could barely see anything.

"Are we going in?" Deren asked.

Holding up my finger, I put it to my mouth, quieting him. Then I made a fist, showing him we were going to use tactical hand signals, and he nodded in response.

After going to the door, I lifted my hand and slowly turned the knob. To my surprise, it was unlocked.

Shit. Now I would have to go in.

The door made a small squeak when I inched it open. As I entered the darkened space, I stopped to let my eyes adjust and Deren ran into my back like an idiot.

I wanted to holler "watch it," but it would be the same as yelling "vampire bait."

My heart sped up as I stepped further into the darkness of the room. It seemed to be an old storage area. I could faintly make out a mop bucket, sink, trash can, and some old boxes. The only other thing in the room was a door, and it was closed.

Venom members go through extensive combat, first aid, and military tactical training. We also have to take a class they call Perception of Senses. The name never made sense to me because perception in that phrase *is* the senses, so I always thought it was a tautology.

In the class, they taught us how to use most of our senses—touch, smell, sight, and hearing. They didn't teach us about taste, presumably because they preferred we not go around licking objects . . . or at least, I hoped. They just kind of pretended that sense didn't exist.

For weeks straight, we would work on one of the different senses. One month, they took our sight away during business hours—dusk until dawn. We had to bathe, eat, drink, fight, and even use the bathroom blindfolded. At the time, I hated the training, but at this moment, I was grateful.

My feet were silent as I made my way to the door. I laid my ear against it and closed my eyes, listening for sounds on the other side. All I could hear was the sound of Deren's ragged breaths. He needed to work on his breathing techniques—another required class.

After cracking the door open, I entered with cautious steps. This room was lit by moonlight spilling through the giant floor-to-ceiling windows, making it easy to avoid the old gym equipment resting there.

Remembering there were massage rooms and tanning beds upstairs, I figured I would check them out. Making my way over to the windows, I stopped in the brightest part so Deren could see my hand signals. I told him I was going up, and for him to stay down here and investigate the other rooms.

With each step I took up the stairs, I was afraid any little creak of the wood would give me away, so I was careful not to trip or make noise. Relief filled me when I made it up quietly.

There was a double-wide hallway at the top. Looking to the right, a door was standing open, so I went in. The room was empty, but I did notice the window was open. My heart started to race, so I did my breathing techniques to slow it down.

After standing there for a good minute, I contemplated going back down and getting Deren, but Sorin said we rarely come across a vamp on missions. Since I ran into one last night, I assumed my chances of it happening again were slim to none. Unless that fucker I met last night had a tracker on me, he would have no idea where I was.

Continuing my journey, I went into one of the massage rooms and found it vacant. I had a feeling this whole mission was going to be a bust. After checking two more rooms, I only had one left—the last one on the right.

The door was already cracked when I slid it open the rest of the way. Nothing moved, so I stepped inside. My eyes surveyed the room. It was completely empty except for a bookcase and a closet door. As gingerly as I could, I made my way over to the closet and opened it. Empty.

With nothing more to check upstairs, I turned around to head back to the main level. My breath caught at the sight of the figure standing in front of me.

"Fuck," I whispered to myself.

"Hello, Sage."

CHAPTER 10
LUKA

The night was quiet as I made my way up to the rooftops, traversing them until I was across the street from the address Finneas gave me. Not trusting the asshole, and possibly entering a massacre he set up, I showed up over an hour early and waited patiently to see what I could find.

Around forty-five minutes earlier than the time I was supposed to arrive, a vehicle approached from down the street of the next block over. I jogged over to the side of the roof and crouched down. A black van pulled up, parked on the side of the street, and three Venom members got out.

Holy shit! I couldn't believe my eyes. The girl, Sage, was with them.

The older man, who seemed to be their leader, headed to the back of the van and opened the doors. He handed them both what looked like flashlights and then led them into the building below me.

Twenty minutes later, the door to the back of the building opened. They were in discussion as I watched. The one with a Russian accent, seemed to be pissing the girl off. After a few minutes, he went into the building I was supposed to investigate while the other two stood there.

After the two were done arguing about who was going to lead who, Sage led the other member toward the alley between the buildings.

"What the fuck," I mumbled to myself.

Even *I* knew it was a stupid idea to leave two young members alone on a mission. This smelled like a trap to me—Finneas was either trying to get me captured or killed. I was supposed to enter the building where the leader was, but I sure as hell wasn't going in there. Instead, my body was drawing me to *her*. She needed to die, as Drag instructed. I descended the side of the building and landed on the ground.

After crossing the street, I climbed up to the roof of the structure she had entered. Peeking over the side, I spotted a small ledge, so I slid down onto it hoping to gain access through the window. To my surprise, it was unlocked.

Tanning bed bulbs were the only thing occupying the space I entered. Staying as quiet as possible, I made my way down the hallway and went into one of the other rooms. There was an old bookcase inside, so I waited in the shadows beside it.

My mind raced with the possibilities of what could happen. She was trained, but she was young. Being an older vampire, I was strong, so I highly doubted she could take me. The weird thing about missions is you never know what's going to happen.

Her scent alerted me she was on the same floor as me now. As she wandered from room to room, it got stronger. She entered with caution before making her way to the closet. Stepping out of the shadows, I stood in the middle of the room, waiting for her to notice. She turned around, her heartbeat speeding up as we locked eyes. Music to my ears.

"Fuck," she whispered.

"Hello, Sage."

She reached into her jeans pocket, and I knew immediately she was going for the flashlight. Not wanting to smell like burned toast, I smacked it out of her hand. Not wasting time, she lunged for me, and I caught her in mid-air, pinning her arms between us. She didn't hesitate to headbutt me in the face. *Fuck.*

This girl was spunky—a true fighter. I liked that about her, but it was time for me to end this and get the revenge my brother deserved.

Letting go of her, she fell to her hands and knees in front of me and immediately tried to crawl away. She had a nice ass from this angle, I'd give her that. I grabbed her ankle, yanking her back toward me.

After throwing myself onto her back, I grabbed her wrists and pinned them above her head. She rested her cheek against the hardwood floor as she tried to catch her breath.

"Get off me, fucker!"

"If I did, you would try to kill me again. We can't have that, can we?"

"Fuck you!" Her being feisty was amusing for me. I also found it rather sexy.

"You would like to. Vampires are amazing in bed. We never tire."

"You are extremely immature for someone who is probably fifty years old!" She squirmed as much as she could, but my weight and strength kept her under me.

"More like two hundred and seventy-six." Her face stilled with fear, as did her body. "My age scares you, doesn't it, Sage? You know you couldn't take a vampire that old without the help of a light."

"I already told you I'm not scared of you!"

I grinned at her lies. "Your racing heart says otherwise."

Leaning my face close to her neck, I blew her hair away, ran my nose across her skin, and took a big sniff. She smelled delicious, and I was glad she wasn't lustful. Her lure would have knocked me on my ass. I was already having to concentrate on keeping my cock from getting hard as it pressed against her ass. I may want—more like need—to kill her, but I'm not a creep, even if it seemed like it in this situation.

"I could kill you right now," I whispered. Her scent was mesmerizing as I breathed her in again.

"You keep saying it, but I don't think you have the balls to do it!" she retorted.

I couldn't help but grin. "Believe me, sweetheart, I have plenty of balls."

"Then do it!"

Thinking about her sweet-smelling skin, I wanted to bite her, feel her blood pour down my throat as I drained her. It would be a quick euphoric death. One couldn't ask for anything more. Fortunately for her, even though I was running on anger and going against every moral code I had, I hesitated.

The wood in the hall creaked, alerting me someone was coming. I let go of only one of her wrists and yanked my gun from my waistband.

"Sage?" a man's voice said in a whispered panic.

"Deren, no!" she screamed as he stepped inside the room. I quickly stood up.

As he raised a mini crossbow, I raised my gun. He released his weapon, making the arrow hit me in the arm at the same exact time I pulled the trigger and shot him in the chest. I quickly yanked the arrow out of my arm before my skin sealed it inside my body.

She scrambled across the floor over to him. "No!"

She yanked her shirt off and pressed it tightly over his wound. Seeing her shirtless made my senses light up. Her face, her smell—her body. This girl was doing shit to me.

Seriously, what the fuck was wrong with me?

Fast breaths were coming from me as I thought about how I should have just killed her.

"You're going to be okay, Deren." His only response was the blood he coughed out.

"No, he's not."

"Shut up!" she screamed. Her bloody hands were shaking as she clicked a button on her watch. "I just alerted them. Help is coming, buddy, just hold on."

"He's going to die," I said matter-of-factly.

"You're a heartless bastard!" She sniffed back tears as she pulled his head into her lap.

"An eye for an eye, I guess."

"It was supposed to be me," she whispered. "Not him! Why didn't you just kill me?"

Honestly, I didn't know. The same thought ran through my head as I stepped over the almost-dead guy.

"Help him, please! I know your blood can save him."

"Why would I?"

"Because I'm begging," she whimpered. "Please." Her big hazel eyes stared up at me, pleading for help.

"My blood will turn him. Then what? You guys will either kill him or send him to that fucking lab!"

Deren went completely still. He was dead.

"No, Deren. Please, no!" she cried.

"I'll see you around, Sage."

"Fuck you! I have never hated someone so much in my life!" she screamed as I left the room. "I'm going to fucking kill you!"

The fear and disdain in her voice rang through the hall, and I couldn't help but feel uneasy. Deren didn't die because I was a prick, I killed him out of instinct in a do-or-die situation. So, why did I feel so shitty? Why did her tears make me want to comfort her?

Banishing the thoughts from my head, I quickly went back to the window I had used as an entrance. I needed to leave before the Venom clean-up crew showed up.

As quickly and stealthily as I could, I made my way down and got on my bike, speeding off. After getting far enough away, I pulled over.

Thoughts of the situation ate at me, making my head feel clouded. Deren wasn't the first person I had killed to save my life or someone else's. Why was this different?

Was it *her* making me feel this way?

Reaching my hand in my pocket, I pulled out my cell and called Drag.

"Hello."

"I'm pretty sure we have a rat."

"Fuck," he whispered.

"Meet me at Winnie's in twenty minutes."

CHAPTER 11
SAGE

"**F**uck you! I have never hated someone so much in my life!" I screamed as the vampire left the room. "I'm going to fucking kill you!"

Uncertain whether they got my distress call, I lifted my blood-soaked hand and pushed the button on my Bluetooth. "I need assistance immediately! I have a man down!"

"We know. We got the alert and they're on the way," a voice said from the other end.

Looking back at Deren, I knew there was no helping him. I sat quietly with his head in my lap, stroking his hair as I said my goodbyes. My chest was tight when I closed my eyes, tears streaming down my face.

"What the fuck happened?" Sorin asked as he flew into the room. My anger took over when I turned my attention toward him.

"Deren's dead and it's your fucking fault!"

"You better watch your tone with me before you get another infraction!"

Was he seriously threatening me with an infraction while I held my dead friend?

"Fuck you!" I screamed. "I couldn't care less about you, infractions, or this stupid society. My friend is dead!"

"That's the price we pay. Born with Venom, dies with Venom."

"I fucking hate you," I whispered as his stare burned a hole through me. He seemed to have the same feelings about me.

My attention went to the door when I heard stomping coming up the stairs. An older woman pulled me away as the medical team checked out Deren. She took me by the arm, making me feel like a criminal as she led me out to a van. It was hard not to cry on the ride back to the compound.

Once we arrived, I was escorted into a small interrogation room where I sat quietly at a table. My body shivered in shock from the trauma.

"Would you like a cup of coffee?" Zeke asked. He was a tall, dark, and handsome man. He was Marcus' brother and always kind to me.

I shook my head.

"How about some water?" his wife, April, asked as she rubbed my shoulder in an attempt to soothe me. She was my mom's best friend, and was like an aunt to me.

My eyes were pleading as I looked up at her. "I just want my mom."

"I will see if I can find her." April's blonde hair swayed slightly as she left the room.

"Can't I just go home, Zeke? Please." This was the tenth time I had asked him in the last five minutes while we waited for the rest of my interrogation team to come get my story.

He gave me a sympathetic smile. "You know I can't let you go, Sage."

The locking device clicked before the door flung open and my father walked in. I didn't even attempt to keep the look of disdain off my face as Sorin trailed in behind him like a good dog.

"Do you need medical assistance, Sagelynn?" my dad asked. No hug, no worried face, just a simple question which made my skin crawl. Oblivious to him, I didn't need a bandage, I needed emotional support.

"Where is mom?" I asked.

"She isn't technically a member of Venom, so you can't see her until after we get your story."

"What about Erik, or Lyric? Can I see one of them?" My emotions were overwhelming, and I just wanted a hug.

I needed someone to comfort me for five damn minutes while my brain caught up with the traumatizing events.

"Lyric is on guard and can't leave her post. Erik was asking to see you, but you aren't allowed visitors until we get all the information we need."

"Then let's get this over with," I mumbled, then sniffed back tears.

He took a seat at the table across from me as Zeke and Sorin sat next to him.

"Start from the minute you stepped out of the van and tell us word-for-word exactly what happened."

Zeke opened his laptop to take notes. My eyes immediately went to Sorin, who was stone-faced.

Reliving the whole story wasn't what I wanted to do right now, but I had to, so I told them everything that happened until Sorin left us alone.

Still angry from the events, my eyes darted over to him. "Then he walked away, leaving two rookies alone!" The passion in me made my voice go higher than I intended.

"Sorin had other obligations. It isn't his job to babysit trained members."

My mouth gaped open when my eyes shot to my father. Glancing over at Zeke, he looked stunned as well. Sorin's face hadn't changed.

"Are you fucking kidding me?" I asked. "That's not what we have been taught!"

"Lower your voice when talking to me!" my father said sternly. "I know how my society works. Let's move on. What happened after Sorin left you two?"

After swallowing hard, I shook my head before I continued. "I led Deren into the building Sorin told us to check out."

"What happened once you were in there?"

My lip quivered as I tried to hold back tears. Every detail was explained until the point where Deren walked in on me and the vampire. My heart was heavy, tears finally breaking free when I told him the part where Deren died.

"Then I was brought back here," I said, finally finishing my story.

"You left Deren, a rookie, alone as you went upstairs? That would have normally been an infraction, but I have a feeling his death will be enough to teach you what you did wrong."

"What *I* did wrong? I'm a fucking rookie, too! You mean, what *he* did wrong?" More anger filled me as I pointed to Sorin.

"Sagelynn, you need to lower your voice before we have to sedate you." I noticed when my father pushed a button on his watch and I knew he was calling for Doc Jayne.

"You can't be serious! Am I fucking dreaming right now?" Pushing myself away from the table, I stood up. "I didn't do shit wrong!"

"Sit down!" my father yelled.

"No. Fuck that and fuck this. I'm not going to get blamed for this when it's *his* fault!" Sorin's face stayed blank. He didn't even try to deny it as I angrily pointed at him again.

"Sage," Zeke said calmly, bringing my focus to him. His eyes were sad as he shook his head, silently telling me if I didn't sit down then there would be consequences.

This wasn't our first member to be killed, it wasn't even the first this year. I knew our members died all the time. The trauma some carried with them daily was undeniable. I also knew what happened to them when their emotions got high, but I didn't care.

"Where's Mom? I want Mom now! I can't do this. I can't live like this! Let me out of here!"

Ready to escape, I headed to the door and yanked on it but it wouldn't open. My heart raced and I couldn't breathe as my emotions spiraled out of control.

"Please, Mom!" I pounded my fist on the door. "Mom!"

Not having a high level of security, I didn't bother using my fingerprint because I knew the door wasn't going to open for me. I moved away from it and began pacing back and forth in the room. All I kept thinking was Erik or Lyric could die next. Zeke watched me sympathetically while the other two stared at me like my actions were confounding to them. How could they not see how cumbersome this was? How could my own father not comfort me?

"You don't know what it's like out there! What it's like holding your friend until they die! You have no idea!"

Doc Jayne entered the room, and I stopped with quickness. "No, no, no. I don't want a shot!"

"It's too late now, Sagelynn," my dad said.

In a panic, I backed away not wanting to be sedated.

"Please, no." My eyes were begging, pleading.

Doc Jayne moved toward me and my body stiffened. She was a nice woman, but I was willing to punch her if she came any closer.

"Don't touch me!" I screamed with balled fists.

"Sorin." And that was all my dad had to say. Within seconds, Sorin grabbed me from behind, pinning my arms.

"Stop! Don't!" Kicking and screaming, I begged for them to leave me alone. The doctor had a hard time sticking me with the needle, I was moving so much.

My father stood to leave. "Inject her and then put her in a room so she can sleep it off."

"Dad," I whimpered, hoping he would understand by the cracking of my voice I needed him.

With his back to me, he stood there for a few seconds before he shook his head. After placing a finger on the security reader, he opened the door. I could briefly see my mother standing in the hallway. She appeared to be crying as April was consoling her.

"Mom," I cried out as I gave up fighting.

The doctor took her opportunity and stuck me in the arm with a needle.

"This will make you feel better."

That was the last thing I remembered before Sorin carried me to a room and I fell asleep.

CHAPTER 12

LUKA

We were sitting in Winnie's cave drinking beer. I had just finished telling them the whole story about me killing the Venom member and my thoughts on the situation.

"No fucking way!" Winnie said as he typed on his keyboard. "You think Finneas is some kind of rat for Venom?"

"It was definitely a trap. I have a feeling he wants me dead."

"Why would he want you dead?" Drag asked. He was sitting at the desk next to Winnie.

"I don't know. Maybe because I run my mouth. He has called me insubordinate so many times."

"He has also called you an anarchist on multiple occasions," Winnie added.

I smirked. Fin had no idea what a real anarchist was.

"So, you didn't kill her?"

"I tried, Drag. I was going to, but I don't know what the problem is." The stress was getting to me, so I rubbed my eyes.

"You can't just kill people, that's the problem," Winnie blurted.

"I have killed tons of people and you know it!"

"Only in defense, Luka. You have never gone out of your way to actually kill a person. Well, except . . ." Drag stopped, knowing it was a touchy subject.

"Yeah, except for him. I killed him out of cold blood." I swallowed hard at the memories of what I did many years ago. A story I wasn't ready to relive.

"He deserved it, man. What he did to your mom was—"

"I don't want to talk about this, Winnie." I headed to the kitchen to grab another beer.

"It's Winston," he protested, and I smiled.

"So, what are you going to do about the girl?" Drag asked when I returned.

I took a seat in the recliner. "I don't know, man. My choices are shitty. Either I kill her and dishonor myself, or I don't and dishonor my brother."

"That's deep, bro."

"Shut up, Winnie." I grabbed a pillow from behind me and threw it at his head.

Drag turned toward me. "Maybe we should work on getting some information about Finneas and worry about the girl later."

"I already got some info." Winnie pointed at his screen. "And it's some good shit."

I hopped up and headed toward the desk. "What am I looking at?"

"These here are the records of events. When Save has any leads come in, they're documented on this spreadsheet. They also track who investigates, the outcome, and so on."

"You broke into Save's system?" Drag asked.

Winnie smiled proudly. "I did."

"And what is it showing us?" I asked as I leaned down.

"Do you remember Michael?"

My brows furrowed in confusion. "The dude a Venom inductee staked a few months ago?"

"This spreadsheet tells who sent him into the field. It was Finneas."

"That's one incident," Drag said. "It may not mean anything."

"Do you see whose name is on this one?" Winnie pointed at the screen and I read the info.

"Andrei? Finneas acted like my brother went out on his own to hunt the Venom members."

"By this spreadsheet, Fin sent him the night your girl staked him." Winnie hit a button and the printer revved up.

Shock and anger flooded through me. "You have got to be fucking kidding me!"

"He sent him on missions randomly, but I don't think it's random. About a year ago, this note says he killed a Venom member named Renee in defense. Fin also sent him that night."

"Look up the girl who was taken around six months ago," Drag said. "When was that? March, I think?"

Winnie scrolled through the spreadsheet and stopped. His eyebrows raised as he turned toward us. "Fin."

"Fuck," Drag whispered, running a hand nervously through his beard.

"I need you to look up one more, Winnie." Thinking about all this new information, I decided to say what I knew everyone was thinking. My other brother was taken by Venom over a year ago and I needed to know who was on the order. "Look up Strike."

"One second." Winnie scrolled up for a while and his face paled. "Fin."

"That motherfucker. I'm going to kill him!" I turned away and both of my friends were immediately in front of me.

"You can't say or do anything," Drag said. "Not without more proof."

"Yeah, man. Especially not after I hacked into their systems. You go screaming through the streets without more info, we might disappear, too."

"Exactly," Drag added.

"What I need to know is what system Venom is using so I can hack into it and see if there are any matching records."

My eyebrows rose and a smile spread across my face. "I know a person I could get info from."

"Fuck. Come on, Luka." Drag shook his head, a knowing look on his face. "There's no way she's going to give you any information."

"I don't need her to, I just need to get into her apartment."

"Have you tried breaking in yet?" Winnie asked.

"I checked it out and it's efficiently guarded. I would probably have to kill a few people to get in."

"I could get you in the front door, but I don't know what apartment she's in. I can't find info without a name."

"Her name is Sage," I said and Winnie immediately took a seat back at the computer. "At least, that's what your dad said." I looked at Drag and he sighed.

"Do you need me to go with you?"

"Nah, Drag. I can handle it on my own."

Winnie's fingers moved with fast precision as he typed shit into the computer. "There is no one named Sage listed."

Pulling out the debit card, I sat it on the desk in front of him. "This is hers."

Winnie picked it up. "Marie Adams, hold on." He searched her name. "Nope."

"I'll just figure it out once I'm inside."

"The sun will be up soon, so it won't be tonight," Drag said. "And we're leaving town tomorrow night."

"Fuck. I forgot about the festival."

Winnie and I had both promised Drag we would go to the Autumn Equinox. It was a weeklong witches festival where a lot of vampires and wolven attended.

"I can go alone," Drag said, but his face told me he didn't want to.

"Nah, dude. We'll help you find your intimate."

In wolven terms, an *intimate* meant someone you mated with for life. Ever since Drag's cousin found his intimate at a festival, he was hoping he would, too. Being the romantic man he was, we were off to a new party every few months.

"Thanks. I appreciate it, Luka."

"Anyone want another beer?" I asked as I left the cave.

Thoughts of her entered my brain while I headed for the fridge. Maybe going a week without seeing her would do me some good.

CHAPTER 13

SAGE

It had been seven long, excruciatingly boring days since I got locked up, and I was going insane. The entire week was nothing but meds, therapy, sleeping, and eating. I wanted out of here—needed out of here.

After the first two days, I managed to talk a nurse into letting me have a TV, which helped to pass time. She told me they had already had Deren's funeral and I wasn't allowed to go, which pissed me off.

As I was sitting on what I called The Couch of Doom in my therapist's office, the only thought I had was that Venom was going to be the death of me.

"With the progress you have made this week, I think it's time to send you home," my therapist said, bringing my attention away from the pillow I was picking lint off of.

The progress to which she was referring to wasn't real. It was clear early on what they were looking for, so I gave my father exactly what he wanted. I got extremely good at playing the "*I'm feeling better now*" patient, even though I wasn't. I did, however, manage to open up to her about some private things—something I've never done with anyone else.

I sat up, gripping the pillow tightly with excitement. "Really?"

"Yes, Sagelynn. I think it will benefit you to get out of here and get some fresh air."

I smiled brightly. "Me too."

"I have already cleared it with the president and Dr. Jayne. She has some medicine you need to take that she left in your room."

"When do I have to return to work?" I asked. I held my breath, hoping she said a month, a year . . . never.

"I was advised you wouldn't be returning to the field for another week. I will see you next Friday to check in. If you're doing well then, you'll return to the roster. After that, your sessions will be every Monday."

A week is better than nothing. I had a fleeting thought about possibly making sure I *wasn't* better by our next visit.

"Thank you, Steph."

"You're welcome. Now go. Someone has been waiting for you."

Excitement filled me, knowing I was a free woman again. Tossing the pillow aside, I smiled as I stood up and practically bolted for the door.

"Hey, Sage," Stephanie said, stopping me from my escape.

"Yeah?" I looked over my shoulder. Her face had changed to one of discomfort, making my body tense as she headed toward me.

"May I hug you?" she asked.

"Of course."

She reached her hands around me and nuzzled her nose in my hair.

"Sometimes people need to *escape* the reality of this life," she whispered. She pulled away and smiled before her tone changed to a happier one. "You did a great job. I'll see you next Friday."

I refrained from glancing at the camera watching us and smiled, too.

"See ya Friday," I said cheerfully before I opened the door and left.

My house slippers shuffled against the terrazzo floor as I headed back down to my room. I couldn't help but to think about what Stephanie said. *Sometimes people need to* escape *the reality of this life.* What did she mean? Was she telling me the meds would help, or was she telling me I should get out before it's too late?

My thoughts were interrupted and joy filled me when I opened my bedroom door.

"Erik!"

"About time!"

My eyes filled with tears as he plowed into me.

"Where's Lyric?" I asked as we hugged.

"She's downstairs taking inventory today."

"Man, they just stick her anywhere."

Erik pulled back and gave me a sympathetic look. "How was it?"

"Good. Can we get out of here? Like now?" I kicked my house shoes off.

"What's wrong, Sage?"

"Nothing. I'm just ready to go home and see Chewy."

"He missed you. Lyric and I have been taking turns staying at your apartment, so he wasn't alone."

"Thanks." I took my pajama pants off, making Erik cringe. He swiftly turned around.

"I know what you're thinking, Sage. Don't worry, we had the apartment cleaned today, so everything should be in perfect order."

During one of my therapy sessions, I had mentioned how anal I was about my apartment being in pristine condition. Stephanie told me it was because I needed control of something, since I felt like I had no control over the rest of my life. It made total sense to me.

"Good." I grabbed the jeans and shirt I was wearing when I was admitted and threw them on. I was grateful someone washed the blood off them. They would be going in the trash when I got home.

After shoving my feet back in the house shoes, I headed for the door, grabbing the bottle of pills off the dresser on the way out.

"Are you riding with me?" Erik asked as we headed toward the nurse's desk.

"No, my Jeep is here, but you can call me when you get in your car."

Stopping at the nurse's station, they gave me a small bag which contained my personal items like my cellphone, watch, and stake. I peeked inside to make sure everything was there before we left.

After parting ways with Erik, I headed to my Jeep. The moment I started it, my phone rang.

"So, what's going on? You seem off," Erik asked.

"Something my therapist said got to me."

"What did she say?"

"She hugged me and said *sometimes people need to* escape *the reality of this life,* and it gave me chills."

The gates to the compound opened and I drove through them with a small wave to the guard.

"I mean, she's not wrong. We all need a little something to escape reality sometimes. Especially people who hunt vampires for a living when the rest of the world is oblivious to the fact they even exist."

"I know, but her emphasis on *escape* made me feel like she was trying to secretly tell me something. Like I needed to *escape* Venom."

"Why would you need to escape Venom? I think maybe you misinterpreted it."

"I don't know. It's just a feeling, Erik."

Our conversation had gone silent and I knew he was in deep thought about everything.

"Take all the time you need to think about it and call me later," I said. "Love you."

"Love you."

I hit the end button on the steering wheel.

Music was a part of my everyday life and I had missed it in the last week. I turned the radio on and rolled the windows down while I let the music and fresh air heal my soul.

CHAPTER 14

LUKA

The festival was a good time, especially since Winnie and I got to feed. Unfortunately, Drag didn't find his intimate, but he was sure he would find one at Winter Solstice.

After picking Annie up from my friend Peach, I headed home and got settled in for the night. Since I was determined to find out more information, I woke up with the sunset and got ready.

My friends were also determined to understand the conspiracy which was transpiring within Save. They were at Winnie's place while I was making my way to the Silver Pine Apartments. I had my Bluetooth in and was on the phone with Drag.

"Are you almost there?"

"Yeah. I'm only a block down."

"Okay. I'm going to put you on speaker so Winnie can give you the instructions."

"In exactly three minutes, the guard will head outside for his nightly smoke break. When he does this, Laren is going to have the desk attendant preoccupied. Hopefully, she can get her to leave her station unattended. Once that happens, I will unlock the front door. You will only have fifteen seconds to go through it so I can rearm it before a silent alarm goes off. Then you will hide for roughly thirty minutes. After the desk attendant shift-change, you can start the second half of the plan. You got all that, Luka?"

"Yeah, I got it, man. Are you sure she isn't home?" I asked, before jumping to the next building.

"I did a facial recognition search on all the cameras on the property. She hasn't been there since you killed that dude."

"And you don't think she moved out?" Drag asked.

"Come on, man, you know me." Winnie made a *pfft* sound. "I checked the front and back cameras, no one has moved in or out in the last week."

"You heard him, Luka. You're set to go."

"Two minutes until his smoke break," Winnie alerted me.

"Heading down." I went to the edge of the roof and made my way to the ground.

"And he is outside . . . now." Winnie said. "Laren is calling, I'm listening in on my earpiece."

"How?" I asked as I rounded the corner to her building.

"I traced her phone."

"You really are a beast, Winnie."

"It's Winston."

I completely ignored his protests. "I'm almost to the door, man. You got me?"

"Slow down, bro. Laren is having trouble getting her away from the desk. I'm watching the lobby camera and the girl looks frustrated as fuck. Oh, she's up and moving. Get by the door."

After about thirty seconds of listening to Winnie typing, he said, "Disengaged. Get in now."

I slid through the door of the lobby. "I'm in," I whispered.

"I know. I got eyes in the sky."

Glancing up, I looked for a camera.

"Left side," Winnie said.

My eyes darted to the left and spotted the little black camera. I raised my hand and flipped him off and he laughed.

"That wasn't very nice."

"Which way do I go?"

"Stay along the right wall and take the first right."

I did as Winnie instructed and stumbled upon an elevator.

"Take it up to the fourth floor. It's currently the quietest."

"Got it." The elevator doors opened and I stepped inside. "What about me being on camera?"

"I have them blocked from security right now. I put a loop of no activity on each one of them and you have about three minutes before I have to restart it. Go left when the doors open. There is a stock room at the end of the hall. It's locked, but I'm going to open it. Once inside, you know what to do."

Four floors later, the doors opened and I stepped off heading left. I found the room he was referring to and went in.

After grabbing a towel off the shelf, I removed my clothes, leaving myself dressed in only underwear, then wrapped the towel around my waist. "I'm ready."

"Now, we wait."

Thirty minutes seemed to drag by. I stayed mostly quiet while listening to Winnie and Drag discuss everything from politics, to football, fucking, American conspiracy theories, and back to politics.

"Wakey, wakey, motherfucker. Now's your time to shine," Winnie said. "The hallway and elevator are clear. The desk attendant has changed shifts, so you're good to go. Work your magic, sexy thang."

"Shut up, Winnie." I emerged from the room I was hiding in. "Will this Bluetooth work if I get too far away?"

I had to leave my phone behind because there was nowhere to put it in my towel.

"I checked the range and I'm pretty sure you can reach the lobby," Winnie said as I stepped onto the elevator. "If not, then you're on your own, but you know what to do."

"If we get disconnected, Luka, make sure you text us immediately when you get back to your phone. If you don't message us in an hour, we're coming to get you."

"Got it, Drag."

The elevator doors opened and I stepped off. As I rounded the corner, the desk attendee glanced up at me. Her eyes widened and her heart sped up at the sight of my bare torso.

"Can I . . . umm, help you?" she asked with a squeak. The lustful smell radiating off her was delicious. I had to work to keep my fangs from elongating.

"I hope so, sweetheart. I got locked out of my girlfriend's room and wondered if there was a way you could give me an extra key?"

"Oh, I can't—"

"Or at least, let me back in." I locked eyes with her and smiled, making her blush.

"I can call your girlfriend so she can come down and get you."

"That would be great if she were home, but she works nights. I rarely stay over, but she just got back into town, and I missed her." I gave her my best sad boyfriend face.

"You sound like a pussy right now, Luka," Winnie said into my earpiece. I ignored him.

The girl shifted uncomfortably as she was trying to decide what to do.

"I'm begging, love. I'm completely naked and vulnerable here." I pointed at my towel as I tightened my ab muscles. Her eyes darted down, and then back to my face before her cheeks reddened. "Please. It can be our secret." I gave her a wink, hoping to seal the deal.

A slow smile radiated across her face. "Okay, but you can't tell anyone or I'll get fired."

"Thank you so much. You're a lifesaver. What's your name?"

"It's Angeline."

"I promise not to tell anyone, Angeline."

"I appreciate that. What's the room number?"

"My girlfriend is Marie. Marie Adams."

If her apartment wasn't under the same fake name as her debit card, I was screwed.

"Oh, that's the penthouse. Come on, I'll walk you up."

"Shit. That's eleven floors up, bro. Your Bluetooth won't work."

I glanced at the camera, letting Winnie know I heard him.

Angeline came out from behind the desk and headed toward the elevators. The girl had an ass you could bounce rocks off, and she made sure I noticed. Every step she took was more and more hippy. Since I was an ass man, I didn't mind.

She walked to the service elevator, swiped her card, and we both entered. She hit a button and the elevator moved.

She was being quiet as her lure filled the air of the small compartment. Which had me thinking she was envisioning stopping the elevator and ripping my clothes off. If she stood any closer, I was willing to give her the fantasy she wanted.

The ride was painful for me as the lure seeped into me with every breath. Her natural scent was berries with woodsy background notes, and it was intoxicating, making me work to keep the bulge under my towel in control. My fangs wouldn't listen and elongated on their own. *Shit.*

The elevator doors opened, ripping me back to reality.

"We're here," she said as she stepped off. I immediately fell into step next to her, so it seemed like I knew where I was going.

"I appreciate you doing this," I said with a toothless smile. I didn't want my fangs to scare the shit out of her, or make her hornier than she already was—I wasn't sure which would be worse for me.

"You're very welcome." She stopped at a door and inserted her card. She held it open, and I stepped into the room like I lived there. "Let me know if you need anything else."

I nodded and shut the door. "Fuck me," I whispered to myself. "Are you there, Winnie?"

No answer. Winnie was right, the Bluetooth didn't work at this range. I was on my own now.

My eyes darted around the dark room, and I immediately noticed it was immaculate. A small meow came from around the corner and a few seconds later, a fat cat came purring up to me.

"Hey, buddy."

After a bit of belly rubbing—I couldn't resist—I looked around. The living room was pristine, with no desk or drawers to go through, so I walked over to the kitchen. I opened every drawer there was and only found utensils and other random kitchen essentials.

After flipping on the hallway light, I entered the bedroom, the cat following me. There was a desk in the corner, so I immediately went to it, opening each drawer. I pulled out folders filled with papers and flipped through them, finding nothing but bills and personal records with her fake name.

My gaze swept around the room, trying to see if there was any other place she could hide something. After walking over to the bed, I opened the nightstand drawer. There were handcuffs, condoms, lube, a vibrator, and a silver stake.

"Oh, shit. I guess she stays prepared for anything." I laughed to myself. The cat jumped up on the bed and started purring. I patted his head. "You don't need to see this, kitty."

The sounds of footsteps thudding lightly on the carpet in the hallway halted me. My sensitive ears captured shuffling sounds—a nylon bag—and then a beep.

"Shit," I whispered to the cat.

A *click* of the lock, and a *clank* of the door shutting, and someone was in the apartment.

CHAPTER 15
SAGE

The security guard said hello to me as I stepped onto the elevator inside the parking garage of my apartment building.

I decided to take it down to the lobby first.

The receptionist was typing away on her computer as I walked up. "Hey, Angeline."

"Good evening, Miss Adams. I thought you were at work tonight."

"No, I'm off for the next week. I was just wondering if there were any staff in the kitchen who could make me some food? I'm exhausted and don't have the energy to cook."

"Unfortunately, there isn't anyone past midnight on weeknights, but if you order takeout, I can get someone to bring it up when it gets here."

"Okay, thank you."

Defeated and hungry, I slowly made my way back to the elevator. I berated myself for not stopping and getting a greasy drive-thru burger—which sounded extremely good right now. With a sigh, I pushed the elevator button and rode it up to the penthouse.

Freedom was only fifteen feet away as I shuffled down the hallway. The excitement I had in anticipation of seeing my cat was almost uncontrollable—as was my enthusiasm to binge watch crappy shows on Netflix.

My body and brain were tired, even though I had just woken up a few hours ago. I had a feeling it was the new meds I was on. After loving Chewy for a while, I would be going back to sleep.

As I stood outside my apartment door, I dug in my bag to find my card. One small swipe and the lock clicked—I was finally free!

"Chewy! I'm home."

Everything seemed in order as I looked around the room. I dropped my bag on the table next to the door and drifted into the kitchen. After opening the fridge door, I knew for a fact I was going to order food. With a sigh, I slammed it shut.

An uneasy feeling came over me as I looked around and didn't see my cat. "Chewbacca?"

Heading down the hall, I opened my bedroom door and there was Chewy sitting on my bed. "There you are, I missed . . ." I stopped dead in my tracks as I noticed my nightstand drawer half open.

My friends and I were close. We hung out a lot at my apartment and they both knew my special drawer was off limits. They would never invade my privacy. The desk clerk words replayed in my head, *"I thought you were at work tonight,"* which left me thinking, who the fuck is in my apartment?

Completely unarmed and trying not to draw attention to myself, I pretended I got choked up as I finished my sentence.

"I missed you, Chewy." I petted his head while I tried to ease my breathing.

My eyes glanced into the drawer as I turned around. *Fuck.* My stake was gone. After a few seconds, I toed off my shoes.

"I'll be right back," I said to my cat as I made my way to the bathroom. "I have to shower, then we can watch TV and cuddle."

There were hidden weapons in each room of my apartment, and I hoped I could get to one before the intruder got to me—if they hadn't already taken them all.

After turning the lights on, I steadied my breathing and opened the shower curtain. No one was hiding in the tub, so I turned the water on while I thought about my plan.

Fuck, fuck, fuck. Why did I leave my cell phone in my bag?

Quietly, I opened the bottom drawer and guided my hand between two towels. My fingers found the coldness of the silver stake soothing as I yanked it out. After deciding I had no plans to get out of this situation, I figured I would meet the intruder head on.

I took a deep breath and slung the bathroom door open. "I know you're here, fucker, so just come out!"

The room was quiet. Nothing moved, not even my cat. Was I losing my shit? Was it a weird coincidence my drawer was left open?

My eyes darted around the shadows of the room, waiting for movement. I couldn't help but wonder, for a split second, if my friends hid the weapons from me. Then came a familiar voice.

"Put down the stake."

"In your dreams, fuckface!"

"Can we have a pleasant sit-down conversation? There are some things you need to know."

The moonlight lit the side of his face as he stepped out of the shadows, making my heart race uncontrollably. I lost all ability to stay calm and focus as I stared at the evil immortal who killed my friend.

With an almost feral screech, battle cry, whatever, I lunged for him. He quickly side-stepped me, making me tumble to the ground. With one foot planted on each side of my body, he peered down at me with an amused face.

Coming down a little from my battle lust, I noticed he was only wearing a towel.

Why the fuck is he naked?!

"Seriously, this would be easier if you were just compliant for two fucking minutes!"

"Fuck you!" I grabbed his ankle with one hand while the other buried the stake into his calf muscle. He jerked his leg away, giving me enough space to hop to my feet with proficient speed.

My stake was in the air, heading for his chest when he caught my wrist only inches short of target. His grip loosened when I kicked him in the balls, so I yanked my arm away and went for the kill again. He twisted at the last minute and my stake plunged into his arm. My hand let go of it when he shoved me away, and I landed flat on my ass.

My eyes darted under the bed, and I glimpsed something useful. Rolling to my stomach, I grabbed the mini crossbow I had hidden. It was cocked and ready to go as I rolled to my back again. The smell of burning flesh filled the air as he ripped the stake from his arm and threw it.

He was reaching for me as I pulled the trigger. The first mini stake got him in the leg and sizzled. He jerked back, making the second one I fired hit him in the stomach. With a loud grunt, he fell to his knees.

That was the good thing about silver, the longer it was in a vampire's body, the more it weakened them. I sat up, ready for this kill.

Pure hatred flooded my body as I stared at him. My finger tightened on the trigger and the third stake landed in his chest. Placing my bare foot on him, I shoved, making him fall onto his back.

"Murderer," I screamed as I stood up.

Unfortunately, the mini crossbow was only the size of my hand, and the silver stakes it shot were slightly larger than a screw. They were super sharp and small enough to get embedded in the skin. Once they were implanted, the vampire's quick healing powers sealed the silver in the body, weakening them. It wouldn't kill them, but it would incapacitate one for a while.

My eyes scoured the room, looking for my stake, when a shimmer caught my eye. There was a slight reflection of moonlight bouncing off it like it was revealing itself to me. Taking a few strides across the room, I yanked it off the ground.

"This is for Deren," I whispered as I kneeled next to him.

Lifting my arms high in the air, I yanked the stake down, but halted mere inches before hitting my cat. He had grabbed Chewy mid-swing and was holding him next to his chest, blocking my path to his heart. Which was the only lethal spot, unless I wanted to behead him or burn his remains.

"Let him go!"

"Drop the . . . stake . . . and . . . I will," he said in between gasping breaths.

"Let him go or I will kill him to get to you."

"No . . . you won't."

He was right. It may be just a cat to some people, but Chewy was like my child and I would die for him. It pissed me off that my motherly instincts were going to be what killed me. I had fought hard and was now going to lose by default.

"Let him go and I will let you go."

"You . . . won't."

I swallowed hard because my plan was to kill him as soon as Chewy was safe.

"Pull . . . stakes out . . . then . . . I will."

"You've got to be fucking kidding me."

Chewy let out an angry hiss and a low growl because he didn't like being held still. My thoughts were all over the place. Should I try staking him and hope I didn't hit my cat, or should I pull the stakes out and risk being killed? I didn't know what to do.

"Can we make a pact?" I finally asked.

"What . . . kind?"

"I will pull these out, and then you let Chewy go. I will promise not to kill you, but you need to leave me alone and stop stalking me."

A knock at the door startled me. "Shit. Don't move."

He let out a painful laugh because he knew he wasn't going anywhere in his condition.

After shoving the stake into the back of my waistband, I made my way to the front door. I ran my hands through my tousled hair before looking out the peephole. I sighed when I saw Angeline. A look of worry was plastered on her face when I opened the door.

"Yes?"

"I'm sorry to bug you, Ms. Adams, but we got a noise complaint. The neighbors swore they heard screaming." She glanced over my shoulder before whispering, "Are you okay?"

"Yes, I'm fine." I forced a smile, hoping to ease her.

"Are you and your boyfriend arguing?" she asked in a hushed voice.

Boyfriend? So, that's how the fucker got in. I figured I would play along if it got rid of her quicker.

"Yes, actually, we are, so if you will excuse me . . ." I started to shut the door.

"Is it because I let him in?"

That bitch. I had the half a mind to punch her, but now wasn't the time.

"No, it's because he's a cheating whore and went and got crabs, so you should probably stay away from him." I slammed the door shut, hoping she would leave.

My eye immediately went to the peephole, watching as she walked away. I flipped all the locks and made my way back to my bedroom with a sigh.

"How the fuck did you talk Angeline into letting you in? Honestly, don't answer. It will take you ten minutes to spit it out, anyway."

He let out a wheezing laugh.

"I don't know how you can find this situation funny, vampire."

He grinned arrogantly at me before the look quickly morphed to one of pain.

"Arrangement," he whispered.

"Do you agree?"

He nodded.

"Fine. Hold on."

After turning on the bedroom light, I walked over to the closet and pulled out a black medic kit. I dropped it next to his side and took a seat. I laid the stake in my lap before unzipping the bag.

"You know, you really shouldn't go around fucking with people. Maybe . . ."

My eyes landed on his half-naked body and I lost my train of thought. He must have lost his towel during battle because he was only wearing a pair of snug boxer briefs. I swallowed when I saw the nice-sized bulge in them.

My inappropriate gaze drifted up his body, noticing he was extremely muscular. His stomach and arms were covered in tattoos. I assumed his chest was too, but currently, my fat cat was covering it. He was sexy as fuck, to say the least. I tried to put the thought out of my head as I continued.

"Umm, maybe this will be the . . . um, incident which makes you stop."

Avoiding looking at him, I dug in the bag and pulled out a pair of hemostats, a metal bowl, and a surgical blade. My eyes searched his body, looking for entrance wounds. I swallowed hard at his sexiness.

"Umm." My eyes lingered to the arrogant smirk on his face. "Where are the holes?"

"Blade," he said as he held his hand out, so I handed it to him. "Be quick . . . I'll close."

I nodded.

He lowered his hand to his stomach and sliced it open. I immediately leaned in and stuck the hemostats into his skin as he winced.

"Sorry."

What the fuck! Why did I say sorry for hurting him when I was just trying to kill him? I pretended like I didn't say anything as I leaned in closer.

"Left," he said.

Moving the hemostats to the left, I felt something hard. I maneuvered them around, grabbed the stake, and pulled it out.

"There's one," I said as I dropped it into the metal bowl. "I'm like Meredith Grey or some shit." I laughed as I glanced at his face. He didn't seem amused. "Not a Grey's fan, I take it?" He furrowed his eyebrows at me, and I shrugged.

Looking back at the wound, it was already closed. I had missed it.

"Next?" I asked.

He shifted Chewy to the left before using the blade to cut into the right side of his chest.

My hemostats were working their magic within seconds. I moved them around, trying to find the stake. After what seemed like forever, he hissed, and Chewy hissed back.

"What?" I asked.

"Use . . . fingers."

"Seriously? That's disgusting."

"Do it," he whispered.

"Hold on."

Digging in the medical bag, I searched for gloves. After snapping on a pair, I turned back toward him.

"Okay, I'm ready. Fuck, the hole closed."

He sighed before he lifted the blade and cut another hole, this one bigger.

Gently as I could—mainly because I was grossed out—I stuck one of my fingers in the hole and dug. Eventually, I felt the hardness of the metal.

"There it is, but I can't get it. I think I'm going to have to use two fingers."

"That's what . . . he said." He snickered and I rolled my eyes.

"You're so immature." I slid another finger inside him. Maneuvering them around, I finally got a grip on the stake, so I pulled it out and dropped it into the metal bowl.

My eyes went back to the wound, watching as it closed. My body tensed as it seemed a little too familiar to me. It was exactly what the wound on my hand did when Erik sealed it with bondcoat.

"Before we continue, we need to talk. You can just nod or take your time answering my questions. You also said there were some things—"

"You needed to know," he finished.

"Oh, you can talk again." I shifted uncomfortably as my hand went to the stake and gripped it.

"I'm not going to hurt you or your cat. I will keep my promise in the hopes you will keep yours."

"Fine. What do you know about bondcoat?" I asked.

His eyebrows furrowed. "What the fuck is bondcoat?"

"You've never heard of it?"

"Would I ask you what it was if I had?"

"Stop answering my questions with questions."

"God, you're annoying," he said with a grin.

"Fuck you!"

"So, are you going to tell me what it is or not?"

"Hold on." I dug in the bag and pulled out a can and handed it to him. "It's this stuff."

He looked it over for a few seconds. "Like I said, I've never heard of it." He dropped it into my hand like he didn't care.

"Hey, this is important shit and when I watched your wound heal, it made me think . . ." I stopped myself from finishing the sentence because honestly, I wasn't sure what all it made me think, but some of it wasn't good.

"Made you think what?"

"Nothing, just forget it."

"Let me see it again." He yanked it out of my hand, and I rolled my eyes at him.

He pushed the nozzle on the top and some squirted out. It looked like hairspray in the air. The sound must have scared Chewy, because he hissed and started clawing. He slipped out of the vampire's arms and my hand immediately tightened on my stake.

It was a stand-off, well, a stare-off. Both of us were waiting for the other to make a move or to blink.

"So, what does this shit do, anyway?" he asked before spraying it again.

"Don't waste it! That *shit* is expensive." I yanked it away from him. He laughed, and I swallowed hard from the fact he was acting like a normal human being.

A part of me wondered if I should stake him and my eyes glanced down at his chest—right where his heart was. I wasn't sure if I was quick enough to do it before being caught. I was also unsure if I should, considering he kept his word. Could I forgive myself for being less noble than a vampire?

"I wouldn't hurt him," he said, and my eyes shot back to him.

"What?" I whispered.

"Your cat, Chewbacca. I wouldn't have hurt him."

I bit my lip as my eyes trailed over his face—the face of a killer. My heart sped up as my temper took over.

"No, but you had no problem killing Deren, did you?"

"What was I supposed to do?"

"Maybe not fucking kill him!" My tone softened as sadness took over. "He was my friend." My eyes filled with tears, so I looked away.

"I'm sorry about your friend, but he was going to kill me."

"Yeah, and yet, here you are, alive and in my house, trying to kill me." I quickly wiped a tear.

"I didn't come here to kill you. I came here to get more information on Venom."

"Why? So you can kill all of us?" I asked as I looked back at him.

"No. So I can find out who the fuck is working with the vampires and why."

My eyes widened. "Explain."

"I'm not telling you shit. Tell me what *you* know."

"I'm not telling you shit either. I don't even know your name."

"My name is Vampire, remember?"

"God, you're so damn childish!"

"Whatever. Are you going to remove this last piece of silver, or what?"

"Actually, I'm not. You can just hobble the fuck on out of here." I took the gloves off and tossed them on the floor.

"We had a deal!"

"Well, the deal's off!"

"Then I can kill you?" he asked with a grin.

"I would like to see you try!"

My breathing was heavy as I stared, once again, at his arrogant smile. I swallowed hard before shaking my head. "Just leave."

"I will after you remove the stake."

I stood and crossed my arms. "You can sit here until the sun comes up, for all I care!"

A knock at the door brought my attention away.

"Shit, that's my friends."

"What do you mean, it's your friends?" I asked.

"I had one hour to get out of here." He glanced over at the clock. "Times up."

"What does that mean?"

"It means you're going to have to let them in."

"How many?" I asked.

"Two."

My heart raced as panic set in. "I can't. They'll kill me."

"Look at me," he said, and I ignored him.

"Fuck. Oh, fuck. What am I supposed to do?" I paced the room, wondering how the hell I was going to get out of this situation.

"Look at me, Sage!" The sound of my name made me turn my attention to him. "I won't let them hurt you. Go to the door and I'm going to tell you exactly what to say. You have to trust me."

I stood there in contemplation. Either I let them in and hope he wasn't lying, or I don't, and they kill me. I didn't have much of a choice.

"Go, or they're going to come in and I can't guarantee you anything if they do." His eyes seemed honest, pleading.

"Fuck." I held the stake to my side as I made my way to the door.

Looking out the peephole, two tall men were whispering back and forth.

One of them had golden brown, fully tattooed arms and was holding a pile of clothes I assumed were for the naked vampire. His hair was short, dark, and a little messy. With his style, gauged ears, and tattoos, I would have thought he was hot under different circumstances.

The other one looked like he frequented a biker bar. Big and rugged. He had lighter skin, with brown hair, and a semi-long beard. He was covered in tattoos and hot too, but in a middle-aged dad kind of way.

"Hello. Are you there?" I asked. They didn't answer.

"Ask them for a riddle," the vampire called out.

"I have your friend. He said you should tell us a riddle."

"What's the difference between humans and security systems?" the younger one asked.

"They want to know—"

"The answer is, one of them is for snacking, and the other is for hacking."

"Well, that's just fucking stupid!"

"Tell them, Sage!"

I let out a deep sigh. "One of them is for snacking and the other is for hacking."

"Open the door," dad bod said.

I hesitated for a few seconds before I released all the locks.

Both men barged into the room, the younger one glancing down at my stake. "Keep that shit to yourself, or I'll kill you," he said, and I gave him a dirty look. Since I didn't know his name, he quickly became an asshole in my head.

"Hi, Sage, is it?" Dad bod asked, and I nodded. "I'm Drag, it's nice to make your acquaintance." He held out his hand and I hesitated, so he pulled away.

"Where is he?" Asshole asked.

"He's in—"

"I'm right here." the vampire said, as he walked into the room with an arrogant smile.

"Fuck." I swallowed hard as he headed toward me. I was definitely going to die.

CHAPTER 16
LUKA

As soon as Sage left the room, I grabbed the hemostats and dug the last chunk of silver out of my leg. It healed just as my friends walked in.

"Where is he?" Winnie asked as I strolled down the hallway.

"He's in—"

"I'm right here."

"Fuck," Sage whispered as I walked toward her.

"Thanks for, uh . . ." I nodded my head towards the bedroom.

Winnie glanced between us with suspicious eyes. "What the fuck is going on?"

"Nothing. We were about to discuss the conspiracies within our societies."

Winnie's eyes narrowed on me. "In the bedroom?"

"I didn't fucking sleep with him, if that's what you're insinuating, asshole!"

"Asshole?" Winnie stepped in close to Sage, going nose to nose. "You shouldn't run your mouth to people you don't know."

"Or what, *Asshole*? If you're going to kill me, then come on. I'm waiting!" She held up the stake and shook it, taunting Winnie.

I have to admit, her attitude was sexy as hell.

"I got twenty bucks on the chick," Drag said.

"Same," I agreed.

Sage's glare whipped toward Drag. "You can't call me a chick. Do you know what year it is?"

"I'm sorry. I didn't mean to offend you."

"Don't apologize to her, Drag. She doesn't deserve it." Winnie was still in her face, and I was extremely amused by the situation.

Sage scoffed. "It's *literally* a derogatory term, you can't say it!"

"It *literally* means young woman. I know because I was around when it became popular." Winnie grinned, showing her his fangs.

"Whoopty fucking do. You're an old-ass pretentious vampire. No one cares!" she said, and I couldn't help but laugh. It was extremely amusing.

"Make that a hundred bucks on the, um, can I say woman?" Drag asked with a concerned face. Sage rolled her eyes and sighed.

Winnie narrowed his gaze on her. "A thousand bucks says I can kill her in under a minute."

Sage whipped her attention back to Winnie. "A thousand bucks says you can't!"

Winnie let my clothes fall to the floor. "Bet?"

"Bet!" Sage immediately went into a defensive stance.

"Are you two almost done? We got shit to do."

"Don't interrupt them, Drag, this is fun to watch!" I crossed my arms and grinned at the two feral beings.

"Well, if we don't get out of here before the sun comes up, you two will be toast," Drag reminded us.

Sage eased her body as she glanced at him. "Are you a wolven?"

Drag smiled proudly. "Yes."

"What pack?"

"I would rather not disclose at the moment."

"Fair enough." She turned toward me. "So, what are we doing, Fucker?"

"Do you have any beer?"

She rolled her eyes before she went into the kitchen. A minute later, she came back with four beers, and I noticed she had put the stake in her waistband. She handed us each a drink before opening one for herself.

"You know, you can put your clothes back on now," she said before taking a swig. "Asshole brought them in just for you."

"My name isn't Asshole!"

Sage shrugged. "Well, I don't know your name, so for now, it's Asshole."

"His name is Winnie," I said as I slid my pants on.

"Like Winnie the Pooh?" she asked, and I laughed.

Winnie looked irritated. "It's Winston!"

"Sage, we have some questions, if you don't mind," Drag said. He was always the good cop in our trio.

"Ask away." She wandered over to the couch, pulled her stake from her waistband, and held it as she plopped down. She motioned to the loveseat across from her. "You guys can sit. But if any of you try anything, I won't hesitate to kill you."

"Such great hospitality," Winnie said as he sat down on the loveseat. Drag took a seat next to him.

"I'll be right back." I took off toward the bedroom and grabbed the spray she was showing me and tossed it to Drag. "Have you seen this before?"

He caught it and inspected the can. "What is it?"

"It's a medically engineered wound bonding solution," Sage said.

Drag's eyebrows furrowed. "What does that mean?"

"It seals wounds almost as fast as vampires."

"Can we test it?" Winnie asked as he took the can from Drag.

"It wouldn't work on vampires. You guys heal too quickly."

"I was thinking more like ripping your arm off and seeing if I can heal the wound before you bleed out," Winnie said with a grin.

"I could cut my hand," Drag said. "Just to see how it works."

Sage shook her head. "You're a self-healer, too, even if it's slower than vampires, so I'm not sure it'll work. It's made for humans, not supernatural creatures."

"Then why don't you try it?" Winnie suggested. "Or are you scared?" They locked eyes as the room got quiet.

"Give it here!"

Winnie threw the can a lot harder than was necessary. Sage must have had cat-like reflexes because she caught it. She stood up and headed toward the kitchen and we followed. She set the can and stake on the counter, then pulled a knife out of the drawer.

"Can you two control yourselves if I bleed?"

I nodded, and she immediately looked at Drag. She obviously trusted him more than us.

"They can," he answered.

She looked back at her hand and sighed before running the blade across it. She hissed, and my fangs elongated when I smelled the blood. It was a natural response, similar to when a human's belly growls when they smell food. I made sure to keep my mouth closed.

After running her hand under cold water, she dabbed it with a paper towel. We all moved in curiously as she picked up the can of spray. One squirt, and the wound sealed itself.

"What the fuck?" Winnie whispered.

"Where is bondcoat made?" I asked.

"I don't know. In a lab somewhere."

"Do you know who makes it?" Drag asked as he picked the can up.

"The government, I think."

"Where did you get it?" I asked, even though I was pretty sure I already knew the answer.

"Venom."

"Can you get us a can so we can have it tested?" Drag asked.

"Why?" She narrowed her eyes at him, waiting to hear what we were all thinking.

"Because I have a feeling they have somehow found a way to put vampire blood in it."

Winnie grabbed the can and sprayed some on his hand. "But it's clear."

"I know, but what else could it be?" Drag wondered aloud.

Winnie shook his head with a look of disgust. "I bet they make it at the testing facility."

"No. The only thing VRC researches is a cure for vampirism."

All our eyes widened at Sage's words before we started laughing.

"What's so funny?"

"They starve and torture vampires there. They are nothing more than lab rats," I said.

"Oh, what do you know, shirtless wonder?" She crossed her arms like she was annoyed, causing Winnie to laugh.

"Obviously more than you know, and you work for the assholes who run it," I retorted.

"You don't know what you're talking about! They're not assholes."

"Oh, really?" Her natural scent filled my nostrils more as I moved in close to her. "They took my brother! He's one of their lab rats, so to me, they're assholes!"

She stared at me like she had something snarky to say but at the last minute a look of empathy settled on her face. "I'm sorry about your brother."

I wasn't sure if she was talking about the one who was captured or the one she killed. Looking into her eyes, I had a feeling she meant Andrei.

"Do you know where the lab is located?" Winnie asked.

"No. That's a level seven clearance and I'm only a level two. They don't tell me anything."

"Can you find out?"

Her eyes wandered to Winnie as she bit her lip. "Honestly, even if I knew, I wouldn't tell you. I'm not going to sentence a bunch of Venom members to their deaths."

"We will figure it out on our own," I said, and her eyes narrowed on me.

"So, what else did you need to talk to me about?"

I downed the rest of my drink and held the bottle out to her. "You got more beer? This one will piss you off."

CHAPTER 17

SAGE

The old saying *"if you play with fire, you're gonna get burned"* played over and over in my head as I sat across from a vampire and a wolven. The other vampire—I still didn't know his name, probably Arrogant Fucker—just handed the other two their beers before taking a seat next to me. He grinned arrogantly as he handed me mine.

Definitely Arrogant Fucker.

I scooted away from him in disgust before twisting the top off. "Is someone going to tell me what's going on or what?"

Taking a swig of my beer, I made a face. Erik liked beer, so I kept it stocked for him. Even though I hated it, sitting in a room with people who could kill me, I needed something to relax.

Asshole and Fucker both locked eyes before looking at the wolven.

"Go ahead, Drag," Fucker said.

"There was an incident between you and Luka a week ago and it resulted in your partner getting killed."

"Luka?" My eyes drifted to Fucker.

"That's me," he said with a grin.

I gave him a look of disdain before I turned back toward Drag. "Continue."

"We have evidence proving you both being there wasn't a coincidence."

"Really?" I glanced back at Luka. "He was stalking me, so it just made sense for him to be there."

"You killed my brother!" he screamed.

"He was trying to kill me!" I hollered back.

"Yeah, and your partner was trying to kill me when I shot his ass, so what's the fucking difference?"

My mouth dropped open and anger filled me. "Fuck you!"

"Luka," Drag warned.

The fucker's jaw clenched as I stared him down.

"Anyway, Sage. We have a lot of evidence we want to discuss," Drag said, bringing my attention back to him.

My brows furrowed in confusion. "What kind of evidence?"

"I broke into some specific files," Winnie said. "I could show you, but I don't have my laptop. We thought this was a rescue mission. What we found showed someone in Save sent Andrei to—"

"Who's Andrei?" I asked.

"My brother you staked," Luka said, bringing my attention to him.

"Oh." I wanted to apologize, but I swallowed hard and turned my attention back to Winnie as he continued.

"They sent Andrei to the bar you were at."

Thoughts of that night filled my head, and I wondered if it was a set up. "Now you mention it, he arrived at the bar not long after me and kept his eyes on me the whole time."

"How did you end up at that bar?" Luka asked.

"We are directed to locations when missions come in. That was mine for the night."

"How do you get missions?" Winnie asked.

"All Venom members have a tablet which has the roster schedule, missions, email, etc."

"Do you have it here?"

"I haven't gotten mine. I'm technically not supposed to be on the roster yet, but since my dad is the president, I . . ."

Everyone's eyes widened with the bomb I accidentally dropped.

Fuck.

"You're the president's *daughter*?" Drag asked.

My hand tightened on the stake as I bit my lip in fear of them using me for leverage.

"Your dad sucks at protecting you," Winnie said, and I snickered.

"You're like the princess of Venom," Luka said, and my head whipped toward him.

"I am not. Shut up!"

"You actually are an incredibly important asset to people who might want to use you against Venom," Drag said with a shake of his head. "How is no one protecting you?"

My vulnerability defense kicked in. "I don't need anyone to protect me!"

"But you do, Princess," Luka said. "Otherwise, you wouldn't be sitting in a room filled with enemies."

As I locked eyes with him, I couldn't help but realize he was right, and so was Drag. People could—and would—use me against Venom.

I stood up, ready to fight. "So, are you going to kill me now? Or just use me to get to my dad?!"

"I'll kill you," Luka said, grinning arrogantly at me.

"Don't listen to him, Sage. We aren't your enemies," Drag said, interrupting me from murdering Luka with my eyes. "We don't kill people unless we have to. We also don't take hostages or anything."

"When you get the tablet, could I possibly take a look at it?" Winnie asked.

"Umm, maybe." I slowly lowered my ass back in my seat, feeling a little embarrassed by my outburst. "Depends on what you need it for."

"If I knew what program Venom was using, I could hack into their systems and see who is sending out the missions. Then I could cross-analyze them and find out who the rats are on both ends."

"I have a feeling the bulky douchebag guy you were with is a rat," Luka said, bringing my attention back to him.

"Who?" I asked.

"The Russian leader who left you and Deren alone on a mission."

"Sorin. I don't think . . ."

My mind wandered quickly into treacherous territory. Sorin left two rookies alone and showed no emotion when he saw Deren's body. Was he a rat who was working with vampires?

"Say what you're thinking." Luka's voice brought me out of my head.

"I was about to defend Sorin, but I couldn't. My brain was only giving me red flags to support your theory."

"Like what?"

"Like you said, he left me and Deren alone. He also wasn't surprised when he was killed. Then . . ." I wasn't sure if I should say it aloud, but how else would we find the traitors if I didn't. "My dad defended him during my interrogation. I got so upset I got knocked out, but after a week in the psych ward, I—"

"Hold on a second," Luka interrupted. "What do you mean by interrogation and psych ward?"

"And knocked out?" Winnie added.

"Umm." I took a sip of my beer, buying me time to think.

"If you feel comfortable enough, would you mind telling us everything that happened?" Drag asked. He seemed like a genuinely nice person, but I wasn't going to let my guard down.

I shrugged. "I guess I could."

Once again, I had to completely relive the trauma of one of the worst nights of my life. I told them everything that happened until I was released from the hospital. When I was done, I glanced around and all three of them looked like I had told them a horror story.

Drag seemed the most concerned as his eyes locked on me. "Is that normal Venom procedure?"

"Yeah. It's for our safety."

The room got quiet, and I felt like shrinking into myself as I thought about all the Venom procedures. *Was it normal?*

"Well, this has been a great discussion," Drag said as he stood. "We appreciate the hospitality, but we must get going before the sun comes up."

Winnie and Luka stood up, so I followed suit.

"Let me know when you get the tablet," Winnie said. I nodded, though I was still unsure if I was going to let him see it.

A lot of information was thrown at me, and I was having a hard time wrapping my head around the fact my society could be in bed with vampires.

"It was nice meeting you, Sage." Drag extended his hand. I hesitated for a second, but figured I could muster myself enough to at least shake his hand since he had been benevolent. He smiled before heading toward the door.

When I looked at Luka, his eyes narrowed on me. He said nothing as he turned away.

"Oh, Sage," Drag said from the hallway. "Give Luka your number so we can keep in contact."

He smiled again before walking away, leaving me alone with Fucker. When we made eye contact, we both gave repulsed faces.

"Can we just email or something?" I asked.

Luka's face went deadpan and he held out his hand. "Just give me your phone."

With a sigh, I handed it to him. He added himself as a contact before handing it back. After seeing what he named it, I rolled my eyes.

"You couldn't come up with anything better than *Sexy Vampire*?" He grinned arrogantly at me. I immediately hit edit and changed his contact to *Fucker* before showing him my phone. "There, that's better."

"Mine was true," he said with a wink, and I gave him a look of hatred. "Text me so I can save your number."

With a sigh, I sent him a text which said *Fuckface.* He grinned as he saved my contact in his phone and then showed it to me. My mouth dropped open when I saw what name he assigned me.

Princess Badass.

"Goodnight, Princess." He smirked before he walked away.

"Good night, Fucker!" I shook my head and slammed the door.

After making my way back to the couch, I plopped down.

What the fuck just happened? How did I go from almost killing a vampire to putting my number in his phone? It wasn't so we could go on a date, but still.

My mind was going a mile a minute. I needed to tell my friends what happened, but a part of me wondered if I should keep it secret. I truly had no idea what to do.

A few weeks ago, my life was mundane, now I was trying to keep from being murdered. Surrounded by conspiracy theories and death, my first week had been like cold water to the face. Concern about what was going to happen settled in me. I was willing to help them if it meant helping Venom find the rat, not to mention the possibility of me getting answers to some questions I've had about my society.

I guess I would rather play with fire and get burned than die of boredom.

CHAPTER 18

LUKA

"What time was her appointment?" Winnie asked.

"It was at ten." I let out a sigh as I checked my phone for the tenth time.

"Shouldn't she be out by now?"

I shrugged. "I have no idea how long therapy takes."

We were chilling in Winnie's cave while he was doing research. Tonight was Sage's first night back to Venom. If her therapy appointment went well, she would be returning to the field. Winnie was dying to get his hands on her tablet and was annoying the shit out of me because of it.

"If she's on the roster, she won't be able to get the tablet to you until after work," I reminded him.

"Can you text her and ask if she's done yet?"

"Why do I have to be the one who communicates with her? Can't one of you do it?" My stare went from Winnie to Drag. He didn't even look up from the magazine he was thumbing through.

"It's just a simple text. What's the problem, bro?"

"She killed my brother, Winnie!"

"And you killed her friend."

"Whose side are you on?" I asked as I pulled out my phone for the eleventh time.

"I'm on your side, like always. I was just stating the obvious. This is probably just as uncomfortable for her."

I gave him a dirty look. "I honestly don't care about her comfort level."

"What's everyone doing tonight," Drag asked, finally engaging in the conversation.

"If you would have been listening, you would know I'm hoping to meet up with Sage and get her tablet," Winnie said. "What about you?"

Drag mindlessly turned a page. "It's the first Friday of the month."

"Oh, family safety night at Save." Winnie turned back toward his computer. "Have fun with that."

"You should come out one night, it's a lot of fun." Drag glanced up at me. "You should come, too, Luka."

"It's Friday night feed for me," I said with a smile. "Winnie?"

"No, thanks, Drag. I'm not willing to ruin a Friday night watching kids play board games while the council talks about safety."

My phone dinged and Winnie's eyes darted to me. "Is it her?"

I nodded before I read the message.

Princess Badass: *Meet me where we first met.*

The message was vague, but I answered her.

Luka: *K*

Princess Badass: *I hate when people say K, it sounds uneducated.*

I grinned at her last message.

Luka: *Okay, Princess.*

Princess Badass: *Shut up!*

I laughed aloud.

"What is she saying?" Winnie asked impatiently.

"She wants me to meet her at Drifter's."

"Why?" Drag asked. I'm sure he was extra concerned for his father.

"I don't know. The message was vague. Do you wanna come?"

"I promised Laren I would help her tonight, so I can't, but you two need to be careful." He laid the magazine down before he rose from his seat.

"We will let you know what happens," I said before we left the apartment.

When we got to Drifter's, we sat at the bar. Ollie and Libby were bartending.

"How's it going?" Ollie asked as he slid two beers in front of us.

"It's been good," Winnie said before taking a swig.

"Good, good," Ollie mumbled as he wandered off. Unless angry, he was a man of few words.

The door opened and I smelled Sage before I saw her. My head whipped in her direction when another scent hit me. To my utter astonishment, she had brought a friend.

"Who is that?" Winnie asked.

"I don't know." My eyes narrowed on the two women. They were both beautiful but looked lethal. "I bet she's Venom."

"Probably, but I like it. She smells good, too." He grinned as they headed toward us.

"We have a working relationship to keep," I reminded him before the women got closer. "Be respectful."

"I'm always respectful."

"Hey," Sage said.

"Hello, ladies. Looking good tonight, Sage. Did you do something different with your hair? It looks less bitchy." Winnie grinned, showing off his fangs. I shook my head and sighed.

"I did, Winnie. Thanks for noticing."

"You're not going to comment on *my* hair?" he asked.

"No, but I am going to comment on the balls you left in my apartment," Sage said, and her friend's eyes widened.

"Is this normal?" the brunette asked. She was a pretty girl, with tan skin and a sweet-looking face. Her hair was French-braided on each side of her head.

"Yes," Winnie and Sage said in unison, causing Winnie to smile with amusement.

Sage pointed to Winnie. "This here is Pooh Bear or Asshole."

"Hi, I'm Lyric."

"Nice to meet you, Lyric. My name is actually Winston. Winston Rodriguez." He held his hand out and the new girl shook it with a smile.

Then Sage pointed to me. "His name is Fucker."

Lyric narrowed her eyes and nodded. She had a knowing look, and I was sure Sage had been talking smack on me.

With a grin, I stood up from the barstool. "You can call me Luka." I winked at Lyric, and Sage made a gagging sound.

"How was your therapy session?" Winnie asked. I could tell he was dying to ask her about the tablet but was trying to be patient.

"Extremely interesting. Is there a private place to talk?"

"Hey, Ollie, can we—"

"You can use it." Ollie let us use his office more often than I liked to admit.

"Thanks, man." I turned toward the women. "Follow me." I headed behind the bar and into the office.

Taking a seat behind the desk, I gestured for the women to sit. There were only two chairs so Winnie sat on the short filing cabinet close to Lyric.

"So, what's going on?" I asked.

Sage pulled a folder of papers out of her bag and dropped it on the desk. "This may be deeper than we thought."

CHAPTER 19
SAGE

Walking into Venom after being gone for a week was anxiety-inducing, but thankfully, Lyric was off today and came with me for emotional support. I was grateful since I was nervous I would run into my dad. He called once to check on me—probably because my mom made him—but I hadn't seen him since the night of my breakdown. My mom, on the other hand, called every day and stopped by a couple of times. Just like Erik and Lyric had.

"Okay, I will be out of therapy in an hour."

"I'll wait for you in the cafeteria. Good luck." Lyric walked away and I sighed.

When I stepped into the therapist's office, I was shocked to see a man sitting in Stephanie's chair.

"Hi. Sage, I'm presuming?" The short, older man stood up and held out his hand.

"Yes." I closed the distance between us and shook it.

"I'm Mr. Johnson, your new therapist."

Surprise filled me as I stared at the white-haired man. It took me a good three days of straight therapy to get used to Steph and be able to open up to her. Now I have a new therapist and he wants me to call him Mr. Johnson. At least Steph was only a little bit older than me, and I knew her from seeing her around the compound. This man I had never seen before in my life.

"Where's Steph?" I asked.

"Ms. Parker is no longer working for Venom. Have a seat."

After I took a seat on the Couch of Doom, I had to do my breathing techniques to relax my body. He wasted no time and dove right in.

One hour later, I was saying goodbye to my new therapist, having decided I didn't like him. The only good thing he did was give me another week extension on my time off.

"I'll see you next week, Ms. Argent."

I nodded and left the room.

During my entire therapy visit, red flags were going off. What Steph said, *sometimes people need to* escape *the reality of this life,* played over and over in my head. I immediately pulled my phone out and called her.

All I got was a recording that said, *"The number you're calling is no longer in service."* My heart sped up and I was glad I didn't wear my watch today. The *health monitors* would have known something was up by the giant spike in my heart rate.

As fast as I could, without looking suspicious, I went to the cafeteria and found Lyric. She was sitting alone at a table, reading a book.

"Oh, hey," she said as I approached. Her smile immediately dropped when she saw the look on my face. "Oh, no, what's wrong?"

Nodding my head toward the cafeteria's outdoor patio, she stood up and followed me out the door. Hoping the distance would put us out of earshot of anyone around and out of range of the cameras, I wandered over to the mimosa trees by the edge.

"What's wrong?" she whispered.

"Are you off tonight?"

Her face was a cross between confusion and concern. "Yes. Why?"

"I need help."

She laid a hand on my arm. "You know I would help you with anything, Sage."

"You won't like this. It goes against our morals . . ." I lowered my voice, "and the society."

Lyric's eyes widened before she took a deep breath. "Blood of the coven." I nodded, knowing exactly what she meant.

Lyric, Erik, and I had made pacts when we were younger. We vowed to be there for each other, no matter what, and let no one come in between us—not Venom, not family. We also vowed to never lie to one another, because the blood of the coven was thicker than the water of the womb.

"Can you pull the roster and see who is monitoring the security cameras for the basement?"

"One second." Looking down into her bag, her dark hair fell forward, blocking her face. She pulled her tablet out and got into our system. "Jimmy."

"I need you to flirt with him and make him think he has a chance."

She made an unpleasant face. "Why?"

"I can't tell you here, but I will tell you everything as soon as we get off the compound. It will take me less than two minutes to get down there, then I have to sneak past Linda, before I come back up. I would say try to keep him occupied for at least ten minutes. I need to borrow your bookbag, too. Are you in?"

Without hesitation, she handed me her bag.

"Now walk next to me and talk about everyday normal life things." Lyric nodded before we headed into the building. She immediately started rambling about how we needed to go shopping for our Halloween costumes.

What I was going to attempt to do could get me in a hell of a lot of trouble. I would definitely get an infraction for it—possibly worse. But if my suspicions were right, the Venom-Save conspiracy theory was bigger than we thought.

As we got close to where we needed to part ways, I said,. "I have to go down and see about getting a file from Linda." I gave her an exasperated face like I hated my job because anyone who might have been watching would expect nothing less from me.

"Okay, I need to go talk to Jimmy." She smiled mischievously.

I widened my eyes and gave her an accusing look. "Why?"

"He's asked me out a bunch of times, and I think I should give him a shot."

That was the good thing about Lyric. We had been so close for so long we just got each other. After being in multiple situations where we would have to make up stories on the spot when guys would try to hit on us, we became great at it.

"He's a weird guy, but okay. Meet me by my car when you're done. We can go costume shopping."

"Okay," she said before rounding the corner, heading toward the security room.

As I strolled down to the basement, I wondered how the hell I was going to pull this off. After taking a quick right, I headed straight for the files room.

Linda was sitting comfortably at the desk behind the window. She was an elderly woman, probably in her late seventies. Even though she was way past retirement, she refused to leave. The society let her stay because she still did her job, just slowly.

"Hey, Linda," I said as I peeked over the counter.

She looked up from the crossword puzzle she was doing and gave me a huge smile. "Hello, Sagelynn. I'm so happy to see you. I heard about what happened on your first and second nights out. It's such a tragedy what happened to Deren. Your mother was so upset over the whole thing. I told her you would—"

"I hate to cut you off, but I'm on strict orders to hurry. I don't want to get another infraction." I felt terrible because I knew she loved to talk to me.

"Oh, my. No, you don't," she mumbled as she grabbed her cane. "What are you needing?"

"A file. Last name is. . ." I needed to get to the files that started with a P so I could steal Steph's folder. It was vital to get her to the opposite side of the room so I blurted a random name. "Baker. Olivia Baker."

"Baker. I don't think I have a Baker, let me see." She slowly, and I mean glacially, headed toward the back-right side of the room. What seemed like an eternity later, I made my move.

Opening the door to her office, I slid inside and quickly went to the left side of the room. After roughly twenty seconds, I found the filing cabinet with a P on it. I dug through it and found the folder I was looking for. Stephanie Parker. I shoved it into the bookbag and headed back through the door, shutting it quietly behind me.

A few minutes later, she strolled up. "I'm not sure if you got the name wrong, but there is no Olivia Baker."

"That's odd. I will confirm and come back if I need to."

"Okay, honey. You come see me anytime you need to."

"Bye, Linda," I said before quickly making my way out of there.

My heart was racing from the adrenaline rush I had as I headed up the stairs. I tried hard not to look suspicious as I made my way out to my Jeep. Lyric wasn't at my car when I got there.

After hitting the unlock button, I got in, sat the bag in the seat next to me, and stared at it. I wanted to dig into it so badly, but since there were cameras everywhere, I didn't.

Lyric opened the car door, drawing my gaze. She picked the bag up and slid in. Neither of us spoke as we made our way off the compound's grounds. I waved to the security guard when the gates opened.

Once we were on the dirt road which led to the highway, I pulled over. "Can you hand me the file out of the bag?"

Lyric did and I frantically thumbed through it until I got to the personal information page. Venom kept records of the phones they gave us, including our personal cell phones and addresses if we didn't live on the compound grounds.

"Here it is," I mumbled as I pointed at the paper. I dialed the number and got the same message. It was disconnected. "Fuck."

"Are you ready to tell me what's going on?" Lyric asked.

"I will tell you on the way to this address." I handed her the folder and pointed to where we needed to go. "Can you pop it into the GPS for me?"

Lyric typed it into the navigation system as I pulled back onto the dirt road and headed for the highway.

Fifteen minutes later, I was almost at the house we were looking for and I had told Lyric everything. Her mouth was agape when I glanced over at her.

"What the fuck, Sage! Why didn't you say something sooner?"

"I don't know! Honestly, I didn't want to involve you or Erik. I figured it wasn't what it seemed, but the more that happened, the more it became this big thing and now I'm freaking out!"

"I can't believe you had two vampires and a wolven in your house."

"The shifter was super nice, and I actually thought Winnie was cool after a while. I fucking hate the other one. Luka."

The navigation said we arrived at our destination, so I pulled over. There was a sign in the yard of Steph's house, and I couldn't believe they found a realtor that quick.

"Fuck. Her house is already up for sale. How, if she is missing?"

"I don't know. It seems odd." Lyric shook her head with a confused expression. "What do we do now?"

"I have to go meet them. You don't have to come."

She sighed. "Of course, I'm coming. I'm one hundred percent in now. I want to find out what's going on just as bad as you. Also, I don't want you getting murdered. Two stakes are better than one."

I laughed as I pulled up Luka's contact info to text him.

Lyric laid her hand over my phone screen. "Wait."

"What?"

"Be vague about the message. Venom tracks everything we do, and with all these conspiracy theories, how do you know they don't read our texts?"

"I don't, but thanks for freaking me out. I'm definitely getting a personal cell after this. I'll just tell him to meet me where we first met." I sent the text.

"At that bar?"

"Yeah." My phone beeped. "Ugh, I hate people who text 'K.'"

Lyric laughed because she knew how much I despised it.

After telling him to shut up, I handed her my phone in case he texted back. Pulling away from the curb, I headed downtown to Drifter's bar.

CHAPTER 20

LUKA

"What the hell is this? Nineteen eighty?" Winnie asked as he picked up the file. Sage had just filled us in on what happened and how she got it.

"Venom does everything electronically except for personal files. That way if any asshole like you ever hacked into our system, we won't all be found and murdered."

"This folder even *smells* like nineteen eighty," Winnie said before sniffing it. "Ahh, it brings back memories."

"Give me that." I yanked it from his hand. "So, you think your therapist went into hiding?" I asked suspiciously.

"Maybe. Like I said, she moved, her house is for sale, and both her phones are turned off."

"Have you tried her emergency contact?"

Sage's brows rose as her brain seemed to light up like she didn't think of that. "No. I was still running on adrenaline when we got out of there."

"Winnie, get me a burner." He hopped off the filing cabinet and opened the top drawer. I eyed the two women. "Is anyone good at acting?"

"I'm fantastic at it," Lyric answered.

Winnie handed me the phone before he slid back onto the filing cabinet, continuing to make googly eyes at her.

"This is a burner phone. It's untraceable. Do you think your acting skills are good enough to pretend to be someone looking for the therapist?"

"Her name is Stephanie Parker, not *therapist*," Sage corrected with a dirty look. I grinned in return. I loved tormenting her.

"Yeah, I can do it," Lyric said. I handed her the phone and she dialed the number.

"Put it on speaker, so we can hear," Sage whispered.

"Hello," an elderly sounding man answered.

"Is this Mr. Parker?"

"Yes, it is."

"Hello, this is Olivia Baker, badge 87501. I'm one of the security members at your daughter Stephanie's work."

Lyric was a quick thinker, I realized. She had used the same name Sage used when she told us her story. I also noticed her badge number was a zip code from a nearby city.

The line went silent for a minute. "Did you find her? Is she dead?"

Lyric's eyes widened as she glanced at Sage. She quickly composed herself and continued. "We haven't found her yet, sir. I'm assuming you haven't had contact with her, either?"

"No, I haven't. It isn't like her just to take off like this. When your people called me and told me she disappeared, I just couldn't believe it. I didn't know what to think." The man let out a long, hard sigh.

"It was a shock to us, too. She has always been a loyal worker."

"She has. Her entire life has revolved around that place. I just wished her mother was around, she would know what to do. She died a few years back. Cancer."

Lyric had a look of empathy even though the man couldn't see it. "I'm so sorry for your loss."

"Thanks. So, what can I do for you? The guy who called me last time said he would call back if they heard something, but he hasn't."

"Who did you speak to last time?" Lyric asked.

The line went silent again, and then he snapped his tongue. "Ah, I can't remember his name. He spilled off a set of numbers, too. He was rather short with me on the phone. He seemed annoyed that he had to call."

"Well, I apologize, sir. I'll make a note in the file." Lyric opened the folder, purposely making a rustling sound with the papers.

"Oh, no need to do that, sweetheart. I wouldn't want the Russian man getting in any trouble."

Sage and Lyric's mouth were both agape as they made eye contact. Lyric quickly composed herself.

"I will pretend like you never said it." The tone of Lyric's voice was soothing. She actually *was* good at this.

"Thanks. I wish I had the strength to go to Vegas. Stephanie has a house there, and I keep wondering if she just had to get away for a while. Life does get stressful sometimes."

"It really does."

"So, what was it you needed?"

"We wanted to make sure you didn't need anything." Lyric smiled as if he could see her.

"That's so kind of you, but I'm good right now. I'm not going to make you drive all the way to San Francisco to get me some milk." The man laughed hard, and Lyric played along. He let out another sigh before continuing. "If I need anything, I'll let you know."

"You take care of yourself, Mr. Parker."

"You too, sweetheart. Bye now."

Lyric hung up the phone and smiled proudly.

"That was sexy as hell," Winnie said as he looked adoringly at her.

"Eww, put your tongue back in your mouth, Pooh Bear," Sage said before her eyes darted to me. "The Russian guy he was talking about was Sorin!"

I nodded because I already figured it out. "The douchebag who left you two alone."

"Yep!"

"Why would Steph just leave?" Lyric asked. "It makes no sense."

"Did she actually leave or was she removed?"

Sage narrowed her eyes on Winnie. "What do you mean?"

He crossed his arms, leaning back against the wall. "Removed, as in maybe they killed her, or had her killed."

"Do you think that's what happened?" Lyric asked.

Sage shook her head. "Why would they kill her? She is in her thirties and has never been in trouble. Her file shows she doesn't even have an infraction. Not even a parking violation from security. I have three."

"Bad driver, huh?" I grinned and Sage's nose scrunched up in anger.

"Fuck you! I know how to drive."

"When was the last time you saw her?" Winnie asked, completely ignoring us.

Sage gave me a dirty look before turning her attention to Winnie. "A week ago at therapy."

"That's the last time I saw her, too," Lyric added. "Right after Sage left, she left. I saw them both on camera because I was downstairs taking inventory in the monitoring room."

"Did she seem off or anything?"

Lyric shook her head. "She seemed to be in a hurry, but it wasn't abnormal."

"So, the last time anyone saw her was right after your appointment?" I asked.

Sage shrugged. "I guess so."

"Was there anything different about that day than any other?"

"Sometimes people need to *escape* the reality of this life."

"What?" I asked, confused by the statement.

"She whispered it to me right before I left, but the way she said it was like she was hinting at something."

"Lyric, you said there are cameras at Venom. Are there microphones, too?" Winnie asked.

"There are."

"Do you work in the security department?"

"I do." Lyrics narrowed her eyes suspiciously on Winnie. "Why?"

"I'm going to need access to those cameras so I can see if I can find out anything. Unless we want to take a trip to Vegas?" Winnie smiled at Lyric and Sage rolled her eyes.

Lyric turned toward Sage not saying anything as they stared at each other. After a few seconds, Sage nodded, and Lyric turned back to Winnie.

"I can get you access to the cameras."

Winnie smiled with excitement. "Sweet."

"But I'm going to need to be there when you access them, and you'll have to use my laptop."

"What?" Winnie's smile dropped as he hopped off the filing cabinet. "I like my equipment. I don't want to use some old ass—"

"Well, that's the deal, Winston. Even if I wasn't part of the security team, I'm not going to put the lives of many people in danger because I handed off valuable information to a vampire."

"But—"

"You use my laptop and I'm there with you, or you don't get access to our cameras."

Winnie huffed. "Can't we just use mine and—"

"Deal or no deal?" Lyric asked sternly. Winnie stared at her with a furrowed brow and she gave him a sweet, innocent smile.

"Fine, whatever." Winnie's annoyed expression turned to one of excitement. "When can you come to my apartment?"

Sage shook her head. "She isn't going to your apartment, Pooh Bear."

"How else will I hack?"

"I can go, but Sage is coming with me." Lyric grinned as Sage gave her a look of disbelief.

Needing to break the seductive eye contact and smiling contest that Lyric and Winnie were having, I cleared my throat.

"Winnie will let you know what information he needs from you. Once you get it, let us know."

"Can I get your number, Lyric?"

The way Sage's forehead wrinkled in anger before she spoke, was amusing. "That's unnecessary—"

"Sure!" Lyric pulled out her phone and exchanged numbers with Winnie before they engaged in a conversation about what kind of laptop she had.

My eyes wandered over to Sage, the look on her face told me Lyric was going to get an earful when they left.

As I watched her side-eye the flirting pair, the beauty in her hazel eyes was mesmerizing. The black eyeliner seemed to accentuate them, as did her long dark lashes. Her cheekbones were high and slightly pink, giving her a sweet and beautiful face—even if she was snarky as shit. My gaze traveled down to her mouth as she bit her bottom lip nervously. Her lips were full, kissable, and for a split second, I thought about how they would feel against mine.

With quickness, she whipped her head toward me like she felt me staring. "What the fuck are you looking at?"

I let out a snicker at the way her eyes were suspiciously narrowed on me. "Nothing, Princess."

The muscles at the corner of my mouth had a mind of their own when they tightened, making me give her a genuine smile. Her eyes locked with mine and she briefly smiled back before stopping herself. Her brows furrowed in confusion, then she shook her head and quickly looked away.

"We have to go, Lyric," she said, interrupting their conversation.

"Already?" Winnie asked. "We were making plans to go get dinner."

"Do you even eat food?" Sage questioned.

Winnie looked appalled as he crossed his arms. "Of course, I do."

"I mean, other than people."

"It holds no nutritional value, but it still tastes good." Winnie smiled and Lyric let out a small laugh. "But we have to drink blood regularly to survive."

"Gross," Sage said as she stood up. "We will be in contact." She headed for the door and Lyric gave Winnie one more smile before following her.

As soon as the door shut, I turned toward Winnie. "What the fuck is wrong with you?"

"What?" With his arms still crossed, he leaned against the filing cabinet with a pompous grin.

"You can't fuck her, Winnie. She's a Venom member. Plus, we need to keep a friendly working relationship between us and them until we figure this shit out. We don't need you breaking some girl's heart."

"But it's okay for you to eye-fuck Sage?"

I shifted uncomfortably in my seat. "What are you talking about?"

"I glanced over while Lyric was talking, and I saw you, Luka. You couldn't keep your eyes off her. You have a thing for her, bro."

"I can't fucking stand her."

"You can't stand her because she killed your brother. That doesn't mean you're not attracted to her."

"Believe me, I'm not." I stood and headed for the door.

As I wandered back to my seat at the bar, I couldn't help but think about what Winnie said. There was no way I was attracted to someone who killed my brother, no matter how gorgeous she was.

CHAPTER 21
SAGE

Halloween was only a week away and I was shopping with Lyric, trying on costumes when my mouth dropped open at her remark.

"You can't be serious, Lyric?"

"What, you don't think he's cute?" It had been three days since we met with Luka and Winnie, and I was surprised she kept the secret that long.

"Lyric, he's a," I lowered my voice, "vampire."

"Just because he's a, you know, doesn't mean he isn't cute." She grabbed a couple of garments off the rack and handed them to me.

"I like Winnie and all, but it's weird."

"I didn't say I was going to marry him. I just said he's cute." She grabbed a pair of fishnet stockings and handed them to me. My eyes widened as I piled them on top of the handful of clothes I was already carrying. "I think Luka is cute, too."

I made a disgusted face. "Eww."

"Oh, my god!" She whipped toward me with wide eyes. "You think he's cute, too!"

"No, I don't!"

"I know you, Sagelynn. Anytime you say *eww* about a guy, you think he's cute."

Was I attracted to him? I mean, yeah. He had a nice body, was covered in tattoos, rode a motorcycle, and was drop-dead gorgeous, but he also was an arrogant prick who killed my friend.

"Whatever, Lyric. Agree to disagree."

"Let's try these on." She handed me *another* garment before heading to the fitting room. I trailed behind her.

"I'm not wearing a slutty outfit for Halloween. I already told you I wanted to go as the Mandalorian."

Lyric stopped and turned toward me. "Sage, you're not going out with me dressed as the Mandalorian! We chose from the bowl what our group costume was, and the theme is Little Red Riding Hood. Star Wars didn't get picked!"

We had a bowl and all three of us put two ideas each in, giving me a thirty-three percent chance of winning. It was amazing how, almost every year at Halloween, I got screwed. My ideas haven't been drawn in four years!

"It never does!" Taking a deep breath, I sighed. "I would be fine if I could have been the grandma."

"We chose those from a bowl, too. Erik is the grandma, I'm the wolf, and you're Red Riding Hood." She turned into the fitting rooms. "Stop complaining."

I held up the tiny skirt she'd picked out for me. "That doesn't mean I have to dress in provocative clothing."

"You will look amazing in that. Oh, here's an open one."

We went into the biggest dressing room and locked the door.

"I just feel like I shouldn't have to show a bunch of skin to have fun on Halloween."

She turned toward me with a sad frown. "Wear whatever you want, but can you, at least, try it on first?" Lyric had an adorable look on her face that she knew I wouldn't say no to.

With a sigh of exasperation, I stripped down to my undergarments. After throwing on what Lyric considered being an appropriate costume, I sauntered over to the mirror.

"You have got to be kidding me!"

"You look amazing!" Lyric let out a squeal of excitement as I stared at myself.

The black skirt was barely past my ass and the fishnets didn't help to cover it. The top was a black strapless corset with silver buckles and my breasts . . . well, my breasts looked amazing in it, but that's beside the point.

I shook my head. "I can't wear this, Lyric."

"Here, you forgot your cape."

"Cloak. Cape sounds like I'm a superhero."

She laughed as she clasped it on me. "There, you look perfect!"

Seeing her smiling face in the mirror, I knew damn well I was going to wear it to make her happy. Guess I would just keep my cloak closed the entire night.

"Fine, I'll wear it."

"Awesome! How does mine look?" I turned to look at her as she was putting on a wolf mask.

"You look warm and comfortable."

"Thanks!" She made a growling sound and I laughed.

After changing back into our clothes, we quickly went to check out before they closed. That's one thing that sucked about being on a night shift. We either went places late or missed sleep.

"When is Erik getting his costume?" I asked.

"He said he was going tonight or tomorrow." Lyric's phone rang and she handed me her things so she could dig in her bag and find it. "Oh, it's Winston. Hello?"

As she engaged in a smiling conversation with Winnie, I rolled my eyes. The person in front of us left, so I stepped up to the cashier and put our items down. After the girl was done ringing us out, I paid and headed for the door. Lyric trailed behind me, still on the phone.

"Of course. We will be there soon. Okay, bye." She was grinning like a fool when she hung up.

"What was that about?" I asked.

"He was just wanting us to come by his apartment tonight, so I told him we would. He said not to bring our phones. He just texted me his address."

Lyric started texting him back while I opened the trunk of my Jeep. After throwing our costumes in the back, I wandered around to the driver's door.

"So, you want us to go to a vampire's apartment and not even take our phones?"

"Do you want to figure out what's going on or not?"

An enormous sigh escaped me. "You know I do."

"Then let's go." Lyric grinned before jogging around the car and hopping in.

Looking up at the stars above my head, I wondered if I wanted to even know what deep secrets Venom had. Not because I would rather be blind to what was going on, but because my father was the president. If there was a deeper conspiracy, then he more than likely knew about it. Could I handle knowing one of the people who brought me into this world could be a villain?

"What are you doing, stargazing?" Lyric's muffled voice brought me back to reality. "Come on, Sage!"

"I'm coming." I slid into the Jeep and headed to Lyric's place.

She took our phones inside and grabbed her laptop before we drove to Winnie's.

We pulled up to an apartment building on the south side of town. There was a motorcycle out front I recognized as Luka's, and another one parked next to it.

"This is the place. That's Luka's Harley."

"Sexy," Lyric said as I turned the engine off. "Is the other one Winston's?"

"I don't know."

We got out of the car and headed into the building. Once we found his apartment, I raised my hand to knock and the door flung open. Winnie was grinning from ear to ear.

"Good evening, beautiful," he said as he looked at Lyric, then his eyes wandered to me. "And Sage."

"Move, Asshole." I shoved past him and went inside.

"Welcome to my humble abode. Did you bring your laptop?"

"I did!" Lyric pulled the bag off her shoulder and handed it to Winnie.

"Sweet. Follow me." Winnie strolled off with Lyric in tow, leaving me standing by the front door.

Shaking my head, I was about to follow them when a voice stopped me.

"I'm glad you're here," Luka said, and my eyes drifted toward him. I hadn't seen him standing in the kitchen.

"Eww, why?"

He laughed as he grabbed a bag off the counter and held it out to me. "I got you something."

Wondering what the hell he could have possibly bought me, I narrowed my eyes on him. "Once again, eww, why?"

He snickered. "Just take it, Princess."

"Whatever." Stepping into the kitchen, I took the bag from him and peeked inside. There was a box with a brand new cell phone. Confused by the present, I looked up at him. "You got me a phone?"

"Lyric told Winnie you were both worried about Venom tracking your phones. So, I figured you would need it to keep in contact with us without them knowing. There's also a case in there for you."

"Thanks. I'll set it up when I get home."

"I already set it up. I added Lyric, Winnie, and myself to your contacts as well."

My eyebrows rose in surprise. Setting the bag on the counter, I took out my present and opened it up. There was a shiny, extremely expensive iPhone. Taking it out of the box, I turned it over to check the color.

When I looked back at him, he shifted uncomfortably before clearing his throat. "You seem like the type of girl who mostly wears black."

"It will do, I guess." When I pulled out the case, it was also black. I didn't want to tell him it was my favorite color. "I appreciate the gesture, but you didn't have to do this. Venom pays me extremely well."

He grinned, and for once, I didn't find it disgusting. "I don't have to do anything I don't want to, Princess."

I gave him a half smile. Taking the case out of the package, I tried to put it on the phone. Luka watched as I struggled before he stepped closer to me.

"Let me." He took the phone, slid the case on with ease, and then handed it back.

"Thanks."

"You're welcome," he whispered, his voice deep and low.

As I stared up at him, I realized how gorgeous he was. If we'd met under different circumstances, I would have been severely attracted to him.

He smiled, making my heart speed up. Without even trying, I smiled back. His eyes seemed to glaze over and I couldn't help but wonder if he was attracted to me.

He held my eye contact as his smile melted away. The look on his face turned to one of confusion, making me wonder what kind of inner struggle he was having. My lips parted slightly as I tried to suck in the air, which seemed to have escaped from the room.

"Sage! Look what Winnie got me!" Lyric's voice brought my attention away from Luka. Taking a deep breath, I turned toward her. She held up the same phone I got, but her case was pink.

"He even got your favorite color."

"Yeah. I told him the other day what it was."

How close were they getting, I wondered? *They text, call, and he even knows her favorite color.*

"Winnie said you got one as well."

"I did." I held up my new phone, showing it to her.

"Oh, you got your favorite color, too!" She smiled before taking off back to Winnie.

My teeth bit down over my lip as I looked back toward Luka.

"It will do, huh?" He grinned arrogantly. "I knew black was your favorite color."

"Shut up." I punched him in the arm and he laughed.

"We're going to dinner," Winnie informed as he stepped into the kitchen. "Do you guys want to come?"

Dinner? So, they are close. "What about the security footage?" I asked.

"It's running, but it's going to take hours, so I figured we could get a bite to eat and maybe a drink while we wait." Winnie grinned with excitement as Lyric entered the room.

"It'll be fun! You guys should come," she encouraged.

A slow smile radiated across Luka's face. "Come on, Princess. Let loose for once."

"Hey, I am loose!" Everyone laughed at me.

"Sure!" Winnie left the apartment and Lyric followed.

Luka smiled as he held the door for me. "Are you coming?"

Shaking my head, I headed toward him. "I fucking guess so."

Once we were outside, Winnie handed Lyric a helmet.

"What are you doing?" I asked.

"I'm riding with Winnie!" Lyric put the helmet on and slid onto the back of Winnie's bike.

"We're going to the Mexican restaurant on 5th Street," Winnie informed us. "See ya there."

My mouth was agape as he started the engine and they pulled away from the curb. I threw my hands out in exasperation.

"What the fuck! Those two barely even know each other." I shook my head. Looking over at Luka, he was grinning. "Why are you smiling?"

"Because you're adorable when you're angry."

Shock filled me, making my brows rise. "Oh."

"Are you riding with me or what?" He mounted his bike and I bit my lip.

Anxiety filled me and I swallowed hard. "No, thanks."

"What are you scared of?" he asked.

"I'm not scared of anything!"

He held out a helmet and I shook my head. Even though I loved the sound of motorcycles, and I thought it was sexy when people rode them, I had never been on one.

He smirked. "So, you *are* scared."

"No, I'm not!"

"Sure you're not."

My eyebrows scrunched in annoyance. I'll be damned if I let him think I was scared of anything.

"Give me that." I yanked the helmet out of his hand, stuck it on my head, and latched it. "This doesn't make us friends."

"Of course not, Princess."

When I slid onto the back of his bike, I noticed there wasn't a seat behind me. "How do I hold on?"

Luka's hands reached back and grabbed mine, wrapping them around his waist. "Like this."

My heart thundered in my chest when I felt his hard muscles beneath my palms. He started the bike and it rumbled below me. My breath caught as he pulled away from the curb.

At first, I was scared, but once I relaxed, it got better. A few blocks away, we hit a red light.

Luka laid a hand on top of mine before glancing over his shoulder. "Are you okay?"

"Yeah!" I was more than okay, I was enthralled.

He smiled and grabbed the bars again when the light turned green. The wind in my face was exhilarating until he took the highway on ramp and my breathing sped up in fear. Leaning into him, I laid my cheek against his back and closed my eyes. Three miles later, he took the exit. After getting held up at a few more red lights through downtown, we pulled up at the restaurant. Winnie and Lyric were standing next to his bike, talking.

Luka stopped beside them and killed the engine. Both their eyes widened when they saw me.

"I figured you would drive yourself," Lyric said, a shocked look on her face.

I hopped off the bike and took my helmet off. "I decided not to."

"How was it?" Luka asked.

My smile was huge as I met his face. "It was kind of amazing." He smiled in return, causing some unexpecting feelings in me.

"Come on." Winnie took Lyric's hand as they headed into the restaurant.

I let out a large sigh. "So, are we the chaperones?"

"Do you want to be a chaperone?" Luka asked.

"Not really, but they look like they need one."

He held the door for me and laughed. "It's just dinner."

The hostess set us at a booth. Lyric slid into one side, and of course Winnie sat next to her. Nervousness filled me and I glanced into Luka's eyes.

"We can ask for a table," he said, in an attempt to make me comfortable.

"It's fine." After sliding into the booth, Luka followed.

"There are only two drink menus." Lyric handed me one with a smile before her and Winnie started talking about what they were going to order.

Opening the one I was holding, I skimmed it, checking out my options.

Luka leaned in and pointed to a fruity drink. "This one is delicious." His voice being so close to my ear, sent shivers down my spine and my heart racing.

When I turned my head, his face was close to mine. He held my eye contact for a few short breaths before his gaze traveled to my lips.

I quickly shut the menu and handed it to him, avoiding any feelings he was giving me. "I'll try it."

The server came by and took our order. Winnie and Lyric were in a conversation of their own. They were both laughing and smiling while Luka and I quietly watched.

A few minutes later, the server returned with our drinks. Picking mine up, I took a sip.

"How is it?" Luka asked, bringing my attention to him.

"It's delicious." He smiled and I smiled back before stopping myself again.

Two weeks ago, this vampire killed my friend after I'd killed his brother. Now I was breaking bread with him and his vampire best friend, who my friend was flirting with.

What the fuck is going on in my life?

CHAPTER 22

LUKA

S age's smile was bright and sweet, making her actually seem happy for once, but it dropped too quickly leaving me wanting more. She was focusing all of her attention on Winnie and Lyric. When I glanced toward them, Lyric was holding her drink up so Winnie could taste it. Looking back at Sage, she seemed unamused.

"So, what do you do for fun?" I asked, trying to distract her.

She turned her attention to me, shaking her head. "You don't have to do this."

"Do what?" I took a swig of my beer.

"Pretend like you care about me or my hobbies."

"Who's pretending, Princess?"

She gave me a scrutinizing look. "Stop calling me that. It's annoying."

I smirked because that wasn't going to happen. "What should I call you?"

"You know my name, Fucker. Don't act like you don't." She picked up her drink and took a sip.

"And you know my name isn't Fucker, yet you still call me that."

She set her drink down, locking her eyes back on me. "It's different!"

I was dying to hear her answer. "How?"

"You really are a fucker." I snorted out a chuckle. She laughed before turning her body completely toward me. "Do you have a job?"

"Unless you call feeding off random women, partying, and killing assholes a job, then no."

Her brows scrunched together. "Then how do you afford things?"

"I used to work and most of my money went into savings. When your money compounds interest as long as mine has, you don't need to work. I could live off the interest alone."

"So, you're retired?"

My eyes widened. "More like I choose not to work. Saying I'm retired makes me sound old."

She laughed, causing a beautiful smile on her face. "You *are* old."

"Shut up." I slammed my beer and glanced around for the server. Catching her gaze, I held my empty bottle up, letting her know I'd take another.

"I'm not riding on your bike if you have more than one beer."

"I could drink ten of these and still be sober."

"How is that possible?" she asked. Her genuine interest made me feel some sort away.

Despite being a vampire for so long, I still didn't have an answer to that question. "It's just how we metabolize."

"Hmm." She seemed to be processing the information as she picked up her drink and continued to stare at the flirting pair across from us.

After our food came, we conversed about random topics. Once we were done eating, I pulled out my credit card and paid for dinner. Winnie and Lyric thanked me, and Sage complained that she was an independent woman with a job who didn't need me to buy her dinner. She insisted on tipping the server, herself. Her stubbornness made me laugh, so I let her.

Once we were in the parking lot, Lyric hopped on the back of Winnie's motorcycle and they took off. Sage watched until she couldn't see them anymore.

"Are you ready?" I asked.

She bit her lip as she looked back at me. "I don't like this."

"You already rode on it once."

"Not the bike, Fucker." She shook her head with a giggle. "I don't like them getting too close. We're supposed to be doing business and taking down rats in our organization, not flirting."

"Are you jealous?"

Her eyes widened. "What? No!"

"Do you need me to flirt with you so you don't feel left out?"

She smacked my arm. "Shut up, Luka!"

She yanked the helmet up and put it on. I mounted the bike with a grin on my face.

"I will flirt with you if I have to. For the greater good."

She snorted before sliding on behind me and tapping my back. "Let's go, Romeo."

Something about her thighs being open and so close thrilled me. My heart raced as her hands glided across my abs before she pressed her breasts against my back. Hearing hers speed up as well made me smile.

"Whatever you say, Princess."

I started the engine and headed for the highway. Once we were on it, I sped up to eighty and she let out a squeal. Her grip on me tightened and she laid her head against my back. After taking the exit, we got stopped at a red light.

"Hey, Luka!"

Don't think I didn't notice she said my name twice in ten minutes. "Yeah?"

"That was fucking awesome!" The light turned green, and I smiled as we continued our ride.

When we pulled up to Winnie's a few minutes later, I was disappointed it wasn't longer. Our friends were nowhere in sight.

"Where the fuck are they?" Sage asked when I killed my bike engine. "We left after them."

"I don't know."

She removed her hands and got off the bike. I immediately missed the feeling of her body against mine.

"Do you think they're okay?"

I swung my leg off and stood next to her. "They're fine, I'm sure."

She took off the helmet and handed it to me. "Why don't you wear a helmet?"

I took it from her and set it on the seat. The fact that she asked whatever question crossed her mind had me smiling. "Because you were wearing mine."

"Oh." Her eyebrows furrowed like she was thinking. "Would you die if you wrecked without a helmet?"

"No. It would just hurt like a mother fucker."

She giggled before stopping herself by biting her lip. For a brief second, I thought about biting that lip myself and then swiftly pushed the thought away.

Needing to break the tension, I kept the conversation going. "Winnie told me you guys were out shopping for costumes before you came here."

"Is there anything Lyric *doesn't* tell Winnie?"

I laughed. "It doesn't seem like it."

"We are supposed to be partners, not friends."

I nodded in agreement. "So, what are you going to be?"

"It's a surprise. We do a group costume every year, but our rule is we don't tell anyone."

"Where are you guys going?" I asked, curiously tilting my head.

"Lyric wants to go to this club over by the east bridge that's having a Halloween party. They're supposed to have great music, so I'm excited."

"Sounds like fun." I knew exactly what club she was going to, so I smiled, making her smile, which dropped when she heard a motorcycle.

She turned toward Winnie and Lyric as they pulled up. With her hands on her hips, she glared at them until he killed the engine.

"Where were you two?"

Winnie's eyes widened. "Sorry, Mom. We were just having fun."

Sage's mouth was agape while Lyric laughed. "Don't call me Mom!"

"I told him to take the long way, Sagelynn. It's fine." Lyric took her helmet off and dismounted the bike.

Sagelynn? I thought to myself.

"Whatever. Let's get what we need." Sage stomped off toward the apartment building and Lyric followed her.

"If she's the mom, does that make you the dad?" Winnie asked, and my eyebrows rose.

"We're just acquaintances."

"Sure you are."

With a shake of my head, I turned and went into the building. Once we were back in the apartment, Lyric and Winnie went to check on the files, leaving me alone with Sage.

"How has your therapy been?" I genuinely asked.

She smirked. "You know we aren't friends, right?"

"Yeah. I honestly can't stand you."

She gave me a playful smile as we stared at each other. "Good, because same."

The eye contact was intense, sending the sound of her racing heart to my ears. Her teeth bit down on her bottom lip, a quizzical look on her face.

For the first time ever, I smelled her lure. The citrus and vanilla caressed my senses, making my blood pump. Even though it was only a hint of the lustful scent, it was delicious. I wanted to taste it . . . taste her.

Not sure what I was doing, I held her gaze as I stepped in closer. "You smell good," I whispered mere inches from her face.

She stared up at me, lips parted. Her chest rose and fell, her breathing getting heavier.

The sound of Winnie and Lyric talking as they left the cave brought me back to reality.

What the fuck am I doing? I quickly stepped away from Sage.

"Hopefully, I will get some results tonight," Winnie said as he rounded the corner to the kitchen. He stopped dead in his tracks, his eyes glancing from Sage to me. He smelled her lure.

Fuck.

"Okay, text me," Lyric said.

"Sure." Winnie nodded, but his eyes were locked on me.

Lyric opened the door and stopped. "Bye, Luka."

The intense feelings kept me from moving. Sage blinked a couple of times, her beautiful eyes penetrating mine. Whatever shift just happened, she felt it, too. She said nothing when she left.

As soon as the door shut, I let out a deep breath and opened the fridge.

"What the fuck was that about?" Winnie asked.

"I don't know." I popped the top off a beer and downed the whole thing before grabbing another.

"Acquaintances, huh? I smelled her, bro."

"Let it go, Winnie."

He got quiet and I slammed a second beer.

CHAPTER 23
SAGE

It was Halloween night and I was driving to the club when I got a call from Lyric. She was supposed to be meeting me there in twenty minutes.

"What do you mean, you can't go?"

"The roster changed at the last minute due to someone being sick or something. I'm on tower duty for the night."

"This is bullshit! My father knows we always go out on Halloween!"

"I'm sorry, Sage." Her voice was sad.

I knew she was upset and I was completely willing to skip the party if she wanted.

"Do you want me to come hang out with you in the tower?"

"No, it's fine. You and Erik will have fun. I'll see ya tomorrow. Love you."

"Okay. Love you."

I hit the end call button on the steering wheel and pulled into the parking lot of the club.

There were no texts or calls from Erik when I checked my phone. I slid it into a small red velvet pouch that matched my cloak before heading to the door.

After standing in line for twenty minutes, I was finally in. My eyes were scanning the mass of people dressed up and ready to party when my phone buzzed in my bag. I pulled it out and read the text.

Erik: *Can't come. Got put on a job because they needed an extra person. You two have fun and be safe.*

"Damn it!" I shoved my phone back in my bag and shook my head. Apparently, Erik didn't know Lyric was also forced to work.

As I was making my way through the crowd, I locked eyes with someone I knew and my brows furrowed in frustration. Luka gave me an amused smile when I approached.

"What are you doing here, Fucker?" A smidgen of jealousy filled me as I eyeballed the woman he was talking to. She was dressed—if you call a bra and panties dressed—as an angel.

"Celebrating Halloween by partying. What about you, Princess?"

"Can we talk?" I stepped a few feet away from the girl and he followed me. "You don't have to tail me. I don't need your protection."

"You think I'm protecting you?" He laughed, shaking his head. "Unless I'm keeping my dinner safe." He tilted his head and grinned.

"Whatever, Luka. You don't have to use the tough vampire act when your friends aren't around."

"Act? This is who I am. Take it or leave it."

I scrunched up my nose in fake disgust. "I'll leave it."

Turning away, I smiled as I headed toward the bar. Wondering if he followed me or went back to his date, I nearly looked back over my shoulder, but I wouldn't give him the satisfaction of knowing I was jealous. Once at the bar, I sat my bag on it and took a seat.

"Can I get two shots of tequila, some lime, and a jalapeno margarita, please?"

"I'll have the same," Luka said before taking the stool next to me.

"Coming right up." The bartender turned away.

"What the fuck do you want now, stalker?" I asked, my head turning toward him.

He ran his fingers over his beard, looking me up and down.

"What is," he waved his hand toward me, "this thing you're wearing?"

Confusion filled me. "It's called a Halloween costume."

"Yeah, I got that part, but what are you supposed to be?"

"I'm Little Red Riding Hood." Not wanting to look into his beautiful eyes, I glanced over to see how much longer the bartender would be.

"A red cloak doesn't make you Little Red Riding Hood."

I side eyed him. "I have an outfit under it."

"Let me see."

My head whipped toward him in shock or excitement, I wasn't sure which. "Eww, no!"

"Not like that. Believe me, I have absolutely *no* attraction towards you, Princess." His smile was flirtatious and sexy, leaving me wanting more.

"Good, because same, Fucker." His eyes locked on mine and I swallowed hard.

Okay, maybe I was *slightly* attracted to him, but I sure as hell wasn't going to let him know.

"Here's your drink," the bartender said, breaking our intense eye contact. "That'll be thirty-two dollars."

"I got it." Luka pulled his wallet out and threw forty bucks down. "Keep the change."

"You didn't have to pay for my drinks."

He slid a shot of tequila in front of me. "I don't have to do anything I don't want to."

"This doesn't make us friends," I reminded him before picking it up.

"Of course not, Princess." He raised his shot with a cheerful expression. "Happy Halloween."

"Happy Halloween." We clinked our glasses and then threw them back. My throat burned when I swallowed the liquor.

"So, are you going to show me your costume?" he asked.

"I don't want to show anyone, especially you, since I have no desire to appease you." I picked up a lime and sucked it.

His eyes narrowed on me. "Why not?"

I shrugged. "I don't know, maybe because I don't like you. You're kind of annoying."

He laughed and shook his head. "No, Princess, I mean, why don't you want to show anyone?"

"Oh, because I let Lyric pick it out, and it's, umm, rather revealing."

His eyes traveled seductively to my breasts. "I'm even more intrigued now."

"You're a disgusting waste of space." He smirked at my remark and I felt a light tug at my mouth as I gave him a half smile.

"The feeling is mutual." He held up his second shot to me. "To hating each other."

"To hating each other." I clinked my shot against his. After downing it, I grabbed another lime.

He picked up his margarita and took a sip then stuck his tongue out like a wussy. "This is spicy."

I let out a half suppressed laugh. "It has jalapeno-infused tequila in it."

"I mean, I don't hate it." He smiled and my eyes drifted down his body.

He had on a black t-shirt and dark wash jeans.

"So, what is your costume supposed to be?" I asked.

"I'm a vampire." He opened his mouth and his fangs elongated causing a hitch in my breath. My lips parted as I intensely watched him run his tongue over the pointy tip of one. "Close your mouth, Princess."

Snapping my mouth shut with quickness, he laughed.

"Where did your date go," I asked, trying to distract myself from the fact the tongue on the fang was a little hot.

"Date? She was going to be my dinner, but she was annoying me. If I'm going to be annoyed, I would rather be annoyed by you, since you're prettier."

My eyebrows rose at his words and I scrunched my nose up in disgust, but deep down, a small amount of pleasure filled me.

He laughed before turning his head toward the bartender. "Hey, Tim. Can you start me a tab and can we get two more shots? "

"Coming right up, Luka."

After Tim walked away, I finally turned half my body toward Luka. "You know the bartender?"

"I know everyone."

"You're so arrogant." I gave him a dirty look, causing him to grin again.

"Here you go," Tim said as he set the shots down.

Luka handed me one and then picked up the other.

"What are we toasting this time?" I asked, as I graciously took the shot from him.

"I don't know, to getting drunk?"

"To getting drunk." I slammed my shot, then picked up a lime.

He watched me with curious eyes as I sucked on it, more seductively than I previously had. His brows rose and the pleasure I got from it excited me.

At this point, I couldn't help but turn completely toward him. "So, what do you do other than drink blood and terrorize people?"

His expression seemed amused by my question. "Not much. I usually just hang with my friends, listen to music, watch movies, or get drunk. What about you?"

"My whole life revolves around Venom, but when I'm not training or working, I do the same things you do."

"You should come over and watch a movie with us sometime." He picked up his margarita and took a sip.

"No, thanks. I've seen Nosferatu."

Luka choked on his drink and almost spit it on me, making me bust out laughing.

"You're an idiot!" I said in between laughs. The drinks had me feeling good and I couldn't stop giggling at what happened.

"I'm an idiot? You're the one who thinks we only watch vampire movies. We don't sparkle, by the way."

More giggles came from me, making me fall forward toward him. As I laughed uncontrollably, I put one hand on his thigh and the other on the bar to keep me upright.

The giggling immediately stopped when his hand laid on top of mine. "Fun looks good on you."

My gaze shot up to his, excitement filling me. "Thanks," I whispered.

My breaths were shallow, my throat dry. His beautiful eyes burned into mine, leaving an imprint on my soul.

Needing to break eye contact, I removed my hand from his thigh and twisted my head toward the bartender. "We'll take more shots, Tim!"

Refusing to look back at him, I bit my lip while I waited patiently. As soon as the bartender set our shots down, I slammed mine without toasting. Obviously, I was trying to drown out some feelings, which had been trying to claw their way to the surface, but I wasn't going to let them see even a snippet of daylight.

"Do you have a place for purses?" I asked Tim.

"Free lockers for the ladies." He pointed to the other end of the bar, at a set of lockers.

"Oh, that's awesome." I held my velvet satchel up to him and he took it.

After putting it in a locker, he came back and handed me a bracelet with a small key on it. "Put this around your wrist and try not to lose it."

"Thanks, Tim." I turned toward Luka. "I'm going to go dance." I guzzled the rest of my margarita before standing. "Thanks for the drinks, Fucker."

He gave me a flirtatious smile. "You're welcome, Princess."

With an eye roll, I walked away. A slow smile spread across my face as I headed through the club.

The music was blasting, and lights were flickering, lighting my senses on fire. After pushing my way through the crowd, I finally made it to the dance floor. The music they were playing was mostly alternative—my favorite genre—so I was in a great mood. Lifting my hands above my head, I started dancing as I melted into the pool of overly intoxicated humans dressed like supernatural creatures. If they only knew.

Three girls pulled me into their dancing group. They seemed to have good vibes, so I was happy to dance with them. After a handful of songs, I was ready for another drink.

"I'm going to take a break," I told the trio. They smiled and nodded.

Turning away, I headed toward the bar. Before I got off the dance floor, someone completely invaded my personal space by grabbing my arm and halting me. Looking up into my captors' eyes, my heart raced with fear as I recognized him. It was Beer Jack from Drifter's bar.

"I remember you because I never forget a pretty face, but the question is: Do you remember me, Sage?"

Forcing myself, I smiled as kindly as I could because I remembered him. I also remembered how creepy he was.

"It's Jack, right?"

"That's right. How about a dance?" he asked.

"Actually, I just got done. I'm tired."

"Come on, one dance won't hurt."

The same uneasy feeling I had the first time we met, filled me. As I tried to come up with the words to say without offending him, I bit my lip.

"Please."

My fear of angering him made me give in. "Just until the end of this song," I said, knowing it only had a minute left.

Since it was a fast song, I kept my distance from him, dancing two feet away.

The song ended and I had never been more relieved. "Thanks for the dance, Jack."

"Creep" by Radiohead came on and he slid his arms around my waist.

He pulled me in close with an evil grin plastered on his face. "Last one, I promise." Something about his words and stare set off my inner alarms.

Last one? Was that a threat? Had he planned on killing me? My heart thundered in my chest and I briefly contemplated punching him in the face or head-butting him. Then I wondered if I should stake him. I didn't care if he was human or not, but the room was filled with people and I had left my stake in my satchel.

"There you are," Luka said, bringing me away from my murderous thoughts. Relief filled me when he narrowed his eyes on Beer Jack. "You might want to get your hands off my girlfriend."

"Oh." Jack immediately let me go.

His girlfriend?

Oh, he's saving me.

Do I want to be saved?

Quickly deciding I *did*, at least from this asshole, I turned toward Luka and stepped in close and smiled. "Hey, babe."

"Hey, gorgeous." Luka leaned in and my heart raced as he pressed his perfect lips against mine.

What the fuck?

"My bad, Luka. I had no idea she was with you," Jack said.

"No worries, man." Luka laid a hand on my lower back.

"Where did you guys meet?" Jack asked with an extremely suspicious tone.

"I can't remember, but I'm glad we did." Luka smiled at me before his eyes shot back to Jack. "You have a goodnight," he said dismissively.

Jack narrowed his gaze on Luka, then at me. "You, too." He strolled off, leaving me anxious.

In a panic, I started to bolt, but Luka snaked his other hand around me. He leaned in and kissed my neck and before I could smack him, he whispered, "Taking off is too suspicious. Dance with me."

Looking up into his gorgeous blue eyes, I nodded.

"Are you okay?" he asked.

I swayed slowly in his arms, pretending to dance. "I'm fine. Did you have to kiss me?" I scrunched up my face, letting him know I was displeased.

He laughed. "Yes, otherwise, he wouldn't have believed us."

"I'm still punching you later for it."

"I wouldn't expect anything less from you." He smiled and it made my heart skip a beat. Deciding to pretend like it didn't, I continued the conversation.

"So, how do you know Beer Jack?"

"Beer Jack? His name's Mannie and he's a vampire."

"Oh, fuck," I whispered. I looked around until I found Mannie, and he had his gaze locked in our direction. "He's watching us."

"Look at me, Sage."

I did as he said, glancing into his beautiful eyes.

He pushed my hair behind my ear and leaned in close to my neck sending shivers down my spine. "I think he knows who you are," he whispered, his hot breath bouncing off my skin. "Can you act like you *want* me for a few minutes?" He kissed my neck again before he pulled back and gave me one of his notorious arrogant grins.

Instead of rolling my eyes or punching him, I slid my hands around his neck and continued dancing. My head started to wander back toward Mannie, but Luka placed his hand on my cheek, stopping me. He ran it slowly across my face and under my chin, tilting my head up toward him.

"Look right here, Princess." His thumb brushed lightly over my bottom lip, causing a hitch in my breath.

Since I feared being stalked by yet another vampire, I figured I would play along. I closed my eyes and slowly rolled my tongue around his thumb before sucking it into my mouth. My eyelids drifted open and I stared at him as I pulled my head back, making a sucking sound when I released his thumb.

Luka's eyes widened, and then he smiled as if he was saying *game on*. His hand dropped to the front of my cloak, running his fingers down its velvety softness and brushing slightly over my nipple, making me gasp. My heart sped up with excitement when he grabbed the edge of the fabric and slid it open, revealing my half-naked body.

"I like it." I wasn't sure if he was talking about my costume or my body, but either way, I was slightly turned on. His eyes were seductive, the gorgeous blue calling my name. He was damn good at this game.

"Sweet Dreams" by Marilyn Manson came on, and I swallowed hard as our eyes stayed locked. Both of his arms slithered inside my cloak, then hands pressed against my skin as he pulled me in closer to him.

His knee was between my legs, giving me perfect access to grind on him. At first I refrained, but his leg kept brushing lightly over my pussy making my clit throb. The more I swayed, the throbbing pain became too much to bear, so I gave in and let my body move seductively against his.

It was just a dance, right?

One of his hands moved to my lower back . . . I didn't stop him. The other hand came out from behind me, and he laid it on my chest before running it down the front of my body. When it grazed my lower abdomen, a gasp left me and I let my head fall back in ecstasy. His hand traveled over my hip and down my leg before lifting it, holding it across the front of his body. Something hard pressed against my inner thigh and I wondered if it was his cock. But my train of thought disappeared when the hand on my lower back went down to my ass and squeezed.

A breathy moan escaped me, and he leaned his face into my neck again.

"You smell like citrus and vanilla," he whispered, and I wondered what he meant because I wasn't wearing perfume. His nose followed down my jaw line as he sniffed. "It's the most delicious scent I have ever smelled."

His voice was deep and seductive, enticing me, so I tilted my face towards his, leaving my lips only a few inches away. My breaths were hard and fast and, before I even realized what I was doing, my mouth closed the distance. My lips worked against his with an angry hunger as his lips pushed back against mine with the same need. One of his hands held position on my ass and the other pulled my thigh higher, making me have to hold on to keep from falling backward. My tongue rolled around his in desperation because I needed this. I wanted this, I realized.

As his soft lips consumed me, I moved one hand to his hair and tightened as the other dug into his shoulder. My chest was pressed against him, my sensitive nipples being brushed with every move we made. Time seemed to stand still as the need, the hunger, took over us both. The hand that had been on my ass was now on my breast, squeezing, so I pressed into it, wanting more.

We were both yanked back to reality when the song changed to a fast one, making me pull slightly away. Our eyes locked as we both panted in each other's faces. What the fuck was I doing, and why was I enjoying it?

"Fuck," I whispered before swallowing hard.

"Are you okay?" he asked, his eyes concerned. I glanced at the hand on my breast and then back to him. Shaking my head, he instantly let go of me, making me stumble. "Sorry, I guess we got carried away with pretending." Luka's eyes darted around the room. "I think he's gone."

My brain wasn't even thinking about Mannie anymore. It was stuck on what he said. Pretending. Was that what he was doing? At first, I was role playing too, but at some point, I shifted to doing it because I liked it. Was he pretending the whole time, because if so, he was damn good at it? The thought angered me, and I pulled my cloak tight before stomping off.

"Sage!" he called out, I ignored him.

Squeezing past people, I headed straight to where I knew he wouldn't follow: the women's restroom. The anger consumed every inch of me as I slammed the stall door shut. What the hell was I thinking, making out with a vampire? And why was I mad for him being fictitious when that was the plan? Or was I mad at myself for liking it?

"FUCK. FUCK. FUCK!" My outburst made some girls giggle as they left the bathroom. I leaned against the stall door, attempting to calm myself.

Why was I so angry? Did I like Luka? His hands felt good on me and I let him go further than I would anyone on a first date. But no, there was no way I liked him, not like that. Even if he was hot. Maybe I was just sexually frustrated, or *I'm just a fucking fool who likes to play with fire.*

After a few minutes of internal struggle, I relieved myself and washed my hands. Taking a couple of deep inhales to calm myself, I left the bathroom and headed straight toward the bar.

"Can I have some water, please?" I asked the bartender, then set down the key. "And my purse."

"Absolutely," Tim said with a smile.

He set a glass of water in front of me, then retrieved my purse.

Realizing I needed to sober up so I could go home, I needed something in my stomach. "Thanks. Do you have some pretzels, or crackers, or something?"

"Here you go." Tim dropped a two-pack of crackers on the bar and I immediately opened the package.

"Are you okay?" Luka asked from behind me. Not wanting to speak, I hurried up and stuck a cracker in my mouth. Turning toward him, I nodded. His face was concerned, and slightly disbelieving. "Are you sure?"

After I swallowed the bite and took a sip of water, I answered him, "I'm fine. I'm just trying to sober up so I can drive home."

"I can drive you home if you need me to."

The anger toward myself reflected out to him. "I don't need you to take care of me, Luka." I slid off the barstool and headed toward the door.

Once I was outside, the cool night air hit me and I felt better. Figuring I wasn't sober enough to drive yet, I decided I was going to sit in my car for a bit. After my stumbling journey through the parking lot, I stopped a few spots away from my vehicle. An uneasy feeling came over me when I noticed a black van, similar to Venom's, was parked directly next to me. It had backed in, which meant its driver's side door was next to mine. It also meant it was parked for a quick exit.

Deciding to be safe, I turned on a dime to head back into the bar, but it was as far as I got.

"Hi," Mannie said, and before I could scream or grab my stake, his hand was over my mouth.

CHAPTER 24
LUKA

Last night was great until it wasn't. Sage dropped some of her barriers and I saw a glimpse of who she was. Her laugh, her smile—amazing and gorgeous. When she got turned on, her intoxicating scent took over my body, making every nerve I had light up. The world could have burned to ash around us, and I wouldn't have noticed. Since smelling her lure the first time at Winnie's apartment, I couldn't stop thinking about her. She had no idea I could smell her lust, and I felt bad for keeping it from her, but didn't want to upset her anymore. It was bad enough I had killed her friend. She would never forgive me for that.

After she left the club, I had to settle the tab before leaving. When I went to the parking lot, her Jeep was gone. Letting myself get carried away, I guess I went too far on the dance floor. After getting home, I messaged her and apologized. No response. When I woke up with the sunset, I messaged her again. No response. I figured she was pissed off.

Standing in my bedroom, I was drying my body when my phone rang. Yanking it off my dresser, Winnie's name showed up.

"What's up, man?"

"Have you heard from Sage?"

Fuck. How was I going to explain we practically fucked through our clothes on the dance floor? Deciding I should avoid the conversation, I stayed vague.

"I haven't heard from her today."

Winnie got quiet for a minute. "Should I track the phone you gave her?"

"Nah, she'll eventually make contact." I put my jeans on and buttoned them.

"Just tell him she's missing!" Lyric's voice in the background halted me from sliding my shirt on.

My heart sped up as a fear I didn't know existed hit me. "What the fuck do you mean, she's missing?"

"Put him on speaker!" Lyric said frantically.

"There," Winnie said.

"Luka, it's Lyric!"

"What do you mean she's missing?" I put my phone on speaker as well and tossed it on the bed while I put my shirt on.

"The last time anyone talked to her was before she went to the Halloween party. I don't even know what time she left the club."

"Two am. I was there and saw her." I put my socks on.

"Oh," Winnie said, his voice suspicious.

"Did you see her leave?" Lyric asked.

"She went outside, and I came out only a few minutes behind her. Since her Jeep was gone, I assumed she got in it and left." I frantically yanked my boots on and laced them.

"Well, she's not answering her phone or door. I also had the security check the garage and her car isn't there. So, where the hell would she go?"

"Winnie, pull up the club parking lot cameras." I grabbed my leather jacket and bike keys before heading for the garage. "I'm on my way."

After a bit of reckless driving, I pulled up to Winnie's, jogged up to his apartment, opened the door, and went straight into the cave.

"Did you find anything?" I asked.

"No, there are no cameras on the street, and none that go anywhere near the parking lot."

My anxiety was high as I paced back and forth. Lyric was sitting in the chair, gripping a pillow with a panicked face.

"Now I'm in the cameras that are a block away. Shit, there's her Jeep." Winnie paused the video. "I can't see who's in it." He pressed play and a black van was following close behind. "Who the fuck is following her?"

The van looked similar to the one I saw the night I killed Deren. "It looks like Venom."

"Let me see." Lyric stood up and made her way over to the desk. "Oh, it does."

"Did Sage recognize anyone at the club?" Winnie asked.

"No, but I did. Mannie was there, and he tried to force Sage to dance with him."

Winnie's eyes shot to me. Mannie was a sadistic fuck and we knew it. Winnie said nothing in front of Lyric, but I could tell by the look on his face he thought the same thing I did. She would be tortured to death.

"Can we search her phone?" Lyric asked.

"I searched for the one we gave her. Its last location was her apartment before nine pm, so I'm assuming it died."

"Search her work phone," Lyric said.

Winnie turned his head toward her. "She'll get mad because we promised her we never would."

Lyric leaned over the desk and pointed to the screen. "I consider that girl to be my sister, so I don't give a fuck if she gets mad. Find her phone!"

"Yes, ma'am!" Winnie ran a search. "It's outside her apartment."

"What?" Lyric asked, a confused expression on her face.

"Hold on." Winnie went back to the screen with the cameras and pulled up the one on Sage's street.

"Oh, there's her Jeep!" Lyric pointed to the screen. "Why did she park on the side of the building? Maybe she's sleeping and I'm freaking out for no reason."

My thoughts and hers were not the same. It looked like someone dumped her Jeep there. "Rewind back to when the Jeep got there," I said.

Winnie rewound the camera for a few minutes while we watched.

"There." He slowed it down and ran it forward a little. When her car pulled up, he hit play.

A man dressed in all black got out. The hood on his sweatshirt was up so we couldn't see his face.

"What the fuck! Who's that?" Lyric asked.

A black van pulled up next to the hooded man, he got in, and they sped off.

"Hold on." Winnie rewound the camera again and paused it. He zoomed in on the passenger's face and it was blurry, but wasn't covered. Using some advanced technology I knew nothing about, the face slowly got clearer.

It was Mannie.

"Oh, fuck," Winnie whispered.

"I will fucking gut him!" My fangs elongated with the anger that was surging through me. Lyric glanced at me, a fearful look on her face as I let out a low growl. "Get me Mannie's address!"

"Who the fuck is Mannie and why does he have Sage?" Lyric had a panicked expression as she stared at us.

"He's a vampire we know," Winnie said, giving her little information. "We need to find her now!"

"Get me his address, Winnie!"

"One second." Winnie was clicking fast. "There!"

The address popped up on the screen. I typed it into GPS before leaving the cave.

"I'm coming with you," Winnie said, following me.

"Me too!" Lyric said.

Winnie made a hard stop. "No, you're not."

"The fuck I ain't, that's my—"

"You're not going!" My voice was louder than I intended, making Lyric jump.

She crossed her arms with a huff. "Why not?"

"Because we don't know how many vampires there are. It's not safe."

"But—"

"No. You're staying here. I'm not getting another one of her friends killed!"

Lyric scowled at me.

Winnie took the nice guy approach. "Drag is on his way and I need you to let him in so he can send me reports off the computers. Can you do that and help him if he needs it?"

Lyric swallowed hard before nodding.

"Thank you."

Opening the door, we left the apartment.

"Is Drag actually coming here to send info?" I asked.

"No." Winnie grinned as we descended the stairs. "I called him right before you got here, so he's on his way, but you know he has a key and sucks at computers."

"Lyric will probably stake you when we get back."

"That will be a sexy way to die!"

I couldn't even laugh at his joke. My mind was going insane, thinking she was hurt—or worse.

Once we were outside, we mounted our motorcycles. Looking down at the GPS, Mannie's place was thirty minutes away.

Fuck.

We started our bikes, pulled away from the curb, and headed to Mannie's place. I hoped she was still alive when we got there.

CHAPTER 25

SAGE

Cold water slammed into my face and I gasped for air. My head was pounding, and I had extremely vague memories of what happened. Drinking, dancing with Luka . . . Mannie.

Oh, fuck.

As I tried to move my body, I could immediately tell I was sitting up in a chair with my wrist and ankles bound to it.

No.

"Wake the fuck up, beautiful!" Another splash of ice cold water to the face.

My breaths were fast as I gasped for air. Peeling my water-logged eyes open, I could barely make out the figure in front of me. But by the sound of his voice, I knew it was Mannie. Trying to remove my grogginess, I closed my eyes and shook my head.

"I said wake up!" Burning pain radiated across my cheek as the sound of a slap filled the room.

Forcing my eyelids open, I looked up at the blurry figure.

"Finally. Now we can play." Mannie walked away and set the bucket in a sink.

Pulling on my wrists, they were super secure, completely wrapped in duct tape. If I could get Mannie out of here, I might be able to gnaw it away—or at least I would try.

Leaning my head over, I tried to clear the water from my eyes with my shoulder. I looked around and realized I was in a basement. Not any normal basement, this one was made for torturing people. One side of the room had an old bloodstained cot, and I didn't want to know what that was for. The other side was where Mannie was standing in front of a workbench, staring at a wall of tools. He lifted his hand and pulled down random items, setting them on a metal tray—pliers, something shiny and small, and a handsaw. Coming back toward me, he set the tray on the table next to me.

"Did you think you could get by with secretly hanging out with vampires?" His laugh was atrocious. Husky and evil.

Not giving him the pleasure of agitating me, I stayed quiet. The sound of metal scraping against the concrete floor filled the air when he pulled a stool over.

"I asked you a question."

My eyes drifted to his with no response.

Pain radiated through my jaw when he slammed a fist into it, making blood pool in my mouth.

He leaned in close and ran a thumb over my cheek. "Aww. Your pretty face is going to get fucked up, sweetheart."

My temper took over and I spat a mouth full of blood at him.

"That's sexy!" He grinned sadistically, leaving my blood on his face. "Let's see how much more blood we can get out of you."

Turning toward the table, he picked up the saw. "No, that will kill you too quickly. We'll wait until the end for this one." He set it back down and picked up the small surgical blade—so that's what the shiny object was. "This is a good start."

He raised it toward my face and my heart raced with fear of being tortured for hours. He ran the flat part across my cheek and, as he pulled the icy blade away, he turned it, making it slice my skin. A small, painful moan left me.

"Oh, so you're not mute. I was worried the shit I knocked you out with might have given you brain damage." He let out another evil laugh before taking the blade to my hand and cutting.

More pain radiated through me, making me scream. Looking down with panting breaths, I watched as my blood dripped onto the floor. He leaned down and licked my wound before pulling away.

"Oh, you taste amazing." Taking the blade, he raised it to my throat, and I gasped. "Where is Venom located?"

I didn't respond.

He dug the blade in slightly, causing blood to roll down my neck and across my chest. "Where is it?"

Not being able to keep quiet anymore, I screamed, "I'm not telling you a fucking thing!"

"Wrong answer." He removed the blade from my throat and ran it across the top of one of my breasts popping out of the corset, making me scream. He laughed before dropping the knife on the tray. Leaning in, he lapped up the blood and I sucked in a breath before whimpering.

"Don't start crying yet. We have two more hours before the sun comes up and I have to sleep."

Grabbing the pliers off the tray, he clamped it on my middle finger and bent it backwards. The sound of my bones breaking rang through the room a second before my screams.

"Are you ready to talk yet?"

My face fell forward as sobs left me. There was no way I could handle two more hours of torture.

"Seriously? I thought you were strong!"

Taking the pliers, he moved toward my breast. Through my corset, he clamped it on my nipple and I sucked in a painful breath. He twisted slowly and I hissed as I tried my best not to give in. Unfortunately, my nipples were pierced, so the metal on the inside was being twisted along with my nipple.

I relented. "Stop! Stop!"

He pulled the pliers away and dropped them on the tray, the sound of metal on metal rang through the room.

"Are you ready to talk?" he asked.

My mind wasn't much more focused than it was when I woke up, but I tried hard to dig through my memories of places I could say were Venom.

"Yes," I whimpered.

"Go ahead." He crossed his arms, waiting for me to spill the secret most vampires wanted. I wasn't dense enough to give him the actual address, so I gave him a location I knew would take him far away.

"It's an old farm, way off highway nine."

His eyebrows furrowed. "That's almost an hour from here."

"Yes, but if you take me with you, I can show you where it—"

"Do you think I'm stupid?" he interrupted. He grabbed the duct tape and wrapped it around my upper torso, taping me to the back of the chair before heading toward the door.

Fuck!

My thoughts of gnawing the tape away wouldn't work now.

"I have to go now or I won't be back before the sun comes up. Don't go anywhere." He laughed hard, and then slammed the wooden door shut.

Tears instantly ran down my face as I let go of all the emotions I had been holding in. After a good ten-minute crying session, I realized he wasn't coming back.

Offering to go with him was just a ruse. I was hoping he would get suspicious and deny me. He had done exactly what I wanted him to do, and now I was alone.

With no proper plan since my chest was taped, I pulled and squirmed until I was exhausted. Figuring if I broke the chair, I might have a better chance of getting free. I rocked back and forth until it finally tipped. As the chair slammed into the ground, my head bounced off the concrete, making me dizzy. No matter how much I pulled and squirmed the tape never loosened.

The cold air washed over my wet body as I laid there in a skimpy Halloween costume covered in blood and water. Resting my head against the concrete floor, I cried until I fell asleep.

Not long before the sun was about to rise, Mannie returned and he was pissed off.

"Wake up!" He smacked me across the face before putting my chair back upright. "You're a lying bitch!" Another stinging smack and then a punch.

Though I didn't escape while he was gone, I did manage to save myself from two straight hours of torture.

Grabbing the blade, he stabbed it straight into my right shoulder and my screams filled the room.

"That was for the hour ride there." He dug it into my left shoulder and more of my screams echoed through the basement. "And that's for the hour back!"

He dropped the knife on the table and walked away. My head was dizzy—probably from blood loss—as tears streamed down my face. Sliding the bucket under a faucet, he turned it on and filled it up before returning to me.

"You look like shit!" He splashed me with water again. "This would have been easier if you had just complied!"

My body shivered from the cold and trauma.

"The sun is almost up, so I have to sleep for the day. When I wake up, we will play some more. Then I'll show you what the cot is for." He grinned sadistically again before slamming the basement door.

Sobs left me.

There was no hope in me of being rescued because no one knew where I was. The only hope I had was

I would bleed out while he was sleeping, but I had a feeling he knew what he was doing. Staring at the tiny basement window, a hint of sunlight eventually came through. It had to have been hours of me staring at it, hoping someone walked by before I gave up. Eventually, exhaustion hit me, making my eyelids heavy.

The sound of metal clinking woke me from my sleep. Mannie was back and was gathering a multitude of tools from the wall.

A feeling of dread overcame me as I remembered he promised to show me what the cot was for. My mouth was dry and my throat felt like it was full of razor blades as I swallowed hard. My bladder was extremely full, adding stomach cramps on top of the multitude of pain I was feeling.

"I would have been down here as soon as the sun set, but I had shit to take care of first." He brought over the metal tray filled with tools and set them down. I refrained from looking at them, not wanting to know what came next.

"How are you feeling?" He tilted his head with a sympathetic look. If my eyes were daggers, he would have been dead.

He barked out a creepy laugh and shook his head. "You're pretty funny, Sage. I might keep you around for a while." He smiled maliciously at me. "So, where were we? We did face, hand, and breast last night. Then you pissed me off, so I had to do both shoulders. Which, by the way, is completely out of order for me." He shook his head.

Small whimpers of fear left me and his smile dropped.

"Shut the fuck up or I will tape your mouth! I hate it when you guys act weak. Especially when we've barely even started." As quickly as possible, I sniffed back tears and tried to compose myself to make him happy.

"So, what do you like to do? Well, when you're not out killing us vampires."

My heart thundered in my chest when he picked up an even bigger scalpel.

"I asked you a question!" My ears rang from the loudness of his voice.

"I . . . I like . . ." My mouth was too dry to talk.

"Oh, just forget it." He let out a hard sigh. After setting the scalpel down, he looked at me with sympathy. "Do you need some water?"

Worrying I would get soaked again, I was hesitant to answer.

"It's a simple yes or no, Sage."

A part of me wanted to say no so I could die of dehydration as quickly as possible, but my aching throat wouldn't stop screaming, so I nodded. With a smile, he stood up and headed to the sink. After filling up a glass, he came back and pressed it gently against my lips.

The water felt good as it poured down my achy throat in slow gulps. He pulled the cup back.

"Not too much. You don't want to fill your bladder."

Too late you fucking asshole.

Unfortunately, my bladder was extremely full and screaming.

He set the cup on the tray and turned toward me. "I think we'll skip straight to the cot for now."

Pure panic shot through me at the thought of being raped. "You don't have to do this," I whimpered. My voice was barely above a whisper.

"But I do."

He picked the scalpel up again and went for my right hand. I immediately looked away while I waited for the pain. When I felt the tape being cut away, I looked back.

Going into defense mode, I immediately wondered what I could do with one free hand. Not much. He cut the other one free as I watched closely. All I needed now was my back and legs released and it was on.

His eyes met mine like he knew what I was thinking. "I don't trust you." He laid the scalpel down and picked up a roll of duct tape.

He lifted my arm and taped my right wrist to my left forearm, securing them together. Then he went behind me and removed the tape, freeing my chest from the chair. Sitting back in his stool, he bent down and cut both my legs free.

My survival instincts kicked in hard and I went into an almost feral state. Swinging out my leg, I kicked him in the stomach, hoping he would fall back—he didn't. I stood up and whacked him in the face with my bound arms as I let out a battle cry. When I lifted my leg to kick him in the chest, he caught my foot. He twisted my ankle and I lost my balance. With bound hands, I had no way to brace myself as the concrete floor slammed into my side. In a flash, he was in my face, punching me multiple times. Pain radiated through my eye sockets and I felt like I was going to be blind forever—if I lived.

"You try that shit again and I will keep you alive for the most miserable month of your life!" Fear from another punch to my face kept me from retorting. That and the fact I was pretty sure I had a broken jaw.

It was like I was weightless when he yanked me up, threw me over his shoulder, and headed toward the cot. He slammed me down on it and my fight or flight once again propelled me to defend myself. I kicked my feet as much as possible.

"Sit still!"

"Fuck you!" More kicks, and then screams of terror left my body.

Reaching his hands down, he ripped my fishnet stockings right at the apex of my legs. Remembering what someone once told me, I did the unthinkable.

Hoping to turn him off, I let my bladder go, and my urine flooded the bed.

"What the fuck?" he exclaimed, then jumped back seconds before he was whipped away.

Shock filled me as I watched two blurry figures brawl. Scared it was another vampire fighting over who was going to eat me first, I covered my face and crawled into the corner.

CHAPTER 26

LUKA

Anger and worry were still flooding me when we arrived at Mannie's house. Our motorcycles were loud, so we parked a block away and made the rest of the journey on foot. Sneaking up to the back of the house, we checked for movement and saw nothing.

"Are we going in?" Winnie asked. We were both crouching on the back porch.

"I didn't come this far to *not* go in." I stood up and was reaching for the door handle when her scream pierced the air.

Unhesitatingly, my boot kicked the door open. I followed the scream through the kitchen and into a hallway. There was a door to the left and I opened it. Her screams of terror were loud as they poured up from the basement, sending a painful chill through me.

"What the fuck?" Mannie said as I flew down the stairs.

Grabbing him by the head, I flung him across the room. He was immediately on his feet, fangs bared. Baring my own, I lunged for him.

Mannie was strong. He had over a hundred years on me, so when he punched me, it felt like my jaw broke. Swinging back, I slammed a fist into him, then immediately kicked him in the stomach, making him fly backwards into the concrete wall.

Deep-seated anger flowed through me as I grabbed his feet and I pulled him to the middle of the floor. Time seemed to not exist as my feral instincts took over and controlled my body. I hopped on top of him and punched, punched, punched, punched, punched. I punched repeatedly until his face became a puddle of broken bones, tissue, and blood.

"Luka!" Winnie screamed and my head whipped toward him. "I called your name seven times!"

"We need to cut his head off," I said with panting breaths.

"We need to take care of Sage first. She needs blood!"

I hopped up and ran over to where she was curled up in the corner. One of her wrists was taped to her other arm and she had them covering her face. Her breasts and shoulders were oozing blood. My chest felt like it was squeezed when I saw her fishnets were ripped between her legs. Thoughts of my mother flooded me. I shook my head, trying to clear the horrific memories.

The sounds of her rapid heartbeat and breaths filled my ears. Not wanting to scare her, I sat on the edge of the bed as gently as I could. "It's okay, Princess. We're here."

She slowly lowered her arms, and I swallowed hard when I saw her face. It was extremely swollen and bruised, with gashes and cuts everywhere. With all the damage Mannie did, she didn't even look like Sage anymore.

She scrambled to me and fell into my arms. My hands went around her, holding her tight as she cried.

Shaking my head in disgust, I glanced over at Winnie. "Get this shit off her!"

He grabbed the tape and ripped it, freeing her. After lacing my hands around her, I pulled her onto my lap and held her like a baby.

"I'm going to take care of Mannie," Winnie said before he walked over and picked up a saw.

"Text Lyric first and tell her we found her and she's safe." I lowered my voice to a whisper. "Sage, I'm going to take you upstairs because Winnie is going to do something you may not want to see, okay?"

She let out a whimper. I stood up and quickly ascended the stairs and headed to the kitchen. I took a seat in a chair and shifted her until she was sitting on my lap.

"You need to be healed with my blood or you're going to be scarred."

"No," she whimpered into my chest.

"Either I can heal you and all your external pain will go away, or I'm going to have to call Drag to bring a car to pick you up. You can't ride on the back of my motorcycle in this condition." I prayed she took the easy route, but I understood not everyone was comfortable drinking vampire blood.

She pulled back slightly and looked at me through swollen eyes, then nodded. My heart hurt for her as the memories of my mother flew through my mind again. I swallowed hard.

Wanting to make sure I understood her, I asked her again for her consent. "Are you saying it's okay to feed you my blood?"

She sniffed back tears and nodded again.

Keeping one arm around her back, I lifted my other to my mouth and bit into my wrist before turning it toward her face. She carefully opened her mouth as far as she could in its extremely swollen state. She latched onto my wrist, making small swallows as she sucked.

Her rapid heartbeat steadied to an almost normal level within seconds. The swelling around her eyes slowly disappeared, along with the gashes all over her body. She grabbed on to my forearm as she desperately sucked for more. After a minute, I stopped her.

"That's enough, Princess. You're going to get sick." She pulled back and gasped for air. Her color came back and, if it wasn't for her being covered in blood, she would look exactly like herself again.

"Whoa," she whispered. Her glossy eyes were dilated when they met mine.

"The euphoric effect wears off in an hour or two, but until then, you're going to feel good." I pushed the hair out of her face and behind her ear.

"Will the pain come back?" she asked.

"No. At least not the physical pain. You're healed."

"It's done," Winnie said as he came into the room. He gave Sage an empathetic smile. "You look much better."

"You don't," she retorted, making Winnie laugh.

I slid my leather jacket off and put it on her. "Are you ready to go?"

After nodding, she shifted until she was straddling me, and wrapped her arms around my neck. She held on tight, like she would fall off of the Earth if she let go. It wasn't sexual, or love, it was pure fear which drove her into my arms.

Using the alley, I carried her until we got to our motorcycles. "We didn't have time to get a car," I said apologetically as she stared at my bike.

"It's okay." She dropped her legs from me and let go of my neck.

Grabbing my helmet, I put it on her. My thumb brushed lightly across her chin as I latched it.

I mounted my bike. "Come on." I held my hand out and she took it without hesitation. After hopping onto the back, she wrapped her arms around me and laid her cheek against my back.

"I don't want to go home," she whispered. "Can I stay with you?"

Winnie stared at me bug eyed.

"Of course, Princess." I started the engine and headed to my house.

When we pulled into the driveway, it was a few hours before daylight. Winnie had gone home to let Lyric and Drag know what happened. After pulling out my phone, I opened the garage door with the app and then pulled in. Sage didn't let go, or move when I shut off my motorcycle.

"Sage?"

"Yeah," she whispered in a sleepy voice.

"We're here."

She released a long sigh before she let go of me and got off the bike. I put the kickstand out and stepped off. She removed the helmet and set it on the seat before she reached her hand out and took mine. I said nothing as I headed for the door, unlocked it, and stepped inside.

"Alexa, lights." Annie came running up to me with a wagging tail, then started barking at the sight of Sage. She let go of my hand.

"It's okay, Annie." I picked the little chihuahua up who sniffed the air curiously.

"Hi, Annie." Sage's voice was gentle as she held out her hand for a closer sniff. "You're a pretty girl."

"Annie's a boy."

Sage's eyes widened. "Why would you name a boy dog Annie?"

"His real name is Anakin."

Her eyebrows rose. "Like Anakin Skywalker?"

"Yep." I grinned because I knew her cat was named Chewbacca.

"This doesn't make us friends," she whispered.

"Of course not, Princess."

Her eyes were drowsy as she gave me a half-smile, which quickly faded. "Can I shower?"

"Yeah, follow me." I set Annie down, and before I started walking, Sage's hand was in mine again. Not wanting to make a big deal out of it, I ignored it and led her into the main bathroom off of my bedroom.

"You can shower here. I will get you something to wear and lay it on the bed."

"Okay. By the way, I kind of peed on Mannie, so you may want to wipe your Harley seat down and probably shower yourself."

Being a gentleman, I wasn't going to say anything, but I already knew.

"I have another bathroom in the hallway. I'll shower real quick."

She nodded before shutting the bathroom door. I had nothing for a girl in my closet, so my clothes were going to have to work. Figuring I would let her decide what to wear, I put a t-shirt, sweat pants, boxers, gym shorts, and socks on the bed. Worried she may be cold, I grabbed a hoodie and laid it with the rest of the clothes. It may have been overkill.

After grabbing some sweat pants and a tank for myself, I headed into the hallway bathroom and took a quick shower. Sage was still showering when I got back to the bedroom, so I went out and cleaned my bike. Heading back inside, I laid on the bed while I waited for her to be done, in case she needed me. Ten minutes later, the water turned off, so I left the room to give her some privacy.

I went into the kitchen, fed Annie, and filled his water bowl. Figuring Sage was probably hungry, too, I heated the deep fryer. Digging in the fridge, I pulled out some thawed ground beef, and quickly made a pattie. After dropping the hamburger in a skillet, I grabbed a potato and cut it up, then threw it in the hot oil.

The scent of Sage's freshly cleaned skin filled my senses as she came down the hall. Annie barked when she entered the room.

"What are you doing?" she asked.

Glancing back at her, she was wearing a pair of basketball shorts which was way past her knees and a hoodie. I smiled at how adorable she looked in my clothes.

"Feeding you. Sit." I pointed to the table and she slid into a chair.

After grabbing two glasses out of the cabinet, I filled one with water and the other with orange juice, then set them in front of her. She immediately grabbed the water and started downing it.

"I know you're thirsty, but you'll get sick to your stomach if you drink too fast," I said, before flipping the burger.

I popped a bun into the toaster and pulled a plate from the cabinet. Once her food was prepared, I plated it and sat it in front of her.

"Do you need condiments?"

She shook her head, so I headed to the wet bar and poured myself a glass of scotch before taking a seat across from her.

"You're not going to eat?" she asked.

I held up my glass. "My dinner's right here."

She picked up her burger and took a huge bite.

My phone rang and I answered it. "What's up, Winnie?"

"Lyric wants to talk to Sage."

"Let me see if she's awake." My eyes met hers, asking a silent question. She shook her head before shoving a fry in her mouth. "She's sound asleep."

"Alright. I'll let her know."

Winnie hung up, and I turned my attention back to Sage. "You can take my bed and I'll sleep on the couch."

She nodded.

"Would you like me to wash your clothes or . . ."

Her eyes met mine in a panic. "I don't need a reminder of . . ." She shook her head before picking up her burger and biting into it.

The conversation got quiet.

While she finished eating, I immediately threw her clothes into a garbage bag and took them out to the trash. When I came back, she was done eating. She said goodnight before heading to the bedroom. Annie was a traitor and went with her.

After cleaning the kitchen, I grabbed a blanket from the hall closet and laid on the couch. A little while later, I was just about to close the shutters when her footsteps creeped down the hallway.

"Luka."

Turning my head toward her, I met her eyes. "What's up, Sage?"

"I have an odd question." She shifted uncomfortably

"Ask away."

"I know we aren't friends or anything, but I can't sleep, so I was wondering if you could, umm . . ." She hesitated as she bit her lip.

"What do you need, Princess?"

She walked further into the room and stood next to the couch.

"I was wondering if you would sleep with me?" she whispered, and my eyes widened. "Well, not *with* me. I mean, I guess it's with me, but, like, sleeping in the bed, so I feel safe." She shook her head, her eyes filling with tears. "Nevermind, I shouldn't have asked."

Wanting her to feel safe, I flung the blanket off and stood up. "I can sleep in there."

"Thank you," she whispered.

"Alexa, shut it down." The steel shutters closed and Sage's eyes widened. "Come on." As we headed toward the bedroom, her hand slid into mine again. I didn't say a word.

Once we were there, she stopped and waited for me to lie down. After taking my normal side, I laid on my back, put my hands behind my head, and got comfortable. The bed moved slightly as she crawled on and pulled the blanket over herself.

"Alexa, sleep." The lights went out, and a sigh escaped her. "Are you okay, Princess?"

She scooted in close and laid her cheek against my chest. "You have a heartbeat," she whispered.

She couldn't see my face in the dark, but I was smiling. "I do."

"It sounds nice." She laid her arm across my stomach and snuggled in.

No matter how strong a person is, after the atrocious things she went through, anyone would be traumatized and want comfort.

Out of instinct, I put an arm around her and laid my hand on her back. I trailed my fingers in small circles, soothing her.

A short while later, her breathing slowed and she fell asleep.

CHAPTER 27

SAGE

A wet tongue on my face woke me from my sleep. When I popped my eyes open, Luka's dog was licking me to death.

"Good morning, Anakin." He happily wagged his tail while I stroked his fur.

The smell of bacon filled my nostrils, making my stomach growl. Sliding out of bed, I used the bathroom and threw on a pair of Luka's socks before heading out to find him.

Luka was standing at the stove . . . shirtless. When I saw his strong back muscles covered in tattoos, my eyes widened.

"Good morning, Princess. I'm making breakfast."

Since he never turned around, I immediately wondered how he knew I was there.

"You don't have to do that." I glanced at the dining room table. There were two places set. A glass of orange juice and a small bowl of cut strawberries were at each one.

"I don't have to do anything I don't want to. Plus, you need it for strength." He grabbed a loaf of bread and took four slices out before popping them into the toaster. "How do you like your eggs?"

"Over medium."

"Me too. I'm not sure if you like coffee, but there's a fresh brewed pot."

Excitement filled me as I made my way over to it. After making a cup, I leaned against the counter and blew on it.

"Did you sleep well?" he asked.

"Yeah, thanks for everything." My mind was still processing what happened and I had no desire to talk about it yet.

"No problem."

I watched curiously as he made two plates of food and headed to the dining room table.

"You coming?" he asked, before taking a seat.

"Yep." Taking my coffee with me, I sat across from him.

Immediately going for the bacon, I picked up a piece and took a bite.

"Do you want, or need, to talk about what happened," he asked "Or would you rather talk about the weather?"

Shifting uncomfortably in my seat, I shook my head. "Neither."

It was hard to focus on his face when his tattooed-covered chest was right in front of me.

"I talked to Winnie. He said Lyric called him when she woke up. She's worried about you."

"Fuck. I hope everyone else isn't wondering where I am."

"Lyric told some dude named Erik and your mom that you went to the farm for the weekend."

The place she was referring to was an old family farm which belonged to Erik and Lyric's grandparents. All three of us use it to get away from reality when needed. Sometimes, we went together, sometimes, we went alone. There was only one rule, if you went alone, no one bothered you.

"She's brilliant." I smiled before picking up another piece of bacon.

"So, the only ones who know are Winnie, Lyric, and Drag."

"Is Mannie dead?" I asked.

Luka's eyes met mine. "Abso-fucking-lutely."

With a nod, I returned to my food, and we finished eating, mostly in silence.

After breakfast, Luka let me pick a movie and we lounged on the couch. The movie had just ended and I was getting cold from lack of movement.

"Do you have a throw?" I asked. "I'm chilly."

Luka stood up and wandered off. When he came back, he threw one at my face and laughed.

"You asshole!"

"Hey, now. That's Winnie's name."

"Oh, sorry, Fucker."

"You're forgiven, Princess." Luka grinned and I smiled back for a brief second before it dropped. It almost felt wrong to be happy after everything that had happened.

"Do you want some popcorn?" he asked.

"Hell, yeah!" Throwing the blanket next to me, I hopped up.

Luka headed toward the kitchen and I followed him like an excited child. He put some popcorn in the microwave and then started washing the breakfast dishes.

Leaning against the counter, I watched. "I guess I have to go home."

"Whenever you want. Just let me know."

I nodded. "I just don't want to be alone."

"You can stay as long as you need to."

My eyes stayed on his for a few short breaths. The intense feeling I had made me look away and pick at my nails. "I don't want to impose. Plus, Chewy will need to be fed." I wasn't sure if I was trying to convince him of the reasons I needed to go home, or myself.

"Winnie said Lyric was going there today to take care of him."

"Oh, good."

It was only Saturday night, and I had nothing planned until my therapy session on Monday. Unsure what Luka thought about me staying, I didn't want to impose by asking him to stay another night. He may not be my favorite person, but I would rather stay here than go home. Even though Mannie was dead, I was still scared to be alone. For some reason, Luka made me feel safe.

"Maybe I should go stay with Lyric or Erik until Monday. That way—"

"I know what you went through was traumatic and you're probably scared to be alone right now." He turned the water off and dried his hands before facing toward me. "Even though I'm your least favorite person, I know you feel safe here because I saved you. If you want to stay, then stay."

"Can you read minds?" I asked in a panic, and he laughed.

"No, not at all. I just know how trauma works. I'm almost three hundred years old, remember?"

"Yeah. You're old as shit."

He snickered and I gave him a half smile.

Luka grabbed the spoon by the coffee pot and dropped it in the sink. The metal on metal sound reminded me of Mannie's tools when he dropped them on the tray. All the memories of the torture flooded into my mind. My screams rang in my head. I shut my eyes tight and placed my hands over my ears, trying to block out the memories. My body uncontrollably shook and small sobs left me as I gasped for air.

"Sage, I'm going to hug you." Luka's warning came seconds before he wrapped his arms around me.

As soon as I felt the warmth of his body, I wrapped my arms around him and laid my ear against his chest. The sound of his beating heart helped drown out the visions.

"He cut me, Luka."

"I know."

"He beat me . . . he tortured me. He tried to rape me!" My chest tightened with pain. It felt like the mourning pain you feel when someone dies. Maybe I was mourning the death of a piece of me—a piece of my soul.

"You're safe now." Luka ran his hands soothingly up and down my back. He held me until my crying stopped. It could have been two minutes, it could have been twenty, I wasn't sure, but I had a lot more respect for him after that.

After letting go of him, I wiped away tears. "Sorry."

"Look at me, Princess." He tilted my chin, forcing my eyes to his. They were a beautiful blue, filled with compassion. "Don't ever be sorry for having emotions."

I swallowed hard and nodded. "Is my popcorn cold?" I asked, trying to pretend like I didn't just have a breakdown in front of him.

He smiled. "Go sit on the couch and get the next movie ready. I'll make us another one."

After cuddling up in the blanket, I scrolled through movies until I came across one of my favorites. It was cheesy, but I loved it. Luka came and sat next to me with a bowl of popcorn. Before he could complain, I quickly hit play. It took him less than a minute to turn his head toward me.

"Did you seriously put on Buffy the Vampire Slayer?"

I grinned mischievously. "It's an iconic movie! The show wouldn't even have existed without it. Plus, it seemed fitting."

He laughed and set the bowl of popcorn between us.

Half way through the movie, I shifted to my side with my head close to Luka. After a few minutes, he ran his fingers through my hair and it sent tingles down my scalp making my eyes feel heavy.

CHAPTER 28

LUKA

Sage fell asleep not long after she laid down. I covered her with a throw, and went about my night. Annie and I went out to play, I did my laundry, played games on my phone, and took a quick shower. She was still asleep. Not wanting to wake her, I headed to the garage and called Winnie.

"It's about time you called."

"Sorry. I've been busy."

"How is Sage?" he asked. "Did you take her home?"

"Not yet." I took a seat in a lawn chair. "I don't think she wants to go home."

"Is there something going on between you two?"

I let out a sigh. "Seriously, Winnie?"

"I was just asking, bro. She seemed awfully attached to you last night."

Stress filled me and I rubbed my eyes before answering. "She's just in shock, man. She's scared."

"Yeah." Winnie let out a long breath. "Call me tomorrow."

"Later." I hung up the phone.

Sitting there with my thoughts, all I could think about was Sage. What she went through had to have been traumatic and I was willing to give her a place to stay, even if I couldn't stand her, or at least, that's what I kept telling myself. The few brief moments she was happy, played through my memories making me smile.

With a large sigh, I stood up. "Stop being a pussy," I told myself before shoving my phone in my pocket and going inside.

As I went through the living room, I stopped next to the couch. Sage was still asleep, and my traitorous dog was sleeping with her. A slow smile radiated across my face while I watched them. My eyes drifted around Sage's features. Her long lashes, her high cheekbones, her luscious lips. For someone so snarky, she was gorgeous.

Confusion filled me as I headed to the bedroom.

"Alexa, shut it down." Since Sage wasn't sleeping in here tonight, I stripped down to my underwear and laid down. "Alexa, lights."

My thoughts were so loud, it made it hard to relax. After tossing and turning for a while, I finally fell asleep.

Sage's screams woke me, and within seconds, I was kneeling on the floor next to the couch.

"It's okay, Sage." Reaching my hands out, I touched her shoulder, trying to calm her.

"Don't touch me!" She flailed her arms as more screams left her.

The last thing I wanted to do was hold her still, but I didn't have a choice. Placing my hands on her arms, I pulled her close to me, then wrapped my arms around her. She fought and kicked, and even tried to bite me.

"Sage, open your eyes! It's me. Luka!" She fought for another fifteen seconds before she started to slow down. Then her head fell forward on my chest as sobs left her. "It was just a nightmare, Princess. You're safe."

Her arms went around my neck, so I stood up and carried her to the bedroom. I tried laying her on the bed but she wouldn't let go, so I ended up crawling on with her in my arms.

We were both on our sides, facing each other. She stayed as close as she could to me. Her body trembled under my embrace as she cried herself back to sleep.

A few hours later, I woke up with the sunset, with Sage still in my arms. Her hair was fanned across her face so I pushed it to the side. She stirred and let out a large sigh before her eyes fluttered open.

"Oh," she squealed. "I'm sorry."

She let go of me in a panic and rolled off the bed, landing on her feet.

"It's okay, you just had a nightmare."

"I need to go home." She crossed her arms in front of her like she was trying to hide from the world—trying to hide from me.

"Okay." I yanked the covers off and jumped out of bed. Her eyes drifted to the front of my underwear. Unfortunately, I was sporting some morning wood.

"Oh, God!" Her hands immediately covered her face.

"Sorry." Grabbing a pair of sweatpants, I slid them on.

"No, it's okay. I'm in your space, you're allowed to have, umm, that."

A small laugh left me as I smiled. "I'm dressed now."

She dropped her hands and shook her head. "I'm so embarrassed."

"You're embarrassed? I'm the one with the—"

"Yep, you win. Stop talking!"

I laughed.

A random thought popped in my head, and I had an idea.

"You want to do something fun?" I asked, and her eyes widened as she glanced back at my crotch. I guess I should have waited until my dick went down to ask. I shook my head with a laugh. "Not that. Do you want to get out of here?"

She peered down at what she was wearing and shook her head. "I'm not dressed for that."

"We can swing by your house."

She narrowed her eyes on me for a second as she pondered the idea before she smiled. "What the hell, why not?"

We both took quick showers and, after letting Annie go out, I mounted my bike. Sage got on the back and we headed to her house.

"I'll be right back," she said as she took off into her apartment building.

She came back downstairs ten minutes later, dressed in her own clothes. Sporting a black tank top, a short leather jacket, some dark jeans, and combat boots, she looked like Sage again.

"Let's go, Fucker." She crawled onto the back of my bike and wrapped her arms around me.

As I pulled away from the curb with a smile, I reminded myself not to get used to this. She wasn't my woman.

Thirty minutes later, I took a back road and started ascending a hill. Once we were at the top of the lookout point, I pulled the bike over and killed the engine.

"Oh my god," she whispered. "How have I lived here my whole life and never seen this?"

She jumped off my bike and set the helmet down before walking to the edge of the cliff.

"It's gorgeous, isn't it?"

"It is." Her eyes sparkled in the moonlight as she took in the lights of the city shining below.

Moving in close, in a hushed voice, I said, "Look up, Princess."

The night sky was void of clouds and, as she tilted her head up, a small gasp left her when she took in the countless stars.

"It's the most gorgeous thing I have ever seen," she whispered.

As I stared at her perfect face, I had the same thought.

Her head whipped toward me with a large smile. "How did you find this place?"

"My house used to be over there." I pointed to an empty field behind us.

"You lived with this view?"

"Well, it wasn't quite this view, since the city was just a small town back then. There were no lights so, at night, all you had were thousands of stars. Way more than you see now." I took a seat on a boulder and rested my elbows on my knees. After hesitating for a second, she slowly lowered herself next to me.

"What was it like living back then?" she asked, a look of wonder on her face.

"Boring." I grinned and she laughed before letting out a deep sigh.

"I bet it was peaceful, though."

"Not as peaceful as you think, Princess. Maybe I'll tell you about it someday."

She smiled and nodded. "I would like that. Thank you, Luka. For everything." For once, her smile stayed longer than normal.

"You're welcome."

She leaned in to me, and as her lips pressed against my cheek, my heart raced.

Why am I reacting like this to a fucking kiss on the cheek? Seriously, what the fuck is wrong with me?

She pulled back and stared at me with those beautiful eyes of hers. A light scent of citrus and vanilla seduced my senses, and I quickly got off the rock.

Fuck, fuck, fuck! Why does she have to smell so good?

"Are you ready to go?" I asked as I quickly made my way toward the bike. I had to get away from her, away from that smell.

"Umm, yeah." She stood up and strolled toward me.

After cracking my neck, I tried to pretend like I didn't want her and started the engine. Grabbing the helmet, she put it on before sliding onto the bike and wrapping

her arms around me. Enjoying the moment, I drove as
slow as I could back to her apartment.

294

CHAPTER 29
SAGE

Two weeks later, I was lounging on Winnie's couch, eating all his snacks. Somehow, I had managed to convince my therapist I still couldn't come back to work. I'm sure the crying I did the last two Mondays helped. It wasn't fake. I had been going through a lot of emotions. One of them, unfortunately, was me realizing I was severely attracted to Luka. As usual, I pretended it wasn't true.

Since I was tortured, I had spent almost every night at Winnie's apartment hanging with the guys, and almost every day sleeping at Lyric's. Sometimes she was here with us, too. We had all become, I wouldn't say friends, but good acquaintances.

Drag was sitting on the lounge chair playing some game on his tablet, like always. I was a little too comfortable, sprawled out like I owned the place as Luka sat at the end of my feet.

Okay, maybe we were friends.

Winnie came out of the kitchen and popped open a beer. "You remember the old man Lyric talked to? Well, I called him."

"Steph's dad? What did he say?"

"After a long conversation on fishing, hunting, and power tools, he finally trusted me enough to give me her address so I could check it out."

Surprise filled me and I shot up. "What?"

"Lyric isn't the only talented actor." Winnie smiled proudly as he grabbed a file off the coffee table and handed it to me. "Do you still want to check it out?"

"Abso-fucking-lutely!" I opened the file and my eyes caught the address. "So, this means I'm going to Vegas?"

"We're going to Vegas!" Luka grinned with excitement and I wanted to vomit looking at his face, or at least, that's the look I gave him.

"What do you mean, *we*? Like, all of us?" I asked.

"Actually, Winnie and I are going to stay here so we can monitor things," Drag said. "It'll just be you and Luka."

"How long will we be gone?"

"It's about a nine-hour drive to get there. Then Luka will have to sleep for the day. Once night hits, you guys can investigate. There won't be enough nighttime hours to drive back after that, so another day of sleeping, then you can drive home."

"Geez, Pooh Bear, I didn't know I'd be doing algebra or some shit today." My eyes rolled in exasperation." Just tell me how many days it is."

"Do you work this weekend?" Winnie asked.

"Nope. I'm still on mental health leave." I dug in the bag, grabbed more chips, and shoved a handful into my mouth.

"If you guys leave Friday at dusk, you can be back Monday before dawn."

Two nights, well, days, sleeping in the same room as . . . I immediately swallowed the chips, the crunchy corners scratching my throat.

"I want my own room!" I blurted. "At the hotel, or whatever. I snore loudly." I shrugged, trying to play it off.

As I glanced at Luka, he seemed suspicious. I looked away, trying to keep my secrets to myself.

"Of course, you'll get your own room. Why wouldn't you?" Drag asked with a look of confusion.

"I was just making sure. So, when do we leave?"

"I'll be at your house at nine pm," Luka said.

"I'm not riding on the back of your motorcycle for nine hours." Even though it sounded sexy, my hair would never be the same.

"We aren't taking my bike."

Even though I knew what the answer was going to be, I asked it anyway. "What are we taking, then?"

"Your Jeep." Luka winked and I rolled my eyes.

"Fine, but I'm driving."

"Whatever you want, Princess."

"Stop calling me that, Fucker!" I had half a mind to throw a chip at him, but I wasn't going to waste my snack.

"Are you two sure you won't kill each other before the mission gets completed?" Drag asked.

"No," Luka and I both said in unison and then glared at each other with wide eyes before laughing.

"Don't hurt my boy, Sage Stick," Winnie said as he walked toward me. Sage Stick was his new nickname for me. He thought it was hilarious.

"Or what, Pooh Bear? Are you going to kill me?" Looking up at him, I grinned.

"No, but I won't share my snacks with you anymore."

Winnie ripped the bag of chips from my lap, and I pouted. "Asshole."

"Way to have my back, dude," Luka said with a wry smile.

"You're welcome, *Fucker*." Winnie strolled into the kitchen and I busted up laughing.

Luka glanced at me with a serious face, and I wondered what he was thinking. I bit my lip and he immediately looked away. Putting his hands behind his head, he leaned back and struck up a conversation with Drag.

The muscles under his tattooed arms were big and sexy, and I thought about how they felt around me at the Halloween party.

The room got quiet, and Luka closed his eyes tight, inhaling deep. Drag cleared his throat and when I glanced at him, his eyes were wide.

"What?" I asked, my eyes darting between Luka and Drag.

"We were just wondering what time you were leaving," Luka said. "We were about to head out."

"Fuck." Winnie's eyes widened when walked back into the room. He glanced at me, and then at Luka.

"Yeah." Luka nodded. "It's hard to ignore."

"What is?" I asked as I stood up and grabbed my purse from the coffee table.

"We're just out of beer." Luka stood with me. "Heading out?"

"Yeah. I'll see you Friday. Bye, guys." I flung my bag over my shoulder and left the apartment.

CHAPTER 30

LUKA

When Sage closed the door, Drag and Winnie both stared at me. Her lure was getting stronger, making it harder and harder for me not to touch her. Every time I smelled it, my body would react on its own, leaving me completely out of control, leaving me wanting more—wanting *her*. Even when she wasn't around, which was becoming rare, I still thought about her. She acted like she couldn't stand me, but her lure—her needs, her wants—said otherwise. Winnie has smelled it before, but this was the first time for Drag, so I knew I was about to get an earful.

"What the fuck was that?" Winnie asked. "Her lure is super strong!"

"Yeah, I know." I shook my head, trying to get thoughts of her out of it.

"Why did she suddenly get turned on?" Winnie took a seat on the couch and stared at me. "What did you do?"

"I don't know, man. Go ask her!" Feeling like I was being accused of something, I needed to get out of here. "I'm headed to meet Peach."

"I'm coming with you," Drag said. "I need to talk to Laren."

"Later, Winnie." I left the apartment with Drag in tow.

The walk down the hall was excruciatingly quiet. I could tell he was thinking hard about what happened with Sage. After hopping on the elevator and pushing the button, I turned toward him.

"Just say what you're thinking, man."

"I was just concerned about the trip. If she is attracted to you—"

"She's not. She's made it blatantly obvious."

Drag's eyebrows furrowed together in confusion. "You've already talked about this with her?"

The doors popped open, and we stepped off. "Nope."

As quickly as possible, I headed through the lobby and out the front door. Drag caught up with me when I was almost to his truck.

"Luka, I don't know if this whole Vegas trip is a good idea."

"Why?"

Stopping at the back of the truck, he hit the unlock button. "We need to keep the Venom members as acquaintances."

"Again, I know." Opening the truck door, I got in. I wanted to tell him he should be having this conversation with Winnie, but I wasn't going to throw him under the bus, even out of anger.

Though I knew I needed to stay platonic with her, I wasn't going to be able to. This Vegas trip might actually be a bad idea, but deep down, I was excited as fuck to be alone with her.

The drive to Save was quiet. Drag knew I wasn't in the mood to talk about it, and unlike Winnie, he wouldn't push me into conversations I didn't want to have.

Once we were at the church, we headed toward the office to find Peach sitting behind a desk, staring at a computer screen. The beautiful, voluptuous woman was scratching the short hair on her head like she was in deep contemplation.

"Peachy keen jelly bean," I said with a smile.

"Well, if it isn't my favorite arrogant prick!" Peach's smile was bright as she stood for a hug. "What are you doing here on a non-meeting night, Kid?" She insisted on calling me Kid, since she had a few hundred years on me.

"I was wondering if you could watch Annie? I have to go out of town for some business."

"Of course, I will. When are you going to drop him off?"

"Thursday. I should be back by Monday."

"Perfect! I miss his little butt! I'm sure he will be happy to see Auntie Peach."

Her excitement and love for my dog had me giving her a kind smile. "Can you do me another favor and keep watch on Laren for me while I'm gone?"

She tilted her head in concern. "What's going on, Luka?"

"We can't talk here, but if you come by Winnie's later, they will fill you in on everything."

She narrowed her eyes on me. "Big or little, problem?"

"Rat-sized," I whispered.

Her eyes widened, then she nodded. "Well, I will definitely be looking forward to it." With a sigh, she took a seat back at her desk.

"Bring Viviana with you," Drag added.

"Why do I need to bring Vivi?" Peach asked.

"Because she's your best friend and, since you have a big mouth, it'll save you the trouble of telling her later." Drag laughed and Peach threw a pen at him.

"Get out of my office, wolf."

"See you Thursday," I said as we turned to leave.

"Should I bring Laren?" Peach asked when I was halfway out the door.

The last thing I wanted to do was tell Laren I was working with the woman who killed her husband.

Swallowing hard, I turned back toward her. "She can't know yet."

Peach nodded. "Got it, Kid." She gave me a sweet smile, which dropped immediately when the office phone rang. Giving her some privacy, I waved bye before shutting the door.

CHAPTER 31
SAGE

Friday had finally come, my bags were packed, and it was almost nine pm. While I waited for Luka, I finished getting ready by putting on some black eyeliner and a second coat of mascara. My phone beeped, so I picked it up and read the text.

Fucker: *I'm outside, Princess.*

I quickly texted him back.

Sage: *Be there in five minutes.*

With a smile, I pocketed my phone.

After saying goodbye to Chewy, I grabbed my things and headed down. When I got to my car, I threw my suitcase in the back and got in. Parking security opened the gate and waved me out. Pulling out onto the main drag, I took the first right. Luka was standing on the curb when I pulled up and rolled down the window.

"I have a riddle for you!"

"Oh yeah, Princess, what's that?"

"Why are vampires like vacuums?" I smiled as I waited to tell my joke.

"They both suck. Now, are you going to unlock the door?" His face was deadpan as he yanked the handle.

An evil smile spread across my face. "Tell me you're sorry for ruining my joke and I will."

He let out an exasperated sigh. "I'm sorry. Now let me in."

"That didn't sound very sincere," I said as I tilted my head like he does.

"Sage!"

"Fine, fine." I hit the unlock button, and laughed while he got in. "Where's your suitcase?"

He held up an Adidas backpack. "Right here."

"That's all you brought?" I nervously stared at him, biting my lip in shame.

"We aren't going to be gone that long. Why, what did you bring?" He eyed me suspiciously before glancing over the seat at my luggage. "You brought a suitcase, a backpack, and another bag?"

I shrugged. "I needed it."

"Chewy isn't in there, is he?" he asked, making me giggle.

"No. I thought about it, but I didn't want him throwing up in my car." He laughed and I pulled away from the curb.

Once we were cruising on I-40, Luka reached down to turn the radio on, and I swatted his hand away.

"Hey, I'm driving, so I get the radio."

"No way, Princess. I'm not listening to Justin Bieber, or whatever you kids listen to for the next eight hours."

"Justin Bieber? Really? You sound like a grandpa. I mean, you're old enough to be like a great, great one."

His head whipped toward me with a wrinkled forehead. "Shut up."

Since music was my life—my music anyway—I had a wide variety of it, so I tried hard to plead my case. I wasn't going to listen to crap for anyone. "My iPhone is already hooked up, so it will be easier if you just play my music."

"Let's see what you were listening to last and then I'll decide." Luka turned the radio on and "Whore" by In This Moment was playing. His eyes widened and I wasn't sure if he thought my music was revolting or not.

"What?" I asked. "You don't like them?"

"They're a great band, not to mention Maria Brink is hot as fuck."

I smiled proudly at my music choice. "She definitely is!"

"So, this is what you normally listen to?"

"Pretty much anything alternative. I also like rock and some seventies classics. What about you? Did they even have music when you were born?"

Luka busted out a laugh. When I glanced at him, his face was amused. "Of course they had music."

"Do you, like, listen to orchestra music and shit?"

"I listen to mostly alternative music, but nineties alt is my favorite."

"Oh my god, me too!" I may have gotten a little too excited because when I glanced at him, he had a mischievous grin.

"You almost sounded like a real girl there for a minute."

"Shut up!" I rolled my eyes, but deep down, I was loving the interaction we were having.

"What's your favorite band?" he asked.

"Oh, I have a variety. Alice in Chains, Pearl Jam, Rage Against the Machine, Pink Floyd—"

"Pink Floyd?" His voice sounded suspicious.

"Yeah, it's my mom's favorite band, so when I hear them, I feel at home. I know it's lame, but—"

"It's not lame. I saw them live in the UK in seventy-two."

"What? I would have died if I had seen them!" I glanced over at him, and he was smiling whimsically. "This doesn't make us friends."

"Of course not, Princess."

A slow grin spread across my face as he turned up the song and started singing.

CHAPTER 32

LUKA

We had just arrived at the hotel in Vegas and Sage was infuriated.

"What the fuck do you mean, you only have one room? My, umm, other brother booked two rooms."

The guy behind the counter was frantically typing on a keyboard before he swallowed hard. "I'm sorry, ma'am. There's an MMA fight in town and everything is booked up. I don't have anything else available."

"Well, put the money back on my brother's card then and we'll just find another hotel!"

"We won't find a room anywhere else, *sister*. He just said there was an MMA fight."

Sage stared at me with squinted, accusing eyes. "Fine!" She yanked the keycard from the desk clerk's hand and aggressively thanked him.

She was still pissed when we got into the room.

"This is so ridiculous! Winnie better not have done this on purpose. I'm calling him right now and I'm going to put him on speaker so you can yell at him, too."

With a sigh, I took a seat on the bed. Honestly, I didn't care if we had one bed or four. As long as I didn't catch on fire when the sun came up, I was happy. What I *was* worried about was sleeping in a room with a woman I was trying hard not to fuck.

"Hello," Winnie said over the phone's speaker.

"Winston, Winston, Winston." Sage clicked her tongue. The look on her face was amusing, and I couldn't help but laugh.

"Uh, oh. What happened?" he asked.

"I have an issue."

"I'm assuming you killed Luka and are having trouble dragging his heavy ass out to the car so you can bury him in the desert."

She plopped onto the other side of the bed. "Oh, you wish, Pooh Bear. *Somehow,* we only got one room!"

"That's odd. I reserved two."

"So, you say. I can't trust you after you ate my snacks!"

"First thing, you ate my snacks too. Also, screenshot incoming."

My phone beeped and I opened the message from Winnie. It was a screenshot of the reservation, so I held it up so Sage could see.

"Oh, you got two rooms."

"Obviously, I'm not an asshole, Sage Stick. Well, not to you, anyway."

Sage fluffed out a pillow before leaning back. "Well, fuck. They owe us a room!"

"You owe me an apology."

"I'm sorry, Pooh Bear." She stuck out her lip mockingly, it was adorable.

"Apology accepted. Speaking of snacks, I have one waiting for me in the bedroom. Try not to kill each other."

"Gross. Bye." Sage hung up the phone with a large sigh.

"I can sleep on the floor if it makes you more comfortable, Princess. I would offer to sleep in the car, but I don't want to die."

"I may not like you, but I don't want you to die."

My brows raised. "You tried to kill me."

"Well, I don't want you dead anymore." We both laughed before her face softened. "I still don't like you, though," she added, before biting her lip.

Lies. She could pretend like she didn't like me all she wanted to, but I would never believe it.

Our eyes were locked and her breaths became faster, more ragged. The happy expression faded when she realized the same thing I did. We were laying on the bed together.

She hopped up with quickness. "I'm going to shower."

She bent over and dug into her bag, granting me a beautiful visual of her ass. It was big, perfect, and looked amazing in a pair of stretchy yoga pants. Taking her clothes with her, she headed to the bathroom.

I released a hard breath before taking off my shirt and pants, leaving myself in only my boxer briefs. Sage had already seen me in underwear on multiple occasions, so I didn't give a fuck. I also had no problem with her eye-fucking my body.

After finding some extra blankets in the closet, I made a makeshift bed on the floor. There wasn't much square footage in our room, so I put it on the side of the bed closest to the window. Making sure I didn't die, I closed the drapes, pulling them as far as they would go. The sun would be up soon, and I would start getting weak if I stayed awake during the daylight.

My eyes landed on the mini fridge, and I figured some alcohol might help me sleep in a room with a girl I was starting to yearn for but couldn't touch.

I had just grabbed two mini bottles of liquor when the bathroom door opened. When I glanced at Sage, my heart sped up. She was wearing a spaghetti strap shirt with a pair of extremely short shorts and I couldn't take my eyes off her.

She looked me up and down, taking in every muscle and tattoo I had. Once again, citrus and vanilla lit up my senses when her lure filled the room.

"I see you made yourself at home already," she said with that snarky attitude of hers.

Between my lack of feeding and the smell of her lure, my fangs elongated on their own. I closed my eyes and focused hard to get them to retract.

"Are you okay, Luka?"

A few deep breaths and my fangs went back to normal. "Uh, yeah, sorry. The sun's about to come up and I get spacey. Shot?" I held up one of the bottles.

"Sure, I'll take two." She stalked forward and snatched them out of my hand with a mischievous grin.

When she walked away, I couldn't help but watch her ass. She bent over digging in a bag and her cheeks came out the bottom of her shorts. I was the one now eye-fucking her.

She pulled her laptop out and stood up. "What?" she asked, when she turned toward me.

Between the smell of her lure still lingering in the air and her flirtatious smile, I was aware of the fact that she knew what she was doing.

"Those were the last two Jägers," I said, trying to talk about something other than me ripping those shorts off her.

"Boohoo." She gave me a fake pouting lip and took a seat on the bed.

Turning my attention back to the fridge, I grabbed two bottles of vodka and then headed to the bed where she was sitting up with her laptop open across her thighs.

"I'm going to pull up the map of the area we're going to tomorrow. Do you want to look at it?" she asked.

"Sure." I slammed a shot before crawling onto the bed.

As I laid on my side, leaning on one elbow, my eyes drifted to her face, and I couldn't help but admire her beauty. She had her dark hair up in a messy bun, her long lashes blinking as she focused on what she was doing.

She pointed to the screen. "The address Winnie gave me goes to a gated community. How will we get in?"

I leaned in to see the map and my cheek brushed against her arm. She glanced down at me and our eyes locked. Her heart sped up as she nervously bit her lip. It may be repugnant, but I took serious amusement in giving her feelings.

"I'm sure between the two of us, we will manage," I said, trying to break the sexual tension.

She cleared her throat and looked back at the screen. "You're probably right."

She grabbed a Jäger shot from her lap and cracked it open. Never in my life have I thought about being a tiny bottle of liquor, but as she pressed each one against her lips, I contemplated it.

"Well, I guess we should sleep." She glanced back at me. Her eyes stayed on my face for seconds before they drifted down my chest, following the trail of inked skin to my stomach. "I like your tattoos."

"Thanks."

Her sensual gaze wandered down to my underwear and widened at my bulge. She turned her head with quickness and closed the laptop. "Goodnight, Luka."

When I smelled her lure again, I had to refrain from laughing. "Goodnight, Princess."

Needing all the alcohol I could get to survive this trip, I slammed my second shot. Unfortunately, I needed about thirty more.

After hopping off the bed, I turned the light off before laying on the floor. She shifted a few times like she was trying to get comfortable before she finally stilled.

My thoughts were loud as I wondered if she would ever give into those urges. She still had no idea I could smell her lust, but I was letting her work through her feelings on her own. She may never give into them and the thought of it fucked my head up. She was a vivacious, gorgeous woman and I wanted nothing more than to tell her so. With a sigh, I rolled toward the window and closed my eyes.

CHAPTER 33
SAGE

The rustling sound of panic woke me from my sleep.

"Fuck, fuck!" Luka screamed.

Jumping out of bed, I ran to that side of the room. He was in the corner, holding his arm to his chest and leaning into the wall. The smell of burning flesh was thick in the air, flaring my nostrils.

"Oh, no! What happened?" When I got closer, I saw what the problem was. His entire left arm and leg appeared to have third-degree burns. "Oh my god, Luka, are you okay?" I reached my hand out to help him.

"Don't touch me, please!" He made a shivering sound like he was cold and I felt bad for him.

"It's okay," I whispered as I squatted next to him.

Compassion filled me when he leaned his head into my chest. While I figured out what to do, I brushed my fingers through his hair, trying to calm him. Even with only a small amount of sunlight coming in, I could tell his burns were horrific. Some parts of the skin were white, and some a burgundy red. Chunks of charred flesh barely covered his left biceps. Looking down at his leg, it was worse. My heart raced in panic when I noticed his fibula bone was exposed. I took slow, deep breaths to calm my breathing so I didn't freak out . . . or vomit.

My gaze wandered to the heavy drapes. A bit of sunlight was coming in from under the bottom because they were slightly too short for the windows. Following the rays of sun, they landed directly on the side of his makeshift bed. He had gotten burned because he wanted to make me feel comfortable. It was my fault, and I felt like a piece of shit.

"Come sit on the bed so I can look."

Clasping my hands around his uninjured arm, I pulled him to his feet. He leaned into me, hobbling to the bed. After I helped him sit, I ran and turned on the light and quickly came back.

"This is bad, Luka."

"It'll heal," he groaned.

"It doesn't look like it's healing. Do burns take longer?" Having the light on showed how bad he actually was, and I kept my eyes on his face because I didn't want to look anymore.

"No. I haven't fed in a few weeks, so it's going to take a while."

I immediately wondered why he hadn't fed in weeks. "How long is a while?"

"I don't know. Three or four hours, if I'm lucky."

"Three or four hours?"

There was no way I was letting him suffer in excruciating pain for that long. I had to do something.

There was a knock at the door, and I jumped. "Who could that be?"

He nodded his head to my stake on the nightstand. "Be careful."

Yanking it up, I made my way to the door and looked out the peephole. A hotel employee was standing there.

Holding the stake behind me, I cracked the door open. "Yes?"

"The neighbors complained of screaming."

"Sorry. There was a big ass spider in here. My, um, brother killed it."

"Okay. We have to check these things out, so I apologize."

Luka grunted loudly, and the employee looked over my shoulder with a curious expression.

"Did you ever get my second room?" I asked, distracting him.

"Oh, um." His face paled slightly, like he was afraid of getting yelled at again.

"Yeah, I didn't think so. Have a good day." I slammed the door shut.

Luka had moved and was now laying on his back. His face was pained, and I didn't know what to do.

"I have to pee, but I'll be right back."

As stealthily as I could, I dropped the stake on the nightstand and grabbed my phone before heading into the bathroom. There was only one person in my contacts who would know what to do, so I called him.

"The sun is up. What's wrong?" Winnie asked.

"I have a problem. Luka got burned by the sun and he's not healing."

"Did he say when he fed last?"

I took a seat on the edge of the tub. "He said a few weeks ago."

"Why would he wait that long?" The line went quiet. "Oh, fuck."

"What, Winnie? What's wrong." More silence. "Are you there?"

"Yeah, I'm here, Sage." He let out a large sigh. "Where is he now?"

"He's on the bed and I'm hiding in the bathroom. What should I do?"

The last thing anyone needed was for me to take care of them. This one time, when we were younger, Erik fell off his bike and scraped his knee. I was the only one around to help him, so taking the phrase "rub some dirt on it" literally, I did just that. It got infected and I got yelled at by my parents. So, I was *not* the right person for the job.

"You only have a few options. You can either find someone to feed him, which is probably impossible, or let him heal on his own, but it'll take longer."

"Those are *literally* my only options?"

"Yes, unless . . . nevermind."

"Unless, what?" I was willing to do anything to help Luka.

"You won't like this option."

A thought hit me, and I realized what he was going to say. "Oh, no. Don't say it, Winnie."

"Unless *you* feed him."

"Fuck." My heart raced with the idea, and I swallowed hard. "I have to go check on him. I'll figure it out."

"Text me and let me know what happens, Sage."

"I will, thanks."

After I hung up the phone, I gingerly returned to the bedroom. Luka had his eyes closed, so I quickly set my phone on the nightstand.

"How are you feeling?" I asked.

"You could have called him right here."

"What?" I swallowed hard as he stared at me.

"Super vampire hearing, remember?"

"Yeah, sorry. I didn't know what to do, Luka." I kneeled nervously on the bed.

"I'm assuming he said get me a feeder, which is impossible, or let me tough it out."

"Pretty much." I managed to not mention the part about him feeding off me because I was still struggling with how I felt about it.

"Can I have something to drink?"

"Of course." I scrambled off the bed and grabbed a bottle of water from the mini fridge before crawling back onto it. "Sit up a little."

He turned to his good side and leaned onto his elbow. Placing the water bottle to his lips, I held it there as he drank.

"Thank you," he said. "You should try to get some sleep."

He hissed out a painful sound as he rolled onto his back and tried to get comfortable. After tossing the water bottle on the bed, I scooted closer to him. My heart raced as I thought about what I should do. What I was going to do.

"Feed from me," I blurted. *Fuck, what did I just say?*

"What?" He had a surprised look.

"Feed from me, Luka," I whispered. The thought of a vampire feeding from me scared the shit out of me, and my heart felt like I had downed three Red Bulls, but I didn't have a choice.

He shook his head and looked away. "You don't understand what you're asking for."

"Yes, I do. I'm asking you to use me, use my blood to heal yourself. You saved my life and took care of me, so let me help you."

When his eyes drifted back to me, his face was deadpan. "No."

"You said it yourself. You feed off random women all the time!"

"Yeah, during sex."

My eyes widened, shock filling me. I was willing to save his life, but I didn't know where my stance was on getting naked with a guy who was half burned. I blinked repeatedly, before pushing the thought away.

"Can you feed without sex?"

"Of course I can."

"Then what's the problem?"

"It's not going to happen, Sage. Just drop it."

"Why not?" I asked as I shifted even closer to him.

"Because you're not a fangster looking to get a *thrill* out of being bitten."

"So, what? You need it, Luka." My eyes were pleading.

"It doesn't matter. You don't want it and I would never do something you didn't want."

Hearing those words come from his mouth was like a shock to my system. He would never do anything I didn't want and the gesture made me more attracted to him. Then I had a sudden moment of clarity—he was right. I didn't want to be bitten or, at least, I didn't think I had until that moment. As I stared at his gorgeous face, I wanted him to bite me. Honestly, I wanted more than biting.

"Ask me! Ask me if I want to be bitten and then listen to my heart and tell me if I'm lying."

He said nothing. Picking up his hand, I laid it on my chest.

"I don't need to feel your heart. I can hear it."

"Ask me, Luka!"

He let out an enormous sigh, his eyes locking with mine. "Do you want this?"

"Yes, I want you to bite me," I whispered.

Our eyes stayed locked for a few breaths before he slid his hand up my chest, then behind my neck. He pulled my face down to his, and I sucked in a breath.

"Are you sure this is what you want?" he asked in a hushed voice. He opened his mouth and his fangs elongated, sending shivers through me.

"Yes."

"It will hurt for a second, but then you will get this euphoric feeling like the one you got when I fed you, but a thousand times stronger."

"I'm okay with it," I admitted, now breathlessly panting.

"Then you're going to orgasm."

"What?" I pulled back from him with widened eyes. He let out a half-suppressed laugh before he groaned in pain. "What do you mean?"

"My venom can make you have an orgasm, even if I'm not touching you, but you're going to *want* me to touch you."

I shook my head. "No, I won't."

"Yes, you will, Princess. Even if you had absolutely no attraction to me, you would want it."

This new revelation had me swallowing hard. An instant, euphoric orgasm in return for helping someone. I struggled to believe it was a terrible deal.

I lifted his good arm and scooted as far as I could, lying next to him. "Do it."

"Are you sure you—"

I laid my finger across his lips. "Shhh."

My mouth was only inches from his when I let my hand fall to his chest. His pecs were hard beneath the soft skin of my palm, but what caught my attention was his heart thundering against it. He was just as nervous as I was. His breathing seemed to speed as we stared at each other. My eyes went to his full lips, and I wanted to kiss him, but this wasn't about me.

I tilted my head, exposing my throat to him. To my surprise, he placed slow, deep kisses on me, causing a light moan to escape my mouth.

"You smell like citrus and vanilla," he whispered against my skin. Before I could ask him why he kept saying that, I felt the pain of his strike.

When his fangs sunk into me, I let out a gasp. As the burning pain from his venom ate at my veins, I wanted to pull away, but his hand tightened on my back, holding me in place. Then a calming warmth spread through my body, sending my blood pumping.

The euphoric feeling hit a few seconds later, and I was horny. The horniest I had ever been in my life. My nails dug into his chest and I moaned.

Without even realizing what I was doing, my thigh slid over his body, allowing me to straddle him. Then my clit pulsed and I was coming hard. His hands went around me, holding my lower back. He was still latched onto my neck when I started rubbing on his hard cock beneath me.

My orgasm seemed to last forever, and I was still coming when he let my neck free. His mouth was open as he took fast breaths of ecstasy. My blood stained his fangs and his luscious lips. Focusing hard, I took every detail of him in for a few breaths before I slammed my mouth onto his.

Our kissing was fast, frantic, passionate. A dire need, a hunger, took over us both. We were like caged animals that were starving.

He let me continue my dry humping and consuming his mouth, never once removing my clothes, or touching anywhere other than my back. His hard cock felt amazing through my thin shorts, and it made me curious to see it.

After a few more minutes, my high was fading, and my body seemed more satisfied than it ever had before. Exhaustion hit me, and I fell against his chest. He grazed his hands up and down my back, soothing me. I noticed my panties were soaked as I tried to catch my breath.

"Did it work?" I asked in a hushed voice.

"I'm healed. Thank you."

I let out a breathy laugh, because I should have thanked him for the orgasm. Noticing he was still hard beneath me, I felt bad.

"Do you want to have—"

He rolled to his side, taking me with him. We were now face to face, my eyes meeting his.

"It wasn't about sex. You owe me nothing." He brushed a piece of hair behind my ear and then pulled my body close making me feel extremely protected. "Goodnight, Princess."

CHAPTER 34

LUKA

The sun had gone down and, as always, I immediately awakened. Sage's warm body was pressed tightly next to mine as I watched her sleep. I knew what happened was going to haunt her for the rest of the trip, and I was trying to mentally prepare myself for the fact she was going to shut down.

Her cell phone rang, making her stir. She nuzzled in close to me and let out a happy sigh. Her eyes fluttered and she blinked a couple times before they popped open in shock.

"Oh, my god!" For as fast as she moved, you would have thought the bed was on fire.

"It's okay, don't freak out."

"I'm not." She glanced at her cell phone before yanking it off the nightstand. It stopped ringing. "Shit, it was

Winnie. I forgot to call him back and tell him you were okay."

"Sage."

"Let me call him back first."

Before she had a chance to hit send, I was standing in front of her with my hand on her upper arm, trying to soothe her.

"Calm down. It's not that bad."

She leaned to the side, pulling away from me. "I know. It's fine, I'm fine. I just have to call Winnie."

"Can you stop for one fucking second?"

She rolled her eyes. "What, Luka? What?"

"What happened this morning was—"

"What happened will never be mentioned again. We will tell Winnie you healed on your own and that's it. Nothing has changed between us. Now, can I call Winnie, or would you like to talk about your feelings first?" She gave me her best annoyed face.

"Why are you so cold-hearted?"

Her mouth fell open with my words. "I'm cold-hearted? You murdered my friend!"

"And you killed my brother." I threw my hands up. "So, we're at an impasse."

"It wasn't my fault. I was doing my fucking job!"

"I know it wasn't your fault, just like it wasn't my fault Deren died. We have both lost someone we cared about because of the people who are controlling us. The sooner you get your head out of your ass and realize it, the better off you'll be!"

Her eyes narrowed on me as she bit her lip. It wasn't the way she usually bit it. It wasn't out of frustration, concentration, or secretiveness. This time, she was trying to keep from saying something she may regret.

"Whatever, Luka." She shook her head and looked away, refusing to make eye contact with me.

"What you did—"

"I said I don't want to talk about it!" she yelled.

Stepping in as close as I could, my chest accidentally bumped into hers. She tried to get away from me by backing up, but ran into the wall, so I stepped closer, my face inches from hers.

"What? Are you going to kill me now?" Her eyes drifted around my face. Don't think I didn't notice when they kept going back to my lips. I could tell she was fighting her inner demons and keeping those feelings buried.

"No," I whispered. "I'm going to say what I want to say and you're going to listen."

Her breaths were almost faster than her heart as she stared up at me. I wanted to grab her and shake some sense into her, but I wouldn't. What I *was* going to do was whatever I could to make her comfortable. She looked down at the ground, so I placed my fingers under her chin, lifting her face back up.

"Look right here, Princess." She blinked from under her plush lashes, and it took all my strength not to kiss her when her lure seeped into my lungs . . . *fuck*. "What you did last night was to help me, and what you did after I fed from you was only because of my venom. Nothing more. So you can stop acting like you did something wrong."

The truth fell out of my mouth, and for some reason, it was painful.

"I don't want it to be weird," she mumbled.

Letting go of her chin, I took a step back and gave her what she calls one of my arrogant grins. "It's not weird."

She gave me a half smile then nodded, but I could tell she didn't believe me. "What should I tell Winnie?"

"Tell him I healed on my own."

"Are you sure?" She bit her lip, and I had to stop thinking about biting it myself.

"Yeah, I'm sure. I'm going to take a quick shower. Once you're off the phone, you need to get ready. We have a mission to complete." Turning away from her, I grabbed my backpack.

"Thank you, Luka. I appreciate it."

"This doesn't make us friends," I said with a wink, making her laugh.

"That's my line, Fucker!" She laughed and the sound was so beautiful, it made me smile.

As I headed for the bathroom, my smile melted away with the pain of knowing I was so close to having her, but yet so far away. Thoughts of her luscious lips and memories of her sweet scent were haunting me.

This was going to be a long night.

After showering, I called Winnie and went over the plans. He didn't say anything about me not feeding for weeks, but I knew he was aware. He also knew why.

Sage had showered and was running around the room with a towel on while she gathered her clothes. I swear she was torturing me on purpose at this point. Not being able to take it, I told her I was going to wait outside. Wanting to make sure I drove this time, I swiped the keys to the Jeep on the way out.

Twenty minutes later, she came out of the hotel and looked around, momentarily confused when she saw her car was gone. Her thick thighs looked amazing in the black leather pants she was wearing, and I was dying to see her from behind. Pulling up next to her, I rolled down the window and grinned.

"Get in, Princess."

"You're not serious?" she asked with an exasperated face. She jumped into the car and shut the door. "Don't dog Lucille!"

"You named your Jeep Lucille?"

"Yeah, after Negan's bat. Well, and his wife I guess since he named his bat after her. His back story is interesting. I mean, for an anti-hero he . . ." She glanced over at me and caught me grinning at her rambling. I loved it when she nerded out. She let out a large sigh as she shook her head. "You wouldn't understand."

"Actually, I would."

"You like the Walking Dead?" She shifted in the seat, her body almost completely facing me as she smiled with excitement.

"No, I don't. I just read the comics and watched most of the series just so I can say I have." I laughed and she rolled her eyes. I conceded, "It's actually one of my favorite shows."

"Me too!" Her smile was huge when we locked eyes. "This doesn't make us friends." It was the first time she said it with a smile.

"Yeah, yeah. I know."

Her gaze wandered down my body for a second before she cleared her throat. The scent hit me like a rock to the face. Citrus and vanilla filled the car, making my balls tighten instantly. My breaths were fast and my heart rapid as she shifted forward and latched her seatbelt. The side profile of her gorgeous face was almost too much to bear as the scent took over my senses. My eyes trailed down her body to the perfect lumps of her breasts and stopped when I got to her thighs. My fangs elongated, ready to taste her from the inside out.

"Luka?" The sound of her beautiful voice brought me back to reality. "Are you okay?" she asked.

I wasn't okay. Her scent made me want to rip her clothes off and lick every inch of her body, toss her up on the hood of the Jeep and then fuck her until she screams my name. Why did she affect me so strongly?

Looking down at the radio area so she didn't see my fangs, I said, "Yeah, I'm fine. I was just wondering where the button is to make the top go down."

"Why? Do you need some fresh air?"

"Something like that," I mumbled.

"Why don't you just roll down the window?"

My throat felt like it was full of razor blades when I remembered what her blood tasted like. Her eyebrows scrunched together as she stared at me and even *that* was sexy. My fingers couldn't get to the window button fast enough. The fresh air seeped in and after I took a couple deep breaths, my fangs disappeared.

"Are you better now?" she asked with a concerned expression.

"Yeah." I pulled away from the curb as I focused on calming myself.

Our first stop was for food. We had no time for dine-in restaurants since we were on a mission, so I pulled in a drive thru and got us both a burger. Unlike some girls who pick at their food, Sage smashed hers like she had no care in the world. I thought it was adorable.

After we ate, we headed for the therapist's house.

Thirty minutes outside of Vegas, we found the place we were looking for. It indeed was a gated community.

"That fence is over ten feet," she said. "How the fuck are we going to get in there?"

"You'll see."

After parking the car a block away, we headed off to hike around the community. Since the fence was made of black steel with spikes at the top, it wasn't going to be easy to climb, but Winnie had a plan.

Clicking my earbud, I called him. "We're here."

"I'm tracking you now. Keep going until you get around to the back side. Once you pass a bunch of trees, there will be another gate. It's used by garbage and delivery companies. It's programmed to only open during daylight hours."

Making sure Sage followed me, I nodded my head in the direction we needed to go and kept walking. "Can you open it?"

"I tried, but they have amazing security on it. If it opens, it automatically sets off the alarms for an inside security system, which I can block, but it also sets off alarms for an outside one that I can't. I did manage to find the camera feed path and record ten minutes of non-movement, which I'm going to play for you guys to get past the cameras. I recorded it from around this time last night, so the moonlight will be shining on the same spots. I already tested it before you two left the hotel and there were no alerts on their security system."

"You're extra as fuck."

"Yeah and you love me for it." He laughed. "You're almost there." A minute later, the gate came into view. "There should be stone masonry, or concrete pillars in between the fence and the gate."

Stopping in front of them, I looked up. "There is, and they're about twelve feet tall."

"Get your asses up there. Once you're in, there's a small tree line on each side of the road the cameras can't reach. Just let me know when you're there."

"Got it." Turning toward Sage, I held out my hand. "Come on, Princess."

She reluctantly placed her hand in mine, and I led her up to the pillar.

"What are we doing?"

"How is your grip?" I asked.

"Why?" She looked up. "Are you going to throw me?"

"Pretty much. Are you okay with that?"

Her face lit up with excitement. "Absolutely!"

"Face that way." I pointed at the pillars and she turned toward them. Placing my hands on her waist, I leaned in and whispered into her ear. "Are you ready?"

She looked over her shoulder, her lips close to mine. "Yeah," she breathed.

"Squat and jump." I squatted with her and as she jumped, I threw her toward the top of the pillars. Reaching out, she missed the edge by an inch. She fell back down with a gasp and my hands were there to catch her.

"Thanks," she said as I set her down. She rubbed her hands together and I could tell she got scraped a little. "Let's try it again."

That was one thing I liked about her: her perseverance. She turned away from me and backed up, making her ass touch my cock. Even in the darkness, I saw a small grin on her face. She was amused by seductively torturing me, and I was happy to let her.

Placing my hands on her waist, I smiled. "Again."

She squatted and I threw her but this time she caught the ledge. As she held on, she pushed her feet against the concrete for support, giving me a perfect view of her ass when she climbed up.

I grinned with pride. "Atta, girl!"

Sage raised her hands in the air, excited for her win.

Jogging ten feet back, I ran as fast as I could and jumped. My hands caught the edge of the column and I pulled myself up. With it only being two feet wide, as soon as I stood up I put my arms around her so I didn't knock her over.

"Whoa," she whispered. "How did you do that?" My eyes went to her face, and I wondered if now, during a mission was a good time to kiss her. Probably not. She would definitely smack me off the pillar.

"Tell her because you're a badass vampire," Winnie said in my ear.

"Shut up, Winnie."

"It's Winston."

Completely ignoring him, I continued to stare at the beauty in front of me.

"Now what?" she asked breathlessly.

"Hold your balance." I let go of her and jumped, landing with only a small thud. Turning toward her, I held out my hands. "Your turn, Princess."

She shook out her arms like she was preparing herself, then took a deep breath and jumped. I caught her and pulled her close to me.

"That was cool," she said and I smiled. Eye eyes were like magnets, locking on each other.

"Did you guys make it?" Winnie asked, snapping me back to reality.

"Yeah. We're in."

After I set Sage down, I grabbed her hand and headed for the tree line.

As I squatted, I pulled her down with me. "We're under the trees."

"Perfect. I'm engaging the camera replay. You have exactly ten minutes to get into her house starting . . . now."

Seeing the neighborhood watch signs on the street, I figured lurking in the shadows as much as possible was for the best. I pulled Sage with me and headed for the first backyard I spotted that was dark and easy to get into.

The third yard we traversed had a short picket fence. It was the target house. Stopping next to the fence, I lifted her over it before I hopped it with ease.

"We're here," I whispered.

"The house isn't online for any security systems, so her locks are probably manual as well. You and Sage are on your own for this one, bro."

"Alright. Thanks." Clicking the ear piece, I hung up with Winnie.

Looking around, I noticed the lights above the porch had motion sensors on them.

"Those motion lights may come on, so we have to be quick getting in the door without making a lot of noise. Are you ready, Princess?"

She nodded with a sly grin. I had a feeling she got a thrill out of what we were doing.

Hunkering down, we made our way to the back porch. Just as I stepped under the motion lights, they turned on. Then lights from three other directions hit me, locking me in place since they were UV lights. My skin burned and my body felt sluggish as pain scattered across every piece of exposed flesh. Not being able to run, I turned my back toward the one closest to me and squatted

"What the fuck!" Sage jumped in front of me, trying to block the lights from killing me. She frantically took her leather jacket off and laid it over my head. The sound of a screen door opening filled my ears moments before I heard a cock of a crossbow.

"Stop, Steph!" Sage screamed. "It's me!"

"Sage?"

"Turn the lights off!"

"What are you doing here?"

"Please, Steph! I'm begging you!" Her voice was desperate and I felt a ping of satisfaction knowing she cared for me. "Turn the lights off!"

The screen door squeaked again and then the UV lights faded.

Sage yanked her coat off me and squatted down. Her face was filled with fear and empathy. "Are you okay?"

"I'm fine. I just need a minute to heal."

"Is it going to take three hours?" she lowered her voice, "because I really don't want to feed you, umm, in public."

A small, painful snicker left me. "No. I'm still good from last night."

"What are you doing here, Sage?" the therapist asked.

"Go." I nodded my head toward the porch. "I'll be fine in a few minutes."

Sage stood up and headed toward the house. "I just wanted to talk to you."

"You come any closer and the lights are coming back on!"

Sage's footsteps stopped. "I don't mean any harm. It's actually the opposite. I was worried about you."

"If you were worried about me, then why did you bring a vampire with you?"

My wounds were almost healed, and this therapist was starting to annoy me.

"There's a lot we need to discuss. If I could come in and—"

"You think I'm going to let you in? You're a trained killer and you brought *him* with you!"

Moving as fast as I could, my hand was on Steph's throat before she even knew I moved. Making sure her lights didn't get me again, I pushed her back into the house.

"Be quiet and listen to what she has to say," I said through gritted teeth. It was possible I was a little on edge after getting burned twice in less than twenty-four hours.

"Luka!" Sage ran up to us.

Noticing immediately Stephanie didn't have a human scent, my eyes widened. She bared her fangs at me and hissed.

When I realized she was weak, a superior grin spread across my face. "I'm much older than you, so I wouldn't try anything!"

She took a few breaths before closing her mouth. "What do you want?"

"Do you promise not to do anything stupid and listen to what she has to say if I let you go?" I asked, and she nodded. "Crossbow." I held my hand out and she handed it to me.

Letting go of her throat, her hand immediately went to it and rubbed.

"Okay, I'm listening."

CHAPTER 35

SAGE

"What the fuck!" I bursted out. "How long have you been a vampire?"

Steph said nothing as she glanced at me.

Luka narrowed his eyes. "By her strength and slow reflexes, if I had to guess, I would say less than a few months."

My mind couldn't wrap around the fact she was a vampire. "When did it happen?"

"Does my transition have anything to do with the reason you're here?" she asked, and I shook my head. "Then it's not important."

My eyes saddened as tears threatened the rims. "Why didn't you tell me? I thought we were friends."

She let out an exasperated sigh. "You're a vampire hunter, Sage. What was I supposed to do?"

"Is that the reason you left Venom?" Luka asked.

Her face was somber and sadness lurked behind her eyes. "Do you guys want to come in for a cup of tea and we can talk?"

Luka focused his eyes on me, waiting for my response. Even though I was upset and felt betrayed, I nodded.

"Follow me," she said before strolling away.

Luka shut the back door and turned toward me. "Come on, Princess." With a sigh, I followed him.

Steph gestured to a small dining table with four chairs. "Have a seat."

Luka pulled out a chair for me before taking the one next to it.

My eyes never left Steph as I watched her fill a teal colored kettle with water and set it on the stove. Luka's hand landed on my thigh and I glanced toward him.

"Relax," he said with a calming smile.

"Indeed. Your heart is racing," Steph added.

More anger filled me. "It's kind of hard to relax when you feel betrayed!"

She took three dainty matching tea cups out of the cupboard and headed toward us with them. Her eyes met mine as she set them on the table.

"How have you been, Sage?"

I shook my head. "I trusted you. I told you deep secrets that . . ." That I would never tell anyone, was what I was going to say, but I couldn't bring myself to finish the sentence.

"I'm sorry. I never meant for you to find out."

I snickered. "Well, obviously!"

She set three tea bags on the table before she took a seat across from us. "My decision to turn had nothing to do with you."

My mouth was agape, and I couldn't believe my ears. "You chose to become a vampire?"

"Yes, but I didn't have a choice."

"If you made the decision, then you had a choice!" I yelled, my voice was much louder than I intended.

She sighed in exasperation before her eyes drifted to Luka. "Can you help me here?"

Luka shook his head, then looked at me and grinned. "No, I think it's adorable when she's mad."

Trying to keep my feelings suppressed, I turned my attention back to Steph. My face was emotionless as I stared at her. "Tell me why?"

"Venom." The teapot went off like an alarm to the name.

"What do you mean, Venom?"

Steph sauntered over to the stove and grabbed the kettle. "For many years, people have told me their emotional experiences. After a while, I became suspicious." Heading back toward us, she set the pot on a trivet in the middle of the table. She grabbed a small wooden tray and set it next to the pot. "Here's cream and sugar," she said before retaking her seat.

"Suspicious of what?" I asked.

"Some of my patients' stories didn't add up with others. There seemed to be a lot of cover-ups after incidents, and after seeing and hearing it repeatedly, I knew I had to get out." She poured hot water into all three cups.

"And you had to become a vampire to do that?" I asked as I opened a tea bag.

"Since I've been in Venom since birth, I know it's a ruthless society. I figured if I wanted to get out of it, I would have to make sure I did it right. I bought this house a few years ago under a false name. I'm assuming you spoke to my father, since he is the *only* one who knows this address." Her eyes saddened as she swallowed hard. "Was he harmed?"

"My friend spoke to him, and no. He's fine."

"Good." She dunked her tea bag up and down repeatedly as she spoke. "So, as I was saying, I had been planning on leaving for a while. Unlike you, I haven't been trained to defend myself. I'm thirty-five now, so it's a little late in the game to quickly become a lethal weapon. The only way to make sure I could take care of myself was to become a vampire. If Venom came for me, I would at least have a chance. But when the time came, I couldn't bring myself to do it. It took you walking into my office and hearing you speak about Deren, and listening to Sorin basically lie and half-ass threaten me, to make me realize I needed out fast."

"Hold on." I shifted in my seat and leaned in. "What do you mean, he lied and threatened you?"

She picked up her cup and took a sip before answering. "After you were put into holding for your mental breakdown, and I use that term loosely because having emotions that are being ignored, and then being accused of something which wasn't your fault is *not* a mental breakdown. I don't care what your asshole father says." Her eyes were filled with empathy as she shook her head. "I'm sorry that happened to you, Sage." She sighed and took another sip of her tea. "Where was I? Oh, yes. After you were put into holding, your mother asked me to check on you. I went down to the nurses' station to get a pass and was stopped by Sorin. He said you were still knocked out and no one could see you."

"That's what he lied about?" I asked confusedly since I had been knocked out.

"No. I asked him what had happened to Deren and his side of the story didn't match up with yours. He said he told you two to wait by the van, but that's not what you told me later that week."

"I'm not trying to defend him, but he could have been lying to cover his ass," Luka said. His manly hand picked up his tea and took a sip. I couldn't help but internally laugh at him holding such a dainty cup.

"Yes, but it was almost the same story he told a year ago when another life was lost while he was the one in charge."

I sucked in a breath. "Renee?"

"Yes. Renee. It set off some internal alarms, making me suspicious, so I started doing some digging. After pulling out Renee's records, and refreshing myself on her case, I noticed she had similar experiences to yours. She managed to make a kill on her first night out, which is rare by the way. It seemed like someone was sending you guys to the exact location they knew a vampire would be."

"We have suspicions a vampire is working with Venom," Luka said.

Steph nodded, a knowing look on her face. "Renee also took therapy for a while after her teammate was killed. She told me at one point, she was getting suspicious about some things. She was murdered by a vampire not long after that. If you're both right, it makes total sense they wanted to get rid of her."

"Did you say a year ago?" Luka asked.

"Yes." Steph looked at him suspiciously. "Why?"

"It was my brother Andrei that killed her."

My focus shifted to Luka as well. "How do you know?"

"I saw it when Winnie was looking at those records trying to find the rat. It seemed Andrei was used as a pawn. Someone was sending him to take care of loose ends."

"So, was Venom trying to have *me* killed or Andrei?" I asked. I was getting confused.

"Andrei had been insubordinate toward Fin shortly before you killed him, just like I had when he tried to set me up, so I'm assuming Andrei. I could be wrong, but it seems like they had him killed to make sure more loose ends were taken care of."

"Wait," Steph said. Her eyes went from me to Luka and back again. "You killed his brother? Was he your entrance into Venom?"

When I glanced at Luka, his eyes were sad, so I laid my hand on his leg in a silent way of saying I was sorry.

"Yes. Why?" I asked as I looked back at Steph.

"I thought you two were dating," Steph said and Luka busted out a hard laugh.

I yanked my hand off his thigh. "God no!"

"Absolutely not!" Luka added with a shake of his head.

Steph's eyebrows rose as she glanced back and forth between us again. The look on her face said she still thought otherwise. Luka shifted uncomfortably in his seat, clearing his throat, and I quickly took a sip of tea.

"So," Steph said, breaking the silence. "After comparing the files at home, I took them back to work the next day, which was the last session we had. Sorin stopped me in the hall when I was on my way to meet you. He told me to make sure I wasn't doing or saying anything I wasn't supposed to. I asked him what he meant and he said to *just be careful.* After our session, I decided it was time to pull the trigger on the plans I had. I called the vampire I had been talking to and had him turn me. I stayed with him for a couple days so he could teach me some things about my new senses, then I came here."

"What was the vampire's name, if you don't mind me asking?" Luka asked and I wondered what he was thinking.

"Ravage." Steph picked up the pot and filled her cup with more hot water.

"Do you know him?" I asked Luka.

"Yep. Nice guy. He's my tattoo artist."

This wasn't the first time I wondered how he got tattoos when he was a vampire, but I would wait to ask him later.

"He really is," Steph said with a friendly smile.

Looking back at her, I cleared my throat. "How did you meet, Ravage?"

"I went to the vampire bar by the east bridge. Eternal Night." I sucked in a breath because that was the same bar Mannie abducted me from.

My eyes shot to Luka. "You let me go to a vampire bar without me knowing?"

"I wouldn't have let anything happen to you, Princess."

"But something *did* happen! I was . . ." A million red flags went off. "Oh fuck. I was supposed to die. Venom *was* trying to have me murdered."

"Do you think that's why your friends didn't show up?" he asked.

I shook my head as I tried to ponder the situation. "Maybe. I don't know."

"You said Lyric found that bar. Are you sure you can trust her?"

"Absolutely. Blood of the coven," I said and Luka nodded like he understood.

"Does someone want to fill me in on what you guys are talking about?" Steph asked.

We told her the whole story of Halloween night. When Luka's hand landed on my thigh, I realized I had been crying while telling my part of the story.

"I'm so sorry, Sage," Steph said with empathetic eyes.

"Did Lyric say how she found the bar?" Luka asked.

"No. I told her I wasn't ready to talk about anything from that night. Why? Do you think Sorin told her to go there?" Sorin wasn't the clubbing type, so I had my doubts.

"Maybe. You could ask her."

Pulling out my phone, I dialed Lyric's personal cell.

Luka's eyebrows shot up. "I didn't mean right now."

Lyric answered the phone and I put it on speaker. "Hey, are you at work," I asked, wanting to make sure I didn't get her in trouble.

"No, I'm off until Monday, so I stayed the night with a friend. What's up?"

"I'm a friend now?" Winnie asked in the background and Lyric shushed him.

"You were Winnie's snack?" I blurted. "I'm gonna kill Pooh Bear!"

Winnie laughed. "You love me, Sage Stick!"

"Shut up, Winston." Lyric sighed. "It's not like that, Sage. Can we talk about this later? We are about to have breakfast with Drag and go over some things."

"Oh, we will definitely be talking about this later!"

"So, what's up?" she asked. Her voice was small because she knew I was going to be upset that she didn't tell me.

"How did you hear about the club I went to?"

"From Erik. Why?"

"I have to call Erik. I'll fill you in later."

"Okay. Love you."

"Love you." I hung up the phone and met Luka's eyes.

"Who is this Erik dude?" he asked. "I've heard his name twice now."

"It's my brother, well, Lyric's brother." With no time to explain right now, I dialed Erik's number and waited for him to answer.

"You're alive. Where the hell have you been? You barely talk to me anymore, Sage."

A part of me felt bad since Lyric knew I was tortured and was working with vampires, but Erik didn't.

"I'm fine, but we definitely need to talk soon, just not right now. I have a random question for you. Who told you about the club I went to on Halloween?"

"Oh, that was Naomi. She was going to go with us, but she got pulled into work. Why?"

My heart sped up at the name, so I immediately changed my breathing to calm myself. I had been slacking on it.

"I was just wondering. I'll call you on Monday and we can meet up to talk. Love you."

"Love you." After hanging up the phone, I glanced at Steph.

"Do you think Sorin told Naomi to tell Erik?" she asked.

"A month ago, I would have said no. Now I'm not so sure."

Luka cleared his throat. "Is someone going to tell me who Naomi is?"

"She's Sorin's sister."

His eyes widened as he nodded slowly. "The plot thickens."

CHAPTER 36

LUKA

Steph was extremely hospitable during our visit. After getting the information we needed, I exchanged numbers with her in case she needed anything. Sage also gave her new number to her.

"Please keep in contact, Sage. I worry about you and I hope you guys figure this out soon." The two women hugged while I exited the house. They stepped onto the porch and Steph looked at me. "It was nice meeting you, Luka."

"You too. Sorry I had to choke you," I said, causing her to laugh.

"Are you guys sure you don't want me to drive you out of the neighborhood?" she asked.

"Nah. We got this." I gave her a wink and stepped off the porch.

"Be safe!" she called out as we made our way to the fence.

Clicking my earpiece, I called Winnie. "You got us?"

"Absolutely." The clacking of typing was clear from the other side of the line.

"I thought you were going to breakfast?" I asked.

"Nah, Lyric cooked for me and Drag. It was delicious."

"About time someone used your kitchen." I held my hands out. "Come on, Princess." Sage stepped forward and I placed my hands on her waist. She stared into my eyes, a lustful look on her face as I lifted her and set her over the fence.

"All set. You guys should be good until you're out of there. Call if you need me."

"Thanks, man." After hanging up with Winnie, I hopped the fence.

Sage and I strolled through the backyards until we got to the gate again. She stopped in front of the pillars and smiled.

"I'm ready!"

"Shh. I know you're excited, but don't be so loud."

She giggled and turned around. Placing my hands on her waist, she leaned back into me and tilted her head slightly. Citrus and vanilla filled my senses, and it took all my control not to whip her around and kiss her aggressively.

"Squat," I said instead.

She squatted and jumped, and I threw her up to the pillar. After watching her ass with a smile as she crawled up, I jogged back ten feet. Wanting to be near her, I couldn't get to her fast enough. Running and jumping, I caught the ledge and pulled myself up. My hands went around her and she let out a small gasp as I pulled her into me. As I stared down at her, I noticed the smoothness of her lips. They were full and perfect—slightly parted like they were ready to be kissed.

I swallowed hard, trying to keep my dick from hardening. "Hold your balance."

After I let go of her, I hopped off and landed on the outside of the gate before turning back toward her. She jumped, landing in my protective arms. Not being able to resist her beauty, my eyes trailed her face. Ragged breaths left both of us as we fought the hunger.

"Thanks," she whispered.

If the sexual tension got any higher between us, it would reach the stars.

Setting her down, we took off toward the car. We walked mostly in silence since it was the dead of the night.

Once we were outside the Jeep, Sage went to the passenger side. "You can drive," she said.

"Thanks, Princess."

She leaned against the vehicle and shook her head. "Stop calling me that."

Her smile told me she didn't want me to stop. Citrus and vanilla once again filled the air and I couldn't contain myself anymore. Putting both hands on the Jeep, one hand on each side of her, I leaned into her face.

My nose went to her neck as I breathed her in. "You smell good," I whispered in her ear. I pulled back and gazed into her beautiful eyes.

"Why do you keep saying that?" she asked in a hushed voice.

"Because I can smell you. Smell your . . ." Fear of her being mad stopped me from telling her.

"Smell my what?" Her lips parted again and this time, I took it as a sign. My mouth closed in and I pressed my lips against hers.

She took in a deep breath and I felt the air from her nose brush across my cheek as she released it. Her hands pressed against my back and she pulled me into her before relaxing into the kiss. Our tongues rolled around each other, desperately searching for what we both needed.

Then she stopped and her eyes met mine. "I'm sorry."

"For what?"

"For not stopping it sooner." She ducked down under my arm and opened the car door. She said nothing as she got in and slammed it shut.

"You've got to be fucking kidding me," I mumbled to myself as I made my way around the Jeep.

I hopped in and started the engine. Her heart rate went up and down repeatedly while she sat alone with her thoughts.

Once I couldn't take the silence anymore, I glanced toward her. "Are you mad that I kissed you?"

"No. Let's just drop it." She pulled out her phone and put on a nineties alternative playlist. After cranking up the radio, she stared out the window.

We didn't talk the whole ride back to the hotel. Once in the parking lot, I killed the engine and she reached for the door handle.

"Wait."

She let out an exasperated sigh. "What, Luka?"

"Look at me." I laid my hand on her arm and she turned her head toward me. "I kissed you because—"

"You don't have to explain yourself. I understand we have been hanging out a lot and you may find me attractive, but my feelings aren't the same."

My brows rose at her lies before I grinned with arrogance. "Really now, Princess?"

"Really. We are just acquaintances. Nothing more. We are going to finish this trip like civilized adults and that's it. We don't even need to talk about the kiss. We'll just pretend it didn't happen."

"Like Halloween?" I asked and she nodded.

"Just like on Halloween."

"And the feeding?" At this point, I was being a sarcastic asshole because I knew she was lying.

"Yes, and the feeding. No one needs to know those things, because they were just moments that happened. They don't mean anything, for real, like we just had things happen and stuff."

Tilting my head, I smiled at her rambling. My hand went to her face and her eyes stayed locked on mine as I ran my thumb across her lips.

"You tasted good, by the way." Her breathing sped up as did her heart. Her lure filled the car and I took a deep breath, letting my hand fall away from her mouth. "I can smell you again. Citrus and vanilla."

"Why do you keep saying that?"

"I can smell your lure."

Her eyebrows furrowed in confusion. "My what?"

"Your lure. Your lust."

Her mouth was agape for a few seconds while she was thinking. "What do you mean you can smell my lust?"

"Anytime you get horny, I know because you release a hormone only vampires and wolven can smell."

It might make me an asshole, but I wanted her to know that I knew. Not because I wanted to be honest, but because I was hoping she would want me back. It was selfish, and I knew it, but I hoped she would be excited to finally be able to give into her feelings. When her face angered toward me, I realized I was wrong.

"You have got to be fucking kidding me! You lied to me!"

"I didn't lie, I just failed to mention it!"

"That's the same damn thing, Fucker!" She flung the car door open and practically fell out.

I jumped out and followed her. "Sage, wait!"

"Don't speak to me!" She walked into the revolving door of the hotel.

"Why not? Because you were caught and now you're embarrassed?"

"Embarrassed?" She whipped toward me, her cheeks red with anger. "I'm not the liar, so why would I be embarrassed?"

I smirked. "Because I know your secrets. You fucking want me and you know it!" My voice rang through the foyer and some people in the lobby stopped to watch.

"Um, excuse me," the desk clerk interrupted. "Can I help you two with anything?"

"Maybe. Do you have a lie detector?" Sage asked sarcastically.

The clerk seemed confused, her brows furrowing. "What?"

Sage rolled her eyes and walked away. She pushed the button to the elevator, crossing her arms while she waited.

"I'm sorry I didn't tell you."

"I said, don't talk to me!" The elevator opened and she stepped on it. I followed as she frantically pounded the button to our floor.

"Sage, I—"

"Hold the elevator!" a man yelled as he ran up.

"This one is full!" I gave him a dirty look and hit the button to close the door.

"That was rude!"

"Do you want to know what's rude?"

She crossed her arms and glared at me. "Not really. I can't stand your voice and would prefer not to hear you talk!"

Putting one hand on either side of her, I locked her between the elevator wall and me. "It's rude when someone lies, Princess."

"You would know, since you're a liar!"

"You want to fuck me just as bad as I want to fuck you, so why don't you just admit it!"

"No, I don't," she whispered. Her heart raced with the lies she couldn't hide anymore.

Her lure was strong and thick, filling the small space. Leaning in, I inhaled deeply. "Then why do you smell like lust?" I whispered. "Why do you smell *so fucking good*?"

Turning my head, my mouth was only inches from hers when I met her eyes. Her breaths were fast and her lips were parted, desperately trying to suck in air. Both of us, pushed forward by desire, leaned in for the kiss. It was frantic and needy, making our kissing sloppy, but satisfying.

Her hands snaked around my neck and gripped me. Mine left the wall and immediately went to her ass, pulling her from the floor. She wrapped her legs around me seconds before the elevator doors popped open.

We continued our frantic kissing as I carried her down the hall. Once we were at the door of our room, I pulled away. "Hold on."

Her mouth went to my neck, sucking and kissing while I pulled the keycard out and tapped it on the lock. As soon as the door shut, I slammed her against the wall. She broke away from my neck and gasped for air.

Pressing my hard cock against her, I leaned in and inhaled her lure. Intoxicating. My fangs elongated, ready to taste her again.

She dropped her legs from my waist, then her hands went to my shirt and yanked it off. Her fingers trailed down my stomach muscles, stopping at my waistline before she unbuttoned my pants. I kicked off my boots, and as I pulled my pants off, she removed her shoes.

The anticipation of seeing her naked had my heart racing when she slid her shirt over her head and dropped it. My eyes went to her perfect breasts. The bra she was wearing was black and lacey, but what caught my eye was the large tattoo on her ribs. A snake with lots of flowers around it. My fingers trailed over the edge of it and she sucked in a breath. Goosebumps formed on her skin as my hand traveled down her stomach, stopping at the top of her leather pants. I undid the button and then slid the zipper down.

She released the front clasp of her bra, letting it fall open. When I saw her pierced nipples, a sultry grin spread across my face. Ready to taste them, taste her, I leaned in and sucked one into my mouth. The metal piercing clinked against my teeth as I rolled my tongue around it, making her moan.

I wanted to explore every inch of her, so I left her breast, kissing my way down her stomach before I fell to my knees like I was begging her—begging to worship her. She was a Goddess and I wasn't worthy.

My hands traveled up her thick thighs and stopped at her wide hips. Gripping her leather pants, I yanked them down, and she stepped out of them. Her panties were black lace matching her bra.

Wanting to see what her ass looked like in them, I spun her around and pressed her into the wall, making her gasp. Now eye level to that beautiful round ass of hers, I noticed her panties were cut like a thong, leaving both cheeks bare and easily accessible. My mouth went to one, kissing and nipping as she moaned. Sliding my hand between her thighs, I rubbed on her pussy, making her let out little squeals of pleasure.

Wanting to hear more sounds from her, I gripped her panties and glided them down. She wasted no time kicking them off.

"Spread 'em," I commanded.

She spread her legs apart, and from this angle, I could see a little bit of her glistening lips. Putting my hand between her legs, I guided my finger between her folds and found her silky wetness. She was ready for me.

Not being able to wait, I grabbed her hips and turned her again. Her perfect, almost-bare pussy was now in my face. When I glanced up at her, I found her looking down at me with hungry and anticipating eyes.

"Are you okay, Princess?"

Her response was to twine her fingers in my hair, put one leg over my shoulder, and pull me closer to her. She was practically commanding me to eat her pussy. Even completely naked and vulnerable, she wasn't shy, and I loved that about her.

My hands snaked up and spread her lips apart as my mouth closed in on her. As I sucked in her clit, she moaned. Wanting to taste her—needing to taste her—I slipped my tongue down to her entrance and lapped up her juices, which tasted amazing. That was the moment I realized I never wanted to go a day without tasting her.

I ran my tongue up to her clit, she gasped and pulled my hair tighter. My finger slid inside of her before I curled it forward, pressing on her swollen g-spot. She grinded against my hand and face while I consumed her.

"Oh, fuck. Don't stop!"

Not wanting her to lose her orgasm, I stayed at the same exact speed and motion. Her muscles clenched around my finger as her hands tightened in my hair.

"Oh, god," she moaned breathlessly. Her body quaked, and warm wetness surrounded my finger as she came for me. Once her muscles were lax, I pulled back and sucked her juices off my fingers before standing up.

My eyes trailed her face as I waited to see if she was going to let me continue.

"Do you have a condom?" she asked and I snickered.

"Vampires can't reproduce and we can't get diseases." Leaning in, I kissed her neck.

"Oh," she whispered. She jumped into my arms and wrapped her legs around me. "Then fuck me."

My mouth met hers as I gripped her ass tight. I took her to the bed and slammed her down on it before laying on top of her. My hard cock pressed against her and I growled out a moan. My tongue darted into her mouth as I explored every inch of it.

She moaned in desperation as she scratched her nails down my back. Her fingers trailed down my underwear. She yanked them down, releasing my ass cheeks before digging her nails into my flesh. Freeing her mouth so she could catch her breath, I went to her tit and sucked it, bringing more moans from her.

Ready to explore more of her, I supported myself with one forearm as I pulled my boxers off, letting my cock free. Not wasting time, she reached down, slid me inside of her, and gasped. Her pussy was warm, wet, and snug, making my balls tight and ready to release my cum. She raised her knees up high as I grinded in a way I knew would hit her clit, making her moan.

Our fucking was greedy and primal with a desperation to it. A demand that our body was requiring. It was shameless, needful, and intense, and I was enjoying every fucking second of it. Never in my many years had I ever felt this free with someone, and I had a feeling she felt the same way.

My tongue ravaged her mouth once more as I hammered into her. Her body was wet beneath mine as we both sweated out the lust we had been carrying since shortly after we met. My mouth left hers and went to her neck as I kissed and sucked. The pulsating of her veins pumping blood beneath my lips made me want to plunge my fangs into her. As if she knew what I was thinking, she moaned loudly when one of my fangs scraped against her skin.

Pulling back, I looked her in the face. My mouth was open as I panted, fangs visible, ready to strike.

"Do it," she whispered. "Fucking bite me!"

Without hesitation, I sunk my fangs into her. Her warm blood pooled in my mouth as I took hungry gulps. She screamed in ecstasy, her body convulsing below me. As she came, the walls of her pussy pulsated around my cock, making me ready to explode. Releasing her vein before I killed her, I let out a loud moan of my own. Every nerve in my body felt electrified as my cock pulsed and warm cum shot into her.

With a racing heart, my forehead fell against her chest as I tried to catch my breath. Her fingers glided through my hair and she rubbed them in soothing circles.

Not being able to hold my feelings in, my eyes trailed across her face before I ran a thumb across her lip. "You're beautiful, Princess," I whispered, making her breath catch.

She removed her hands from my hair, placed them on my cheeks, and pressed her lips against mine. After another long kiss, I finally rolled off her. She immediately got up to use the bathroom before I had a chance to attend to her.

When she came back, I was lying in bed waiting to see if she freaked out. It surprised me when she crawled into bed, still naked, and curled up by my side.

"Goodnight," she whispered. She snuggled into my armpit and closed her eyes.

My hand pushed her hair out of her face. "Goodnight, Princess."

I savored the moment, wrapping my arms around her. When she wakes up naked in my arms, and my venom has worn off, I knew she was going to freak out again. I wasn't prepared for that.

CHAPTER 37
SAGE

My alarm going off woke me from a deep sleep. After fumbling for it on the nightstand, I grabbed it and hit snooze. Laying my head back on the pillow, Luka's arms curled around me and my breath caught as the memories of last night flooded through my mind.

"Fuck," I whispered. My body reacted, ready to bolt, but his arms tightened.

"Don't freak out," he said into my hair.

"I'm not, I just need to . . ." I tried to get up again, but it didn't work.

"Don't bother. I'm stronger than you. You're not going anywhere."

"I have to pee, Luka!"

"Hold it."

"What? No!" I pulled away again. "I'm naked, I need my clothes."

"No, you don't." He yanked me closer to him. "You need to shut up and enjoy this." His lips went to my neck and, as he kissed, my mouth betrayed me by letting out a moan.

"Stop," I whispered, but I didn't want him to.

"Do you really want me to stop?" he asked, and I didn't answer. "That's what I thought."

More kisses and moans.

"Okay, I won't bolt, but I have to pee." With a sigh, he let go of me.

Sliding slowly off the bed—so he didn't think I was bolting and tackle me—I headed into the bathroom. After relieving myself, I washed my hands. As I looked in the mirror, I thought about last night and smiled. Every touch, every kiss, every moan . . . it was the realest and most natural sexual experience I had ever had. There was no awkward first time, or weirdness afterwards. It was safe, comfortable, and thrilling. It left me feeling like I could be vulnerable, demanding, or needy, and he wouldn't judge me.

After drying my hands, I headed back into the bedroom, picked his t-shirt up off the floor, and put it on.

"Seriously, Sage? Are you going to act like nothing happened again?" His face was frustrated.

"No, Fucker! I'm just cold." I crawled into the bed and laid down next to him.

His arms immediately went around me. "Let's stay another day," he mumbled.

"What? Why do you want to stay?"

"Because I want to show you some of the beautiful parts of Vegas."

I wanted to see that too, but I didn't think it was a good idea. Rolling over, I stared at his gorgeous face. "We are trying to solve a mystery here."

"Okay, Scooby Doo."

My eyes widened. "Scooby? If anything, I'm Daphne!"

"You're not Daphne. More like Velma."

I scrunched up my nose. "Why?"

"Because she's intelligent, curvy, and not afraid to be a nerd. Like you." I smiled at the fact he called me intelligent. "I'm Fred, obviously. Good looking, charming, the true leader."

I rolled my eyes and shook my head. "You are *no* Fred! You're more like Scrappy Doo."

Luka's eyes widened before he cocked an eyebrow at me. "I'm six-foot-two, woman! How am I Scrappy? He's, like, a foot tall! Closer to your height."

"First of all, I'm five-foot-four. That's tall for a girl."

He furrowed his eyebrows. "That's not tall."

"Shut up!" I smacked his arm. "I'm trying to compliment you here."

"Continue, Princess."

"Secondly, he's super brave and never backs down from a fight. Like you."

Luka smiled at my comparison. "I'll accept that. So, are we staying?"

A large sigh left me. "We can't stay because I have therapy tomorrow. Plus, we have a job to do. People could be dying while we waste time. We need to hurry and shower. We have to be on the road soon."

Luka let go of me and rolled to his back with a sigh. "As soon as we kill all the rats, we're coming back to Vegas."

"Deal," I said with a grin. His eyes widened as his head turned toward me.

"I'm really liking you in Vegas." He smiled before hopping off the bed, heading into the bathroom. "Are you coming, Princess?"

I froze.

To me, taking a shower with someone was even more vulnerable than having sex with them. I wasn't particularly fond of water play after trying to have sex in a pool one time. So, other than fucking, what do you do while you're in there? For me, the shower was my sacred place where I could cleanse myself in private and not worry about anyone seeing my flaws.

The shower turned on and I sat up. My mind raced as I thought about what I should do. After a minute of contemplating, I decided I would just wait him out and hop in when he was done.

Luka strolled out of the bathroom buck naked and headed toward me like a lion hunting his prey.

"I'll wait until . . . ahh." He yanked me up, threw me over his shoulder without saying a word, and headed into the bathroom. "Put me down, Fucker."

He kicked the bathroom door shut and set me down. Gripping the bottom of my shirt, he lifted it above my head and threw it on the floor.

"Get in!" With a grin, he pointed to the shower. Hesitating, I stared at him. He immediately saw the difference in my posture. "What's wrong?"

"I've never taken a shower with anyone before," I mumbled.

"Me either. So, it's a first for us both."

My eyes widened in shock. "How? You're really old."

"I'm exactly the same as I was when I was turned. My mentality will always be twenty-seven."

"That doesn't answer my question." I tilted my head with a grin.

"Because showers are sacred. I don't share them with anyone." He slid the glass door open and stepped in. "So, are you coming?"

Knowing I was the first person he ever showered with made a huge smile spread across my face. The fact he thought showers were a sacred place like I did, thrilled me.

"Are you sure you can't read minds?" I asked, as I eased myself in behind him and shut the glass door.

"I've already told you, vampires can't read minds."

"I read this book once, and the vampire in it could."

He yanked me close to him, our wet bodies smashing together, "That's called fantasy, love."

He leaned in, his mouth on mine, hungrily consuming it. Thoughts of what he did to me ran through my head and I wanted more. He pulled back, leaving me breathless as he sniffed the air.

"Citrus and vanilla." With a grin, he started washing himself.

My mind couldn't wrap around the fact he knew when I was horny. When he had first told me, I was angry, but only because I was caught. He knew that, too. He had this weird way of knowing what I was thinking, what I needed, and who I was as a person. The kind of connection we had was new to me, and it was going to take some navigating to understand it.

Turning away from him, I grabbed the body wash and squirted it on a washcloth. After cleansing myself, I held it out to him.

"Can you wash my back?" He took it from my hands and ran it in circles. "Harder."

"How hard do you want it?" he asked, with a seductive playfulness to his voice.

"Real hard," I whispered, returning the flirting.

"What are you trying to do, wash away your sins?"

"Maybe." The washcloth hit the shower floor.

His lips went to my shoulder, drawing a moan as he placed kisses on me. "I don't think you have any sins."

"What you did to me last night is definitely a sin," I said and he snickered.

He turned me toward him, his blue eyes roaming my face. "Making you come repeatedly isn't a sin, Princess. It's an honor."

For once in my life, I actually blushed. This man had been there for me more than my own father had. The thought was fleeting, but I did slightly wonder if I had daddy issues. After all, I just fucked an older man. A much, much, *much* older man.

CHAPTER 38

LUKA

It was hard for me not to fuck her in the shower—especially since I smelled her lure four times. But she was right, we had a job to do. We needed to get back home before more people died. After packing our bags, we loaded up the Jeep and hit the road. I got to drive this time. She had been quiet for a while and, when I glanced over at her, she was deep in thought.

Placing my hand on her knee, her head turned toward me. "What are you thinking about, Princess?"

She shook her head and sighed. "I was thinking about what Steph said."

"Which part?"

"All of it. I was supposed to die, Luka. If I hadn't met you, I wouldn't be here right now." She laid her hand on top of mine.

Having no clue on what to tell someone who was set up to be murdered, I nodded and continued watching the road.

"Do you think it's just Sorin?" she asked. "Or do you think it's deeper than that?"

She didn't come out and say it, but I had a feeling she wanted reassurance that her father didn't want her murdered.

"I don't know, but I have a feeling we will find out and, when we do, we'll have to prepare for a war."

For a while, the ride was quiet. Then we talked on and off about random things, like movies, music, books. She was usually excited about those topics, but personal matters, not so much. When she opened up to me and told me about her fears, her passions, her desires, I was astonished.

Hours later, we were back at her apartment.

"Don't I need to give you a ride home?" she asked as I pulled up to the curb and put the Jeep in park.

"Winnie drove my Harley here and dropped it off. It's in the alley."

"Oh. Well, we have a couple of hours before the sun comes up." Glancing over at her, she was smiling excitedly.

An hour wasn't a lot of time to do the things I wanted to do to her, but I was willing to make it work. "Do you want me to come up?"

She laughed. "I was thinking more like a ride on your bike."

"I wanted a different kind of ride." As I grinned at her, her entire demeanor changed. She crossed her arms, biting her lip.

"Luka . . ." she hesitated and let out a long breath. She gave me a small, rueful smile.

Once again, her feelings were hidden, impenetrable.

"Just say what you want to say."

She looked down, avoiding my eyes. "I just kind of figured, what happens in Vegas—"

"Stays in Vegas. Got it." Reaching behind the seat, I grabbed my backpack.

She laid a hand on my arm. "Luka, I'm sorry that—"

"There's nothing to be sorry for. You have a good night, Princess."

My ego took over a little, and I was infuriated when I opened the car door. After hopping out, I slammed it shut. She may not have intended to, but she made me feel used.

As I rounded the corner of the alley, a car door slammed and the pounding of her footsteps against the pavement rang through the night.

"Luka, wait!"

She was coming to apologize again, but I didn't want to hear it. I set the backpack on my bike and sighed as she came running up to me.

"What do you want, Sage?" I asked, without looking at her.

"Please, don't leave mad. I just figured once we were back in town—"

Anger filled me and I whipped around. "You fucking used me!"

She shook her head frantically. "I did not!"

I threw my hands out in exasperation. "Really? Because that's what it feels like! Did you even want me, or did you just want to fuck a vampire?"

Okay, my ego took over a lot.

Her face changed to one of sorrow as she stepped in close and laid her palm on my chest. "I wasn't using you, Luka." Her voice cracked and I swallowed hard from her teary eyes. "I wanted you, I still do, but . . ."

Not being able to say what she wanted to say, she shook her head as stared up at me.

"But I'm a vampire."

My attention was completely focused on her, so I didn't even hear the footsteps until the guy was ten feet away . . . with a crossbow pointed at me.

"What the fuck, Sage!" he yelled.

Fear had me grabbing her and pushing her out of the way before I lunged toward him. An arrow flew past me as I knocked the crossbow out of his hands. He tried to punch me and I caught his fist, then elbowed him in the face.

"Stop!"

Ignoring her screams, I grabbed his wrist and twisted it behind his back and he fell to his knees. Wrapping my arms around his neck, I squeezed. He frantically grabbed my forearm as I cut off his air supply.

"Don't, Luka. Please!"

Looking up, her eyes were filled with panic. A real, deep fear. They burrowed into my soul, pleading, begging, telling me I was about to kill one of the few people in the world she cared for. Possibly one of the few people who cared for her. The tears rolling down her cheeks sparkled in the moonlight—I couldn't look away. Something inside of me shifted, and I knew immediately I never wanted to see her shed another tear again.

What the fuck's wrong with me?

"Please," she cried. "That's Erik!"

So, this was her brother for all intents and purposes. Deep down, I wanted to snap his neck just for pointing a crossbow anywhere near her, but she would never forgive me.

"He could have hurt you!"

Erik tapped my arm in a panic, I slightly loosened my grip so he wouldn't die . . . yet.

"He won't hurt me, I promise!"

My trust in her was strong, so I let go and shoved him to the ground.

"Thank you," she mouthed.

The scent of love a human emits, differs from the smell of their lure. Sage released a scent that smelled like lavender and vanilla as she stared at me.

She loved me.

My breaths were ragged as I tried hard to shift my focus to break the intense eye contact, but I couldn't. Her beautiful brown irises were giving me life. The cock of a small crossbow made me flinch, the fear of death being the only thing that could take my attention from her.

"Erik, don't!" Her fearful scream rang through the chilly night air as she jumped in between us.

This girl, this woman, cared for me—for a vampire. The thought was both enthralling and scared the shit out of me.

"You have got to be kidding me! What the fuck is wrong with you, Sage?" Erik asked.

"Just . . . don't." She placed her hands on the crossbow and he slowly lowered it. "Let me explain what's going on!"

"He was stalking you and killed Deren! What's there to explain?"

"I'll tell you, just back down!"

"Are you fucking him?" he asked before jumping to his feet.

"That's none of your business!"

His face went pale, and he swallowed hard. "Blood of the coven," he whispered.

She shook her head as she backed up toward me.

"You're picking him over me? We're supposed to be family!"

"I'm not picking anyone. I love you, Erik, but you can't hurt him."

"If you loved me, you wouldn't have chosen a vampire over me!" He narrowed his eyes on me before they drifted back to Sage. "Take care of yourself."

He turned away and she grabbed his arm, halting him. "Eric, wait! It's not what you think. We were on a mission together. Call Lyric and ask her!"

His eyebrows squished together, confusion filling his face. "What are you talking about?"

"Come upstairs and I'll explain. Please!" Her voice was frantic, pleading.

Grabbing my helmet, I put it on and threw my leg over my bike. As I started the engine, Sage's head whipped toward me. Her eyes were sad and filled with regret. Not being able to see her like that, I looked away as I twisted the throttle and drove off.

CHAPTER 39
SAGE

My chest tightened when Luka pulled away. I tried as hard as I could to keep the look of pain off my face when I turned toward Erik.

"Are you ready?" I asked.

He nodded.

The silent walk up to my apartment building was uncomfortable. The judgement and disappointment radiating off of Erik were palpable. Trying my best to ignore it, I mentally cataloged all the details of what had happened. I wanted to be sure I didn't leave anything out when I told him the story.

Once we were inside, Erik sat his bag on the table and grabbed a bottle of beer from the refrigerator. He popped it open and took a swig before sitting at the bar.

Pulling out my phone, I texted Lyric.

Sage: *Erik ran into me and Luka. BIG mad. Wants to know what's going on. Come over now!*

Lyric: *Shit! On my way!*

"Lyric will be here soon," I said in a hushed voice, and he nodded.

Feeling like we were going to need something to help us get through this conversation, I headed to the kitchen and grabbed tequila and some shot glasses.

When Lyric finally showed up, I was already two shots in and Erik *still* hadn't spoken.

"Talk," Erik finally said, heading to the fridge to get another beer.

"It's a long story," I mumbled. I glanced nervously at Lyric when she took a seat next to me.

He popped the top off his beer and sat back down. "I have time."

Between Lyric and myself, we explained everything that had happened to that point. I left out the part about Lyric possibly being Winnie's snack, and the part where I was *definitely* Luka's—twice. I was pretty sure his head would have exploded if he would have known.

"Are you both crazy?" he asked, a look of disbelief on his face.

"We didn't know what to do, Erik!" Lyric was on the defense, but I wasn't. I was still feeling bad about him being choked by Luka, so I was being less confrontational.

"We really didn't," I added. "Everything just happened so fast."

His eyes were filled with empathy when they met mine. "I'm sorry you were tortured."

"Thanks." I hung my head down and bit my nail. I hoped it was all he said about the topic, because I still wasn't ready to talk about it.

"So, what do we do now?" he asked. "If someone in Venom is a traitor, we need to find out who it is."

Lyric shook her head and sighed. "That's what we have been trying to tell you!"

"I want to meet the other two you're working with, this Winnie and Dragon guy."

"Drag," I corrected and he rolled his eyes.

"Whatever."

"So, I heard you already met Luka," Lyric said with a smile, and my eyes widened.

Erik rubbed his throat. "I don't think *met* is the word for it."

Lyric's face was confused as she looked at me. I shook my head, so she knew to drop it. I guess I should have mentioned the choking in my text.

"So, what were you and this Luka guy fighting about?" he asked.

"We weren't fighting. We were discussing plans."

Erik gave me a look like he didn't believe me, but dropped the subject.

"Winnie got some information while you were gone. We can go to his house tomorrow to go over it. Erik, you'll come with us."

He rubbed his hands across his forehead and then sighed. "Make sure they know I'm coming so they don't eat me." He grabbed the tequila and poured us all another shot.

"They won't hurt you," I said before I downed mine.

"They're fucking vampires, Sage!"

"Don't yell at me! I know what they are. We have been coordinating with them for weeks now, and they've done nothing but help us!"

"If it was anyone else, this conversation would be different, but since it's you two, I'm going to trust you."

"I appreciate that, Erik."

He gave me a nod before heading off to the bathroom.

The conversation died down. Lyric and Erik both went home to sleep, and I immediately went to find Chewy to get some much-needed love before bed.

The next day, I was walking through the halls of Venom when I was met by my father.

"Sagelynn, aren't you supposed to be in therapy?"

"I'm headed there now, Dad."

"Good. I spoke with Mr. Johnson and he said you have been making progress. I informed him you would be on the roster for tomorrow night."

"What? Why?" My heart thundered in my chest at the thought of returning to work.

"It's light duty. Only surveillance missions, so you won't even be fighting. You're never going to get over what happened unless you get back out there."

"I'm not ready." My voice was shaky, but he didn't seem to care.

"You'll be fine, I even made sure to pair you with Erik. Now get down to therapy before you're late." He leaned in and kissed my cheek before walking away.

Pure panic set in as I continued walking. I wasn't ready to go back in the field. To be honest, I never wanted to go back especially if the allegations against Venom were true. Which they seemed to be.

My therapy was long and unsuccessful, and it made me miss Steph. Ready to get the fuck out of here, I was saying my goodbyes at the door.

"I will see you next Monday, Mr. Johnson."

"Oh, one last thing, Sage. Dr. Jayne wants to see you before you leave."

I nodded and shut the door behind me.

With a sigh, I headed toward Doc Jayne's office. Walking the halls in silence, my mind wandered to Luka, and I realized I missed him. He hadn't texted or called yet, and I didn't blame him. Once again, he had me pegged. He knew I had used him. It wasn't my plan, but I knew when we were laying there, falling asleep, I wasn't going to pursue a relationship with him. Feeling bad, I reached in my pocket and pulled out my phone and texted him.

Sage: *For whatever it means, I'm sorry. I wanted you and still do, but I need to focus on saving people. I hope we can still be friends.*

I sent the message and watched until it said *read,* a few seconds later. An aching pain filled my chest, making it hard to breathe when he didn't respond. Maybe I liked him a little more than I even knew.

I entered the infirmary and Doc Jayne greeted me with a smile.

"Welcome back, Sage!"

"Hey, Doc."

"Your father said you were going back on the roster, so you have to get your booster. Have a seat."

My dad didn't waste time and neither did the doc.

After setting my bag on the counter, I removed my jacket and rolled up my sleeve. Doc Jayne grabbed a syringe out of the drawer and set it down before grabbing a vial out of the refrigerator. Once she came back to me, she filled the syringe with the *super potion.* After she wiped me down with an alcohol pad, she stuck me in the arm.

The small euphoric feeling washed over me and my breath caught. Flashbacks on the night I was tortured flitted through my mind, the memories giving me an immediate realization. I have felt this feeling before, and it wasn't from my last shot, but I was too out of it that night to realize it.

"Fuck," I whispered accidentally.

"Are you okay?" she asked and I did the only thing I could to cover my reaction, I lied.

"I haven't had an injection in a while, so I'm feeling a little sick."

"Oh, it's normal. It'll settle in a second." She stuck a Band-Aid on my arm. "I want to monitor you to make sure you're good, so sit here for a few minutes and relax."

She took the vial over to the refrigerator, placing it inside. Before she shut the door, I noticed there were multiple bottles in there—ones I had never noticed before.

"Hey, Doc?"

"Yes?"

She turned toward me and I had no idea what I was going to say. I swallowed hard. "I'm still feeling nauseous and a little dizzy."

"Let me take your temperature." She grabbed a thermometer, ran it across my forehead, and it beeped. "Hmm. You don't have a fever. Maybe you should lie down."

Before I had a chance to protest or agree, she grabbed my arm and escorted me to the examination table. She helped me onto it and I laid down.

Her hand patted my arm in a soothing manner. "Rest for a while."

She headed to her desk and started inputting information into her laptop while I immediately devised a plan. As I looked around, I realized this was probably one of the few rooms that didn't have cameras in it, which was about to benefit me.

With a plan in mind, I pulled out my phone and quietly texted Lyric.

Sage: *Doc J is gonna call you, don't answer!*

Lyric: *Umm, okay.*

I quickly pocketed my phone before she saw me.

"Doc, can you call Lyric to come up here. I may need her to give me a ride home if I don't start feeling better."

Her head whipped around in surprise. "Are you feeling that bad?" I nodded as I gripped my stomach. "Oh, no. One second." She pulled out her phone and called Lyric. She shook her head as she hung up. "She didn't answer."

"She's in the cafeteria, is there a way you can go get her?" Another lie. Lyric was off tonight, and when I talked to her on the way in, she was at home.

"Do you want me to see if your mom is here?"

"No. I don't want to worry her more. She has had to do enough of that recently." That part was true.

She nodded and then headed for the door. "I'll be right back. Don't get up!"

"I won't."

To make sure she wasn't coming back, I waited a minute before I jumped up, ran toward the door, and locked it. I immediately headed for the fridge, and opened it. My frantic gaze wandered over the three different types of vials. The one I was injected with was on the right, so I grabbed it first. After I looked it over, I noticed a serial number on the label. I grabbed the next one in the row and it had the next number in sequence. There was no way I could steal three vials without it going unnoticed.

Wondering what I was going to do, I looked around and saw her medical cart. I made my way over to it and opened the drawer that Doc always grabbed syringes from. There were multiple sizes and colors, so I took three different colored ones. Once back at the fridge, I filled each one with a different solution. After I popped the caps back on, I grabbed my small backpack and threw them inside. My adrenaline was pumping when I made my way to the door and unlocked it before quickly getting back on the table.

My heart raced as I waited for the doc to come back. Several minutes later, she returned.

"I'm sorry, Sage. I looked all over for Lyric, and I didn't see her."

"It's okay. I'm feeling a little better." I sat up and hung my feet over the side before I hopped off the table. "I think I'm good. I'll find her."

"As long as you think so." She watched me with curious eyes as I grabbed my bag and headed for the door. "I hope you feel better."

"Thanks." I quickly exited and headed for my Jeep.

As soon as I shut the car door, I pulled out my phone. Luka still hadn't answered my text, so I wasn't sure he would answer the next one.

Sage: *I have something you may want. Can you meet me somewhere?*

A few seconds later it showed he was typing. A big smile spread across my face when the text popped up.

Fucker: *Meet me at Drifter's.*

Starting the car, my heart was heavy with anticipation as I headed to meet Luka.

CHAPTER 40

LUKA

After receiving a text message from Sage, I mounted my bike and headed to Drifter's. The need to see her had anxiety filling me as I waited patiently at the bar. The front door opened and her blissful natural scent filled the air. Breathing it in, I savored it. It had only been seventeen hours, yet it felt like it had been years. The more I was around her, the more I wanted to be because she was intoxicating. I had an addiction and she was my drug.

Not wanting to seem desperate, I downed the rest of my beer while I waited for her to approach me.

"Hey," she said in a low voice.

Looking toward her, I smiled nonchalantly. "Hey."

Her smile was small, but the flush on her cheeks and the acceleration of her heart told me she was excited to see me.

"Can we talk privately?"

Glancing over at Ollie, he nodded.

"Come on." I led her back to the office and shut the door. "Have a seat."

"Where are Pooh and Drag?" she asked, sliding into the chair.

Her heart raced faster, and I assumed she had the same realization I had—we were alone.

"They're at Save right now, where I'm supposed to be. Where's Lyric and Erik?"

She tilted her head with a cheerful look. "At home, where I'm supposed to be."

"Touché." I smiled and she smiled back. Our dual stare was intense for a few seconds before clearing my throat. "So, what do you have for me, Sage?" I had planned on purposely not calling her Princess and the more I refrained, the more I wanted to do it.

She dug inside her bag before slamming three syringes down. "This!"

I picked them up and looked them over. "What is *this*?" I asked.

"One is the booster Venom insists we get and I'm not sure what the other two are."

"Why do they give you a booster?"

"It helps strengthen us when we're in the field. When I asked about it a while back, I was told it was vitamins, minerals, and immune boosters. but when I got my shot today, I realized I've felt it before. When she injected me, I got this euphoric feeling. It was the same feeling I had when you fed me your blood, but on a much smaller scale."

My brows furrowed as I wondered what the fuck Venom was up to. "And you get these often?"

"Once a week, but I haven't had one in a while since I've been on leave." She crossed her legs and my gaze immediately went to her thighs.

Clearing my throat seemed to be my only defense against her beauty, so I did it again and looked back at the syringes. "We need to get these to a lab."

"Do you know anyone who has one?" she asked.

"I do. Ravage."

Her brows rose before a puzzled look settled on her face. "Your tattoo artist?"

"Yep. Were these refrigerated?"

"Yeah. Why?"

"I don't know how long they're good for outside of the cold. I need to get them to him immediately."

I stood up and she followed suit. "I'm coming with you!"

A slow, mischievous grin spread across my face. "Fine, but we're taking my bike."

"I'm okay with that," she said with a smile. I handed her the syringes, and she stuck them in her purse.

Holding the office door open for her, I watched her ass as she exited and it took a tremendous amount of restraint for me not to smack it. With a sigh, I followed her.

"I'll be back, Ollie."

"You kids be safe," he mumbled as he scooped ice from the cooler.

We headed for the backdoor and stepped into the alley. Grabbing the helmet off my bike, I handed it to her.

"This is where we met," she said. "But you hated me then."

I smirked. "What makes you think I don't hate you now?"

Her eyes saddened before she put the helmet on. "Do you hate me, Luka?"

Kicking my leg out, I threw it over my bike, then sighed. "I couldn't possibly hate you, Princess. Come on. We have people to save."

It didn't take long for me to give in and call her by her nickname. I couldn't help myself.

When she climbed on the back and wrapped her arms around me, I wondered if this was it for us. I couldn't help but think, *Are the fun times over?*

But when I fired up the engine, she pressed her breasts against my back. The smell of her lure lit my senses on fire. A knowing smile spread across my face. This wasn't the end.

Pulling away from the curb, we headed across town to Ravage's tattoo shop. I parked my bike, wishing the ride was longer.

After removing the helmet, she hopped off and I put out the kickstand then dismounted.

She tilted her head up at the neon sign on the front of the building that said *Blood Oath Tattoos and Piercings.*

"Well, that's obvious." She handed me the helmet and I tucked it under my arm.

"Only if you're expecting it to be owned by a vampire," I said, as I held the door for her.

Ravage was leaning against the counter, flipping through a tattoo magazine. He was a brawny man with dark hair and a full beard. After sniffing the air, his eyes shot up, a slow grin spreading across his face.

"Lukas mother-fucking Draven!" he exclaimed in a deep voice. "How have you been, son?"

Sage's face was surprised as she glanced at me. "Lukas? That's less badass."

"I like her already!" He held out his hand and Sage shook it with a smile. "Name's Ravage. I hope you find it more badass."

"Sage, and yes, I do." She smiled and Ravage smiled back.

"Can we talk privately?" I asked, breaking their eye contact. I may have been slightly jealous.

Ravage's gaze darted back to me, and he let out a sigh. "Every time you say that, I know shit is going down. Come on." He headed toward his office.

I pushed open the saloon door next to the counter and followed him.

"I'm assuming she *knows*, since she's with you." he said before taking a seat behind the desk.

I set my helmet on the desk and sat down. "She knows."

Sage's face filled with confusion as she sat in the chair next to me. "I know what?"

"That we *eat* pretty girls like you." Ravage smiled, showing off his fangs.

Sage tilted her head and grinned. "I'm assuming you know I'm *not* scared of you."

Ravage chuckled. "You're just as fierce as you are sexy. I like that in a woman!"

A small bit of jealousy seethed in me as I let out a low snarl. Okay, maybe it was more than a small bit.

Sage's eyes darted toward me and her mouth was agape. "Did you just growl?" she asked.

Ravage had an apologetic look as he cleared his throat. "Sorry, Luka. I didn't know she was yours."

In the vampire world, snarling over someone meant they were untouchable. Most of us respected it.

Sage quickly looked back at Ravage. "I'm not his! I don't belong to anyone!"

Ravage busted out a full belly laugh. "Okay." He had a knowing smile before his face went serious. "What's on your mind, Luka?"

"We have something we need tested." Looking at Sage, I nodded my head toward Ravage. "Show him."

She quickly dug the syringes out and set them on the desk.

Ravage glanced at them curiously. "What are these?"

"I work for Venom and—"

Ravage was fast to his feet, baring his fangs with a snarl. Baring my fangs in return, I jumped up, immediately blocking him from her.

"After everything I have done for you, how the fuck can you just bring a Venom member here without telling me first?" he snapped.

"She isn't like that!" Being hundreds of years older than me, Ravage could have killed me if he wanted to.

"Hey, hey! Both of you stop!" Sage squeezed between me and the desk. I immediately pushed her behind me.

"Stay back!" I commanded.

"Stop it, Fucker! Let me talk!" She jumped in front of me again and slammed her hands on the desk. "There's a Venom-Save conspiracy going on and we're trying to figure it out! So, if you could put your damn fangs away and sit the *fuck* down, we can talk about it!"

Ravage's eyes widened before he barked out a laugh. "I'm liking you more and more!" He lowered himself back into his seat with a fanged smile. "Explain."

Taking in a deep breath, I sat back down, as did Sage. She told him everything about the solution in the vials. I explained the things Winnie found during the investigation.

Ravage was bug-eyed by the time we were done. "What the fuck?" he whispered.

"Yeah." I nodded in agreement. "I was hoping you could test the solutions and find out what's in them."

Ravage picked up one of the syringes and rolled it between his fingers. "You know I will. I *always* help my family."

"Family?" Sage's expression turned perplexed. "Are you his brother?"

Ravage snickered before a superior grin spread across his face. "More like *father*."

"He's your dad?" Sage's eyes widened and you could tell she had a hundred thoughts running through her head.

"He's not my dad."

"I'm so confused," Sage said and Ravage chuckled.

"I'm his origin."

"His what?"

"He turned me into a vampire, Princess."

"Oh. Like Steph."

"Steph?" Ravage asked, his eyes locking on Sage. I could tell he knew exactly what she was talking about, but he was waiting for more information before he confirmed.

"She was my therapist at Venom. She . . ." Sage stopped herself from giving more information.

"She told us you turned her," I finished because I knew he was trustworthy.

Ravage shook his head. "Silly girl. She's supposed to be hiding. How the hell did you find her?"

"Winnie," I said with a grin.

"That mother fucker could break into the Pentagon!" Ravage laughed before he settled his face, picking up the other two syringes. "I thought you were here for a tattoo, not conspiracy theories."

"I have a question," Sage said, bringing my attention to her beautiful face. "How do you put tattoos on vampires if they heal instantly?"

Ravage snickered. "It took me many years to come up with the method. Even though Luka trusts you, there is no way I'm telling you."

"Fair enough," she said.

"I will get these tested and get you the results as soon as I can."

"Thanks, man." I grabbed my helmet from the desk.

"It was nice meeting you, Sage." He extended a hand to her and she shook it.

"Likewise."

Once we were outside, I pulled out my phone and called Winnie.

"What's up, bro?"

"Where are you?" I asked.

"Still at Save. Drag and I are building the stage for the children's play. You know, what *you're* supposed to be helping with."

I ignored his complaints. "Who's all there?"

"Other than us, Peach and Vivi."

"On my way." I hung up the phone and pocketed it. "Do you want to meet some people?" I asked.

Sage squinted as she pondered the question. "People or vampires?"

I handed her the helmet with a laugh. "Friends."

"As long as I'm not murdered." She put the helmet on and fastened it.

"I can promise you no one will hurt you as long as I'm around."

Kicking my leg over, I lowered myself onto my bike and she slithered on behind me.

"I know," she whispered before wrapping her arms around me.

CHAPTER 41
SAGE

We pulled away from the curb and headed toward the south side of town. I had no clue where we were going, but as long as I was with him, I didn't care. He made me feel safe. I had missed him a lot more than I was letting on. My heart was a little tender from hanging out with him, but I was going to keep pretending like it wasn't.

We pulled up to a building twenty minutes outside of town and he killed the engine.

"Are you taking me to church?" I asked as I slid off the motorcycle.

"This is Save."

My mouth was agape as I removed the helmet. "Luka, you can't bring me here! You saw how Ravage acted. Plus, I don't want to know where this is. What if someone—"

He looped his finger in the top of my jeans and yanked me toward him. My breath caught, his beautiful eyes meeting mine. "Calm down, Princess. It's just my friends."

He let go of me and took the helmet, setting it on the bike seat. The way he had his body turned, caused his back muscles to tighten. Heat poured through me and I couldn't look away. A large grin adorned his face when he turned back around.

My heart raced when his hand went to my neck, pushing my hair aside. He leaned in close and whispered, "You might want to keep that scent contained until we leave," he kissed my neck, "Princess."

He walked away, leaving me breathless. I swallowed hard. My lure was going to give my feelings away and, as I stared at him—one arm stretched in the air while he held the door open—I wanted to let it.

"You coming?" he asked with an arrogant, sexy grin.

With a deep breath, I bit my lip and entered.

The foyer of the church was huge. Luka went straight into the chapel and I followed with curious eyes. The ceilings were the tallest I had seen. The walls, pews, and floors were made of dark wood. There were stained glass windows as well and I had a feeling they were even more gorgeous in the daylight.

"Who brought dinner?" a woman asked.

At the front of the room, Winnie and Drag were standing beside two women I didn't know. Both of the men had widened eyes.

"Be nice, Peach," Luka said as we walked down the aisle together.

"She smells delicious," a curvy woman with long, dark, curly hair said. She was drop-dead gorgeous and a twinge of jealousy hit me as she walked toward us. "Is this her?"

"Yep." Luka turned toward me. "Sage, this is my sister, Viviana."

Oh. His sister.

"You can call me Vivi."

She looked like she was in her mid-twenties, with a heart-shaped face, high cheekbones, and dimples.

"Nice to meet you. I didn't know Luka had a sister." Her face was deadpan as she glared at me. I tried hard to give her a kind smile.

"I'm not his *real* sister. I'm actually his," she pointed to Winnie, who winked at me, "but I am with Luka's brother Strike . . . or at least, I would be if he hadn't been taken to the lab by one of *you*." She scowled at me and I swallowed hard.

The other woman was beautiful and voluptuous, with short, sandy blonde hair. As she made her way toward me, she had a genuinely sweet smile that put me at ease.

"You told *me* to be nice when you should have told *her* to be nice." She put her hand out to me and I shook it. "I'm Peach."

"Sage. It's nice to meet you."

Peach glanced at Luka with an uncomfortable face. "Just FYI. Laren is on her way to drop off the kids."

"Who's Lauren?" I asked.

Vivi stepped in close to me. "It's Laren. Like Karen, but with an L. You murdered her husband, Andrei, and she'll kill you if she finds out you're here." She shrugged like it was no big deal.

"That's enough, Vivi!" Winnie's voice was deep and stern.

"Whatever. It's *her* death sentence." She strolled over to a pew and took a seat as she continued to glare at me.

"We came here to share information," Luka said. "Then we'll leave."

"How much do they know?" I asked.

"These two know everything we know, Sage Stick." Winnie walked toward me with a smile.

"I was wondering when you were going to say hi to me, Pooh Bear!"

"Pooh Bear?" Peach threw her hand over her mouth to stifle a laugh.

"Shut up, Peach." Winnie tilted his head at me, giving me a fanged smile. "I was going to say hi, but I'm not one to get in the middle of a cat fight."

"Nah, you're more like one who *bets* on a cat fight," Drag said, making his way toward us. "So, what's going on?"

Luka's eyes wandered to me. "Go ahead."

Once again, I shared my story about the syringes. Luka then filled them in on our visit with Ravage.

"When will we know something about the solutions?" Drag asked Luka.

"Maybe in a few days."

Winnie's smile faded when he looked at me. "I got some information while you two were gone."

"Like what?" I asked.

Luka sniffed the air and then turned around. "Fuck."

The sound of feet pounding against the wood floors came from behind me.

"Uncle Luka!" A little girl with shoulder-length brown hair came running down the aisle. Her arms were stretched wide as she headed straight for Luka. He picked her up and gave her a hug, then her head whipped toward me. "Who are you?" she asked with a curious look on her face.

Luka's smile was kind and loving. "Her name is Sage."

"I told you not to run!" a woman said as she entered the chapel. She had thick, curly, auburn hair, and a toddler-sized boy on her generous hip.

"Your auntie is mad," Luka said before setting the girl down. His eyes met mine, a concerning look on his face.

The woman stopped halfway down the aisle and sniffed. She pulled the toddler closer, her eyes locked on me. "Who is she?"

"My name is Sage. I'm Luka's, umm, friend."

Her eyes drifted to Luka. "Why is she here?"

"She's been working with us to take down Venom."

Drag and Winnie both slowly made their way in front of me, and I worked hard to do my breathing techniques. The last thing I needed was for her to hear my fearful heart.

She tilted her head as she tried to look around them. "Is *she* Venom?"

"Let's be on our best behavior. There are children present," Drag reminded her.

"Arabelle, come here." The little girl ran toward her. "Viviana, come get Quinn and take him and Arabelle outside."

Vivi moved so fast, I didn't even see her until she was taking the boy from Laren's arms.

Vivi held out her hand. "Come on, Arabelle."

Once she was gone with the kids, a low growl left Laren and I stiffened. "Do you know who killed Andrei?" she asked.

Drag held his arms out in a peaceful manner as he moved toward her. "Let's all sit down and talk."

Laren took fast strides towards us. Winnie and Luka stepped in front of her before she got to me.

"Move!" she ordered. Neither of them did.

"You need to calm the fuck down!" Winnie spat. She shoved him aside.

"Stop it, Laren!" Luka growled. "You're not going to hurt her!"

"Did she do it? Did she kill Andrei?" Her voice cracked with panic, sadness, anger.

"Enough!" Peach shouted as she stepped in front of her. "You're not doing this! Not here, not anywhere!"

Laren's focus moved to Peach as she took fast breaths. Her jaw clenched before she looked back at Luka.

"How can you associate with the person who killed your brother?" She shook her head, tears filling her eyes. "He would be disappointed in you."

Hoping I could help the situation, I decided to speak up for myself. "It wasn't like that. I was just doing my—"

Laren was super fast and had me by the throat before I even blinked.

A large growl left Luka and veins popped up on his face. "Don't fucking touch her! I don't want to kill you, Laren," he whispered low, "but I will."

"You didn't, Luka." Laren's mouth fell open, her hand tightened on my throat. "I can't believe you fell—"

"That's enough!" Peach demanded.

"But she killed—"

Peach grabbed Laren by the throat and she let out a strangled cry. "I said, enough!"

Laren's hand fell from me as tears rolled down her cheeks. "I loved him," she wailed.

"I know you did, sweetie." Peach's hand left her throat, and immediately pulled her into a hug. Once Laren calmed down, Peach led her toward a pew.

Luka's hand went to my cheek and rubbed a thumb over it. "Are you okay?"

"Uh-huh." My breathing was still heavy and my throat was aching, but I was alive.

Remorse filled me as I watched Peach console Laren. I had killed the man she loved. The thought made my chest heavy.

"What the fuck are we going to do now?" Winnie asked.

Luka's hand fell from my face and then grabbed my hand before he turned his attention to Winnie. "I guess we should leave."

"No!" Laren's voice echoed as it rang through the church. "I want to talk to her!"

Unsure of what propelled me toward her, I pulled my hand out of Luka's and stepped forward.

"I'm sorry. I didn't know what I was doing," I choked as tears brimmed my lids. "I didn't know what my society was doing."

Luka stepped in front of me, blocking my view. I immediately side-stepped him.

"That's why I'm working with these guys. To end this!"

Laren said nothing as she glared at me and sniffed back tears.

"Come on. Let's go." Luka grabbed my arm and I yanked out of his grip.

"Stop, Luka! I'm trying to be honest here."

"Honesty isn't going to save you from getting killed!"

"I won't kill her," Laren exclaimed, getting my attention. "I won't do to Luka what *you* did to me!"

Confusion filled me as I wondered what she meant. Laren stood up and everyone stiffened, including me. With a shake of the head, she headed toward the door.

"Laren, wait!" Peach called out, but she kept walking.

"I'm sorry," I whispered. "I didn't mean . . ."

Peach shook her head. She gave me a kind smile as she patted my arm. "It's okay. She's just hurting."

"Can we come back in now?" Vivi asked from the doorway.

Winnie went toward her. "You were no help!" he said, and she shrugged. He took the toddler before handing him off to Drag.

"Sage, this is my nephew Quinn." Drag smiled proudly as he took the boy.

"Hi." I smiled at him.

He wiggled in Drag's arms, so he set him down on the ground.

"Don't do it, Quinn!"

As soon as Drag said the words, a slow smile spread across Quinn's face. He lowered himself to the ground and transformed into a light gray wolf pup. I let out a gasp.

"What the fuck," I whispered and everyone laughed. "I'm sorry. I didn't mean to curse in front of the children." *Or in church.* I threw my hand over my mouth out of embarrassment.

"It's okay," Drag said. "He likes to show everyone he's a wolven."

The wolf pup came up to me wagging his tail, and I was speechless.

"You can pet him," Peach said.

"What?" My mouth fell open as I contemplated it.

"Can I shift, Uncle Drag?" Arabelle asked, bringing my attention to her. "Please, please, please." She pulled on Drag's shirt and he let out an exasperated sigh.

"Go ahead."

In a flash, Arabelle transformed into a steel gray wolf pup who was twice the size of Quinn. My mouth was agape as I watched the two run off, playing together.

"Are you okay?" Drag asked.

I swallowed hard. "Yeah, umm."

"I'm assuming you've never seen a wolven shift before."

I shook my head and Drag laughed.

"I've never seen one in wolf form at all, let alone watched one shift."

Drag smiled proudly. "They're in my pack, but they sure don't listen. Most kids don't. They're my sister's kids."

"I'm confused," I whispered as I glanced at Luka. He moved next to me.

"About what, Princess?"

"She called you uncle, but she's a wolven."

"They call all of us aunt and uncle, but they aren't related to us," Luka said. "Only Drag."

"I hate to break up the fun, but we need to talk." Winnie locked eyes with me. "And you're not going to like it."

I let out a long sigh. "I'm not sure I'll like anything you say anymore."

"I finally got into Venom's security system, which allowed me to get into the roster where I found some things."

"What things?" Luka asked.

"For one, Sage is back on the roster for tomorrow night."

Luka's face angered as his eyes met mine. "What?"

"I already know. I found out before therapy."

"And you weren't going to tell me?" he asked.

I swallowed hard under his stare. "I was going to, I just haven't had time yet."

"There's another thing," Winnie said as he shifted uncomfortably.

At this point, I didn't think there was anything that would surprise me.

"Just tell me, Pooh Bear."

"When I was in the roster schedule, I referenced every suspicious death we had. The missions that the rat in Save sent out match the exact missions the rat in Venom sent out. So, we have *both* rats."

My brows raised. "And?"

"And one *isn't* Sorin."

"Who is it?" Luka asked.

"Erik."

My heart sped up at his name. I guess there was something that could surprise me.

"Impossible. There's no way!" My voice rang through the church as I went on the defense.

Winnie shrugged. "That's what the evidence points to."

"Did you tell Lyric you think her *brother* is a rat?" I asked.

He shook his head before throwing my own words back at me. "I was going to, I just haven't had time yet." He grinned and I rolled my eyes.

"This Erik guy is Lyric's brother?" Peach asked. "She seemed so nice. I couldn't imagine her having an asshole for a brother."

"He's not an asshole!" I shook my head with exasperation before a realization hit me. "Wait, you met her?"

"A lot happened while you two were gone, Sage Stick."

"Apparently, it did, Pooh Bear!" I rubbed my temples in frustration. "So, what do we do now?"

"I say we confront him."

"What good would that do, Peach?" Drag asked. "He could just lie."

My mind wandered to the incident between me and Luka, and I had a thought. "Yeah, but you guys would know, right? Luka knew I was lying in Vegas . . ." I stopped myself from finishing my sentence before I accidentally told everyone we fucked. I glanced at Luka and he was grinning arrogantly. I couldn't help but smile back at the memories.

Winnie's eyebrows furrowed in confusion as he glanced back and forth between us. "We can tell most of the time. It's not a sure process, though. Some people can pass lie detector tests."

"I think it's worth a try," Luka said. "I met him, and he didn't seem like he knew what was going on."

Another surprise. I would have never guessed Luka would defend Erik. I was happy he was giving him the benefit of the doubt.

"Is he working tonight?" Drag asked.

"No, he's off."

"Call and see if you can get him to meet us."

"Where?" I asked.

"My place," Winnie said. "But if we have to kill him and ruin my carpet, I'm going to be pissed."

CHAPTER 42

LUKA

Doubt filled me when Winnie named the rat. When I met Erik in the alley, his reaction seemed genuine. I didn't care how good an actor someone was, it's hard to fake the feelings of heartbreak and betrayal. The look on his face had said it all.

Sage pulled out her phone and I said, "Actually let's do it at my house. Tell him to be there at two a.m."

She had a look of confusion—I'm assuming because it was only midnight. I know I shouldn't be selfish with everything going on, but I needed to get Sage alone. I was pissed she hadn't mentioned going back to work.

"I don't know your address," she said.

"I'll text it to Lyric," Winnie said, pulling out his phone

Sage nodded before hitting the call button, then walked off to talk to Erik privately.

"So, Luka," Winnie said, bringing my attention to him. "Are you going to tell me what the fuck happened in Vegas?"

"I told you most of it."

Winnie crossed his arms and glared at me. "How many weeks did you go without feeding?"

"A few." I was purposely being vague, but the fact was, once vampires fall in love, they only want to feed off that person. When I realized I went three weeks without feeding, I knew I loved Sage. Winnie had also figured it out.

He nodded his head toward her. "Does *she* know why?"

"There's *nothing* to know, Winnie."

"Bullshit!"

"Drop it," I mumbled when I noticed Sage walking toward us.

"I will for now."

Sage had an anticipating look when she approached. "Erik said he'll be there."

"Lyric texted back and said she's coming," Winnie added. "I'm going to pick her up on the way so she's going to text Erik the address."

"Perfect. What are we going to do for the next two hours?" Sage asked.

"I need to do something. See you guys soon." I turned away and headed down the aisle.

"Bye, Luka," Peach said. "It was nice meeting you, Sage."

"Nice meeting you," Sage said before she followed me.

We stepped outside into the cold night air. My mind was fuming as I mounted my bike.

"Where are we going?" she asked as I handed her the helmet.

"My house."

"For what?"

"We need to talk," I said, trying to hold back anger. The look on her face told me she already knew what I wanted to discuss. "Unless you don't want to. Then I can take you back to your car."

She hesitated before she caved. "Let's go."

After she put the helmet on, she got on behind me. I fired up the engine as she wrapped her arms around my waist.

Thirty minutes later, we pulled into my driveway and I killed the engine.

We were both quiet as we made our way inside. Annie came running and greeted Sage with a wagging tail.

"Hey, buddy." She reached down and petted him.

I headed to the bar, filled a glass with whiskey, and threw it back. After refilling it, I turned toward her. "Do you want a drink?"

She crossed her arms. "What do you want to talk about, Luka?"

"Why didn't you tell me you got put back on the roster?" I downed my second glass and poured a third.

"I was going to, I just didn't think it was important right now."

"How the fuck is your safety *not* important?" I didn't mean to yell, but my temper was getting the best of me.

Her eyebrows furrowed together like she was annoyed. "Why do you care?"

I made my way across the room and yanked her into me causing her to release a small gasp.

"Do you seriously think I don't care about you, Princess?" She looked up at me with lustful eyes, the scent of citrus and vanilla filled my nostrils. I leaned into her and sniffed her. "You want me. I can smell it."

She pulled away and crossed her arms again. "What I want has nothing to do with what I *have* to do."

"You can't be with me if you stay with Venom."

"I know," she whispered, her eyes filling with regret.

"You know what they're doing, yet you still insist on staying!"

"Until I find out more information, I can't leave!"

"Then I can't guarantee your protection when we attack."

"I know that too."

"So, you're choosing to stay?" I asked. Her hazel eyes were filled with tears as she nodded. "Then there is nothing else to discuss." I turned away and poured another drink. After throwing it back, a hard breath left me.

"Luka," she whispered as I refilled my glass. "Please, don't be mad."

"What do you want from me?" I asked, without looking at her.

"I just want you to respect my choice."

"How can I respect your choice when you aren't giving me much of one, Sage? I have to choose between saving the entire vampire race and keeping you safe!" I threw back my drink and slammed the glass down.

"Why not both?"

More anger filled me as I thought about the impossible situation she placed me in. "You know that's not an option at this point!"

"Why not?"

I whipped around toward her. "Because I would choose *you*!"

"Why?" she asked in a hushed voice.

"Because I fucking love you!"

I had never said those words aloud to anyone since my mother was murdered, and I swallowed hard waiting for her to acknowledge it. She didn't. Her mouth was agape as she took fast breaths. I closed the distance between us and pulled her into me.

"Do you need a better reason, Princess?" The smell of lavender and vanilla filled my nostrils, and I took in a deep breath. A slow, knowing grin spread across my face. "You fucking love me, too."

"What?" She pulled away from me and went toward the bar. "No, I don't!"

"Admit it!"

"Whatever, Luka!" She poured herself four fingers of bourbon and quickly chugged it. After letting out a cough, she slammed the glass down. "This shit is gross."

"Trying to drown your feelings?" I asked, even though I was doing the same damn thing.

"I don't have feelings." Her heart sped up as she picked up the decanter and poured another glass. I strolled up to her back and slid my arms around her waist.

"Your heart says you're lying, so does your scent."

"Just because I smell like citrus and vanilla doesn't mean anything!"

I pushed her hair to the side, revealing her neck. "You smell like lavender and vanilla."

"What the hell does that mean?"

"When humans love, they release a scent." I kissed her neck and she let out a light moan. "You love me, admit it."

"Luka," she whispered.

Another kiss. "What?"

"What do *you* want?" she asked as I continued to devour her neck.

The decision was a lot easier for me to make than it was for her.

"I want *you*, Princess," I whispered against her skin. "Now tell me what *you* want."

She turned in my arms, her eyes glistening as she shook her head.

I ran my thumb across her lip. "What do you want?"

CHAPTER 43
SAGE

*H*ow the fuck did I get into this mess? Luka loved me, but there was no way I could be in love with a vampire. Right? At least, that's what I thought. When he screamed I love you, I wanted to scream it back—but I didn't. I couldn't. That was a vulnerability I didn't want.

"What do you want?" he asked as his thumb ran across my lip.

I knew what I wanted, but I couldn't answer him. What I wanted was forbidden—or maybe *unimportant* was a better word for it. I needed to get away from him, but my body wouldn't let me. Forcing myself to move, I backed away and bumped into the wall.

He moved in close, his body pressing against mine and avoided his eyes, immediately looking at the ground. His hand snaked out and grabbed my throat, forcing my face upward.

"Look right here, Princess," he whispered.

The thrill of fighting him was addicting—he was addicting. His eyes darkened as he looked at me from under his long lashes. His hand tightened on my throat and I swallowed hard from the pressure, the nervousness now getting to me. He leaned in close, his nose touching mine. His fangs were only a breath away, along with his lips.

"Are you going to answer me?" he whispered against my mouth.

"I . . . I don't know."

In one swift motion, he let go of my throat, grabbed my wrists, and pinned them above my head. I gasped as my heart raced with excitement.

"Yes, you do." He leaned in and sniffed me, his nose grazing my cheek. "I can smell what you want and it's delicious."

My heart thundered in my chest as I looked into his mysterious blue eyes. With his dark hair and hard chin, everything about him was perfect—a perfect man who would kill for me.

But unfortunately, he wasn't a man.

"I'm Venom," I whispered.

"And?"

"And you're a vampire."

He released his grip on my wrists and a huge part of me wished he hadn't. "Go."

"Are you kicking me out?"

"Yes. Get out!"

I crossed my arms, refusing to move. "What if I say no?"

In an instant, he was in my face. "I will remove you," he said through gritted teeth.

"Than fucking do it!"

He yanked me to him and my mouth fell open as I gasped for air.

"Aren't you scared of me?"

I stared up at him, no fear in my body, only lust and a sprinkle of a feeling I was trying to avoid.

"No," I whispered.

"You should be." He opened his mouth, revealing his long, sharp fangs. My breaths were now ragged as I fought for air.

My hands went up around his neck and I yanked his face down to mine. "You won't hurt me because . . ." I swallowed hard.

"Finish the sentence," he said against my lips.

"Because you love me," I whispered.

He took a deep breath before sniffing the air. "And you love me."

Completely avoiding that word, I chose a more appropriate word for what I wanted.

"Fuck me." I slammed my mouth onto his.

My nails dug into his neck with a needy desperation I didn't know I had. He slid a hand into my hair and gripped it tight. Using it as leverage, he yanked my mouth away from his and I gasped. It turned me on a lot more than it should have.

"I'm not going to be your fuck buddy, Princess. You don't get to *fuck* me and not *be* with me."

"Luka, please," I begged. I needed him—needed him inside of me.

"It's all of me or none of me." He pulled on my hair to tilt my head, exposing my neck. His mouth was warm against my skin.

"Come on," I moaned. "Please. I'll do anything."

He released my hair and his face met mine. "Then tell me what you want." His blue eyes begged for the answer. This wasn't the first time they burrowed into me—into my soul.

"I want *you*," I whispered. He tilted his head like he was waiting for me to say more. I swallowed hard as my heart raced. "All of you. I want all of you, Luka."

His mouth was on me, kissing hard. When he lifted me off the ground, my grip tightened on his neck. I wrapped my legs around him, then he carried me to the countertop. After sitting me down, he shoved me back, grabbed my shoes, and pulled them off. His hands immediately went to my jeans and unbuttoned them. I lifted my ass so he could take them off me.

Grabbing behind my knees, he pulled me to the edge of the counter before kneeling in front of me. His eyes darkened, then yanked my legs open and lowered his mouth on my core. Going straight for my clit, he sucked it in, making me moan in pleasure. I twined my fingers into his hair and gripped it tight as he consumed every inch of me.

My moans echoed through the house as my orgasm came fast. Every muscle in my body tightened as the blissful climax took over.

Luka stood up and wiped me from his face before yanking his shirt off. My eyes landed on his fully tattooed chest—it was hard, sweaty, and perfect. He unbuttoned his pants and lowered them with a grin.

He wasted no time grabbing my ankles and placing one on each shoulder before slamming into me. I had to hold the edge of the counter so I wouldn't slide around. His cock filled every inch of me and it felt amazing.

He snaked a hand out, yanked up my shirt, and squeezed one of my breasts. When I was close to coming again, he slowed his strokes. After dropping my legs from his shoulders, he flipped me onto my belly and crawled up on the counter, straddling my back. His cock pressed into my ass as he leaned into me.

"You're so fucking sexy," he whispered. The warmth of his mouth met my skin as he placed soft kisses on my neck.

His straightforwardness made me comfortable—vulnerable—and I was accepting of it. It was the first time I was ever *this* secure with someone—it made me want to tell him my deepest, darkest secrets.

He pulled away and settled between my legs before his hands grabbed my hips, lifting my ass into the air.

"Do you know you have a perfect ass, Princess?"

I let out a breathy laugh.

A stinging pain radiated across my skin when he smacked me hard. My mouth fell open in shock and I wondered how he knew I would like that, because I did.

He swatted my ass one more time before his hand glided between my legs and found my clit. My back arched as he rubbed in small, gentle circles. Right before I was about to come again, he pulled his hand away and I let out a sigh of frustration.

"You're so impatient," he said, before entering me.

His cock slammed against my g-spot. I gripped the edge of the counter and arched my back, a moan escaping my lips. His hands squeezed my ass tight as my orgasm built.

My mind went to the one thing I wanted—other than his cock. The blissful, mind-blowing, out of body, earth-shattering orgasm I had in Vegas.

"Bite me," I whispered, and he stopped moving.

One of his hands moved onto my hip as the other tightened in my hair. He yanked me up onto my knees—his cock still in me. He slowly moved in and out of me.

"I can make you come without it," he whispered into my ear, sending shivers down me.

I panted out fast breaths of pleasure. "I know."

The hand on my hip went to my breasts and yanked my bra up. His finger slowly grazed over my hardened nipple.

Anticipation filled me when he lowered his mouth to my neck. As he kissed and sucked, a fang raked across my skin, causing me to suck in a deep breath.

"Is that what you want, Princess?"

"Yes," I whispered.

He pulled my hair tighter. "Louder."

"Yes!" I screamed.

The pain of his bite stung for a moment before the blissful warmth took over. My orgasm seemed to radiate from every inch of my body. The euphoric feeling was like walking on clouds while the best feeling in the world brought you to the highest climax possible. A climax that lit up every nerve, every muscle, every feeling deep in my soul.

He released my vein and shoved me back to my hands and knees, pounding into me hard. A loud moan left him before warm cum filled me.

Exhaustion hit hard and I fell flat onto my stomach. He laid over my back as we both fought for air. His fingers grazed lightly in circles over my skin, sending goosebumps down my body.

This sex felt different from the one in Vegas. It felt like he had laid claim on me. Or maybe, we had laid claim on each other.

After a few minutes, he got up. "Don't move."

The sound of a kitchen drawer opened and then running water before he smacked my ass. "On your knees, Princess."

"So commanding." I did what he said and got back on my hands and knees.

He slid a warm, wet towel between my legs and cleaned up the mess he left behind. For a second, I panicked. No one had ever done that for me. Before I had a chance to move, he grabbed me around my waist and pulled me off the counter.

"If we hurry, we can rinse off."

"What?"

"Oh, shut up! We're doing this!" He carried me down the hall as I laughed.

We went into the bathroom and he lowered me to the ground before turning on the water in the shower.

"Hop in. I'm going to grab our shit."

I took the rest of my clothes off and stepped into the shower. A minute later, music came over speakers, surprising me. It seemed to be coming from everywhere.

He stepped in the shower behind me. "Your clothes are on my bed."

"Where is the music coming from?" I asked.

"My iTunes playlist. I have speakers in the ceilings of every room."

"That's kind of amazing and I'm extremely jealous."

He pulled me into him and brushed the hair out of my face. "I meant what I said, Princess. I love you."

Being the asshole I am, I couldn't force myself to say it back. "This doesn't make us friends," I said sarcastically. I bit my lip, hoping I didn't make him mad.

He smirked. "Lavender and vanilla," he whispered before his lips pressed against mine.

CHAPTER 44
LUKA

Thirty minutes later, I was laying across the bed, watching Sage with a perma-grin on my face. She was wearing underwear and my t-shirt, her hair flipped over as she ran a blow dryer over it. She might not be able to tell me she loved me, but I knew she did. She loved me with every piece of her body and soul and it scared the shit out of me. I was also fearful knowing she had to go back to work, but I thought I had come up with a plan.

At least for now, I knew she would be safe from *most* vampires after what I did in the kitchen. It was tradition to ask our mates if they were okay with being marked *before* we marked them. When I came inside of her, I released an extra vampire pheromone, marking her with it. I didn't mean to do it, but it happened before I even realized what I was doing. Most vampires would stay away from her now, but it would wear off in a few weeks. If I had my way, I would mark her every day.

She's going to be pissed when she finds out.

She turned the blow dryer off and flipped her head back upright.

"Why are you smiling like an idiot?" she asked.

"You're such an asshole for someone who's so gorgeous."

She laughed. "You knew I was an asshole before you . . ." She hesitated, biting her lip.

Grabbing her hand, I yanked her down onto the bed. "Love. Just say it. It's a four letter word!"

"I have to throw on clothes before everyone gets here." She went to get up and I pulled her back. "Stop, Luka. I have to get dressed!"

"You'll get dressed when I say you can."

She laughed and leaned into me. "I like it when you're dominant." Her lips met mine with a perfect kiss before she rolled off the bed.

"You may regret those words, Princess!"

Her eyes widened and I winked.

Unless I wanted to hang out with my friends in only a towel, I figured I should throw something on too.

Once I was fully dressed, I headed into the kitchen. I had already put on a pot of coffee, and cleaned the counter where we fucked.

Sage came out a few minutes later.

"Do you want a cup of coffee?" I asked.

"Sure."

I poured two mugs and tried to hand her one.

"I want the Star Wars one," she said with a pout.

"I'm going to change your name to Spoiled Princess." She laughed and I sighed before handing her my *favorite* mug. "Come with me."

I went into the living room and grabbed a throw off the couch before heading for the front door.

Sage followed me as I stepped out onto the wrap-around porch. I took a seat in a rocking chair and she took one next to me.

"It's chilly," she said with a shiver. I handed her the throw. Her face was confused as she took it. "How did you—"

"I know you, Princess." I smiled before taking a sip of coffee.

She set her mug on the little table between our chairs and covered herself with the blanket. "It's beautiful out here," she said as she retrieved her mug.

"I like being outside of town. The sound of nature is more soothing than the city."

"It definitely is."

"I may have come up with a plan for tomorrow."

"What's that?" she asked.

"I figured I can have you and Winnie both on an earpiece while I follow you around. He can track you and

I can stay within a block of where you're at. That way we can make sure you're safe."

She took a sip of her coffee before she spoke. "Maybe."

The sound of motorcycles in the distance rang through the night air. I smiled as my friends pulled down the driveway.

"Whoa," Sage whispered. "Peach rides a Harley?"

"Yep." I stood up as did she.

"She's a fucking badass!"

"She is," I agreed, as we headed toward the driveway.

Winnie was in the front of the group with Lyric on the back of his bike. His eyes widened before he glared at me.

Shit. He smelled my mark on Sage.

Peach pulled up and her eyes also widened in surprise before she smiled.

Drag had Vivi on the back of his Harley. Vivi quickly dismounted and headed towards me. The look on her face told me she smelled it, too.

"I guess she's untouchable now."

I smirked. "She always has been."

"You don't have to like me," Sage said to her. "Like everyone else I'm just trying to help find out what's going on."

"Who said I didn't like you?" Vivi grinned before strolling off.

"This is a nice house! It's very country and peaceful." Lyric turned toward me. "I figured you would live in a black castle or something."

Sage laughed and I shook my head. "Nice to see you, Lyric."

"I'm kidding. You know I love you, Luka." She leaned in and kissed my cheek.

My eyes immediately went to Sage as I gave her a look that said, *see how easy it is to say I love you.*

"Where's Erik?" she asked, ignoring me.

"He should be here soon," Lyric said as Winnie took her hand. He said nothing before he led her toward the house.

Peach smiled as she walked up to us. I knew she was happy that I marked Sage. "Nice to see you again, Sage."

"You, too."

"You got coffee, Kid?"

I smiled. "Anything for you, Peachy Keen."

"Perfect! I'm going to go make a cup and say hi to Annie." She gave me a wink before heading into the house.

Drag took one look at me and sighed. "I'll see you two inside."

All my friends knew I marked Sage. Some of them might be disappointed, but I didn't give a fuck.

"Should I wait for Erik?" Sage asked.

"He'll be here in less than a minute."

Her face was confused. "How do you know? Can you smell him?"

I laughed, then shook. "No, but I can hear the gravel crunching below his tires."

A few seconds later, headlights came around the bend. The blue mustang pulled up behind the Harleys and parked. Erik got out and hesitantly walked towards us.

"Hey," Sage said in a small voice.

"Hey." His eyes wandered to me. He held out his hand and I shook it. "It's nice to meet you without being choked."

"Nice to meet you."

His gaze drifted to the Harleys. "Are you in a biker gang?"

"No. Those are my friends."

His heart sped up in fear and I tried to make small talk so he would be comfortable. For Sage's sake—not his. I didn't give a shit about him, but I cared for her.

"That's a sweet-ass Mustang you have."

His brows furrowed slightly. "Umm, thanks."

"I'm more into classic Mustangs, but the custom job on yours makes it stand out."

He nodded before the conversation went silent.

"I guess we should go inside," Sage said. Erik's eyes wandered to her, a look of adoration on his face.

I didn't know why I felt threatened by this guy, but I did. It made me want to make sure he knew Sage was *mine*, since he couldn't smell my mark.

"Come on, Princess." I grabbed her hand and she immediately tried to wiggle it out, but I was stronger than her. I grinned arrogantly at Erik before turning toward the house.

Once inside, Sage introduced everyone to Erik. Some of us grabbed coffee and others grabbed alcohol before making our way into the living room. My house was pretty big and I had plenty of furniture.

Peach and Vivi plopped in the recliners and were chatting away about something. Lyric took a seat on the loveseat and Erik quickly took one next to her. Winnie gave him a dirty look before sitting on the couch next to Drag. He put his backpack between his feet on the floor with a sigh before clearing his throat. The room got quiet.

"We are gathered here today to celebrate—"

"Shut up, Winnie!" Vivi said and everyone laughed, except for Erik. He seemed unamused and extremely uncomfortable.

"It's Winston!"

Vivi rolled her eyes. "You've been saying that for fifty years. Give it a rest, brother!"

Annie was scratching at Lyric's leg, wanting to be picked up. She bent down and put him on her lap.

Erik reached over and petted him before his attention went to me. "So, what's this meeting about?"

Drag leaned forward, giving Erik his attention as he rested his elbows on his knees. "What all have you been told?"

"We told him everything, except for what I was told today," Sage said.

"I got this." Winnie pulled a tablet out of his backpack and clicked around on it. "The evidence shows you're a rat, Erik," he blurted.

"Winston!" Lyric reprimanded. She shook her head in disappointment. "You could be a little more kind."

Erik's face was red with anger. "I'm not a fucking rat!"

"The info I found shows you sent leads to everyone that has been killed or taken to the lab."

"Even though I'm a commander, I don't send that many missions out!"

Winnie headed to Erik and showed him the information.

"This here shows all the tablets and the serial numbers Venom assigns to its members. Over here shows who they belong to. This one is yours. It's the same one that sent out all these missions that are highlighted."

Erik's eyes skimmed the tablet. "Wait. When I'm in the field, someone else sends out the missions. I was on duty that night." Erik pointed to the screen. "And the night after that was when Deren . . ." He glanced at me and Sage.

"Hold on. Let me see." Sage went and looked at the tablet, her eyes wandering over the screen. "This one here was the night I met Luka. Erik definitely didn't send the lead for Drifter's bar. I was with him the whole time. When that lead came into Deren's tablet, Erik was driving."

"You're right. But how could someone send it from my tablet if it was with me?"

"Someone must be good with software," Winnie said. "Do you know any hackers?"

Sage let out a snicker. "Yeah. Naomi."

"Sorin's sister?" I asked.

"Yep," Erik said. "She works in the security system department running all their software."

"Told you he wasn't a rat!" Lyric blurted as she looked at Winnie.

"I just follow the evidence, sweetheart." He smiled and winked at her.

Erik glanced suspiciously between the two of them.

"So, we just kill Sorin, Naomi, and Finneas," Vivi said with a smile. "Problem solved."

"We can't kill people. What if we had killed Erik before we knew he wasn't a rat?" Peach took a sip of her coffee before finishing what she was saying. "We have to give people the benefit of the doubt before we do anything. We need more evidence."

"Maybe we can get some more tomorrow." I turned toward Sage. "Who all are you on duty with?"

"My dad said he put me with Erik to make me more comfortable my first night back."

"Perfect!" Winnie chimed in as he made his way over to the couch and sat back down.. "I can hack into the system and see if there is anything odd going on with his tablet. Since you're with him, you can see what he's doing."

"Is it safe for Sage to be out there knowing that people in Venom and Save are trying to kill her?" Peach asked.

"I was going to have Winnie track her while I followed," I answered.

"And since I'll be with her, she'll be safe," Erik said.

"I'm on guard duty, so I will probably be stuck in the tower again," Lyric added. "Otherwise, I would help."

"I'll go with Luka for backup," Drag chimed in, "since Winnie will be stuck at the computer."

Sage let out an extended sigh before she plopped down on the couch next to Drag. "I'm sick of people wanting to kill me. First vampires, now my own damn people."

"Well, at least you don't have to worry about vampires wanting to kill you as much now."

Fuck. Shut up, Winnie! I said in my head as I glared at him. I reminded myself to punch him later.

"Why not?" Sage asked.

"They won't come near you since you're marked."

Her eyebrows furrowed. "Marked? Like I have a mark on my back?"

"No, like Luka marked you."

Sage's face turned to one of confusion. "What the fuck does that mean?"

"Oh, umm, I thought you knew." Winnie looked over at me and I shook my head.

"Shut up, Winnie."

"Don't say shit to him for telling me something you're *obviously* keeping secret from me. Tell me what you did, Luka!"

I hesitated for a few seconds before I spoke. "I marked you."

"Yeah, but what does it mean, exactly?"

All eyes in the room were on me. The humans looked confused. Peach seemed concerned, as did Drag. Winnie had an apologetic face. Vivi looked amused, with a huge smile on her face.

I took a deep breath and ripped off the bandaid. "I covered your scent with mine."

"Oh. What does covering my scent do?"

"All vampires and wolven would know you were taken," Vivi said with a smile.

"Excuse me? What the fuck do you mean, *taken*?" Sage moved to the edge of her seat with a pissed off face.

"It was for your safety, Princess. Nothing more."

"It's kind of like the 1920s version of a promise ring," Winnie chimed in.

Sage jumped up in a panic. "What the fuck does that even mean? I don't want a promise ring!"

"Winnie, you aren't helping," Drag said.

"Actually, he is because he isn't lying to me." Her eyes drifted to Winnie. "Tell me exactly what marked means, *and* what it does." She pointed at me. "You be quiet!"

"Umm, see, when vampires, umm. We can . . ."

She crossed her arms as she glared at him. "Spit it out, Pooh Bear!"

"It's just a thing we can do to help protect humans, that's all."

"And what does it involve?" she asked.

Winnie shifted uncomfortably. "This should be a private conversation between you and Luka."

"Tell me what it means, Winnie!"

"I'll tell you," Drag said, and all eyes in the room shot to him. He let out a hard breath before he continued. "A vampire can leave their scent on a human so other vampires won't go near them, unless they really, and I mean *really,* want to kill you. The more a person wants to hurt you the stronger the smell is for them. They would have to be pretty old to fight the urge. It's like a vampire deterrent to everyone except Luka."

"Oh. Why didn't you just say that?" Sage asked. "Can't you guys just mark my friends, then?"

Internally, I was laughing. If she had any clue what marked meant, she wouldn't have said that.

"I don't want to be marked," Erik said with an appalled face.

"I will mark Lyric if she wants."

"Winnie!" Peach said sternly. "Now's not the time."

"If he wants to mark her, let him." Sage turned toward Lyric. "Are you okay with it?"

"Whatever keeps me safe is fine with me." Lyric smiled as she looked at Winnie, who was grinning from ear to ear.

This . . . now this was fucking amusing. Winnie was *down* to mark her.

I laughed aloud, as did Vivi.

"So, how does it work?" Sage asked.

"We should talk about this later, Princess."

"For fuck's sake, Luka, tell me!"

"Okay, fine. You want to know so bad. It has to be done during sex!"

Sage's mouth fell open. The room got quiet except for Vivi's laughter.

CHAPTER 45
SAGE

At this point, I realized I didn't know a fucking thing about vampires until I met Luka. Shock not only filled me but also my friends as I took in their gaping mouths.

How the fuck? I had no words. My secrets weren't so secret anymore.

As I glanced around at everyone, I noticed none of the supernaturals seemed shocked.

Peach and Drag both looked sympathetic.

Vivi was laughing hysterically.

Winnie mouthed 'sorry' to me.

They already knew, and I felt like a fool.

"I told you we should talk privately," Luka said, bringing my focus to him. "But as usual, you didn't listen."

He was right. My stubbornness was the reason I insisted on knowing right that second. When the embarrassment flooded me, I wished I would have just kept my damn mouth shut for once.

"I think it's time for us to go," Erik said with a look of discomfort on his face.

"I can't go," Lyric said. "I haven't been marked yet."

My eyes widened—so did Erik's.

"Lyric!" he yelled.

Winnie hopped to his feet. "Hell yeah, I'm ready!"

"Sit down, Winnie!" Peach commanded.

"I was kidding," Lyric said with a small smile. "Tough crowd."

Winnie sat back down with a pained face. "I was kidding, too."

"This is so much fun!" Vivi announced. She laughed even harder as she pulled out the footrest on the recliner.

I'm glad it was fun for her. I was fucking mortified!

Drag cleared his throat, bringing everyone's attention to him. "Anyway. So, the plan for tomorrow is Luka and I follow Sage and Erik."

"While I hack," Winnie added.

"I can help if you need me, Kid," Peach said.

"You can't," Vivi interrupted. "We have the children's play."

"Shit! Well, I can help after."

"I forgot about the children's play," Drag mumbled before looking at Luka. "I may be a little late, but I'll catch up."

Embarrassed, and needing to take a breath, I turned into the dining room and headed toward the bar. With a sigh, I poured myself a shot and drank it. I could hear everyone still talking about plans from the living room.

"Are you okay, Princess?"

I threw back another shot before turning around. "Yeah. I guess."

Luka's face was rueful as he slid his arms around me and pulled me in.

"I didn't realize I was marking you until it happened, since I had never done it before. I was supposed to ask your permission first and I didn't. I'm sorry."

"I'm not even mad you did it. I'm mad at myself for insisting on being told in front of everyone."

"Everyone already knew but Erik and Lyric. They smelled it when they got here."

"Figures." I sighed.

"Is it okay if I mark you again when it wears off?"

A smile played across my face. "Depends. What do I get?"

"Anything you want, Princess." Luka leaned in and his lips pressed against mine.

"Seriously, Sage!" Lyric's loud voice broke up our kissing. "Why didn't you tell me?"

"I'm going to go see if anyone wants a beer," Luka said before letting go of me.

Lyric placed her hands on her hips. "You do that, Romeo!"

He grinned at her on his way out.

"What happened to our motto? Blood of the coven, remember?"

"I remember, Lyric." I stepped up to her and took her hands. "I'm sorry I didn't tell you. I just didn't know how to navigate my feelings. It's weird having them for something you were raised to hate."

"Tell me about it!" she said and my eyes widened.

"You and Winnie?" I asked, even though I kind of knew.

"Not yet. I'm struggling, too. Believe me, he wants to." We both laughed.

"It's hard, isn't it?"

She sighed and nodded. "It is. I really just want to be with him."

"At this point, I'm just going to do what I want. You should, too."

"Erik will flip out if I get with Winnie! He was shifting uncomfortably during the whole marking conversation."

"I saw." We both laughed again. "But he'll either get over it, or he won't."

She nodded. "So, how long have you two been doing it?" she asked.

I bit my lip. "It didn't happen until Vegas."

"I knew it was going to!" She smiled big. "Is the sex good?"

"Fantastic!" We both giggled.

"Did he, umm, bite you?" she asked in a hushed voice.

"Yeah," I whispered. "It was amazing. I'll have to tell you all about it later."

"Hey, ladies," Peach said as she entered the room. "Just so you're aware, we can hear everything you're saying, since we're vampires and all."

My mouth fell open and I dropped Lyrics hands. "What?"

"Luka is in there grinning arrogantly, per the norm. Winnie gave him a nod of approval. They were just going to keep listening."

"Oh god. So, Winnie knows I want to have . . . oh god." Lyric threw her hands over her face.

"Shut up, Peach!" Winnie hollered from the living room. "You're ruining it."

"Maybe you should talk later." Peach grinned before turning away.

"I'm literally not allowed to have any secrets anymore!"

"No, you're not, Sage Stick!" Winnie yelled.

"Shut up, Pooh Bear!" I shook my head. "I hate him."

"No, you don't!"

Lyric and I both laughed as we headed back into the living room.

"Follow me and I'll show you!" Luka said excitedly. Erik stood up and followed him out.

"Where are they going?" I asked.

"To talk about cars," Vivi said. "Luka's showing him his Mustangs."

"Luka has Mustangs?" I vaguely remembered seeing a couple of covered cars in the garage last time I was here, but I was too traumatized to care.

"They're classics!" Drag said before he and Winnie headed to the kitchen.

Wanting to see the cars, I sauntered toward the garage. Luka was pulling the cover off when I opened the door. It was a beautiful Mustang, sleek and black, with two thick white stripes down the middle.

"Whoa! A Shelby GT500! What year?" Erik asked. He had a look of awe on his face that I hadn't seen in a while.

"1967." Luka crossed his arms, leaned back, and admired his car.

"No way! Those are super rare and expensive."

"I got it when it was new. I'm two hundred and seventy-six." Luka told him his exact age and it seemed like a flex to me. I laughed to myself.

Erik's excitement dropped when he heard his age, his posture becoming nervous. "Oh. Well, it's beautiful."

"Want to see the other one?" Luka asked.

"Don't tell me you have two Shelbys?"

"Nah. Candy apple red Mach One." Luka ripped the cover off the second car and Erik's eyes lit up like a Christmas tree.

"1969?" he asked.

Luka radiated pride.. "Yep!"

Pleased that they were getting along, I smiled and shut the door, allowing them their guy time..

As I walked into the kitchen, Winnie and Drag were pulling meat from the fridge.

"What are you guys doing?" I asked.

"Barbequing."

"It's three am, Winnie!"

"If we did it in the daylight, Sage Stick, we'd be the ones getting cooked."

I laughed before heading back into the living room. Peach was telling Lyric about this cobbler recipe she'd been making for years. With Erik and Luka in the garage bonding over cars, Drag and Winnie prepping food, and the girls being social, this serene feeling came over me. It seemed peaceful.

Too peaceful.

That's when the panic set in. Every time I felt good about something in my life, it meant disaster was coming. It was like the calm before the storm. The air felt like it had left the room and I was being suffocated as I tried hard to breathe.

Peach's eyes met mine. "What's wrong?" she asked.

I shook my head. "Nothing."

"You're lying," Vivi said. "Your heart is racing like crazy."

"I just had a bad feeling. That's all. I have anxiety. It happens."

"You're in good hands, Sage. There's nothing to worry about," Peach said with a smile.

I nodded before I took a seat on the couch. Shoving my hands between my thighs, I sat there quietly, trying to calm my racing heart. I hoped the bad feeling wasn't me dying.

CHAPTER 46
LUKA

The sunrise was an hour away. Drag had grilled up some great tasting food and we were all stuffed. Erik opened up a little more after I showed him my cars and he actually seemed like a decent guy. I was trying to be as nice as possible for Sage's sake.

We were all outside, saying our goodbyes.

"Thanks for the hospitality, Kid." Peach pulled me in for a hug before hugging Sage. "It was nice seeing you again, sweetie."

"You too."

"I like this." Peach pointed at us. "You two look cute together." She smiled before walking away.

I grinned at Sage and she sighed.

"Peach! Don't forget to text me the cobbler recipe!" Lyric called out as she hopped on the back of Winnie's bike.

"I won't, Lyric!"

"This is so weird. It's like . . ." Erik stopped talking and shook his head.

"It's like vampires are humans that just live longer?" I asked.

"Exactly. It's nothing like what we were taught."

Drag started up his bike with Vivi on the back.

"Bye!" She waved with a smile and Erik looked at her adoringly.

"Don't let her cuteness fool you," I said, making his eyebrows rise. "She'll snap your neck with that smile."

"Luka!" Sage reprimanded.

"What? I'm just being honest."

"On that note, I'm going to take off. Thanks for dinner." Erik held out his hand and I shook it before he turned toward Sage. "I don't see your Jeep. Do you need a ride?"

"Actually, I'm staying here." She bit her lips nervously, awaiting his reaction.

Astonishing to me, he smiled. "I'll see you at dusk."

Erik got in his Mustang and followed the bikes down the driveway.

I'd been dying to get my hands on Sage all night so I immediately pulled her into me. "You're staying with me, Princess?"

"I am. Is that okay?"

"That's more than okay. I will go to your apartment, pack all your shit and—"

"One step at a time! Geez." She laughed and I kissed her.

Once inside, we got ready for bed. After using the bathroom and brushing my teeth, I set an extra toothbrush on the sink for Sage. When I crawled into bed, Annie whined, so I reached down and picked him up. He burrowed under the covers and scratched before finally settling.

Sage headed into the bathroom and when she came out, she was wearing my t-shirt again. She looked sexy as hell in it. After climbing into bed beside me, she let out a relaxed sigh. I yanked her to me and pressed my lips to hers. The sweet and intoxicating scent of her lure seeped into me.

"You smell good," I whispered.

"I have a hypothetical question."

I knew exactly where this conversation was going, so I grinned. "Ask away."

"Let's say I'm in a room with Lyric and she releases a lure, how do you know it's hers and not mine?"

"Because all lures smell different. Hers smells like sweet lilacs."

Her eyes widened before her forehead creased. "How do you know?"

"Because I've smelled hints of it when she's around Winnie."

"Do other people's lures turn you on?" she asked, and I could tell she was a bit jealous.

"When we smell someone's lure, it makes our body react in a sexual manner. We get this tingling feeling, and sometimes it makes my dick hard." She giggled at my honesty. "The level of attraction to the person determines the strength of the effect. If we aren't attracted, it's just light tingles."

"How do you know the difference between my lure and, umm, the other one?" She bit her lip as she refused to say the word.

"Your love scent gives us a feeling of being safe, protected. It's hard to explain, but it's like you're being nourished and loved. It pulls on your emotional heart strings."

"That's kind of amazing." She lifted her hand and ran her fingers around the hair on my chest.

"I could get used to this, Princess."

"Don't get too comfortable. I have to go home when we wake up."

"Why did you decide to stay?" I asked as I brushed the hair out of her face. The only light in the room was a salt lamp Peach had gotten me and it was dimmed on low.

"I don't know." She bit her lip, her eyes saddening.

I ran my thumb across her lip, stopping her. "Tell me."

She blinked back tears. "I have a feeling I'm going to die."

"There is no way in hell I will let that happen." Tears fell down her cheeks and I wiped them away with my thumb. "We can leave town now and never come back." The words fell out of my mouth before I even acknowledged what I was saying.

Would I leave my friends for her? I had half a mind to talk them all into coming with us.

"We can't just leave, Luka. There are too many people relying on us."

"I could turn you into a vampire. Then you would be stronger." Her eyes widened, as the sound of her thundering heart filled my ears. "Is that a no?"

She laughed before asking more questions. "If I was a vampire, would you still be able to mark me?"

I grinned at the fact that she wanted to be marked. "I would and it would have the same effect."

"What does the marking smell like?"

"It's like an earthy, sweet pepper smell to those who don't want to hurt you. The more someone wants to do harm, the stronger the odor. I have never wanted to kill someone who was marked, so I've never smelled it myself, but Peach explained that when you hate someone and they're marked, it's almost impossible to go near them. The sweet pepper scent turns to more of an ammonia smell that makes your eyes water and burn. The more you try to harm, the stronger it gets. It's literally a deterrent."

She blinked repeatedly like she was trying to figure it out.

"Do you want me to turn you, Princess?" I asked again.

Of course, she completely avoided my question. "How many people have you turned?"

"Just one asshole," I said with a smile.

"Who?"

"Winnie."

Her face filled with astonishment as her mouth gaped open. "You're Winnie's dad?"

"Origin," I reminded her with a laugh.

"That's so weird. Why did you turn him?"

There was no way I would ever tell anyone's story on how they were turned because I would expect the same respect from my friends.

"That's Winnie's story to tell. Not mine."

"Then tell me yours. How did you become a vampire?"

"It's a long drawn out story and it's not even—."

"I have time," she interrupted with a smile.

The story she wanted to hear was one very few people knew—my brothers, Ravage, Winnie, Drag, and Peach. Looking into her beautiful hazel eyes, I couldn't say no. A huge part of me realized that night that I would *never* be able to say no to her for the rest of our lives.

"It was a long time ago. My brothers and I were human then. My mother was a strong, hard-headed woman, but was kind, sweet, and honest to a fault. Not to mention the most amazing person I have ever known. One night she went into town on horseback. She always went alone after our father died of pneumonia when we were in our teens, so she was used to it. I wasn't sure what could have kept her there so late, but she wasn't back by the time the sun was going down. I hesitated to go looking for her, hoping she would come up the hill at any moment. It was a mistake on my part."

I swallowed hard as I relived the memories. Her hand went to my cheek and rubbed. I took a deep breath and continued.

"About thirty minutes after the sun went down, my brothers and I mounted our horses to go find her. When we got into town, the woman who ran the shop mom had been visiting told us she had left hours ago. We talked to a few more people before we found out her horse was stolen, forcing her to leave on foot. With it being almost an hour-long walk into town, we started to panic. Since we'd taken the riding trail in and didn't see her, we assumed she took one of the walking trails home. There were two ways to get to our house on foot. One she took often and one she rarely took. Since I was the oldest, I sent Strike and Andrei on the easier trail together and I took the dangerous one. I found her not long after that."

With sympathetic eyes, Sage wiped a tear from my face I didn't even know was there before I forced myself to continue.

"I jumped off my horse and ran to her. She was barely alive at this point. She was . . ." I cleared my throat. "She appeared to be raped and brutally beaten. What I didn't know was she was almost drained dry of her blood as well. She couldn't talk to tell me who did it or what happened. I held her in my lap until she died."

Sage put a hand over her mouth as she sniffed back tears.

"I alerted my brothers and we found the nearest sheriff, but not much came of it. There were no witnesses and eventually her case went cold. Shortly after the funeral, Andrei was trying his damndest to find out who killed her, talking to everyone in town. That's when he met Ravage. He told Andrei to quit looking or he was going to get himself killed. When Andrei told me and Strike about this, we went looking for him, thinking he was the one who did it. Ravage explained it wasn't him, but something sinister was going on, and we should stop poking around.

"After a few days of following him everywhere he went, which was hard, since we could only find him at night, Ravage caved. He let us know he could help us, but it was a sacrifice of life. Confused by the statement, we pushed him for more information. That was when he finally told us about vampires. There was no TV back then, and the story just seemed unreal, but once he bared his fangs and then showed us how strong and fast he was, we were pretty convinced."

Sage let out a small breathy laugh before sniffing.

"He said he couldn't help us kill the vampire who did it, but he knew who was responsible. He offered to turn us and teach us how to hunt and get strong. The thing was, the vampire who did this to my mother was a few hundred years old, so there was a chance we wouldn't survive if we tried to kill him. We agreed to Ravage's terms, which were pretty simple. Don't kill unless threatened, don't turn just anyone, and don't get caught. After he turned us, we spent years training with him, practically making ourselves lethal weapons. Strike and I were better at fighting than Andrei. Arrogance and a need to taunt were always his downfall. I'm assuming that's how you got him."

Sage swallowed hard. "I'm sorry," she whispered.

I nodded as I ran a finger over her cheek, wiping away another tear.

"Over the years, we formed a bond with Ravage. He was like a father figure to us. We went everywhere with him, hopping from town to town, figuring someday we would get our revenge and we did. Ravage got word from a friend that there was a female vampire with information on the one we were looking for. That's how I met Peach."

Sage's mouth fell open in shock, and I smiled.

"We went to talk to her. She let us know he was only a few towns over, so we quickly devised a plan to kill him. Ravage lied when he said he wouldn't help. He wasn't going to let any of us get hurt, so he helped us kill the asshole. That was the one and only time I have ever killed someone because I wanted to . . . until I killed Mannie. I'm not going to explain what we did to him, but it was way worse than what Mannie got."

I became quiet and Sage's eyes trailed over my face before she leaned in and gently pressed her lips against mine. "I'm sorry, Luka."

I pushed her hair behind her ear and pulled her close.

"Good night, Princess."

"Good night."

"I love you," I whispered into the top of her head.

She let out a settling sigh. "Lavender and vanilla," she whispered, and my heart almost fell out of my chest.

CHAPTER 47

SAGE

The sound of the steel shutters opening woke me. I had rolled over at some point in my sleep and Luka was snuggled against my back.

"I could get used to this," he whispered, his hard cock pressed into my ass.

"What time is it?"

"Almost Seven."

"Shit! I have to get home to shower."

"You don't have to be on duty until nine."

"I'm not sure I even have clean clothes." I tried to get up and his arms tightened around me, making me laugh.

After pushing my hair aside with his nose, his warm lips pressed against my neck. My laughter immediately turned into a moan, which only made his kisses deeper—wetter. His hand moved from my stomach to my breast and squeezed. Pushing my ass back, I rubbed it on his hardness. His hand was quick to move under my shirt, quickly finding my nipple. As he rubbed and squeezed, my clit started throbbing, making me move my ass more.

"You smell amazing," he whispered, his deep voice radiating through me, making me shudder.

When his hand left my nipple, I was a little disappointed until it went into my panties and a finger slid inside me.

"Oh. You're wet already, Princess."

"Uh, huh," I moaned breathlessly.

He pulled his finger out of me, dragging the wetness up to my clit that was twitching uncontrollably, begging to be touched. His fingers traced circles around it, never making contact. With urgency, I grabbed his wrist and tried to make him touch me.

"I'm in control here," he whispered and I let out a breathy laugh. "Actually, don't move."

I wondered what the fuck was so important to stop right in the middle of what we were doing.

He shifted on the bed and reached for the bedpost. From this angle, I had no idea what he was doing. He pulled on the top of it and the wood popped open. Then he flipped up the other one before hopping off the bed and doing the bottom two posts.

He lifted the edge of the blanket, and pulled Annie out before putting him in the hall, and shutting the door.

There was a huge grin on his face when headed to the dresser, where he opened the top drawer and pulled out what looked like rope.

Oh, fuck, I thought to myself as excitement filled me.

"I saw handcuffs in your nightstand drawer, so I assume you aren't opposed to these."

There were leather cuffs at one end of the ropes and metal carabiner rings at the other. I said nothing as he clipped them on the bottom bedposts before his eyes met mine.

"Are you okay with this, Princess?"

"Yes," I breathed as I rolled to my back and spread eagle on the bed, ready for him.

He could do whatever the fuck he wanted to me. In my mind, I could die tonight, so I was ready to go out with a bang.

He grinned, strapping the cuffs around my ankles before moving to the top bedposts where he latched the metal clips, then cuffed my wrists.

"Alexa, play my kinky playlist."

"What?" I laughed as 'Love is a Bitch' by Two Feet came on over the speakers in the ceiling.

After dropping his boxers, he kneeled on the bed. Starting at my foot, he blew a breath across the top of it and as he crawled further onto the bed, his breaths trailed up my leg. He blew a breath across my thighs and

I squirmed, my core aching. When the warm air caressed my pussy, a gasp left me.

Inching his way up, he continued blowing across my stomach. I jumped when the breath hit my side, tickling slightly. His cock brushed over my center as he made his way to my breasts.

He leaned his head down, his mouth was a mere inch from my nipple. I arched my back, waiting for him to suck on it—he didn't. He blew light breaths across it, making me jump in anticipation. He moved to the other breast and repeated the action before bringing his face up to meet mine.

His body was barely pressed against me, as was his cock. He kept pulling back so it wouldn't make full contact with my flesh, making me yearn for more. As his face met mine, he leaned in like we were going to kiss and my lips parted, waiting for it. Instead, he stopped short, his lips brushing lightly against mine. He breathed into my mouth, sending goosebumps down my neck. With impatient lips, I craned my neck forward as I tried to close in the distance. The more I did it, the more he pulled back. At this point, I was panting from lack of contact. My skin felt like it was on fire from the suspense of waiting to be touched—needing to be touched. Every muscle I had was twitching and begging for more.

His hand brushed lightly against my nipple before he trailed his fingers down my stomach. Sticking one finger in my entrance, I moaned. He pulled the wetness up to my clit and I gasped at the glorious feeling I had been begging for. Then his finger trailed in circles around it, still not making contact. I groaned in protest.

"I'm going to teach you patience, one way or another, Princess."

"Touch me," I breathed into his mouth. "Please."

My begging didn't stop his pattern. He continued to go near my throbbing bud, but never even grazed it. The motion had me thrusting my pelvis forward, trying to force the contact. The suspense was killing me.

My arms tightened when I pulled on the cuffs, wanting to dig my hands in his hair and shove his face into my core, but I couldn't. He had my ass locked down—literally. He was in control, and I was giving him free rein to be. He had a road map to my body, but he was definitely going off-road with what he was doing.

His finger went over the top of my aching clit, down one lip, and back up again before heading down the other lip. Surprisingly, my orgasm was building from the unfamiliar action.

"Don't stop," I moaned.

He moved in a steady motion, doing the perfect arches over, and over, and over again. The non-contact contact was new to me and somehow, it was amazing.

In my life, I had never had an orgasm without clitoral or g-spot stimulation—well, if you don't count the bite in

Vegas. But as he continued the magic ministrations of his fingers, I knew I was about to climax.

The pressure was building and I felt like a tea kettle about to scream that I was ready. The muscles in my thighs trembled as my toes curled. My breaths were ragged and my mouth fell open with a gasp.

"Oh, fuck."

Right when I was about to come, his fingers stopped on my clit and circled. Loud moans echoed through the room, and my muscles tightened as I exploded. The euphoric feeling was the best orgasm I'd had in my life . . . without vampire venom. Every nerve in my body tingled like they were dancing in celebration of our victory. My body went lax with satisfaction as my climax ended.

"Was it worth the wait?" he asked in a hushed voice.

"Fuck, yes," I whispered with barely a breath.

His cock slid between my soaking wet lips. I tried to maneuver it in by wiggling my hips around, but failed.

"You have no idea what you being *so greedy* does to me," he whispered against my mouth.

His tongue traced the edge of my lips, leaving me wanting more.

Yanking on the ropes, I tried to reach for his head so I could force him to kiss me, but was met with resistance.

He leaned to one side, moving his mouth close to my ear before he blew a gentle breath, sending shivers down my spine. His knee went between my legs, pushing them further open before he pressed his warm cock against my core. When he sucked in my nipple, I gasped. He bit down lightly on it, making me arch upward. My breaths were hard and fast when the tip of his cock pressed against my entrance, begging him to impale me. Apparently, that was being denied, too.

"Fuck me," I begged. "Please."

He released my nipple and brought his head up to mine. A slow grin spread across his face. With one good thrust, he slammed his cock into me, stealing my breath.

His lips met mine forcefully, smashing a kiss onto me. His tongue darted in and rolled around mine with extreme hunger as he pounded into me. He broke the kiss and I gasped for air.

With quickness, he pushed himself off me, reached down, and uncuffed my ankles. Grabbing my hips, he flipped me onto my belly, crossing my cuffed hands over each other. I now had even less mobility.

A burning pain radiated across my ass as a loud smack echoed through the room. He pulled me to my knees before slamming his cock back into me.

If I was going to die tonight, this was the way to go.

He rolled his hips in circles, grinding against my swollen g-spot as his nails dug into me, squeezing my ass cheeks tight. My orgasm was building once more and I was ready to explode.

"Oh, fuck," I moaned and he pulled out. I let out a whine and he let out a breathy laugh.

He flipped me back over before undoing my wrists. He maneuvered until he was sitting on the bed and pulled me into his lap. Now a free woman, my hands dug into his hair and pulled. A long moan left us both as I lowered myself onto his cock. He squeezed my ass again as I moved my hips. Once I found a nice stride, I stayed there for a while.

Our sweaty bodies smacked together as we fucked to the rhythm of the music. Ready to come again, I shoved him back onto the bed and got on my knees, making sure his cock never left me.

My hands on his chest, I dug my nails in hard as I grinded against him. He grabbed my hips and we moved in unison. Our bodies fit perfectly together like two puzzle pieces made for each other.

The euphoric tingling washed over my body. My head fell back with the extreme ecstasy I was feeling and I moaned as I started to come again. His fingers dug deeper into my hips and he groaned as warm cum squirted inside of me. Our breaths were ragged as I fell against his chest, sated.

Luka trailed his fingers up and down my back as my breathing slowly returned to normal. Glancing over at the clock, I realized we had been fucking for an hour. I sighed.

"I have to shower," I whispered.

His hands tightened around me as he sat up. Realizing what he was doing, I relented, wrapping my arms around his neck. He scooted off the bed, carried us to the bathroom, and straight into the shower.

Once we were both cleaned, we got dressed. Since I had no clothes here, I was wearing some of Luka's. Twenty minutes later, we were hopping on his motorcycle.

"Here, Princess," he said, handing me the helmet.

He started up the motorcycle as I mounted behind him. The rumble of the engine below me was calming. I wrapped my arms around him and he placed one of his hands on top of mine, rubbing for a few seconds before he pulled out of the driveway. I had already come to terms with the fact I was going to be a little late to work as we headed to my house.

He parked in front of my apartment building and I handed him the helmet before I quickly made my way upstairs.

Once inside, I fed Chewy and got dressed. Looking around my apartment, I felt like something was off. My uneasy feeling was getting thicker, stagnant. My eyes landed on the dresser and I realized I hadn't taken my anxiety meds in two nights. Figuring they may help, I grabbed the pill bottle, took one out, and headed into the kitchen.

After taking a water bottle from the fridge, I threw the pill in my mouth and took a sip. I gave Chewy a quick pet before hurrying out the door.

Luka was waiting patiently when I came down. I took the helmet from him and put it back on. As I crawled onto the back of the bike, I wondered if it would be the last time I got to ride with him.

Tears threatened to fall as I wrapped my arms tightly around him. We pulled away from the curb and headed to Drifter's Bar where I had left my car. Winnie was waiting for us when we pulled up.

After dismounting the bike, I took the helmet off and handed it to Luka. Instead of taking the helmet, he grabbed my wrist and yanked me toward him.

"What time do you want to meet up?" he asked as he laid a hand on my lower back.

"Around ten or eleven. I'll text you." I had been pretty quiet since we got in the shower. My brain was *still* stuck on the fact I thought I was going to die.

"Everything will be fine, Princess."

Staring into his beautiful blue eyes, I had a feeling this was the last time I would ever see him again. A huge part of me wanted to tell him I loved him, but I couldn't. Instead, I nodded as I bit my lip.

He pulled me into him, kissing me gently before letting go. I swallowed hard, then turned away.

"Bye, Sage Stick."

"Bye, Winnie." I said in a low voice.

"Winnie?" he asked, and I ignored him. I wasn't in a playful mood.

After I got in my car and started it, Luka smiled at me through the window. I smiled back, reassuring him I was okay before pulling away.

CHAPTER 48

LUKA

Sage pulled out of the parking lot and a sigh left me as I watched her tail lights disappear. It was a quarter to nine, so Winnie and I had at least an hour before we had to follow Sage and Erik around.

"What time did Drag say he would be available?" Winnie asked.

"He said the play ends at eleven."

"Perfect. That gives us plenty of time to talk to Ravage."

Ravage had texted me and said he had lab results to share. Sage had no clue what I was doing because I didn't want to worry her with more bullshit when she was already stressed enough.

After heading across town, we parked our bikes in front of the tattoo shop.

"It's about time you brought my grandson around!" Ravage said, as we entered.

"Dude, it's kind of weird when you say that."

"Shut up, Winston, and come give grandpa a hug."

Winnie laughed as they exchanged a bear hug.

"So, what did you find?" I asked, before Ravage decided to hug me.

He glanced over at someone who was getting tattooed by a woman artist. They were both definitely vampires.

"Follow me." He headed toward his office and we trailed behind. I took the opportunity to text Sage.

Luka: *You good, Princess?*

No response.

We all took a seat and Ravage let out a long, loud sigh.

"First, I wanted to say I'm sorry about Andrei. I know we talked on the phone after, but it's not the same. I was going to mention it last time I saw you, but you had that girl with you and it didn't feel right mentioning it in front of someone who isn't family. Andrei's moral compass didn't always point north, but he was a good man in his own way."

"Thanks." My lips pressed together in a tight line. I wasn't sure if Ravage had realized Sage was the one who killed Andrei, but now was not the time to bring it up. In my head, she was my family, so I didn't know how I would handle it if he tried to hurt her.

"I found this." He threw a pile of papers onto the desk.

I picked them up and my eyes scanned a bunch of words I didn't know. "What is this?"

The office chair squeaked as Ravage leaned back in it. "Ingredients."

"Let me see," Winnie said, craning his neck trying to look.

"The syringes did contain three different solutions and I was fascinated by what I found. Those fuckers have been busy."

"Are you going to explain what all these ingredients are, or are you going to make us Google this shit?" I asked, and Ravage let out a boisterous laugh.

"I'll make it simple for you. One is an antibiotic, one is sodium chloride, and the other is something I'm sure Venom is proud of. It seems they found a way to use vampire blood to strengthen their members."

"But wouldn't they turn if they died with it in their system?" Winnie asked.

Ravage kicked his feet up onto the desk and crossed his arms behind his head.

"Normally, yes, but they have somehow managed to strip the blood of certain qualities. The vampire DNA has been removed, leaving behind specific hormones. Taking these shots can give someone a fraction of the strength we have, but more than what a human normally has. It's like being on steroids without the side effects, or so I assume. I'm not sure how long the effects would last, but it wouldn't be forever."

"Since Sage said they are required to get them weekly, probably not much longer than that," I added.

"Have you told him about bondcoat?" Winnie asked"

I set the papers back on the desk. "Yep."

"I assume some of those qualities they're taking out are being left in for other things, like bondcoat. If it does what you think it does—"

"It does," Winnie said. "We both saw it."

Ravage nodded. "Like I said, I'm sure Venom is proud."

Winnie's phone dinged and his mouth was agape while he stared at the screen. "What the fuck!" he shouted as he stood up. "Someone's in my house!"

Ravage and I both jumped up. "Who?" I asked.

"I don't know. The cameras are black."

"They hacked your cameras?" Ravage questioned. "That's surprising."

"No. It looks like spray paint. I'll rewind the footage." He walked out of the office and I followed. "Yep! Spray paint. I'm going to kill these . . . I'm sorry, ma'am." Winnie smiled at the client who was getting the tattoo before flinging the door open. He put his phone in his pocket before mounting his bike. "These mother fuckers are gonna die!"

"Do you think it's Venom?" Ravage asked.

"Maybe. They won't be able to get into the cave without my voice, so they won't get much."

My phone vibrated and I quickly checked it.

Princess Badass: *Something is going down with Venom.*

My heart thundered in my chest as worry for the woman I was madly in love with filled my body.

Luka: *Get out of there and meet me at Winnie's!*

"It's Venom. Sage said something is going down!"

"Fuck!" The engine roared as Winnie pulled off.

"If you guys need me, don't hesitate."

I started my bike. "I'll keep you updated," I yelled as I pulled away.

Winnie was speeding like hell through town, but I caught up to him at a red light. When we got to his apartment, the door was cracked open. He didn't hesitate, flying through it and I was right behind him. He went one way and I went the other. Twenty seconds later we met back in the middle.

"They're gone!"

"What did they take?" I asked.

"I don't know." With a sigh, Winnie walked to the front door and slammed it shut. A second later, it slowly creaked back open. "They broke my fucking door, bro!"

As I glanced around the living room, it didn't seem like anything was taken. There were a few things knocked over, but it wasn't trashed.

An odd sound fell upon our ears and both our eyes widened.

"That's a fucking rattler!" Winnie said and we headed toward the bedroom.

Right in the middle of Winnie's bed was a big-ass rattlesnake. He was coiled up with a shaking tail—just as agitated as I was.

"Venom was here." I yanked out my phone. No text from Sage. "Fuck!"

"How did they know where I lived?"

I shook my head. "I have no fucking clue."

"Do you think Erik had anything to do with this?" Winnie asked.

I'm not going to lie, it was one of my first thoughts, but I wasn't sure. The only thing I *was* sure about was I didn't fucking trust anyone but Sage and my friends.

"He doesn't even know where you live, unless Lyric told him."

"You should text Sage. I'm going to text Lyric."

"I have." I looked at my phone again—no text. "She's not responding."

I hit Drag's contact and sent him a quick text.

Luka: *Snakes in the cave.*

"Lyric isn't answering, either. Something's off, man. I can feel it!"

I didn't respond to him, but I could feel it, too.

"What the fuck are we going to do with that?" he asked, staring at the pissed off snake.

"Leave it for now. We can come back later and release it in the desert."

Worry and anxiousness settled in me as we left the bedroom. Winnie went straight to the picture hanging next to the hidden entrance.

"Cave, avow."

The picture on the wall clicked and Winnie opened it before entering his code. After the bookcase opened revealing the hidden room, we entered.

"At least they didn't get in here. Fuckers!" He took a seat at the computer and pulled up the cameras. "I want to see what all they touched."

I stood behind him with my arms crossed while he rewound the cameras to just before the intrusion. The door flew open and two characters dressed in all black entered. They both had the physiques of men. The taller one glanced around and immediately saw a camera. Walking over to it, he held up a can of spray paint and blacked out the view.

"That was a thousand dollar camera, you asshole!"

A few seconds later, he found the other camera and did the same.

"Good thing I have a backup camera." Winnie clicked the mouse and pulled up a third camera—one *I* didn't even know he had.

One of the figures searched the room frantically—opening drawers and quickly scanning papers. The other went into the bedroom with a bag. I assumed the snake was in it. They were there less than two minutes before they were heading out the door.

"This was a warning. Shit's going down and Sage and Lyric are both in the middle of it!"

"I'll call Drag. We need to prepare for a battle."

A text came across the top of my screen as I was about to hit send. It was from Sage.

Princess Badass: *Can you meet me at Save?*

Luka: *Yeah, is everything okay?*

Princess Badass: *Just be there.*

My suspicions rose with her text. When we weren't together, we texted back and forth constantly. Sage was never short with me, so it concerned me she *wasn't* okay.

I immediately hit send and called her. After a half of a ring, I was sent to voicemail.

"Fuck!"

"What's wrong?" Winnie asked.

"Hold on." My fingers were typing frantically.

Luka: *You didn't answer.*

Princess Badass: *Can't talk. Just meet me there. K?*

The response set off major alarms. Something was wrong. Sage hated it when people texted 'K' and I knew she would never use it. Either she was trying to tell me something or . . . she wasn't the one texting.

"Look at this shit," I said as I showed Winnie my phone.

His eyes skimmed it as he read the text. "Wait, she said *K*.' She would never say that. I texted her that once and got a ten-minute lecture on how disrespectful it was."

"I know. I have a feeling this isn't her."

My heart raced with fear and I stared at the screen.

"Ask her the code," Winnie said.

I quickly typed out a text.

Luka: *I have a joke for you.*

Princess Badass: *K.*

Every time I saw a 'K,' I got more and more pissed off. Pushing my anger aside, I messaged her the one thing I knew she would remember.

Luka: *What's the difference between a security system and a human?*

The air in the room seemed to disappear as Winnie and I both waited for the response.

Princess Badass: *IDK. What?*

My heart raced as I looked at Winnie whose mouth was agape. I threw my phone onto the desk and a loud growl left me. Anger I had been trying to contain decided to consume every piece of me. It flooded through my body like poison eating away at my blood. Veins popped up on my face and a crawling sensation tingled across my skin as blood pumped through me at rapid speed.

"I will fucking kill all of them if they touch her!" I punched a hole in Winnie's wall. "Fuck!" Another hole. "Fuck!"

"Take a breath and chill, bro! We'll find her!"

My phone rang and I frantically yanked it off the desk hoping it was Sage. The name on the screen surprised me.

"I can't talk, Stephanie. Shit is—"

"Venom found me!" She was breathing heavily, like she was running.

"What?"

"I don't know how, but they did. I managed to get away. I tried to contact Sage, but she isn't answering."

"She's at Venom and shit just got bad. I can't get a hold of her."

A car door slammed and an engine started. "I'm heading there. It will take me a while, but I'll message you when I'm closer."

The phone went silent and I looked back at Winnie. "They found the therapist. She got away."

"This is getting bad quick as fuck!"

"Can you track both of Sage's phones?" I growled.

A huge part of me wanted to run to Save, but since I wasn't sure who had her phone, I hesitated, worried they were waiting for us to leave so they could follow us there.

"One second." Winnie whipped around and started slamming keys. "It looks like the phone we gave her is at the corner of Second Avenue and Sycamore Street."

"That's only ten minutes from Save."

"And her other one is . . . in the same spot."

She wouldn't take her work phone because she knows they're tracking her. I left the cave and headed for the front door.

"Hopefully, whoever has her phone also has her." I dialed Drag's number—no answer. I called Peach and instantly got a voicemail. "Fuck! I can't get a hold of anyone. We have to get there now."

"What if it's a trap?" Winnie asked as we walked down the hall.

"What if it isn't? What if they're going to attack and we do nothing?" I pushed the button for the elevator.

"Oh, fuck, Luka. The play!"

If Venom attacked while Save was full of families, it would be a massacre of women and children.

Pure fear coursed through me as I pulled out my phone and called Drag again—still no answer.

Not wanting to wait for the elevator, I ran for the stairwell. It only took me seconds to clear all three flights. Winnie was on my ass when we made it outside. I called Drag for the third damn time before mounting my bike.

"The play is still—"

"Get the kids out now! Venom is on their way!"

"Code red!" Drag yelled before the phone went silent.

CHAPTER 49
SAGE

Walking into Venom was like walking the green mile but it was a necessary evil because if I didn't come back, more people could die. I figured it would be a good way to help find out what all Venom was doing. Also, I hoped to find the location of the Vampire Research Center so we could find Luka's brother. After hearing the story about his mom, my heart was breaking for him. He had no one left since I had taken his last family member. If I could get Strike back, I might feel less like an asshole. I just hoped he was still alive.

As I walked the halls, I realized how weird it was now. I had been here my whole life, but since I had been on medical leave, I felt disconnected. Almost like I had blinders on and someone finally took them off—that someone being Luka.

Heading to the armory, three people went by in a panic and I wondered what was going on. There were no alarms going off, so I had no idea what the rush was. When two more people quickly passed me at almost a full run, I started to worry.

My phone dinged, so I dug in my purse to find it. Pulling out my work phone, there were no notifications on it, so it had to have come to my personal one. As stealthy as possible, I slid it back into my bag and pulled the other one out.

Lyric: *Meeting spot.*

As quickly as I could—without looking suspicious—I headed toward the less used women's bathroom where we always met when we needed to talk privately. When the group of three I saw earlier passed me again, I froze. This time, they were armed. Someone bumped into my back and I whipped around.

"Sorry, Sage. I was just trying to get to the armory in a hurry," Jimmy said breathlessly.

"Why are you going there?" I asked.

Jimmy worked in security and sat behind a computer every shift he had. Since he didn't work in the field, he wouldn't have any use for the armory.

"Haven't you heard? There is something big going down. I think they're expecting an attack or something. We're all supposed to get armed and meet in the dining hall."

Figuring I should know this information, I decided to play it off. "Yeah, I know. I just figured it was for people in the field."

"It includes everybody." His glasses were sliding off his nose and he pushed them back up with one finger. "I have to go. You better, too!" He took off at a fast jog, as did I, but in the opposite direction.

The bad feeling I had escalated, along with my suspicions. When I got to the bathroom, I slowly opened the door and peeked my head inside to make sure it wasn't a trap. Lyric was leaning against the sink with her arms crossed.

"Get in here and shut the door," she whispered as she waved her hand frantically.

"What the fuck is going on?" I asked.

"We don't know," Erik said, emerging from a stall with a worried look. "But I have a bad feeling."

"Have you talked to Winston or Luka?" Lyric asked.

"I just left them."

"They aren't planning on attacking, are they?" Eric asked.

I shook my head. "They wouldn't do that without our knowledge."

"Agreed," Lyric added. "I was going to text Winnie, but I didn't know what to say since I have no clue what's going on."

"We should at least let them know something is off." I pulled my phone out of my pocket and the door opened, startling me.

Doctor Jayne's eyes widened as they went to Erik. "Mr. 'Muldova, I believe you may have stumbled into the wrong bathroom."

"Sorry, Doc. I had to give my sister something."

Her eyes narrowed on him before bouncing to me and Lyric.

"You three better get down to the meeting." She held the door open, waiting for us to exit. With a deep breath, I slid my phone into my back pocket and headed out the door.

Once we were in the hallway, she stalked next to us, making it impossible to text Luka without her seeing. The silence was deafening as my mind wandered to possible scenarios of what was happening.

As we entered the dining hall, my heart raced at the abundance of people.

"Get to the front with the rest of the field team," Doc Jayne said.

Being the senior in our group, Erik nodded and took control. "Follow me." He headed to the front of the room with confidence.

As we followed, I tried my damndest to hold my head high, like everyone else who was willing to die for Venom. Little did they know, I wasn't that person anymore. I used to think what we were doing was for the greater good—we were going to find a vaccine to help those poor vampires. I was a fool.

Erik stopped near the front of the stage, Lyric and I flanked him. I surveyed the room, my eyes wandering around the many faces. It was a blend of people young and old ready to defend us. A part of me wanted to run up on the stage and tell everyone to save themselves, but now wasn't the time for dramatics—they wouldn't believe me, anyway.

My eyes stopped scanning when I saw Sorin. He was roughly twenty feet away, standing with Naomi. The infamous duo both looked content—no surprise or worry on their faces. Whatever was going on, they knew about it.

Hatred ran through me and I gritted my teeth as I stared at his side profile. It was almost like Sorin could feel my disdain from afar as his head whipped toward me. After locking eyes, he gave me a malicious smile. I had half a mind to give him the finger, or possibly go over there and punch him in the dick, but I refrained and glanced away.

I needed to inform Luka of everything, so I pulled my phone from my back pocket. He had texted me and I hadn't seen it yet.

Fucker: *You good, Princess?*

Sage: *Something is going down.*

I sent the text and waited for his response.

Fucker: *Get out of there and meet me at Winnie's!*

"No phones!" someone yelled, bringing my attention to them. It was a commander—I couldn't remember his name, but I knew he was higher ranking.

"Are these your subordinates?" he asked Erik.

"Yes, sir."

"Then get them under control!"

Erik's eyes met mine. "Put your phone away!" I knew when he yelled, it wasn't what he wanted to do.

Acting like my normal self, I rolled my eyes and stuck my phone in my back jeans pocket. The commander shook his head before strolling away. Erik had a rueful look on his face.

The room quickly silenced as my father took the stage with my mother in tow. She gingerly took a seat at the back of the stage—like a supporting spouse does—as he stepped up to the mic.

"Welcome, members. I come to you with a heavy heart today. We have been doing some investigations and have found surprising revelations."

I shifted uncomfortably, wondering where this speech was going. Erik leaned towards me.

"Stay calm," he whispered before righting himself. I started the breathing techniques I always forgot to use.

"Since the death of Deren, things have been off. I've had the security team pulling camera footage, as well as phone and tablet records. Unfortunately, when our investigator searched the evidence, they found something which hasn't happened in many years." He pulled the mic from the stand before strolling to the front of the stage. He stopped, his eyes scanning the audience. "We have found out there has been someone working *with* the vampires."

Gasps and curses came from the room. Erik took it as an opportunity to whisper, "Don't hesitate to kill these fuckers to get out."

Looking past him, I met Lyric's eyes. "Blood of the coven," she mouthed. I nodded as the uneasy feeling in my stomach threatened to consume me.

There was no air left in the room as I worried if I and possibly my friends had been caught.

"This person had been conspiring *against* us! Doing everything in their power to set up *our people* to be *murdered*!"

There was no way my dad was talking about me. I didn't set anyone up. I was one of the people *going* to be murdered.

"And that person," he took a deep breath, "was Deren."

More gasps filled the room. One of them was mine. Glancing at my friends, they looked just as confused as I was.

"His untimely death was brought down by his own hands!"

The crowd cheered and I leaned into Erik. "Sorin is putting everything on Deren," I whispered and Erik nodded.

"But he wasn't the only one who was a traitor," my dad continued. "And the other person is here!"

My heart thundered in my chest when I looked back at my father. As his eyes locked on the three of us, I wished I had gone to the armory to get weapons.

"Guards!" I stayed as still as possible as Marcus, Zeke, and two others approached us. My father pointed. "Arrest him!"

Him?

Two of the guards immediately pushed me and Lyric aside before grabbing Erik and slinging his arms behind his back.

"What the fuck!" I screamed. "Get away from him!" I pulled on one's arm and when he turned toward me, I swung my fist out and punched him, causing an instant bloody nose.

"Sagelynn!" My name echoed as my dad screamed it into the microphone.

Neither Marcus nor Zeke moved as we fought off the two guards. They stood with their arms crossed, watching closely and I wondered why.

Lyric yanked one into her with a choke hold. I took it as an opportunity to punch him, too. Erik started beating the shit out of the first guard I punched. With Lyric still choking the second one, I lifted my foot, ready to kick him in the face when my dad's words stopped me.

"Marcus, Zeke!"

Whipping my body toward Marcus, I knew I was fucked. I *might* have been able to take him down if he were alone, but there was no way I was taking him down along with Zeke.

Out of the corner of my eye, Erik was being contained by two extra guards who had jumped in. Zeke grabbed Lyric and pulled her off the guard she was pummeling.

As calmly as possible, Marcus walked up to me with his hands out. "You know what I have to do. Please don't fight." He grabbed my arm and my heart raced as I had to make a quick decision. Swinging my arm out, I chopped him in the throat with the side of my hand.

"Sage, stop!" Looking up at the sound of my mother's voice, her face was filled with fear. I froze, giving Marcus the opportunity to pin my arm behind my back. I gave up.

"Take them to interrogation!" My father dropped the mic on the ground and quickly left the stage.

Marcus led me by the arm as we made our way through the crowd. Everyone stared at me with either shock or disgust.

Zeke and Lyric were right behind us but I had no idea where they took Erik.

"This is not what it seems, Marcus. Erik didn't do anything!"

He remained quiet as he stopped in front of an interrogation room and swiped his finger to unlock the door.

"My brother is innocent!" Lyric screamed as Zeke pushed her into the next room over. "He's not a rat!"

"Don't say anything, Lyric!" I yelled as the door to my room shut.

"Sit!" Marcus commanded and I lowered my ass into a chair. He crossed his arms. "Calmly, tell me what you know."

"I can't."

The look on his face was empathetic. "Then I can't help you, Sage."

The door opened and my dad walked in with saddened eyes. He strolled toward me and leaned in like he was going to give me a hug. A part of me felt relieved—until I heard the handcuffs jingle right before he latched a cuff around one of my wrists, attaching the other to the chair.

"What the fuck!"

"It's for your own protection, sweetheart. The last time your emotions spiraled out of control, you had to be sedated."

"Oh, yeah. Cuffing me to a fucking chair will ease my emotions!"

He sat across from me before clearing his throat. Marcus took the seat next to him. "I know you love Erik, but what he did—"

"He didn't do anything!"

He said nothing at my outburst, surprising me. His face was empathetic, and it was rare when I saw that.

"The evidence shows he did, Sagelynn. I'm sorry, but he was sending people on missions to get them killed."

I shook my head and lowered it knowing I was fighting a losing battle.

"Sorin has been tracking him and Deren for a while. He even knows the location to Save and—"

"What?" My heart thundered in my chest as my head whipped up.

"Sorin knows the location. They're heading there now."

Without hesitation, I reached behind me with my only free hand and pulled out my phone to text Luka. I was two words in when my phone was ripped from my fingers.

"What the—"

"Whose phone is this?" my dad asked.

"Give it back!" I went to yank it away and couldn't reach it. The look on his face told me it was too late, as his eyes widened.

"You're a fucking traitor!" He jumped to his feet. His face filled with sadness and disappointment. It made me tear up.

"I'm not a traitor! I'm trying to help!" He walked toward the door and set his finger on the scanner. "Dad, please!"

Without a word, the door shut behind him.

Marcus' face was confused when I glanced at him.

"Marcus, if you don't help me, tons of people will die!"

"Tell me what's going on."

I shook my head. "I can't. Just get me my other phone!"

He slammed his fist on the table. "Damn it, Sage! You know I care about you!"

I took a deep breath before I tried to tell the fastest story possible.

"I met a vampire a while back. He was the one who killed Deren. Him and his friends showed me a shit ton of evidence that proved Sorin was working with at least two vampires. Deren wasn't a rat. Sorin is the one sending Venom members on missions to get us killed, not Erik. He just used Erik's tablet information to do it. He also makes sure problematic vampires are killed. He's the rat, playing both sides!"

My heart thundered in my chest as Marcus stared at me with wide eyes. I thought about the Save members I met and I hoped none of them got hurt. Then last night's conversation came back to me. The children's play was tonight.

"Shit! If you don't help me, kids are going to die, too!" Tears threatened to break free and I blew out slow breaths.

He pressed the button on his ear piece. "Did you get all of that?" he asked and I felt betrayed. I didn't know what the person on the other end said but Marcus replied with, "Agreed."

He quickly stood up and made his way around the table. He leaned in close and whispered, "You have to be my prisoner if you want me to get you out of here, so act like it."

Shock filled me when he uncuffed my hand. Grabbing me by the arm, he pulled me from my chair and led me to the door where he scanned his finger.

Once we were in the hall, Zeke emerged from the other room with Lyric in his grip. Marcus nodded his head in the direction he wanted us to go. Zeke nodded back in acknowledgement. My heart thundered as the two brothers escorted us toward the elevator.

The only thing we had going for us was the fact everyone was in the hall—or so I hoped. If they had already left, people could be minutes from dying. My father did say they were leaving ten minutes ago and fear ran through me.

Marcus pushed the button to the elevator and we entered, but Zeke didn't.

"Where is he—"

Marcus yanked me closer to him. "I said no talking!" His eyes burrowed into mine like they were telling me something. Cameras—there were hidden cameras in the elevator I didn't know about. I refrained from glancing around as I gave him a fake scowl.

The elevator doors opened and we stepped out. The garage was quiet and anxiety filled me when I saw most of the vans were gone. Marcus led us to the high security one. It was the one my father always used. Opening the sliding side door, he motioned for us to get in before taking the front seat.

"Why are you trusting me?" I asked.

Marcus's eyes met mine in the rearview mirror. "Zeke and I have been watching Sorin for a while now. We weren't positive on what was going on, but we knew there was something suspicious. Also, I love you."

I nodded as tears filled my eyes. "I love you, too." He smiled and I immediately turned toward Lyric. "Do you have your phone?"

She handed it to me and I dialed Luka's number—no answer. Then I called Winnie with the same result. I frantically dialed Drag, and then Peach.

"Fuck. No one is answering!"

Glancing over at Lyric, her eyes were filled with worry.

A few minutes later, the van door reopened and Erik crawled in. He took a seat as he sucked in fast breaths. Lyric pulled him in for a hug.

"I'm good," he whispered.

"Did you have to kill them?" Marcus asked as Zeke took the passenger seat.

"Nope. But they're going to have bad headaches when they wake up."

Marcus started the van up with a laugh. "Where to?" he asked, pulling out of the garage.

"It's a church outside of town. I don't know the address, so just head in that direction and I will let you know when we're closer."

I tried Luka again. Panic filled me when he didn't answer.

Fuck! "Drive faster, Marcus!"

"As soon as we are out of here."

Marcus slowed at the gate and I was relieved when I heard it opening. Once he pulled through, he slammed the gas and we headed for the highway.

CHAPTER 50

LUKA

We were almost to Save and my anxiety had a stranglehold on me. No one was answering their phones, so I was in the dark about the condition of things.

Loud pops rang through the night, filling me with panic.

"The humans brought guns!" Winnie shouted, an angry tone to his voice.

Vampires could survive *most* gunshots, but the wolven wouldn't be able to heal fast enough if they got shot in specific locations or multiple times.

As we turned onto the gravel road, there were four black vans out front. They were empty when I passed them. More gunshots sounded as we rounded the side of the church where two more vans were parked. Driving my motorcycle through the grass and towards the sounds of fighting, I almost ran over a dead body. I took a quick glance and was relieved when I saw it was a Venom member—thankfully, nobody I knew.

I had never dismounted so fast in my life. Dropping my bike, I headed straight into the brawl, a standoff was in progress: Vivi fought against three men and a woman. She lunged toward a guy with a gun pointed at her and he shot her multiple times. She let out a screeching cry, falling to the ground. Winnie was on the shooter before he even saw us. Grabbing his neck, he twisted. The cracking sounds filled the air before he hit the ground.

I immediately went for the biggest guy plowing into him with my shoulder. He dropped his crossbow as he fell to the ground. I twisted my body toward the girl and yanked a stake from her grasp. She came at me with fierceness. Catching her mid-leap, I threw her on top of the other dude.

The fourth man's face was panicked. His glasses were sliding off his nose as his heart thundered in his chest. Winnie was about to lunge for him but I halted him by grabbing his arm.

"Wait!" Winnie gave me a confused look as I turned my attention back to the Venom member. "Get the fuck out of here!" I shouted and he took off running. The other two quickly scrambled to their feet and followed.

Veins of anger popped up on Winnie's face. "Why did you do that?" he spat.

"They don't know who they're working for! What if that was Sage or Lyric?"

"Whatever, Luka!" Winnie ripped his arm out of my grasp before turning toward Vivi. To my surprise, she was still on the ground. "Are you okay?"

"I'm not healing," she said in a painful whisper. "I think they have silver bullets."

"Fuck!" Winnie kneeled beside her seconds before more gunshots rang.

"You need to help the kids!" Vivi screamed.

I took off toward the back of the church at lightning speed. Heading down the small set of stairs, I went through the basement door to find Laren fighting two people. Thankfully, neither of them had guns. She jumped on one and bit into her neck. The girl collapsed to her knees as Laren fed. The other member was watching in shock as I tackled him to the ground. One good punch to the face and he was out cold.

Even though I knew it would happen eventually, I was trying my best not to kill them unless I had to.

Hopping to my feet, I met Laren's eyes. "Where are the kids?"

"Hiding," she said as pounding feet came down the stairs.

We looked up to see three more Venom members.

The one in the front was a bigger man. He had a gun in his hand and immediately shot at Laren. His aim was sloppy and imprecise. Luckily, he didn't see me in the shadows until it was too late. With one quick grab, I pulled him toward me and snapped his neck. He fell to the floor, dead.

Another one lunged toward me so I quickly sidestepped, making him stumble past.

Grabbing the third from behind, I put him in a chokehold. Once he went lax, I let him go, hoping he would sleep for a while.

Growling and screaming sounded behind me. Laren was crouched over a body when I turned. She had ripped the throat out of the man who stumbled past me. She released his neck, mouth gaping wide as she took fast breaths. When her head whipped toward me, I noticed her eyes were glazed over, her heartbeat rapid. Bloodlust. No one was safe around her now.

"Fuck!" I headed toward her, and as I got close, she growled.

She was fast to her feet, immediately leaping for me. She plowed into me, almost knocking me down, her bared teeth mere inches from my neck as she snarled. I had one hand on her shoulder, the other on her throat, holding her at bay.

"Laren! Calm the fuck down!"

She issued snarls and growls as my mind raced to figure out how to contain her. I didn't want to hurt a girl—especially a friend.

Another growl came from behind me and, by her scent, I immediately knew it was Drag's little sister, Kimber.

The large gray wolf lunged for Laren, knocking her down, but she immediately sprang to her feet again.

"Enough!" Peach's voice rang through the stairwell seconds before she grabbed Laren her by the throat. Laren snarled and fought. "Go, Luka. I got this!"

I turned toward the gray wolf. "Thanks, Kimber," I said before ascending the stairs.

Following the sounds of fighting, I stumbled upon a fight to the death—literally. There was a dead wolven with a stake in its side, next to a dead Venom member with their throat ripped out.

With no time to waste, or mourn, I continued into the sanctuary.

Fuck.

It was a bloodbath. Multiple members from both sides lay dead. Smelling Drag, I frantically followed the scent. I stumbled upon a glorious sight, but there was no time to appreciate the four large wolves ripping apart anyone who moved. I immediately jumped into the mix and started snapping necks.

A stabbing pain radiated through me as a stake was plunged into my shoulder. I whipped around and met the eyes of my attacker. Since the chunk of silver was still in me, the man was weaponless. He backed away with fear-filled eyes before turning and running off.

The silver had already started to slow my movements. I reached behind me and tried to yank it out to no avail. Looking around, I noticed everyone was dead except for three wolven—one had died. My eyes frantically bounced from each mass of gray fur until I knew my best friend was still breathing. He was the last I saw and I took a large breath of relief.

I wanted to tell Drag I loved him and I was glad he hadn't died, but I didn't. He knew.

I fell to my knees as I got weaker. "Drag! Get this fucking thing out of me!"

Drag's ears rose before he trotted in my direction. Turning back into his human form left me face to face with his dick.

"What the fuck, man!"

"Shut up. It's not like you haven't seen it a hundred times."

"Yeah, but I have never looked it in the eye!"

"Funny." He walked behind me and yanked the stake out.

Heston shifted back into his human form and chuckled. He strolled over to the dead wolven and kneeled next to him. Laying a hand on his chest, he whispered, "Although your soul may be at peace, our vinculum with you will never cease."

"Eternal bond," Drag said.

The third wolf, Demetrius, shifted back. "Eternal bond," he repeated.

A vinculum is the bond a wolven has with their pack—on this plane and beyond. I wasn't sure how it felt to them, but in my head, I figured it was a type of devotion like I had with my friends and Sage.

"Glad you're alive, Luka!"

"You too, Demetrius."

Drag reached a hand out and helped me off the ground. "Are you good?"

"I will be in a second." My strength was coming back fast since the silver had been removed. "We need to check on everyone."

Peach came into the sanctuary in a flash. "Three more vans just pulled up!"

Drag and I followed Peach as she headed out of the sanctuary. Heston and Demetrius were right on our asses when we flew out the front door. Sage's scent hit me before I saw her past a myriad of bodies. A loud growl rumbled from the depths of my soul when I saw the situation she was in.

CHAPTER 51
SAGE

My heart seemed to beat faster and faster the closer we got to Save. During the ride, Marcus and Zeke had explained some of the unusual things they had noticed with Sorin's actions. Which eventually led to them investigating. They were some of the same things Steph said she had noticed. I wondered how a person could go under so many people's radar, especially my father's. I wasn't sure if he was actually working with Sorin—or maybe I didn't want to believe a father would go against his own daughter. The one thing I did know was the look on his face in the interrogation room made me believe he truly thought Erik was working against Venom and had no clue I was a traitor.

"Take a right onto the dirt road!" I was on my feet, ready to burst out the door as soon as we stopped. Luckily, there were some weapons in the van, so I had armed myself with a silver stake and I wouldn't hesitate to use it. "Remember what I said, there are kids in there and they are our top priority," I reminded my friends.

The van came to a screeching halt and I immediately jumped out into a cloud of dust. There were growling sounds coming from behind the church, so I ran toward them, hoping it was Luka. My heart sank as I passed dead bodies of people I knew.

Next I passed a line of vehicles parked in a little gravel parking lot. None of them looked familiar, so I assumed they belonged to Save members. Then I stumbled upon two Harleys I immediately recognized. Using my emotions to propel my body faster, I ran straight into an altercation. Winnie was fighting off nearly a dozen Venom members on his own. Vivi was on the ground, surrounded by dead bodies, killing anyone who came near her.

"Help him!" she screamed when we approached.

My stake was in the air as I lunged forward, slamming it into the back of someone's arm. He let out a cry as I turned toward another person. Lifting my foot, I kicked her dead in the face. She flew back, hitting the ground hard.

Lyric wasted no time smashing a girl's head into her knee while Erik had a guy in a chokehold. When Marcus and Zeke entered the battle, people started being thrown in all directions, and I was glad they were on my side.

Not paying as much attention as I should have been, someone grabbed me from behind and I dropped my stake. Remembering the move I used when Marcus did that to me, I pulled my knees up high and yanked down, making us both tumble to the ground. He scrambled on top of me, pinning my wrists above my head. Lifting my knee, I nailed him right in the dick, making him groan, before I shoved him off.

With quickness, I sprang to my feet and immediately squared off with a different guy—one I have known since I was five years old. We both took fast breaths as we locked eyes in hesitation. He quickly decided what he was going to do and charged me. With no time to react, I braced myself as he tackled me to the ground. Now, with the upper hand, he didn't hesitate to punch me, sending intense pain through my jaw. Lifting my hands, I grabbed the side of his face and pushed my thumbs into his eyes as hard as I could. He let out a scream and a huge part of me felt bad, but at least, it made him scramble away from me in fear.

As I was getting off the ground again, I caught sight of Lyric plunging a stake into a guy's chest. She yanked it out with a remorseful look.

"Erik," she said in a panic.

"You're good! Don't stop fighting!" Erik yelled, repeatedly punching a dude.

"I got them out!" Vivi yelled, and I had no idea what she was talking about.

"Power the fuck up, then!" Winnie threw a man to the ground next to Vivi and she immediately sank her teeth into him. He let out a scream and then a moan.

A person in my peripheral had me quickly whipping around. It was a girl and she lunged for me but I dodged it. We quickly used every move we had on each other. Lifting her leg, she kicked me square in the chest. I landed on my back against the *all too familiar* ground. Before she had a chance to get on top of me, I leapt up. She came at me with fervor, which was dumb on her part at such a long distance. I grabbed her, using her momentum to propel her past me. Finally, someone else was on the ground other than me. Jumping on top of her, I pounded fists into her face as she tried carelessly to block them.

The sounds of squealing tires grabbed my attention. When I glanced up, over a dozen Venom members came around the building.

"Oh, fuck," I whispered. I hopped off the girl I was beating the fuck out of. "Winnie!"

His eyes shot to the direction I was looking before he yanked my stake off the ground. "Here. Kill anyone who tries to touch you." He tossed it to me and I caught it.

As more people joined the battle, I lost track of what my friends were doing as kicks and punches were thrown. A man came at me and I drove my stake into his shoulder. I hadn't killed anyone yet, but it was getting to the point where it was eventually going to happen.

Exhaustion was getting to me as I continued to fight for my life. After fighting off two girls at the same time, one of them ran away. I noticed a few other Venom members did as well, and I wondered how I could stop this fight and explain to them what the truth was.

Thoughts clouded my head enough that I slightly let my guard down. A girl punched me dead in the eye, blinding me for a split second.

"We're supposed to take her back!" A man said as his arms went around me, lifting me off the ground. The woman that punched me grabbed my ankles. Panic surged through and I thrashed and fought, but they prevailed, carrying me away from the battle.

"Marcus! Winnie!" I screamed, but my friends were busy.

Not resisting easily, I craned my neck and bit the man's bicep, causing him to drop me to the ground with a curse. Since the girl still had my feet in her hands, my head hit hard.

"Let her go," he commanded and she did, right before he kicked me in the side. "Bitch!"

I coughed hard and gasped for air before a loud growl rang through the night sky. Luka was on the man within seconds, quickly breaking his neck before kneeling next to me.

"Are you okay, Princess?"

Breathless and exhausted, I nodded and he helped me off the ground.

As I stared at the woman who had been carrying me, I was ready to attack her out of anger, but I didn't have time before Peach grabbed her by the throat and squeezed. She let out a strangled cry before Peach yanked half of the girl's throat out. She coughed on her own blood before falling over.

Without a second thought, Peach took off toward the battle.

"Did you get the kids out?" I asked.

"Not yet."

"Let's finish this." I took off rejoining the brawl.

There were only a handful of people left alive and most of them were my friends. Four of them were wolven, and I had no idea if one of them was Drag. Eventually, the only ones left standing were us.

"Is that all of them?" Marcus asked.

"Fuck if I know," Erik said breathlessly. He put his hands on his knees and leaned over.

"Where's Lyric?" I asked.

"Right here," she said from behind me and Winnie made a beeline for her.

Grabbing her by the waist, he pushed her hair out of her face before slamming a kiss onto her.

"Oh, shit!" Vivi said with a laugh.

Winnie pulled back, leaving Lyric shocked. "The whole battle, all I could think about was you. I was worried one of us would die before I got to do that."

Lyric's eyes filled with tears at the sentiment, as did mine.

"Isn't that precious," Ravage said as he strolled up with a woman I didn't know.

She was a tawny-skinned beauty with gauged ears and short, bright purple hair. If I wasn't with Luka—and surrounded by dead bodies—I would have totally hit on her.

"Where the fuck have you been?" Luka asked.

"Why don't you go ask all the dead Venom members out front?"

"We've got to get the kids out of here before more come," Peach said.

A wolf trotted up to the middle of us, and my mouth fell open when it turned into Drag. "Agreed!"

Of course, I glanced right at his cock out of shock before averting my eyes.

"Why the fuck are you naked?" Zeke asked.

Drag didn't seem shy when he met Zeke's eyes. "Our clothes rip when we transform."

"Let's get everyone out of here now," Peach said before she strolled toward the church.

The other wolven stayed in wolf form as we all followed.

Luka reached down and took my hand, pulling me into him. He placed a quick kiss on my neck as we walked. I knew it was his way of silently saying he was glad I was safe and the gesture made me feel loved.

"Who is the girl with Ravage?" I asked Luka.

"My name is Lynx," the girl answered from fifteen feet behind us and Luka laughed. Knowing she had heard me, I assumed she was a vampire.

Peach stopped at a small set of stairs that led to a basement.

"Luka, Winnie, and, umm, big guy." Peach pointed at Marcus and I laughed. "Stand guard, we are going to bring the people out and escort them to their vehicles. Lyric, you're with me."

"Yes, ma'am," Marcus said with a grin. "I like a woman who takes control."

"And I like a man who listens." Peach smiled before descending the stairs with Lyric in tow.

"Can you guys do a perimeter check?" Luka asked Drag.

In a flash, Drag shifted into a wolf again. Now I knew which one he was, I could see the difference. He took off on a full run as did the other wolven. Once they were far away, they split in four different directions. I wondered how the hell they knew where to go, since wolves can't talk.

"This is fucking wild!" Zeke said and I couldn't help but chuckle.

Ravage walked up with a smile. "Nice to see you again, Sage." He turned toward the girl. "Lynx, this is Sage. Luka's woman."

My face scrunched up at the phrase *Luka's woman.* Glancing at Luka, he was smiling arrogantly and I sighed. I guess I was Luka's woman.

"So, you're the one who killed Andrei?" she asked, curiously tilting her head.

Panic soared through me and I swallowed hard.

"She is, but we overlook it because it wasn't *technically* her fault," Vivi chimed in. She grinned as we locked eyes. "She's kind of cool for a Venom member."

Little feet pounding against wooden stairs sounded as ten children ran up. Behind them were a half a dozen wolf pups.

"Woah," Erik said. He had an astonished look on his face. "Are those kids?"

"Yeah," Vivi said with a frown. "Some of them are probably too nervous and can't shift back."

Erik's eyes widened as a woman came up the stairs holding a tiny pup. I let out an *aww* and she smiled nervously when she passed us.

"They're so cute," I whispered and Luka placed his hand on my lower back.

"You're doing great. Just take it slow," Lyric said in a calming voice. Her head and the one of an elderly woman popped up as they ascended the stairs. "Erik, can you help?"

Erik took the woman's hand and she stepped up the last step. Her eyes widened when she glanced up at Erik.

"Well, aren't you handsome? Would you mind helping an old lady to her car?"

"Of course, ma'am." He held out his arm and she looped hers through it. She held her head in pride as they strolled away.

An elderly man with a cane came up next and glanced around. "Evelyn! Where did she go?"

Vivi pointed toward Erik and the woman. "She went that way, Mr. Fletcher."

He squinted his eyes towards the pair. "That damn woman is a hundred and fifty years old and running off with a young buck." He shook his head before following behind them. I refrained from laughing.

Wait . . . a hundred and fifty? What the fuck?

I glanced at Luka and he smiled like he knew what I was thinking. I still wasn't convinced he couldn't read minds.

A couple more elderly people came out, then another ten people.

Everyone helped by escorting them to their cars. I stood there waiting with Vivi.

"I meant what I said," she whispered. "You aren't that bad, but if you tell anyone I said that, I'll kill you." She smiled, showing me her fangs and it made me giggle.

"I'll keep it between us."

"That's all of them," Peach said, as she finally emerged. "Everything is locked up. Eddie is on his way and we will have to help him load these bodies."

"Who's Eddie?" I asked.

"A guy I know who owns a mortuary." She gave me a sad smile. "We lost two wolven and a vampire."

Sadness filled me, not only for them, but for the Venom members who died. They were sent out with no regard for their lives. For what? Just to take me back to Venom—to my father. I had a feeling he wasn't going to let this go. This wasn't the end.

I needed to go to my apartment and get my cat. I wasn't sure they knew where Luka lived, and I was hoping to stay there.

Erik and Lyric returned from helping people to their car and stood by me. A few minutes later, the four wolven came back from their run. They all transformed one by one, and I was shocked when one was a girl. Erik nervously looked at the ground.

"Hi!" She extended her hand shamelessly. "I'm Kimber."

She was a light-skinned girl with long brown hair.

I shook her hand with an uncomfortable smile. "I'm Sage."

"I know. My brother told me." She patted Drag's back before turning toward Lyric. "And you are?"

"I'm Lyric and this is my brother Erik."

"Nice to meet you, both." She smiled before she strolled over to Erik who was still looking at the ground. "You're a pretty good fighter, for a human."

Erik laughed nervously before looking directly into her eyes, avoiding her naked body. They went into a conversation about fighting.

"I'm Heston." The ebony-skinned man with short black hair extended his hand and I shook it. I was getting good at keeping my eyes above the waistline, but man, I wanted to look.

"And I'm Demetrius. You can call me Demi." The light-skinned male had natural red hair and an Irish accent.

I shook his hand. "Sage. Nice to meet you, both."

The wolven men introduced themselves to Lyric and Erik and I stopped paying attention as Marcus and Zeke strolled up.

"What are you guys going to do?" I asked.

"I was assuming we would be staying with you," Marcus said with a smile.

"Of course you can." I glanced at Zeke. "What about April?"

"I just called her. She went to a friend's house and is waiting for me to pick her up."

I took a deep breath and sighed as Luka and Winnie approached.

"We need to go get Chewy, now," I said immediately. "Plus, we need to figure out who all needs sanctuary." I smiled nervously, hoping Luka didn't mind the extra guests.

He nodded and turned toward Drag. "Can I take your truck and you take my bike?"

"Sure." He handed Luka the keys.

"We have to go get my shit from the cave first!" Winnie said. "My shit is expensive."

"How about I take her to get her cat, then we meet you at your house?"

"Fine." Winnie strolled over to Lyric and took her hand. "You're riding with me."

"What about me?" Erik asked.

"I'll drive you," Kimber said. "I just have to throw some clothes on first."

Erik smiled excitedly. I was dying to see what happened next between the two but Luka pulled on my hand.

"Be careful everyone," I called over my shoulder as Luka escorted me to Drag's truck.

CHAPTER 52

LUKA

"Can I drive?" Sage asked. "I have never driven a truck before."

"Don't kill us!" I tossed her the keys and she grinned before hopping in.

The ride was pretty quiet as we headed to her house. We were only ten minutes away when I noticed we were being trailed.

"Someone is following us. Take a right up here." Sage did what I said and turned. "At the end of the block, take another right."

"But that will take us right back to where we were."

"Exactly." She glanced nervously in the rearview mirror. "Don't look. I'm watching."

She nodded as she took the right and the car followed. "Fuck."

"Is it Ven—"

The sound of metal on metal screeched as the car slammed into the ass end of Drag's truck. Sage yanked the wheel to keep us on the road.

Another slam.

"They're going to kill us!" she screamed. Another slam. "Pull over!"

"You can't be serious, Luka!" Another slam. "Fuck!"

"You're doing great, Princess. Turn here!"

Sage whipped us around the corner. The car sped up and slammed us again. We fishtailed and half the truck went onto the shoulder of the road, which was covered in gravel. Dust surrounded us as if we were in a tornado. She gripped the wheel tight as she tried to regain control.

"Pull over! Call Winnie and tell him what's going on. If anything happens, leave me!"

"Luka, I'm not—" Another slam.

"Pull over so I can kill these fuckers!" I growled.

Sage slammed the brakes, pulling to the side of the road.

"Don't get out, Princess." I tossed the gun in the seat as I exited.

A door on the other vehicle opened as I approached. A guy was halfway out of the passenger side when I yanked him the rest of the way out and put him in a chokehold.

The driver ran around the front of the car, so I let go of the first asshole and engaged in battle with her. She threw a punch, but I caught her hand and twisted it. The sounds of her bones cracking was music to my ears. She let out a cry of pain before falling to her knees.

A crossbow cocked and I whipped around a fraction of a second before an arrow flew past me. The guy shooting it frantically tried to reload. I closed the distance between us and grabbed him by the throat—his eyes widened as he struggled for air.

Another crossbow cocked and then a gunshot. I dropped the guy and turned around. Sage was holding the gun with shaking hands—she had been the one who fired. Footfalls sounded behind me, the guy I had been choking was running away. That only left the driver and she was kneeling on the ground, crying.

"Take off!" I spat. She jumped up from her knees and held her arm as she followed my orders.

"Are you okay, Princess?"

That was a stupid question. Judging by the look on her face, she was *not* okay. Tears filled her eyes and I immediately went to her.

"I . . . I killed him." I took the gun from her hand and stuck it in the back of my waistband.

"You did what you had to do." When I pulled her close to me, her body was trembling. Keeping one arm around her, I took my ringing phone out of my pocket. It was Winnie.

"Sage just called! Where are you guys?"

"Venom ran us off the road. We—" Screeching tires came from all sides as four vans pulled up. "More of them. East side bridge."

I shoved my phone back in my pocket and wrapped both arms around Sage. I was about to run as fast as I could to get her to safety when a bright light stopped me. Letting go of her, I immediately turned toward the fucker with the UV flashlight. After ripping it from his hands, I twisted his neck.

"Stop! Let go of me!"

Turning toward Sage's screams, I saw her fighting off three members. In my peripheral vision, two others came running up. With quickness, I pulled the gun from my waist band and shot them both. I grabbed the girl attacking Sage and pulled her off causing her to tumble to the ground. The next guy got a hard punch to the face. The third one took a roundhouse kick in the stomach from Sage.

Three more members came from one direction and two from the other. Lifting my gun, I took aim, hitting a girl in the chest with my last bullet.

More people joined the melee and I lost count of how many people we were taking out. Sage picked up a stake and stabbed anyone who came near her. I cringed with every blow, knowing she would mentally struggle for the rest of her life with what she had to do.

As the fight continued, I went into a nearly feral state, killing anyone who moved. It seemed to last forever as bodies piled up around us. The sea of the dead in the van's headlights felt almost unreal.

Grabbing a guy's arm, I twisted it behind his back until I felt it break. His screams rang loud as I bit into his neck. He let out a light moan of pleasure as I took a little blood for extra strength. Feeding out of anger was a quick way to go into bloodlust, so I stopped after a few gulps.

The cock of a gun had me dropping the guy and whipping around quickly.

No.

The air rushed out of my lungs and the entire world stood still as I faced one of my biggest fears—Sage had a gun held to her head. I immediately put my hands out in a placating manner.

"Let her go," I whispered. "Please."

"Look who's begging." The evil grin on Sorin's face chilled me to my bones. If anyone could shoot Sage in the head without thinking twice, it was him.

"I'll do whatever you want, just don't hurt her."

"Luka, run!" she screamed.

"Shut up!" Sorin shoved the gun harder into the side of her head.

My heart felt like it was going to explode as her eyes filled with tears. I frantically tried to come up with a plan ... *any* plan to try and save her without the possibility of her getting hurt. If he shot her in the head, even vampire blood couldn't save her—she would be gone forever.

"I will do whatever you want," I repeated.

"Get on your knees, then!" Sorin shouted.

"Don't, Luka! He's going to kill me either way!" Sage's heart raced more with fear for me than it did for her own safety.

"Give yourself up and she won't be harmed!"

Knowing I needed to protect her, I had already made my decision. She locked eyes with me, the hazel surrounded by bloodshot whites.

"Don't," she whispered as tears rolled down her cheeks.

"Lavender and vanilla," I whispered before I fell to my knees.

"Luka!" she wailed. "You should have let me die!"

She was pissed at me, but she'd get over it.

"Never going to happen, Princess."

"Put your hands behind your head!" Sorin commanded.

With his gun still pressed against Sage, I clenched my jaw as I did what the fucker ordered.

Two other members were on me quickly and each dug a stake into one of my thighs. I winced at the burning pain that the silver caused.

"Cuff him, Naomi!"

Sorin's sister nervously approached me. When the handcuffs were latched around my wrists, I was surprised at the pain I felt. There were sharp spikes on the inside of them which dug into my skin. More silver. I winced.

"Leave him alone!" Sage screeched.

Sorin pistol whipped Sage and a loud growl left me. "Don't fucking touch her!" I snarled at him.

A nefarious grin spread across his face. "Not much you can do in your condition."

A low growl left me, even though he was right—my body was getting weaker by the second.

Two members grabbed my arms and assisted me to my feet.

"Lavender and vanilla," Sage whispered. More tears rolled down her face as we passed. My heart—my soul was content giving myself up for her.

"I did what you wanted, now let her go, Sorin!" I yelled as they escorted me toward the van.

Naomi opened the door and stood to the side with an uncertain look on her face. An evil laugh left Sorin as they shoved me into the back. The two members got in and chained me to the seat.

The sound of Harleys in the distance was a symphony of relief. A few seconds later, I saw Peach and Ravage leading a convoy. Their lights shone brightly as they approached. I glimpsed the side of Sage's face before the van doors closed. I had faith my friends would protect the woman I loved.

CHAPTER 53

SAGE

Sacrifice. That's what he did when he fell to his knees. He sacrificed himself *for me.*

Sorin still had the gun pressed against my head when my friends rolled up. Before Winnie's bike completely stopped, Lyric was off of it and running toward me.

"Let go of her, Sorin!"

"This woman has been treasonous. I have been commanded to bring her to her father." Winnie moved in fast ready to kill. "You move again, vampire, and I will bring her body to her father along with yours!"

"Winnie, Luka's in that van!" I screamed as it sped away.

Winnie took off after it and Sorin turned his gun toward him and started shooting. My instincts kicked in and I elbowed him in the face. A loud growl came from behind me and Sorin let out a cry of pain. His grasp on me loosened, so I whipped around. Peach had snuck up behind him and ripped his throat out with her bare teeth. She let go and he fell to his knees in front of me. His hands frantically went to his neck, trying to keep the blood from pouring out of it.

"It's your kill," Peach said as she handed me Sorin's gun. I took it with a racing heart.

"Any of you move, you die!" Ravage yelled when he ran up.

My eyes bounced across each Venom member who was watching—some I knew personally, some I didn't.

"Go home to your families!" I screamed in an angry cry. They stood there in shock, none of them moving. I lifted the gun toward them. "Now!" Screams came from some as they took off running. After hopping in vans, they sped off.

Winnie came running back up to us. "We have to get Luka back!" He paced frantically next to me as I stared at Sorin. He was turning white from blood loss. I knew if I waited, he would die on his own.

"You don't have to do this," Erik whispered from behind me.

"If you don't kill him, I will!" Winnie swore.

After swallowing hard, I lifted my gun to Sorin's head. "This is for Deren."

I pulled the trigger.

Cold blood.

I had killed someone in *cold blood*.

The sounds, the lights, the people all faded away into the darkness as my body went into shock.

CHAPTER 54
WINNIE

It had been two weeks since the attack and we were in a commune located deep in the forest. Since Venom knew where most of us lived, everyone who had been there the night of the slaughter were now guests of Drag's wolven pack. Except for Ravage and Lynx, they came to visit every few days to go over plans.

Lyric plopped down on the wood log I was sitting on and handed me another beer. The flames from the bonfire we sat around danced across her beautiful face as she smiled.

"Thanks," I said with a grin.

"Do you think we have enough people for this?" Peach asked.

"The lab employees aren't trained like we are, so we won't have to worry about them. It's the security guarding the place who will be the problem," Marcus said as he dropped more wood into the fire.

"We have enough people to take care of them." Vivi grinned wickedly.

Peach shook her head. "We only kill if we have to, Viviana."

She rolled her eyes and let out a sigh of annoyance. "That's boring."

Wondering if we did have enough people, I glanced around, judging everyone's strengths.

My sister and I were only in our fifties. We were *much* stronger than the humans, but not as strong as Peach and Ravage—they were old as shit. I hadn't seen Lynx fight, but Ravage said she was good. Laren was staying here with some of the wolven mothers to help with the children and protection.

Kimber, Demetrius, and Heston were all under Drag's command. I knew the wolven had no problem throwing down.

During the battle, I had noticed how skilled Marcus and Zeke were. They were damn good fighters. Lyric and Erik also fought with efficiency.

My attention wandered to Sage. She was standing on the edge of the treeline, staring into the darkness like she did every night. I felt bad for her, but if anyone tried to talk to her—unless it had to do with saving Luka—she ignored us.

Looking back across the campfire, my eyes landed on Steph. Ravage had brought her the second night we were here. She was basically an infant in the vampire world, so she wouldn't be much more help than our only other human, April. She doesn't fight and just happened to be dragged into this mix by her husband, Zeke.

As my mind raced with our plan, there was only one job I thought she could do. "Hey, April. Have you ever raced before?"

The cute blonde shifted uncomfortably. You could tell this whole experience was agonizing for her. "I have driven a Go Kart. Why?"

"I was thinking perhaps you could drive one of the vans—"

"I don't think she should go, Winnie," Ravage interjected.

"Agreed," Marcus said. "We have enough people who can fight without her." He seemed to take on a leadership role for his people. Just like Ravage did for the vamps.

"I don't want to stay here alone," April whispered.

"I'll be staying with the kids. You could help me protect them," Laren said with uncertainty.

April looked at Zeke who tried to comfort her by putting an arm around her shoulders. "That's perfect for you, sweetie. You love kids."

April smiled lightly. "I do. I've always wanted kids but . . ." Her voice seemed to run away with the darkness as her eyes saddened.

"Then you will stay and help with protection," Laren said with a genuine smile.

April nodded before leaning into Zeke.

"Do you have the blood bags, sis?"

Vivi smiled as her eyes met mine. "I do. They're in the fridge."

"Where did you get blood?" Erik asked suspiciously.

"I have a deal with someone who works at a blood bank. They throw out a lot of blood for various reasons. I give her what she wants every week in return. I owe her extra now."

Erik's eyes widened before confusion settled on his face. "Every week? Do you not feed from humans?"

"No." Vivi's almost standing smirk disappeared as a look of sadness filled her face. "Venom took my man, so I have *no choice* but to feed from bags."

Erik shook his head. "I don't understand."

Vivi let out an annoyed sigh before standing. "I need more drinks to deal with this shit!" She stomped off into the darkness.

"I'm sorry. I didn't mean to upset her."

"You're good, Erik." Peach patted him on the shoulder. "She just misses Strike."

"Who's Strike?"

Tears rimmed Peach's eyes. "Luka's brother. Venom took him to the lab a year ago."

"Why can't she feed off humans?" Lyric asked.

"Because she's in love," Ravage said as he swirled the whiskey in his glass. "One of the few bad qualities of being a vampire."

"What does love have to do with blood?" April asked. She seemed to shrink when everyone glanced at her. "I'm not trying to be rude, just curious."

"When a vampire forms a lenxus with someone, they find others' blood almost intolerable. It's not that she *can't* drink it, she can, she just doesn't want to. It's extremely unappealing. Unless it's out of anger," Ravage informed her.

"Can we change the subject?" Sage interrupted.

"Agreed," Vivi said as she retook her seat. She had a bottle of whiskey in her hand and she popped the lid off it. "It's rude to talk about feeding when both of our men are starving for our blood!"

Sage let out a large sigh and shifted. It looked like she was wiping away tears.

"I think I'm going to turn in," Kimber said, bringing my attention back as she stood up. "Goodnight."

Almost every night, like clockwork, Erik left right after her. We all knew what they were doing, but yet, they still acted like we were oblivious.

"I'm going to bed," Erik said and I laughed. His eyes narrowed on me. "What?"

"Nothing." I grinned and he gave me a suspicious look before taking off.

"Leave him alone!" Lyric said as she swatted my arm.

"We all know they're fucking!"

"Yep," Demetrious added. "I smell their lure constantly."

Steph's eyes were wide as she glanced around at everyone. "I didn't know."

Ravage snicked. "Because your situational awareness sucks."

She shrugged and then smiled. "I'm working on it."

"Would you like another drink, Peaches and cream?"

Peach shook her head with an exasperated sigh. "Marcus, if I have to tell you one more time to stop calling me that, I'm going to rip your balls off!"

"When you're being mean, he thinks it's sexy," Zeke said with a laugh.

"That's why she keeps doing it. She's playing hard to get!" Marcus grinned arrogantly. He was definitely my new favorite person. He was funny, brilliant, and even showed me some new fighting moves. We had a blooming bromance.

Peach let out an exasperated sigh before standing. "I'm going to bed."

"Want some company?"

"Goodnight, Marcus!" Peach strolled off as we laughed.

"Do you think this plan will work?" Heston asked as he leaned forward onto his knees.

"It has to work. We have to get him out of there!" Sage's voice cracked with pain, making my chest heavy.

Without saying a word, she headed into her cabin and slammed the door. The entire camp's quietness spoke volumes as our emotions ran high. The fire crackled and frogs croaked. The night sky was filled with clouds, making it as gloomy as we were.

"We're going to bed," Zeke said. He stood up and took April's hand.

"Goodnight!" Steph called out.

"I think I'm going to head to bed, too." I stood up and glanced down at Lyric. She had been staying in a cabin with Stephanie since we arrived.

"Goodnight," she said. Leaning down, I gave her a quick kiss since she was officially my girlfriend now. Heading toward Marcus, I gave him a fist bump.

My thoughts were loud as I strolled into my cabin. This plan *had* to work. Too many people were counting on it.

Making my way to the windows, I closed the steel shutters and the special currents Drag got for us vampires. I had just pulled the covers back on the bed when I heard a quiet knock at the door.

Making my way to it, I smelled her lure, and knew who it was. I flung the door open with a grin.

"Hey," Lyric said with a small smile. She stepped inside and I shut the door.

"What's up?" I asked, even though I already knew what she wanted. Her lure had been getting stronger all week and I was ready to devour her.

"I was just wondering if I could stay here tonight." Sweet lilacs engulfed the room and I took a deep breath.

I yanked her toward me. "I thought you would never ask."

TURN THE PAGE FOR A
SNEAK PEEK OF
SCORNED BY VENOM

SCORNED BY VENOM

SAGE

We had no clue where Luka was or if he was dead. I hadn't told anyone, but I had given up on believing he was still alive.

"Can we even trust this woman?" Lynx asked, bringing my attention away from the pine trees. My painful thoughts had kept me from hearing the beginning of the conversation.

What woman?

Everyone living here usually gathered around the fire every night to talk about random things. But at least once a night, someone would bring up the rescue mission to save Luka and Strike. A mission which I had eventually given up on. This didn't sound like that.

Maybe I *didn't* hear everything.

"I don't know," Ravage responded. "What do you think, Drag?"

"She may have valuable information and we don't have any other leads." The fire crackled, the sound of a wood log being dropped into it ringing through the night. "You know her, Marcus. What's your opinion?"

"I think it's worth a shot. Sage may not come out of the state she's in if we don't."

I whipped toward the crowd of people. "I can hear you, you know?"

"We don't care if you hear us!" Winnie spat. "We know you miss Luka, most of us do too, but you need to get your shit together so we can get him the fuck back."

Glancing around the campfire, most people looked at me with sympathy, like April and Peach. Others blatantly avoided my eyes, like most of the ex Venom members. But not Winnie and Marcus. They stared me down, ready for the battle. They had both been on my ass the past few days. One way or another, they were going to assure I didn't shut down any more than I already had.

"Shut up, Winston!"

He snickered. "Winston? Still hate me, I see." An arrogant grin spread across his face and it made me miss Luka. I fought back tears, determined not to let them fall in front of people. I'd been getting good at it.

"Whatever," I mumbled, before turning back around.

Every night, something inside of me pulled me toward the forest. I stared into the darkness, hoping Luka would magically walk out of it because he *somehow* managed to escape and make his way back to me.

Obviously, I was delusional. Deep down, I *knew* he was dead.

"You can be mad at me all you want, Sage, but unlike most of these cowardly people around here, I won't give up on you," Winnie ranted. "I'm not going to tiptoe around, worried you'll break. I don't give a fuck! I'll continue to give you hell until the fiery girl I know comes back!"

Was I *that* bad? Were people afraid to talk to me? Afraid I would break? Possibly, but I didn't give a shit. Life meant nothing to me anymore.

"Leave her alone," Lyric interrupted. "She misses Luka."

Lyric was constantly defending me. I knew it was out of kindness and love, but it made me look less stable than I already was.

Rage filled me, whipping my body around. "I don't need you to defend me, Lyric!"

With unhuman quickness, Winnie had me by the waist before I even realized he moved. Within seconds, my body plummeted into icy water. I hastily made my way to the surface and sucked in a hard breath.

"What the fuck!" I screamed, quickly standing up in the shallow lake. "Are you trying to piss me off?!"

Winnie flung his arms out, a look of frustrated anger consuming his face. "Please get mad! Please fight me! Do something other than stand there staring into the woods, eat soup, and wither the fuck away!"

A shiver ran through me and I swallowed hard. I averted my eyes and they landed on a lily pad clinging to my shoulder. "This was unnecessary."

Winnie's face was stone cold when my gaze met his again. Colder than the lake I was standing in. "You think? It seems fitting to me since water lilies are a symbol for resurrection and rebirth in many cultures."

"I'm still alive, Asshole. I don't need to be resurrected!"

Winnie's eyes narrowed on me, his face filled with emotion. "Are you sure about that, Sage? Because it seems to me like you died when they took Luka."

The shock of his words hit me like a boulder and I sucked in a hard breath through chattering teeth. An aching pain settled in my chest, tears filling my eyes. Winnie shook his head in disappointment, his own eyes brimmed with emotions before turning away.

Peach was immediately at the edge of the water. She extended her hand with a kind and compassionate face. "Come on, kid."

Kid. That's what she called Luka and it made my chest hurt more. She pulled me from the lake and I did everything in my power to push back my emotions.

"Thanks." Embarrassed and pissed, I trudged off toward my cabin.

Glossary

Fangsters/Fangasizers: A human who fantasizes or wants to be fed on by a vampire.

Fangdom: A group of humans who obsess over vampires.

Intimate: The person which a wolven has a *nexus* with is considered their intimate. *See also, Nexus.*

Lenxus: A bond which a vampire has with their mate.

Lure: The scent a person emits when sexually attracted to someone. Other humans can't smell it, but vampires and wolven can.

Mark: Vampires can mark a person with their scent, showing other vampires they're taken.

Nexus: The bond which a wolven has with their mate.

Nosh Pit: A group of dancing Humans.

Origin: A vampire who *turns* a human into a vampire.

Supernaturals Against Venom Elitists or SAVE — An organization who is trying to protect vampires and wolven from being used for research.

Vampire Eradicating National Organization of Malice or VENOM: A government-funded society who trains its members to hunt vampires for research.

Vinculum: A non-sexual bond a wolven has to their pack.

Vampire Research Center or VRC: A government funded facility and/or laboratory who does investigations, collection, analysis, and experimentation on vampires so they can use the information to make a multitude of products.

ALSO BY P.S. NAIL

Primordial Gods Series

Violet Flames: Book 1

Emerald Skies: Book 2
Silver Storms: Book 3

Argentium Vampire Hunters Trilogy

Raised by Venom: Book 1
Scorned by Venom: Book 2

About the Author

Dreaming of becoming a vampire, I mean author, since she was a youngling, PS Nail finally fulfilled her prophecy by self-publishing her first paranormal fantasy romance novel, with many more to come.

She enjoys playing guitar to soothe the draw of the moon, video games to help pacify her blood lust, reading romance and smut books, since she never sleeps, and having a fangtastic time with paranormal friends. Once a month, when the full moon calls, she and her coven dance naked around a magical blazing fire . . . but don't tell her we told you.

We think she currently lives in the United States, or possibly Romania, with her shifter husband, three hybrid sons, and their pet demons. She lovingly calls them her immortal family.

She will continue to quench her thirst for writing until death, dismissal, or dishonor.

FYI: She hates the sun, but loves garlic.